CYRIL IN THE FLESH

RAMSEY HOOTMAN

In celebration of my Aunt Wendy
and her bold, generous, joy-filled life.

Had your story had been mine to write,
you'd be with us still.

Be proud and bitter to the world, my friend; but, privately, just say, "She doesn't love me."

— EDMUND ROSTAND, *CYRANO DE BERGERAC*, HAROLD WHITEHALL TRANSLATION

STAGE 1

ANGER

CHAPTER 1

NOW

L ots of shit happens after this asshole gets his best friend killed. For the sake of brevity, we'll cut to the day he's released from prison. Lest the reader assume his incarceration unjust—it's always tempting to give the protagonist the benefit of the doubt—it was not. Cyril Blanchard deserved every last moment of those five-to-ten years. The indictment says he exposed thousands of pages of highly classified military intelligence; of that crime, anyone with an internet connection is well aware.

What most will never know: hacking the Marine Corps was just the icing on the shit cake. If there were a hell, the crimes which would condemn this asshole to eternal torment include betraying his best friend, getting him blown to kingdom come, and fucking his widow. Not physically, mind you (yeah, he wishes), but with words alone. He's good with words.

That he is released after five years, three months, and nine days is not due to some saintly reformation or presidential pardon, but the happy accident of a global pandemic colliding with America's overcrowded criminal justice system. No; he worked that prison like a bitch.

Which is how this asshole comes to be sitting at a deserted bus station in Taft, California, wondering where the hell he is supposed to go. His pretentious shrew of an ACLU lawyer said she'd have it figured out, but judging by the season and the sun, it's well past noon. Typical.

It's possible this day will end with him digging in a dumpster. Not for lack of money; his pocket bulges with the two hundred he was allotted upon release, in small bills. The first thing he did when they dropped him off was mask up and hoof it to the nearest burger joint—where he stood like an idiot, staring at a menu so vast it boggled the mind. Eventually, someone asked if he needed help, and he got angry, and the manager told him he could leave immediately, or leave with the police.

His stomach complains. He regrets not having gone around back to find the dumpster when he left the restaurant. Eating someone else's garbage would have been unthinkable, five years thence, but prison has lowered his standards considerably. But he hadn't done it, and now it's too late, because if he wanders off, he may miss his ride. Assuming one is coming.

He sits on the cinder block bench for another hour, maybe two, feeling the smart of sunshine crisping his pale epidermis. It's more trouble to shift his bulk than it's worth to go in search of shade. When, finally, a cherry-red Ford Ranger rounds the corner at the end of the block, he knows it's there for him by the way it slows when he lifts a hand to shade his eyes. You'd think he'd be grateful, but the flash of relief only ignites a powder keg of anger: six hours for his goddamn lawyer to find him a ride? Phone a fucking Uber.

Getting to his feet is not the herculean ordeal it once was, but it still requires more effort than he likes to expend, especially in the heat. The bench sits on a rise, and his deflated gut swings like a fleshy hoop skirt as he negotiates the graded slope down to the sidewalk.

The late summer sun glances off the pickup's windshield,

obscuring his view of the driver. It had better not be a fanboy, or some lunatic script kiddie. He doesn't have any relatives willing to acknowledge shared genetic material, so no worries there. Most likely it's whichever one of his lawyer's west-coast colleagues owes her the biggest favor.

He yanks open the passenger door, mouth open to ask this douche whether he's at least getting a hand job out of the deal, and—

The words stick.

It's her.

Not the lawyer, dumbass. The *other* her. The widow. Jesus Christ.

CHAPTER 1.5

TWELVE YEARS AGO

He took philosophy for her. It was a general-ed class, not even remotely a requirement for a computer science major in his third year. He arrived late and sat in back, most days, ignoring the droning lecture as he committed her image to memory in photo-perfect detail: her hair, which she'd flat-ironed in those days, sleek and lustrous as a blackbird wing. The way the ends had brushed across her bare shoulders, separating like the delicate teeth of a comb. The quirk of her asymmetrical eyebrows as she turned to listen to a classmate's opinion, disagreement registering only in a slight flare of nostrils. Her open-mouthed, utterly unselfconscious laughter, as if nobody in her entire life had ever been able to bring themselves to shush her joyful noise. Every inch of her perfect, except—

Except that she kept saying "all of *the* sudden." This was down in Cal Poly's main study hall—she was not with him, but nearby —and he cannot have been the only one bothered by her butchering of this ridiculously common idiom. He'd leaned across the long table and pointed it out. The way one might do an acquaintance the favor of pointing out a flipped tag or an unzipped fly.

She had not appreciated the courtesy, and told him so in no uncertain terms.

What reaction had he hoped for? A coy laugh, followed by introductions (he already knew her name was Robin) and an invitation to join her little study group? Yeah, probably not. What he hadn't expected was the utter lack of recognition in her withering gaze. The 3 PM section of PHIL 126 was capped at thirty students, and as far as Robin was concerned, she'd never in her life laid eyes upon this slovenly, basement dwelling specimen.

She had just finished telling him to take his negging bullshit and shove it up his ass when Tavis arrived, fresh off the bus from boot camp with nowhere to bunk down but the floor of his childhood friend's dorm. Lanky and lean as a half-starved wolf, he and his crew cut might as well have sucked all the air out of the room. Only Robin, a Navy brat herself, had seen too many earnest young sailors to be impressed by his crisp uniform and confident stride. When she saw Tavis greet Cyril with a hearty slap on the back, she'd gathered her books and headed for the door.

It was not Cyril, then, but Tavis—smitten by the blaze of fury in her eyes—who rushed after her to offer an apology for this asshole's offense. That evening, he'd dropped out of a tree and into her path, with the coy insistence that he'd fallen from the bright full moon. And that was how Robin and Tavis Matheson fell in love.

This is the story everyone knows. It is the narrative their friends and family have become familiar with. It is the tale Robin will one day tell her grandchildren. Mostly, it's true.

The story lacks just one small detail: Cyril had known she would be in the library that day.

Oh. He never mentioned that, did he?

It was not stalking, exactly. Not yet. Robin had simply caught his eye, first outside the student union, and then repeatedly in the campus dining hall. Almost without intent, Cyril had found himself frequenting those spots, hoping for another glimpse of her broad, toothy smile. There were only a few Black students on campus; it had been easy enough to discover her name. Her major. Her dormitory. The password to her university account.

So he'd known when and where she planned to meet up with a few classmates to prep for their final presentations. Robin didn't belong to him, but he'd wanted to share her, somehow, with his best and only friend. Though he would have denied it, perhaps some part of him had hoped that Tav's charismatic presence would, somehow, open the door for him to... what? Step in and stun her with his wit and charm?

How naïve he had been, to imagine Tavis wouldn't fall for Robin, too.

CHAPTER 2
NOW

This now-formerly-incarcerated asshole doesn't speak to Tavis Matheson's widow for two fucking hours. Not only because he's an ungrateful piece of shit, but because she doesn't deserve to hear the things he wants to say. Five years she'd left him to bake in this central Californian hellhole, without a single visit or phone call or even so much as a note jotted on a postcard. He had given himself up for dead. And now—*now* she has the gall to roll back into his life, as if no time has passed at all?

Of course, he has no right to this fury. She owes him nothing. She made no promises. Five years ago, when she'd dropped him off in the prison parking lot, her body had been a freeway sign flashing *sayonara*. He had never expected to see her again.

He adjusts the air vents, and then adjusts them again. A couple years into his sentence he'd obtained a small handheld fan, but this is the first time he has felt genuine AC since he went in. He is still hot. He is always hot. He plucks at his shirt—the musty bin of Goodwill castoffs set aside for graduating felons had contained nothing in his size, so he wears the same unwashed cotton shirt he'd traded for an orange jumpsuit the day he self-surrendered. It is stiff with the salt of her angry tears.

Camarillo, where Robin had lived and laid her husband to rest, was south and west of Taft; now she drives north, past an endless vista of flat yellow fields. This asshole does not ask why she is here, or where they are going, or what the ever-loving fuck she thinks she is doing. He shifts, knocking his head against the roof of the cab as he attempts to find some position in which the seatbelt does not cut into his gut. It is a position which does not exist.

She doesn't speak, either, though he feels her evaluating him out of the corner of one eye. He is good at reading her, but the black cotton mask covering her nose and mouth obscures most of the nonverbal data he might use to do so. No matter. When she wants him to know why she has come, *if* she wants him to know, he will know. She has never had a problem speaking her mind.

Perhaps she is silent now because there are simply too many things to say.

The truck breaks the stalemate, in the end, with a beep of warning.

"Oh, shoot—I'm empty." She flips on the blinker—sunlight flashes off the diamond in the wedding band she still wears—and swerves just in time to make the exit on the right. They're on I-5, so the next offramp could be forty miles.

At the pump she hops out, tugging the mask down to her chin for a breath of gasoline-infused air. He watches through the glass as she plugs the nozzle into the tank and squeegees the windshield, drinking her in with his eyes.

Close-fitted cotton shirt, the outline of her sports bra just visible beneath. Faded, paint-spattered jeans—not a fashion statement, but the real deal. Work boots with leather laces worn thin around the hooks and eyes. She is the same as he left her, but different in a thousand subtle ways. Her body a little thicker, a little more muscle in her arms. Her face harder, leaner, etched with the first few indelible lines. Her thick black curls, once shoulder-length, now cropped close to her head. Only her hands are rough; everywhere else, her brown-gold skin is so fresh it glows. She yawns and stretches, and his eyes follow the arch of her back.

She is beautiful. She couldn't not be. Not ever. Not to him.

She disappears into the station, and then around back, presumably to pee. When she slides back into the cab, she tosses a cheap spandex mask onto his thigh. The tag is still attached.

"Had it," he tells her, adding the mask to the receipts, blueprints, and napkins which clutter the dash. The thin paper covering he had been allotted that morning sits crumpled at the bottom of his pocket. "Tested positive, but all I ever got was a runny nose. And yeah, they isolated and tested me again before release."

She rips her own mask off, the elastic snapping back against her fingers, and closes her eyes as she exhales exasperation. "I'll give you this much, Cyril. You never change."

"Pretty sure I fucking told you so."

He had. She knows.

She inhales again, slowly, and when she opens her eyes, she nods at the Burger King across the street. "I know it's a crappy first meal, but I'm starving. What do you say?"

As if they're just two old friends, catching up after all these years. Why is she here? Why is she treating him like a decent human being, instead of the man who made her a widow? He snorts and turns to gaze out the passenger window.

"Really? You planning to spend the next four hours pretending I'm not here?"

"Sure as fuck gonna try." This is how he speaks to his best friend's wife.

She shakes her head and pulls into the drive-through line.

When the car in front moves forward, she lowers the window and hooks and elbow over the door. "Gimme a bacon cheeseburger with medium coke and fries." She glances over one shoulder. "Last chance."

He doesn't look. Not because he doesn't want the food—look at him; he wants the food—but because he might freeze up again, and then she will know he has not emerged from prison unscathed. He'll pick hate over pity every time.

His stomach betrays him with a long, low growl.

She turns back to the microphone. "You know what, just double my order."

At the window, she dons her mask long enough to accept two top-heavy beverages and a crinkly bag spotted with oil, then lets the truck roll forward a few yards to accommodate the car behind. She wedges the drinks into cup holders and drops the bag onto the console between them before steering back into the street. With one hand on the wheel and her eyes on the road, she reaches into the pocket in the door and retrieves a bottle of hand sanitizer. At the first red light, she pumps a generous glob into her palm and thrusts the bottle toward him in a way that suggests compliance is not optional.

Sanitary precautions seem almost quaint after five years in a human petri dish, but he humors her. The evaporation of alcohol is pleasantly cool on his skin.

Still driving single-handedly—merging onto the freeway now —Robin pulls a burger from the bag and tears back the wrapper with her teeth. The smell makes his mouth water.

"Didn't stop to eat," she explains around a mouthful, though he hasn't asked and doesn't care. "Your lawyer called last night to tell me you were getting out. Wasn't sure I could make it before you got on the bus to Bakersfield."

Is that what he was supposed to do? Fucking lawyers. When he'd asked the woman where she expected him to go in the middle of a pandemic, she'd suggested calling around to his "friends." Seeing as the only person who'd ever deserved that title was five years dead, he'd declined, but she'd apparently taken the initiative.

Robin's left hand leaves the wheel long enough to flip the blinker. "We're up in Healdsburg now." She eases into the fast lane. "Wine country. North of the bay?"

Her window is still open. He rolls his down, too, and drapes an elbow over the door, plucking again at his shirt. The smell of bacon grease mingles with the tang of his own sweat. He clenches and unclenches a fist.

She finishes the burger and then the fries, licking salt from her fingertips before wiping her hand on her thigh. The next time she reaches into the bag, eyes still on the road, she pulls out the second burger and extends her arm.

This is the test, right?

Has being locked in a cage taught this asshole to control his animal impulses, or is he still the same gluttonous fuck he's always been? As if she doesn't know. He snatches the burger, rips off the paper. More than happy to settle that question immediately.

She ate; he inhales.

"You... look all right." She glances at him as she reaches for her soda. "You know, not fantastic, but—all right. Considering."

Considering that when he went to prison, he looked like an overinflated blimp, and now resembles merely a partially melted tub of lard. So much better.

The burger is gone. He wads the paper into a ball and flings it out the window.

"Hey! Don't—"

"Fuck off."

————

ROBIN PULLS INTO A COOKIE-CUTTER STRIP MALL AT dusk, parking out beyond the crush of cars. She sets the brake and sits back, fingers drumming softly on the wheel. "If we go in there," she says, nodding to the big-box anchor store, "are you gonna freak out?"

She'd noticed. At the drive-through. If self-loathing were a liquid, he would drown. Fortunately, he's used to being short of breath. "Dunno. But I'm pretty much guaranteed to be an asshole."

"Good point. Here." She grabs the back of his collar, flipping the tag out.

He shoves her, hard. "Keep your—fucking—*shit*." The watery remainder of her soda sloshes over his pants and the floor of the cab. He fumbles for the handle; the door pops open against the press of his bulk, and he spills out into the lot.

Fucking—fuck.

Fuck.

He hears her, at his back, doing something in the cab. Scrambling to clean up his mess, likely. Then her door opens, and her booted footsteps—

"You know what you don't do in prison?" He spits the words like darts, shaking sticky liquid off his hands. "*That.*" He hasn't experienced skin-to-skin contact in well over a year. Nobody has dared. The hair on the back of his neck prickles where her thumb brushed his flesh.

She holds her hands up in surrender. "Look, it's—" She gestures at the vehicle. "The kids do worse than that on the daily. I'll hose it out when we get home. Okay?"

Like he's offered an apology.

She waits, but when it's clear all he's going to give her is silence she shrugs and turns, hoisting herself into the passenger side of the cab. With one knee planted on the seat, she rummages through the detritus on the dash—providing him, incidentally, with a prime view of her ass. "I'd say just wait and order something," she says over one shoulder, "but honestly you're pretty rank. Oh. Found it." When she steps back down to the ground, she's holding a tape measure. Her eyes drop to his middle as her thumb flicks out a few inches of yellow blade.

He realizes what she means to do. "That's not—"

"Relax. We'll make it work." She gestures with the end of the tape. "Arms up."

He doesn't move. "Odds of them having my size—"

"Let me worry about that. Arms up. Come on."

"I'm not your fucking toddler."

"Obviously. She's got better manners."

"I never asked you to—"

"Oh my God, Cyril." She rolls her eyes skyward. "I've known you long enough not to expect anything so banal as *thank you,* but this is the longest I've been away from the kids since quarantine began, and mom-mode is a little hard to turn off. So maybe cut me some slack?" She yanks out a couple feet of tape. "Look, just hold it—" She stops just shy of touching his side. "There."

"Jesus Christ." He does it, though. He presses the end of the tape measure into the tire of flesh somewhere above his right hip.

While she has never been above commenting on his size—often with scathing bluntness—he is always caught off balance by her apparent lack of disgust. She hums a low note to herself as she wraps the strip of yellow around the back of him, numbers facing inward so the tape bends. Then, not looking at his face: "Over or under?"

His belly, she means. "I don't give a shit." He knows as well as she does that any attempt to make him more presentable is pointless. It's all lipstick on a pig.

She whips the tape around, stretching it across his sagging belly. Loss of mass has not improved its shape. "Got it." She pinches the end of the tape and flips it over, nodding as she notes the number. Then she holds the tape out vertically, standing tiptoe to eyeball his shoulder width and bending, quickly, to measure his inseam. "That should do it." She lets the tape retract and tosses the case into the cab. "I'd ask if you had any preferences, but I think you're gonna have to take whatever you can get."

CHAPTER 2.5

TWELVE YEARS AGO

Tavis had returned to the campus study hall only long enough to pick up his canvas sea bag. "I'm gonna ask her out."

He, Cyril, could have spoken up, then. Claimed her for his own. He had, in the most literal sense, seen her first. But they had both witnessed her reaction to him. He was nothing to her. Nobody. Tavis, ever the optimist, might have said her utter lack of recognition was all in Cyril's head, but she never did remember, in all the intervening years, that they'd shared a class together.

He offered a snort of derisive laughter instead. "You're only here—what, two days? And then you ship out. How's that going to work?"

"I have to try. I *have* to." Of course he did. That's just how Tavis was: no agonizing, no worrying, no second guessing. Just desire, translated directly into action.

This asshole had already combed through enough of Robin's email history to know she'd never fall for an approach like that. She'd spent her teenage years on a naval base in Italy, where an entire fleet of young sailors had vied for the opportunity of throwing themselves at the feet of the commander's daughter.

"Chill," he told Tavis. "I know where she'll be tonight. But if you're gonna do it, for fuck's sake, make it unique." To demonstrate, he had torn a page out of his notebook a tossed off a quick monologue. Or so it must have seemed to Tavis. In truth, Cyril had been plotting the perfect approach for weeks. Maybe he had hoped Tavis would recognize the truth and encourage his friend to take a chance. Or maybe not. "I mean, it only works if you climb the tree," Cyril added, postscript. Which was idiotic. Nobody would do that.

Tavis had.

Cyril celebrated with him, laughing in his dry, half-mocking way when she agreed to dinner and a movie. ("Take her to The Palm," he'd suggested, San Luis Obispo's quirky foreign-film theater house.)

"Your words, dude!" Tavis crowed, cuffing Cyril's shoulder with his soda.

"Your face," Cyril answered, with a clink of his can.

Tavis was not half so happy when he returned.

"What," Cyril joked, "she wouldn't fuck you on a first date? Is it possible she has standards?"

"She wants more," Tavis said. And held up the paper. "Of you."

CHAPTER 3
NOW

It's two minutes to midnight when she pulls up in front of the ramshackle Victorian. Moonlight streaks through the bones of the second floor, stripped clean to the studs. "Keep to the right," she says, when the front porch steps groan. "Wood's half rotten."

Inside, she circles around a boarded-up flight of stairs, kicking a path through toys cluttering the living room floor without regard for the noise. No surprise she's arranged for the kids to be elsewhere; once, he was a securities specialist and a hacker. (A hacktivist, to put it generously, which Tavis usually had.) But now he's a criminal. A felon. Chelsea Manning without the righteous cause.

Through an open-plan dining room and into a kitchen, she flicks on the light and grabs a half-thawed bottle of frozen tap water from the fridge. She extends it toward him—he shakes his head—before cranking off the top. The floor beneath their feet is unfinished plywood; the cabinets are old, topped with cracked tile, and the doors have been removed. A nail gun rests next to a compressor in the corner, orange extension cord snaking out via the laundry room. She tilts her head back and chugs. "I think—"

she wipes her mouth with the back of her hand—"You can sleep in Seth's bed tonight. Assuming a twin's okay."

Though they have spent hours in the truck together, it is this familiar image of her—feet planted, head thrown back—which, finally, catches him off guard. Five years he has horded these small moments like precious gems, never imagining he would bear witness to her casual radiance again. And yet here she is, drinking a bottle of water as he blinks back the sudden sting of tears. He struggles to summon an appropriately acerbic response: "If you saw what I've been sleeping on—"

"Figured." She screws the cap back on before tossing the bottle onto the counter. It lands neatly upright. "I bet you have to pee, but not as bad as I do. This way."

A corridor off the dining room leads to three doors. She ducks inside the second—a bathroom fan spins up—while he loiters in the hall.

She has never been one for artfully arranged photos, but she's strung a haphazard collection of snapshots along a length of copper wire and alligator clips, more half-assed than Pinterest-worthy. At the far left he recognizes her mother, a waifish white woman, half-eclipsed by the embrace of the beloved father who had clearly gifted Robin her smile. Next comes Tavis, changeless as ever in his formal Navy blues, milk-white skin, and fiery hair peeking out from under his cap. This coward tries to avoid his gaze, but he hears the echo of Tav's warm, easy laughter all the same. He always will.

"He's nine."

Cyril blinks. He is staring now at the awkwardly posed school photo of Tavis Matheson's son. The boy's freckled face is leaner, now, than the four-year-old Cyril remembers, made more adult by teeth too large even for his broad, gap-toothed smile. His hair, an unbridled explosion of copper red, remains the same.

"I know." This asshole has had ample time to count every milestone missed.

She holds out a freshly laundered towel, folded around a toothbrush, razor, and an unused bar of soap. "Shampoo's in the shower. Oh—and I'll run out to the truck and grab your clothes."

The bathroom is pristine, newly renovated in glass and granite. The mat on the floor in front of the toilet is, like the towel, large and plush and green. Scented lotion. A box of tissues. Two-ply paper. Mouthwash. Fucking *hand towels*. And a mirror.

A real mirror, not the shot-to-shit scrap of stainless steel so deeply etched with gang symbols and profanity that his reflection had been reduced to a round white blur. He sees, now, running a hand over his flaccid jowls, what Robin saw: he looks old. Not because of the gray flecks in his dark stubble or the looseness in his cheeks and second chin. He looks old because, like war, prison makes you old. While this is no tragedy—he was never handsome to begin with—it is startling. But for his size, he is not sure he could have picked himself out of a lineup.

He reaches over one shoulder to grab a handful of his shirt, turning away from the mirror as he pulls it off over his head. He doesn't want to see that shit any more than she does.

The glass shower stall is spacious enough to have accommodated him at his heaviest. When the water runs hot, he sits on the wide granite bench built along the edge, letting the flow run down over his head. If, here, he were to cry, not even he would ever know.

This is where he is when she knocks, and then cracks the door open just far enough to hook the plastic shopping bag over the inside knob. "Everything all right?"

"Dandy," he says, knowing they both know it's a lie.

He cannot stay. He'll get what he needs—contact with his lawyer, access to his finances, a car—and then he'll disappear. Before she has time to regret offering him this wholly undeserved shred of mercy.

That's what he ought to do. If he were good.

He's not. And he won't. She has driven him home, and he will make her drive him away.

———

She gives him a frank once-over when he emerges. "Not bad."

"Oh, was a clean shirt and a shave all I needed to complete my transformation into Alpha Hero?" He'd half-expected her to buy him a button-up shirt and slacks, but she'd purchased only his standard cotton tee and elastic-waisted sweatpants. They feel alien on his skin.

She rolls her eyes: a gesture so deeply etched into his memory that for a moment he forgets to breathe. "You underestimate the value of not smelling like a flophouse." She leans a shoulder against the door to the right of the bathroom, shoving back a rising tide of toys.

He follows her in, tugging at the shirt which is, in various places, starting to work its way between rolls. "About three sizes too fucking small." This bloated asshole could barely squeeze himself into the sweatpants, even with the waistband tucked under his belly.

"It *fits*. You think nobody's gonna see you if you hide under a tent?"

As if he gives a fuck about anyone's comfort but his own.

"Also, it's the biggest they had. Watch your step, the floor's a Lego minefield." The bedroom is octagonal, with faded floral wallpaper and a bay window looking onto the street. A den, in some other decade. Robin bends over Seth's bed, plucking out stuffed animals and tossing them toward a crib-sized mattress on the floor in the corner. Pretending she has not noticed him noticing the obvious.

Two photocopied pictures, taped to the wall above the boy's bed. One is a portrait, a facsimile of the one in the hall: his father, Tavis, in full Navy blues. The other is a shot from Seth's fourth birthday. The boy sits in front of a giant bowl of ice cream, upturned face radiating adoration for the asshole sitting next to him. Cyril.

She straightens. Seems about to say something, then shrugs. "He remembers you."

CHAPTER 3.5

A t first, it was a thrill. Even if he wasn't in the driver's seat, scripting his best friend's relationship with Robin was the farthest this asshole had ever gotten with a woman. And he was good at it—between Tav's face and Cyril's hastily scrawled missives, Tavis and Robin went from zero to sixty in one weekend flat. She was funny and charming and, thanks to her unique upbringing, by turns both worldly and naïve. Tavis balked when Cyril proposed extending the ruse into his deployment, but what could it hurt? Robin was smart; she'd connect the dots and whip aside the wizard's curtain soon enough. Then she'd either dump Tavis or decide she liked him even if his wit wasn't quite as sharp as advertised. At least Cyril had bought Tavis the chance she'd never have given him. Right?

Lies.

The truth was far more desperate. Every time Cyril wrote, he resolved to eat right, get in shape, and get serious about landing an industry job before he failed out of college. So that when she snatched away the mask—and she would; she *had* to—he would be standing there, ready to be the man she already loved. Then his letters would not be lies, but simply a placeholder. A bookmark slipped between pages in their love story.

Sometimes, he succeeded for days at a time. But then the indignity of attending classes to "learn" skills he already possessed for the privilege of obtaining a piece of paper that said he was worth hiring would overpower him, and he'd say something stupid and get himself kicked out of class and put back on academic probation and then he'd go back to his dorm and spend all night eating Hot Pockets and hijacking some Wall Street asshole's website or bank account or whatever because at least out in the digital wastelands his worth was indisputable.

And then he'd wake up in the morning (or afternoon or whenever) to find another soulful, enchanting note from Robin in his inbox and realize what a fucking moron he'd been, but instead of trying to get his shit together he'd toss another Hot Pocket in the microwave and plunge right back into that hole he'd dug, deeper and farther than before—because he'd failed her again. And again. And again. He wasn't worthy of her, and never would be. Why bother trying? He deserved to fail.

Even so, he never failed to write.

As the weeks and then months of Tav's deployment wore on, it was a relief, in a way, that Robin never suspected Tavis was anything other than what he appeared to be. It meant she was too stupid to be anyone Cyril truly desired. He didn't have to feel guilty when three letters became thirty. Sixty. Two hundred seventy-four. Like his increasingly risky exploits with the Anonymous collective, he could tell himself it was just for kicks. That he was doing it as a favor. Life in Afghanistan was rough, and Tavis needed something to live for, back home.

More lies.

Then Tav's deployment ended, and he returned to the base at Port Hueneme, which meant he could drive up to see her every weekend, once he got a car. He listened with half an ear to Cyril's hastily delivered CliffsNotes on his correspondence with Robin, and then slipped back into her life as effortlessly as if he'd never gone. Whenever Robin strayed into unfamiliar territory, all he needed to do was dash off a text, and good old Cyril would fill in the details. Robin suspected nothing; if anything, Tav's enduring loyalty to the childhood friend who grew more caustic and reclusive with each passing year only made her love him more.

Cyril should have called it quits, then (and a thousand times before and after). But he would have lost her, and he couldn't. He was the one who had needed something to live for, and Robin had become his life. Even if only online.

One deployment became two. Months turned into years. And then one day—on an impulse, as he did everything—Tavis proposed.

Cyril panicked. Dating was one thing, but marriage? He and Robin had discussed it, though only in the vaguest terms, via email. It was no small matter for her, and she felt the pressure to live up to her parents' abiding romance, the afterglow of which continued to sustain her mother long after her father's passing. He couldn't stand by and let her commit her life to a lie. But he couldn't just tell her the truth, either. After having finally given up on college, he was living in the granny unit behind what had been his mother's house, existing on what he made renting the place out and eBaying the free shit companies sent him to eviscerate on his increasingly popular tech blog.

He starved himself for what seemed like weeks. He wrote and discarded a thousand confessions. Because he craved the reassuring high of her instant feedback, he composed vows and sent them to her. She loved his words, she said. She could not wait to spend the rest of her life living happily ever after.

The high lasted only so long as it took to read her enthusiastic reply. Doubt was forever. Inevitably, he allowed himself that one bag of Cheetos, just so he could focus on something other than his hunger, and then it wasn't just one bag, it was three, and then a frozen pizza, and by the time the tux he'd rented for the

wedding arrived he couldn't get it on. He spent nights picking
fights on the internet and didn't sleep for days. When he finally
took a handful of sleeping pills the night before the wedding, he
had nightmarish hallucinations of leaping to his feet in the
middle of the ceremony to declaim the truth and declare his love
for her.

Instead, when the moment came, he buttoned up the clear-
ance-rack suit Tavis had rustled up at the eleventh hour and stood
three feet to the right of where he wanted to be, nails cutting
bloody crescents into his palms. Robin's face was luminous
as Tavis recited the words Cyril had written for her.

After that, his hopes diminished in inverse proportion to the
expansion of his waistline. But even as vanishingly small as those
hopes were, he clung to the belief that deep in her heart of
hearts, Robin knew. That she would recognize the
truth. That's how delusional he had become.

When she graduated, she moved onto the base with Tavis, and
when they'd saved up a down payment they bought a fixer-upper
in Camarillo, the city where he'd been born. Tavis was on leave
again, for a month or however long it was that time, and he'd
walked four blocks to the granny unit Cyril called home to catch
up on Robin's correspondence and play a couple hours' worth of
Counterstrike. He'd overstayed that estimate by an hour when his
phone pinged once, and then again.

"She's gonna be pissed if you're not home in time," Cyril
said, knowing Tavis knew this perfectly well. "Her mom's coming
for dinner, remember?"

Tavis hadn't moved from his position on the worn leather
couch: feet kicked up on one arm, Xbox controller in hand. "Just
one more level. It's fine."

Not two minutes later, his phone pinged again. Cyril knew he
was asking for trouble, but he never was any good at keeping his
mouth shut. "You should let her know if—"

"I'll *deal* with it," Tavis snapped. Then he sighed. "I know you think you know everything about her, but she's my wife, dude."

As if Cyril didn't know. Writing to Robin when Tavis was home was necessary—it was how she had become accustomed to communicating the most important things—but too risky to do more than once or twice a week. Even then, he had to stick to general platitudes and remember to fill Tavis in on every last detail. But if Robin got angry at Tavis, she'd put it in an email, and then it would fall to Cyril to smooth over. It would, at least, be some meaningful contact from her during what was, ordinarily, a lean season for him. So he shrugged. "Fine."

The next interruption was not a ping, but a knock. Before Cyril had time to haul his ass out of his computer chair, the door swung wide, and there she was, framed by the pink-purple light of dusk like some modern-art Madonna. He froze. It wasn't often he saw her in the flesh.

Tavis was on his feet in an instant, sputtering apologies.

Her face was angry—but not *really* angry. Cyril could see that much. "You were supposed to be home half an hour ago," she said, arms folded over her chest in exaggerated outrage.

Astonishingly, Tavis couldn't see the smile hidden behind her eyes. "I'm sorry, Robbie," he said, "I thought—"

"I couldn't wait," she said, raising her voice to drown out his next excuse. "For you to slink in halfway through dinner. Not unless you wanted my mom to figure it out first, Tav."

"Figure out, uh, what?" His electric blue eyes flickered to Cyril's face. Was there something he should have known? Something conveyed by email that Cyril hadn't relayed? It wouldn't have been the first time.

Cyril shrugged. This was news to him.

Robin pulled one hand out of the crook of her arm. Cyril had never actually seen one in person, but he recognized the object she raised like a trophy: a pregnancy test.

Tavis blinked at it for one uncomprehending moment. "Is that —" And then he choked out a laugh. "Robbie, oh my God!"

Robin threw her arms around him, eyes shut tight. "You're gonna be a *dad*."

There had been many final moments—so many Rubicons crossed—prior to their arrival at this place and time. But this moment, here and now, was Cyril's last stand. His final opportunity to repent and wipe the slate clean. What he and Tavis had already done to her was bad enough. But to involve a child? Unforgivable.

Tavis looked at Cyril over Robin's shoulder, one eyebrow raised in a helpless question: What now? Should they confess?

Cyril hesitated for half an instant, and then gave the slightest shake of his head. (What, like it's a surprise? Tavis knew Cyril was a coward, and he fucking left it up him.)

"I—I'm so happy," Tavis stuttered.

And that was it. *Finito*. Robin, fluent in Italian, would have said it thus: *Lasciate ogne speranza, voi ch'intrate*. Abandon all hope, ye who enter here.

Cyril had seen the sign, and stepped through the door.

CHAPTER 4

NOW

He cannot sleep.

The frequent flyers had warned him he wouldn't, and he didn't believe them. He hasn't had a solid nights' rest in five goddamn years. He'd have given his right arm for one night on a good bed. Here it is, and Jesus, apparently there's not enough snoring or jerking off.

As soon as he is sure she is asleep in her room, he rifles through the medicine cabinet. Not because he's an addict, but because pills are currency. Power. Unfortunately, she is a responsible mother who doesn't leave her pills or power tools unsecured. The good stuff, assuming she has any, is probably stashed on a high shelf in her bedroom closet.

Maybe not because of the kids. Maybe because of him.

You don't have to do this, Tavis would have said, leaning his rangy frame against the bathroom door. But Tavis wasn't here—not that his presence ever stopped Cyril in any case.

He goes through her fridge next. Mostly what she's got is fruits and veggies, but there's milk and cheese and half a loaf of bread, too, so he takes it all to the table and sets to work. When his stomach is so full his gut aches, he returns to the kitchen and digs through the cabinets until he unearths a Costco-sized box of chocolate-laced protein bars. He consumes maybe ten, standing at the counter, plucking at his sweat-dampened shirt. Then he finds a couple of ice cream sandwiches hidden in the back of the freezer, and there's room for nothing in his mind but the thought of how full he is and how much it hurts and goddamn, it feels *so fucking good.*

He walks slowly, carefully, into the living room. He turns the lamp on, and then the TV, volume low, before lowering himself to the couch, stabilizing his belly with one hand. His waistband stretches wire tight. When he polishes off the last of the protein bars, the ones he brought with him, he is breathing hard.

CHAPTER 4.5

SIX YEARS AGO

"I can't do this anymore." In all the years Tavis and Cyril had performed this strange, tangled dance, each of them must have said these words a thousand times. It was Tavis who spoke that day, and even over the fragmented Skype connection Cyril had known that this time, he was for real.

Their arrangement, the one where Cyril handled all the complicated emotional labor and Tavis got the girl, couldn't work. Not up close. Not long term. Robin would inevitably discover the truth.

"You can't rush this," Cyril said. "We need a plan. Give me some time."

Maybe he'd even started working on that plan. Or maybe he hadn't. Maybe he'd just been borrowing time. Tavis never found out one way or the other, because the Afghan kid who worked odd jobs for him went missing. His father and uncle killed. When Tav's inquiries unearthed a trail of corruption, his superiors ordered him to look the other way. He declined.

Saving the kid was a phenomenally stupid idea. Cyril told him as much. Repeatedly. "Getting yourself court-martialed or shot to shit is not an exit strategy. What if you get your legs blown off?

Or your arms. You want her to spend the rest of her life wiping your ass? Come home, buy her some fucking flowers, and get on your knees." He knew her. Better than Tavis, it seemed. "Believe me, she doesn't want your blood."

Cyril had given up hope of making this right when Robin got pregnant, but Tavis still thought he could pull it off. He convinced himself this could be his road to salvation. If he bucked command and saved the kid, he'd be a hero. Then, when he told Robin the truth, she'd have to love him in spite of his sins. And if she didn't —well, at least he could face himself in the mirror again. Cyril's letters tumbled to a footnote, in his mind. As, perhaps, they always had been.

Dumbass.

But Tav's mind was made up, and if he was going to do this thing, Cyril couldn't let him go it alone. He did securities work, on an off, for a software company with a defense contract, which meant half the work of gaining access to the information Tavis needed—winning the trust of people with the right clearances— was already accomplished. Tavis knew his command was hiding information involving the whereabouts of the kid, and working from the back end forward, Cyril was able to tell him exactly what to look for in the architecture of the local system.

Would Tavis have gotten himself killed if Cyril hadn't helped him penetrate his command's classified server? If he hadn't shown Tavis how to cover his digital footprints, would he have realized the futility of his efforts and given up before the wrong person caught on and blasted him to kingdom come with an IED?

These are the questions that will torment this asshole for the rest of his life.

CHAPTER 5

NOW

His best friend's widow is perched on the end of the couch. She wears pajama pants and a ribbed tank top over her ubiquitous sports bra, knees pulled up to her chest, hands wrapped around a cup of steaming coffee. Morning light forms a soft halo around her face, and because of this he wonders if he is dreaming. There were a lot of dreams like this, in prison. None of them ended well.

She glances at him. "You sleep all right?" Her eyes flicker back to the morning show, muted with the captions on. She raises the mug to her lips. "After you raided the kitchen, I mean." There is no trace of sarcasm in her tone. Only truth, seasoned with a dash of dry humor. Motherhood has made her unflappable.

This asshole pushes himself upright, tugging his shirt down over his belly, running a hand over his face to clear the sleep from his eyes. "Better than usual." Also truth. "I have to piss."

Strange to say that, and then just... go. Alone. Behind a solid door that locks. He checks it three times.

Even more strange: she is still there when he returns, hugging her knees, sipping coffee. Her toes curl over the welted edge of the cushion.

He lumbers into the kitchen, wincing as his knees crack. Stained-glass sun-catchers, the handiwork of Robin's mother Glennis, cast a rainbow of leopard spots over his pale skin. He hadn't touched the cereal the night before, and there's still a little milk, so he pours them each a bowl of mini wheats. As if this is totally normal for him. "Here," he says, shoving one at her face.

"Thanks." She lets her feet drop to the floor and makes room for her mug on the coffee table, pushing aside design magazines and empty protein bar wrappers.

He watches her lift the spoon to her mouth. Everything still feels vaguely unreal.

She glances up. "Well?"

He sets the bowl next to her mug before lowering himself onto the couch. Then, even however many pounds down he is, this asshole is still too fucking fat to reach his own cereal. Her eyebrow quirks, and she watches, unperturbed, as he rocks himself forward, hooks a foot around the leg off the coffee table to pull it closer, and reaches again.

On television, the morning show hosts are interviewing an epidemiologist. They pepper her with questions about the pandemic but won't let her get a word in edgewise. Five minutes in, nothing of substance has been said, and they cut her off to break for commercials.

Robin spoons a couple of sugared squares into her mouth. Chews. "So here's the thing," she says, swallowing.

He looks at her.

She looks back. "I forgive you."

He does not ask what for. The answer is written in her frank, unwavering stare. *Everything.*

Does he break down, or stammer, or cry? Don't be naïve.

He laughs. Then this asshole heaves himself to his feet and shuffles into the kitchen, still chuckling, as if she's told a rather amusing joke and he's still replaying the punchline in his head.

He pours another bowl of cereal before remembering the milk is gone. He opens the fridge, but there's not much left he hasn't already consumed. Yogurt? Eggs? It's been five years since he's had a decent fried egg. Peanut butter, the real kind. Cantaloupe? Shit, just *pick* something.

And then she is standing next to him, looking in. Her bare skin brushes the hair on the back of his arm. He moves away.

"I mean it," she says.

"I'm sure you think you do." She'd been angry—so angry—when she discovered that Cyril, not her saintly departed husband, was the author and perfecter of their strange romance. For seven years she had shared her most intimate thoughts with him, thinking she wrote to the man who shared her bed. Cyril had hoped to bury the lie with Tavis, but she'd found out the truth the day she drove him to prison.

Robin knows well what he did to her; what she doesn't know is what he did to Tavis. And that's the rub.

He grabs the eggs from the fridge. "Funny how you didn't mention this yesterday."

"You've been gone for five years. I needed to know you were still... you."

The mixing bowls are not above the stove, which is where she kept them in her Camarillo home. Instead, he locates them to the right of the sink, down on the bottom shelf. To pull them out, he lowers himself to one knee and bends, belly brushing the floor. Like everything else, he considers this her fault. "You mean the traitor who killed his best friend and fucked over his widow?"

"Wow." She turns, framed by the rectangle of stainless-steel fridge doors, and sucks a breath in through her teeth. She is beautiful when she does this. She is beautiful doing anything. "You do *not* make this easy."

He said it out loud, and still she doesn't believe him. Not really. He can see it in her eyes. She thinks he's exaggerating. Because, like her husband before her, she will always give him the benefit of the doubt. And look where that got Tavis. This asshole hooks an arm over the edge of the counter, exhaling a grunt as he hauls himself back to his feet. "So now you're expecting... what, gratitude?"

Of course she expects gratitude. It's what any normal, functional human being would feel.

Except that between Tav's death and this moment lie five fucking years of silence. This asshole deserved every hellish minute, it's true; but if she'd wanted to extend an olive branch, why wait until now? He'd had nothing but time, in prison. And now—now, suddenly, he's supposed to believe she's decided to forgive?

No. There is no gratitude.

What he feels is resentment. Fury. Hate.

That's right. He hates her. He has always hated her. He could not have done the things he did, otherwise. Why? That much should be obvious. She is kind and generous and strong. She is all he cannot ever have. He doesn't delude himself. He has known it from the start. And what he cannot have, he will destroy.

He could tell her these things. He could make her weep. He doesn't, because she won't believe. She offers absolution because, all evidence to the contrary, she still believes he's human, deep inside. Like most decent human beings, she can't wrap her brain around the possibility that she might be standing in the presence of a monster. *But he seemed so normal!* That's what they always said about killers, wasn't it? It's not his fault people are idiots.

There are six eggs in a carton which once held twenty-four. He cracks them all into the bowl. The whisk, at least, is where it ought to be. Milk would have made this better, but he's always flexible when it comes to food. He'll make do with cheese.

She stands in the open threshold between the kitchen and the dining room, watching as he heats the oil in the pan and tips in the eggs. When it becomes clear that he is not going to speak, she slips around him and out through the laundry room in back.

He watches through the colored glass over the sink as she tromps down a path worn through the weedy hill of the back yard, disappearing into the barn below.

He is plating the omelet when she returns, hefting a transparent plastic storage bin filled with the things he left behind. She carts it through the kitchen, kicking the laundry room door shut with a heel, and drops it on the dining table. It contains mostly legal documents, obsolete electronics, and a few childhood photographs of Tavis he cannot throw out but will never look at again.

"Thought maybe you'd left some clothes." She glances at him through the open doorway and gives the lid a rap with her knuckles. "Anyway, there's your stuff." She pulls a phone out of her back pocket and pokes at it, frowning. Then she sighs and looks up. "Is it really nothing to you?"

Forgiveness, she means.

He drops the plate on the table and seats himself, leaning forward to plant elbows on either side. Once, the fullness of his belly would have prevented this; now it sags between his knees. "Doesn't change the past." He plunges the fork into the egg.

"No," she agrees.

"Then what does it mean?" More than anyone, she ought to understand the worthlessness of words. He reaches for the orange juice, only to realize he's left it on the counter in the kitchen. With a growl of exasperation, he starts to shove back from the table.

She waves him back to his seat. "I'll get it."

He despises her small, practical kindness. He wants nothing from her, except the hate that is his due. Is that why he got into her truck? To offer her the opportunity for retribution? If he thinks that will make things right, he is a fool.

She sets the glass to the right of his plate and seats herself opposite him. "Aren't you going to ask if I want some?" she asks, when he shoves the fork into his mouth.

He looks up. "Do you?"

"No," she admits, with a half-smile. But she stretches an arm across the table and helps herself to a sip from his glass.

Teasing him. Fucking *teasing* him. He shoves the table. It shudders across the floor with a tooth-grinding screech.

She hops to her feet, narrowly avoiding the table's edge. "Cyril, wait." She extends an arm to halt his retreat.

"Don't," he snarls, and her wrist is in his hand. Her eyes go wide. If he squeezed, he could break it. A snap. He wants to hit her. To make her bleed. You see? This is the kind of man he is become. Perhaps it is who he always was.

Then her hand becomes a fist, and her tendons flex beneath his fingertips. She grins.

He shoves her away. "Keep your fucking hands off me, or I'll—"

"What, break my arm?" She holds it up, unharmed. "You forget this goes two ways now—I know Tav's letters by heart. *Your* letters. Remember the time I got stitches after I nicked my thumb with the power drill, and you wrote me two entire pages about how guilty you felt because you were the one who convinced me to pursue my passion for woodworking?" She snorts. "You'd die before you hurt a hair on my head."

Harming her is not something he cannot do so much as a thing he would very much regret. If she pushes him, she will find there is a world of difference between the two. But when she reaches for him again, placing her hand with deliberate care on his doughy biceps, he cannot suppress a shudder. She already knows he is utterly undone by the flicker of fear in her eyes.

"You poor, miserable bastard," she says, with a sympathetic laugh. "You're shaking."

It's not fair: that's what he wants to say. Like a petulant child. But it's entirely fair. He lived inside her head without permission for seven long years.

"What do you want from me?" He wants to grab her and

shake, hard. "I know what I did. I can't undo it. It's done. So just —fucking *tell* me what you want. I'll do it. And then you can make me go." Because he can't do it himself. Won't. He cannot even pull himself free of her touch. He sucks in a long, rattling breath. "Please."

She looks up at him. Her fingers squeeze his flesh, briefly, and then fall away. "I'm trying to tell you, Cyril, I want you—" She hesitates, and then releases a slow breath, as if in defeat. "To stay."

CHAPTER 5.5

FIVE YEARS AGO

Tavis left a letter. It was the only one he'd ever personally written to his wife—and the idiot had entrusted it to Cyril's keeping.

Here was the problem: Tavis couldn't write for shit. It didn't matter whether he'd used his final communication to confess the truth or take their secret to the grave—if Robin read it, she would realize her husband had been a fraud. To protect her, all Cyril had to do was light a match. Far better to have loved and lost the perfect man than discover he never existed at all.

But this asshole didn't do that, did he? No. He delivered that fucking letter. He could say he'd been driven to it by guilt, or loyalty, or some combination of the two, but he didn't give a shit about preserving Tav's memory, or how devastating the truth might be to Robin. All that mattered was seeing her again.

When he found her at the cemetery, she just stood there, staring at her name written in Tav's sloppy font. "Seriously?" she choked, as despair gave way to anger and loathing. She looked from the envelope to Cyril's face and back again. "He left this with *you?*" And then she snatched it out of his hand, stuffed it in her purse, and stalked away. Alone.

Days passed. He waited for an angry phone call, or a fist pounding on his door. Nothing. He had waited like this when Tavis and Robin had first begun dating, convinced that she'd see through the charade. She never had. Was it possible, now, that she could still be so blind?

Every night, he squeezed himself behind the wheel of his Datsun and hit up a drive-through before parking in front of her house. Hours ticked by as he sat, watching the darkened façade, where, occasionally, a light upstairs might flick on or off. Once, she came out the side door to take a bag of garbage to the can. For ten minutes she stood in the dark, head bent as if in prayer. Weeping.

Knowing she was so close, and yet so unreachable, was torment.

At home, he pored over the intel he'd downloaded from USMC's classified servers, sifting it like powdered sugar. When Tavis had gotten him into the system, he had taken everything he could get his hands on. Anyone who detected the breach would have to think twice about confronting him, knowing the damage he could do with a single Wikileaks dump. But not one byte of all that data offered the slightest clue as to the kid's whereabouts. Tavis had given his life for an exploit doomed to fail.

Invariably, Cyril circled back to Tav's personal email account, re-reading his correspondence with Robin and composing anguished, grief-stricken letters that she would never read. The drafts folder had spilled onto two pages before the obvious solution presented itself: why *couldn't* Tavis have stockpiled a set of letters to be delivered in the event of his death? If Robin found him out, it wasn't as though she could leave him any more alone.

He hit send.

And she showed up at his door.

He'd thought the jig was up—until he'd glanced down to find Seth standing on the threshold. Robin had apologized—to him!—

for the interruption and explained that her three-year-old insisted upon being friends with his father's best friend.

And suddenly he was babysitting the kid and Robin was in his house, in his life, breaking down in his fucking bathroom when she found out she was pregnant with her dead husband's second child. She still hated Cyril—that hadn't changed—but it didn't matter. He could write to her—in a careful, roundabout way—and say all the things she so desperately needed to hear.

But the more time he spent with Seth, the more he couldn't stop thinking about that little Afghan boy. The data made it clear that the kid's abduction by an ostensible ally on the ground in Afghanistan was part of a personal spat between local leaders. USMC had decided that overlooking the matter was necessary to the success of an overall strategy involving several less-than-ethical components. Civilian deaths, questionable interrogation methods, etc. Cyril didn't have access to the specifics, but... he was sitting on a horde of classified intel so massive that leaking it would be a media bombshell. If he packaged the information in the right way, he could shape the narrative into a story the press couldn't ignore. Tavis had taken half a dozen videos of Shafik, and he was a cute little bugger with a million-watt-smile. His would be the face CNN would play on a loop as political commentators and war correspondents discussed evidence of corruption and mismanagement within USMC command. The clickbait potential was irresistible.

The administration would have no choice but to deal with the fallout, and the most effective way to divert public attention—assuming Cyril managed to capture it—would be to find the kid. Command knew exactly who'd done the kidnapping, so retrieving him wasn't so much impossible as it was tactically undesirable. Make a big enough stink, and "rescuing" Shafik would suddenly become top priority. They'd trot him out for press photos with the hero soldiers who'd located him, then send him home with a scholarship fund or something. Just enough of a win to make the public feel like they could, in good conscience, look away. No need to worry about underlying systemic corruption, move along, move along.

Cyril could save the kid. All it would cost was his freedom.

It wasn't much of a sacrifice. At six hundred pounds, quality of life wasn't significantly better in a studio apartment than a prison cell. He even rigged a literal kill switch, which seemed hilarious in a gallows humor kind of way. All he had to do was hit the big red button, and everything went public, immediately. And then he sat on it. For weeks. Months. It was always the same excuse: Just one more afternoon with Seth. One more brief inter-action with Robin. Somehow, without quite understanding what had happened, it was not just Robin he loved, anymore. It was Robin and Seth, inseparable. And leaving Seth would break his heart.

Ironically, it was the letters that did him in. USMC hadn't a clue that Tavis had a partner, but they brought in the Feds to comb through his shit, trying to patch any holes he'd left in the system. When they turned up the emails Cyril was sending from Tav's account, they confronted Robin.

Even then, the magnitude of the thing was too much for her to comprehend. She assumed he had stepped into Tav's shoes posthumously. That revelation alone was more than enough to break her. Certainly it was enough for her to cut him out of her life.

The only thing left, then, was to leak that goddamn intel.

He wasn't stupid enough to imagine, as Tavis had, that saving the kid would redeem him in her eyes. And it didn't. But it was enough for her to invite him back into her children's lives when Nora was born. That, and the fact that he came with an expira-tion date. They let him out on bail (because where was a six-hundred-pound man planning to go?) and after that it was only a matter of months before the lawyers hashed it out and he went to prison. Until then, he cooked and cleaned and read to Seth for hours, and, when the boy nodded off, took the night shift with an ever-colicky Nora so Robin could rest. She ate his food with relish and, occasionally, as she passed by, placed an errant hand upon his arm. Somehow, miraculously, he had blundered into his own personal fantasy. Well—sans sex, but you couldn't have everything. It was enough.

She drove him to Taft herself. She hugged him. She cried. He let her go.

"No," she said, rummaging in her purse. "Wait."

And then, right there at the finish line, she pulled out the envelope. Worn and slightly crumpled, with her name scrawled across the front. She'd kept it with her, always, but hadn't had the courage to open it. Until now. Here, with him, at the very end.

I didn't write any of the letters, Tavis had penned. *You're smart, Robbie, so I am pretty sure you can guess who did.*

CHAPTER 6
NOW

"You want me—" He glances at the dining table and snorts. "You want me to stay. Here."

"Well, you know, probably the couch." She shrugs. "But... yeah. Here."

There is a knock.

"Oh—" Her eyes go to the clock on the stove. "That's the kids."

He lifts an arm, too late to stop her as she sweeps around his circumference and heads for the entryway. "Wait," he calls, with force.

She pauses, hand on doorknob, eyebrows raised.

"The kids. What are you—" In her shoes, even this asshole would not have let her children within five miles of him, forgiveness or no. They are wholly innocent, these biological byproducts of his best friend and the woman he wants to fuck. He may hate her as much as he doesn't want to love her, but the kids share none of that baggage. They do not deserve him.

"What? You're not gonna eat them. At least I hope not." And she opens the door. They rush her, shrieking and jumping with such enthusiasm that they seem like many more than two. "Hold on guys, hold on." She laughs, bending to dispense hugs as they leap into her strong arms.

I want you to stay.

He expects the kids to be chaperoned by Robin's mother, but the woman standing on the porch is not the small, birdlike woman of his memory. This one is in her fifties, easily six feet tall, with the muscular bulk of a linebacker. She is white, but olive-toned, perhaps of Latin extraction. The frown permanently stamped on her unmasked face grows deeper as her eyes rise from the children to his face. She knows who he is. What he has done. Not just the misdeeds which are public record, but his private sins. The things he did to Robin.

Before this asshole can hurl a snide comment in her direction, Seth's attention breaks from his mother. The boy seems taller than his nine years warrant—all knees and elbows, like his father at the same age. His face contracts into a puzzled frown when he sees Cyril, and then his eyes go wide.

The little sister—an infant, last Cyril held her—dashes toward the kitchen, oblivious to his presence until she nearly plows into his thigh. She performs an impressive about-face, poof-ball pigtails bobbing as she barrels back toward the door wailing "Mooommy!"

"Nora," Robin says, attempting to pry her daughter's arms away from her legs, "we talked about this, remember? It's okay!" She glances up, flashing a slightly exasperated smile.

Seth crosses the floor more slowly. He stops a few paces away, gazing up at Cyril with his mother's bottomless brown eyes. It does not even occur to him to be bashful or shy.

I want you to stay.

She could have spoken those words a thousand times, and he wouldn't have believed her. But here, with her children, she has handed him her heart.

Why?

He, Cyril, pulls out a dining chair and sits. Not so much to bring himself to the boy's level as to keep his knees from buckling beneath the weight of the universe. He clears his throat. "Hey, kid." It comes out cool and dry. He is good at this. Pretending not to care.

Seth's mouth spreads into a slow grin, wide and as pleasantly toothy as his mother's. But it won't hold. His lips quaver. Tears drop like pearls from his lower lids.

And then this asshole is holding Robin's precious child in his arms, accepting his tearful welcome like a soldier home from battle. Just one of many priceless gifts he has stolen from his best and only friend.

"I knew it," the boy sobs. "I knew you would come home."

I want you to stay.

"If you're having second thoughts"—this comes in a low voice from the older woman, still standing on the threshold—"I can keep them for another—"

Robin interrupts her with a laugh. "He'd never hurt the kids. Not in a million years." How can she possibly have such confidence in him?

The crease between the woman's eyebrows deepens, as if she's asking herself the same question. "And you?"

"Oh," Robin says, clapping a hand to the woman's shoulder as she ushers her out the door, "don't worry. I can take care of myself." She glances at him, then, and the twitch at the corner of her smile says, *Don't make me regret this, Cyril.*

They both know, without a shadow of a doubt, that he will.

———

LUNCH. ROBIN'S DAUGHTER STARES HIM DOWN ACROSS the table. "Why are you so big?"

"Shoulda seen me before prison, kid."

"Nora," Robin warns, shaking Cheetos from a bag onto Seth's plate. "Let's be nice."

"That's just *Cyril*," Seth says around a mouthful of grilled cheese, his earnest, overly-patient tone suggesting his little sister might be dumb as rocks. In the two hours he's been home, Seth has worn a path from the dining table to his bedroom and back again, a one-kid parade of tiny treasures for Cyril's examination. Sticks in just the right shape. Objects unearthed in forgotten corners of the schoolyard. Drawings. Stuffed animals. Lego creations. T-shirts from a selection of fairs and summer camps and theatrical productions. A binder of meticulously organized Pokémon cards. It is as though he is attempting to account for every hour they have lost. Time that Tavis will never have.

"But he's fat." Half her brother's height, Nora is a condensed, chipmunk-cheeked facsimile of her mother. Her voice, however, is the same unmodulated shout that Seth's was, at that age, tuned to an even higher pitch. She peels the two slices of bread apart and uses her nails to scrape the melted cheese.

"Everyone's different," Seth insists. He's sliding half-off his chair, bouncing on the ball of one foot. No longer four, but still perpetually in motion. "Some people are tall, some people are short, some people are brown, some people are beige. That's just how it is."

Nora holds up an index finger and then levels it, accusingly, at Cyril's gut. "But he's *really* fat."

"Nora!" Robin puts a hand on her daughter's arm and gives it a downward shove, favoring Cyril with a sour eye-roll. "And you thought I was a great parent." She plops herself into a seat and helps herself to a handful of Cheetos directly from the bag. "Turns out it's just luck of the draw."

"Yeah," Seth agrees, affably. "Nora's kind of a jerk."

Nora twists her face into a scowl and screeches. Her gappy baby teeth look like they've been filed to points. Despite her efforts to prove otherwise, or perhaps precisely because of them, she is intensely adorable.

Robin rubs her eyes with her fingertips. "Nora, do you need a time out?"

"No!" She slumps back in her chair, thrusting out a lower lip.

"And Seth, I know Nora can be difficult, but can you please—"

"I know," he says. "Sorry."

"Thanks, buddy." Robin lifts her soda can and peers into it before taking a swig, perhaps wishing for something stronger. Corona had been her elixir of choice, back in the before-times.

Nora meets his eyes with brazen confidence. The instant Seth asks a question and her mother's attention is diverted, she sticks out her tongue.

Cyril tears off a chunk of sandwich and chucks it at her. It hits her square on the forehead and bounces onto the table next to her plate. For a split second her face goes blank with disbelief, and then she opens her mouth wide to let loose a piercing banshee shriek.

Seth laughs so hard he tips his chair over and tumbles to the ground. "I'm fine! I'm fine!"

"It's not funny!" Nora wails.

"Sweetie—" Robin bites her lip to keep herself from laughing until, finally, she fails. She puts her head in her hands and laughs so hard Seth asks if she's crying and all she can do is shake her head.

The first time Cyril had seen her laugh like that—helpless and utterly unselfconscious—Seth had been about two or three. Tavis had brought the kid with him to Cyril's place and stayed too long playing Counterstrike and she'd appeared, not quite angry, to fetch them home for dinner. Seth had turned around, having managed to find a sharpie while the adults were talking, and proudly displayed his "mussache." He'd drawn it across the bridge of his nose. Robin had laughed so hard she'd choked on her own spit and had to go to the bathroom to splash her face with water. Cyril, who had never laughed like that in his entire life, wanted only to make her do it again, somehow, and never ever stop.

It takes a moment for Nora to realize her mother is not, in fact, on her side—but when the realization sinks in, her angry wails turn to grief-stricken sobs.

"Oh, Sweetie," Robin says, using her thumbs to wipe the tears laughter has squeezed from her eyes. She reaches for her daughter, pulling the child into her embrace. "Come here. You gotta learn that not everybody is gonna put up with your nonsense the way we do."

Robin loves her children more fiercely than anything in life, and when she presses her lips to the top of her daughter's head, lifting her eyes to look at Cyril, it shows. "I swear," she says, "someday she is gonna say something to the wrong person and get herself punched in the face."

It would be so easy, now, to surrender to this domestic daydream. But they both know it's bullshit. Robin. The kids. This asshole sitting here, like he's part of the fucking family, like Tavis isn't dead. "Why are you doing this?"

Robin gives her daughter a pat on the behind, sending her back to her chair. She sits back, ignoring the kids as they begin to bicker again, and studies him. Not angry. Almost half-amused, as if to say, really? Here? In front of the children? She rests an arm on the table and pushes her soda can from her thumb to her forefinger and back again. "I told you. I want you—"

"To stay? What, as your nanny?" Just as he had done when Tavis died and Robin was alone and terrified and about to give birth to his fatherless child. Cyril had wormed his way into Tav's family, pretending to be the friend Robin so desperately needed—while privately indulging the pathetic fantasy that he was her husband.

Robin gives him another long, steady look, her eyes slightly lidded. "Well," she says, finally, "if that's all you're comfortable with for now, then yeah." She lifts the soda to her lips. "Sure."

"What the fuck is that supposed to mean?" Only as he speaks does he realize the children have fallen silent. He glances at Seth, who looks stricken. "Sorry."

"Fuck!" Nora exclaims, with relish. It is clearly not the first time she has heard this word. "Fuck, fuck, *fuuuuck!*"

"Oh my God, Cyril." Robin tilts her head back, running her hands over her short hair, and lets out a laugh that is partly a sigh. "Are you really going to make me spell this out?"

Her laughter is infuriating; the more so because he cannot stop his eyes from following the sinuous curve of her neck. "Spell *what* out?"

She sits forward, letting her hand hover for a moment before placing it on top of his. Still, he cannot help but flinch. Her touch is electric. He watches, frozen, as her fingers turn and slide under his soft white palm. She brushes a callused thumb over the dimples on his knuckles. "Cyril—"

"No." He jerks his hand away.

"No?" her voice is amused.

"Don't play this game." She's fucking with him, and he knows it, and she knows he knows it. Trying to get him to lower his guard, to admit he is besotted with her, waiting for the perfect opportunity to insert the blade. But that kind of subterfuge is his forte, not hers. "Because you will lose."

And yet—he cannot pretend he does not see the hunger in her eyes.

They were just letters. Only words. That was what he told himself. Prison was exactly what he'd deserved; she was protected from further harm, and, ultimately, she would recover. Pull her life together. Move on. She might forgive him, sure, in theory. Eventually. But this—no.

The children share a nervous snicker. Her gaze does not waver.

"Fuck!" Nora announces, again.

Robin lifts a hand, slowly, and places her palm on his cheek.

In front of the kids. He feels the warmth of her skin, and the smooth cold line of her wedding band.

Once upon a time, she was a strong, independent woman, and now—could he have damaged her so badly that she thinks she needs... him? Tavis? *Someone?* No. It must be a ruse.

"Oh, Chica," he whispers, covering her hand with his own. "Don't let me ruin you again."

STAGE 2

DENIAL

CHAPTER 7

On his second morning post-incarceration, this asshole is awakened by a cold little finger poking around in his navel. Ordinarily his response to being touched in his sleep would be sudden and violent, but the unfamiliarity of the sensation delays his lunge-and-swing by a fraction of a second. His fist, as Nora darts back, just misses her head. The television remote clatters to the ground, disgorging batteries. "Jesus—"

She giggles, oblivious to her brush with disaster, and dashes out of the living room. A door slams, and Seth's shout comes from their bedroom: "Nora! *Stop!*" Her screeching rejoinder pierces the thin walls.

"If Nora's up," Robin says, shrugging a robe over her shoulders on the way to the kitchen, "everybody's up."

This asshole rubs his eyes with his palms. "Guess I'm not the only one who hasn't changed."

She opens the fridge. "Damn it." Her footsteps come back, past the dining table and into the living room. She tosses her phone, which lands on his stomach with a plop. "If you're gonna keep bingeing, at least order more food." She starts into the hall, then catches the doorframe and leans back around the corner. "Oh, and your lawyer's been texting. I'm free later this morning, so see what you can set up."

It's that easy.

Even having known Cyril since they were kids, Tavis had always assumed, like everyone else, that hacking was about code. Typing in strings of numbers and letters and symbols that magically unlocked digital doors. While this asshole could and did do that, on occasion, hacking was primarily about opportunity. Having the audacity, for example, to open a browser on Robin's phone and download an incognito tracking app. Cyril has no immediate motive for doing so, but that's not the point. Want is weakness. Information is power.

That accomplished, Cyril opens her messages and sees that his lawyer has, in fact, been peppering Robin with a string of half-coherent texts. At... 6 AM. Jesus. Before replying, he peruses Robin's recent texting history. (As if he wouldn't.)

There's a lot of back-and-forth between her and some guy named Charles Dugan, whose roof she has apparently just replaced. Atcha wants a new pergola and is willing to wait until Robin has time. Lydia wonders if Robin knows someone who does plumbing. All recent work requests have been politely declined; after she wraps up her current projects, Robin plans to spend the next few months working on her own house.

The only person she texts with on a personal basis is Greta, no last name supplied. The most recent exchange (*Nora just woke up, we'll come when she's ready*) makes it clear that this is the woman who brought the kids home. He scrolls backward through their correspondence, sees a reference to a "Mr. Cooke," and connects the dots with a twinge of surprise: Greta is the wife of Samuel Cooke. The man Cyril worked for, from time to time— and whose company he had hacked *en route* to the military intel which had landed him in prison. Robin had done some repair work on the guy's condo down in Thousand Oaks and had planned on coming up north to work on his house the summer Cyril went to prison. In the intervening years, Cooke and his wife have apparently turned into something more than employers.

Cyril is about to tap back to the list of Robin's contacts when his thumb stops on a line from Greta. *Have you decided? I need to know in advance if you want me to take the kids.* Surely this is a reference to his arrival, but the timestamp on the message shows it was sent more than a week ago. When Robin had picked him up the day before yesterday, she had complained about the last-minute notification.

He scrolls upward a bit more and, finding nothing more enlightening from Greta, returns to his lawyer's correspondence. The words pop out at him like they're written in fire.

Per our convo yesterday: Your letter was persuasive, but the Bureau will not consider early release without guarantee of housing. If you agree I will send paperwork via DocuSign. If not, we can explore other options.

Robin's answer is one word: *Okay.* The timestamp shows she took a full twenty-four hours to reply.

"Oh look." Robin stands framed in the kitchen doorway, hand on hip. "What is this, forty-eight hours out? And you're already violating my privacy?"

He holds up the phone. "You—you fucking got me out?"

"Oh." She snorts, hand dropping loosely to her side as she crosses the floor. "Right." She plucks the phone from his hand, glances at the screen, and slips it into her back pocket. "You only had a year or two left anyway. Assuming you could keep up the good behavior."

Only. "I fucking know how much time I had left." God, he's an idiot. She doesn't want him. He doesn't know what her game is, but it's a game. And she doesn't seem to be bothered that he's found out. "You're a goddamn liar."

She lets out a bark of laughter. "Gosh, I wonder who I learned that from?" She plucks the phone from his hand, slips it into her back pocket, and turns to yell toward the hall: "Grab your masks, guys and dolls! We're going out for breakfast! You too," she adds, giving him a nod.

This coy, plotting creature is not the scrupulously honest woman he'd once known. Who the hell has she become? He heaves himself forward, to the edge of the couch and then to his feet. "Why are you fucking with me?"

She lifts one eyebrow. "Am I, though?"

———

ROBIN'S DILAPIDATED VICTORIAN SITS ON THE largest lot in a leafy neighborhood filled with cutesy arts and crafts bungalows and immaculately tended gardens. It's only four blocks to the center of town, though the kids do twice that running to each corner and back, apparently unbothered by their masks. This asshole is winded, but not incapacitated. Yeah. What a triumph. So much better than before.

"Is it weird?" she asks, ducking under a low-hanging branch.

Being free, she means. Apparently they're no longer discussing her newfound talent for lying by omission. He casts his gaze down the shady, tree-lined streets. The cool morning air is raucous with birdsong. "Yeah." No guards. No gates. No barbed wire. And no other assholes. "It's weird." His paladin—a repeat offender who'd been downgraded to the camp from a medium-security facility up north—spoke of experiencing a kind of vertigo, out in the open. Cyril doesn't feel that, but he had forgotten the world could be anything but yellow and gray.

They go a few more steps in silence, though his breathing is loud. Their elbows bump. He shifts to the curb.

"Was it bad?" She keeps her voice low.

"Oh," he says, "I know this one. That's code for 'did I get raped.'"

"Cyril."

"I didn't get raped." Stabbed, yes, the once. "They don't put rapists in low-security facilities."

She rolls her eyes and sighs. "Well, good, but—"

"It was fucking prison, Chica. Of course it was bad." He hesitates. "But not in the ways you'd think."

Tavis had complained that the unofficial motto of the Navy was "hurry up and wait." That military life was mostly long stretches of boredom punctuated by absolute terror, and often the boredom was worse. This is also a strikingly apt description of prison.

Most of the terror had been up front, before his commissary funds had worked their way into the system and he'd had nothing but his wits for leverage. But people were people—which was to say, dumb as fuck—and once he'd acclimated to the routines of dormitory-style prison life, the primary challenge had simply been not losing his goddamn mind. He couldn't check enough books out of the prison library to keep himself occupied, and they had a shit selection anyway. The GED and skill certification classes were useless to him, and he was not interested in volunteering to teach a bunch of morons. Eventually they'd realized the fat guy was worth more in the kitchen than out, no matter how much he ate, but food prep had only occupied five hours a day, at most. Without the internet at his fingertips, that left eighteen hours to kill. You could only sleep so long.

Four months in, it hit him: everyone else was as bored out of their skulls as he was.

"Do you want to talk about it?" She asks this quietly, darting a glance at the children.

He tugs his shirt down. It may fit, but only when he's standing still. It's not much of a distinction, but if he's going to be seen in public he'd rather be ogled for being huge than for being unable to fit into his own clothing. "D&D."

"What?" Her head snaps forward, attention shifting lightning-fast. "Seth! See the car in the driveway? Grab your sister's—yeah.

Thanks, buddy!" She lets out a puff of air and lifts a hand, gesturing for him to continue.

"Dungeons and Dragons. The tabletop role playing game. That's how I survived."

"I know what D&D is," she says, giving him a withering glance. "But perhaps you could elaborate a little."

He shrugs. "I didn't have an actual manual to reference, so I had to wing it." He'd recruited a couple of disillusioned ex-army thugs who hadn't adjusted well to civilian life—natural fans of his government-fucking exploits—to start the core of his campaign. Dice were forbidden, but they sold playing cards at the commissary. He'd modified a deck to function as a D20, and paper for character sheets was easy to come by. The story he kept in his head.

Nothing escaped attention. He expected to catch some flak for playing what amounted to a child's game, but in prison, novelty trumped cool, and soon everyone in the unit wanted to know what the hell they were doing, using cards to tell stories about elves and cowboys and cactus-people in a post-apocalyptic wasteland. He let them watch and, when the time was right, permitted a couple more guys to join.

After that, everything came at a price. Nothing so crude as pay-to-play, of course. He never promised campaign success or equipment upgrades in return for commissary, although there was definitely some degree of correlation. No; it was mostly a you-scratch-my-back, I'll-scratch-yours arrangement. Donate a few snacks, and this asshole would lift the purgatorial boredom that makes you want to hang yourself with a bedsheet. If the Oreo supply dries up, maybe your party spends an extra week dicking around in the woods on a planet that might or might not be Earth. It also provided him with a reasonable amount of protection: it was awfully hard to think up new adventures when someone had ganked your shower shoes. So it wasn't only about the food. It was power. Control.

Within weeks, everyone wanted in. Even in low security, the prisoners segregated themselves, so when the Blacks and Latinos started asking questions, he'd had to construct separate campaigns for each group. He synthesized the stories within a single future-fantasy world, borrowing liberally from China Mieville, Octavia Butler, Gene Wolfe, Philip K. Dick, Robert Howard, and Connie Willis. Prisoners were not discerning readers, on the whole, and even if they occasionally identified his sources (usually when he ran out of ideas and started cribbing from Stephen King) they weren't apt to gripe about plagiarism. Balancing everything in his head kept him sharp, while also ensuring he never lost anything of real value in the periodic shakedowns.

Once the guards were satisfied that his goal was entertainment and not revolution—he was, after all, responsible for one of the biggest intelligence breaches in US history—they were happy to let him do his thing. Keeping everyone quiet and content made their jobs a hell of a lot easier. By the time he did cause a small riot, nobody was willing to finger him. If he went down, so did the game; with enough inmates invested, he was too big to fail.

And anywhere—even an imaginary fantasy world—is better than prison.

Robin laughs, incredulous. "Did you not learn anything?"

"Oh, was prison supposed to be an educational experience? My bad." They are standing outside the window of a doughnut shop, a hole-in-the-wall kind of place on a narrow side street off what looks like Healdsburg's main square. The kind of place you don't patronize unless you already know it's there. He does not remember arriving, and he is not sure how long he has been standing on the sidewalk, talking. Things happen so quickly, now.

"No, I mean..." The cowbell hanging from the door by a shoelace clanks, and Robin steps back to let a grizzled, gray-haired bear of a man in biker gear make his exit. "Hey, Joe."

His grunt of acknowledgment, muffled by a paper mask, seems to be all the encouragement the kids need to follow him down the row of parked cars to a big Harley. An old milk crate, strapped to the back with bungie cords, contains a grinning jack-o-lantern made of hard foam. As the kids step up to the curb, expectantly, he reaches into a pocket of his worn leather jacket to produce a small red ball. His fingers close, and when they open again, one ball has become two. Seth and Nora giggle, urging him on, and two balls become three. They begin to appear and disappear from pockets and ears.

Satisfied that the kids are maintaining a safe distance, Robin turns her attention back to Cyril, extending an open palm toward him. Motherhood has made her an expert at rapidly switching gears. "What I mean is, you just... jumped from one fantasy world to another."

"What else was I going to do for five years?" Or, as he'd originally thought, ten? "And," he adds, unable to resist the chance to push her buttons, "seven years was a pretty good run. Longer than most relationships last, anyway."

"What we had was not a—" She puts a hand to her forehead, sighs, and then laughs. Refusing to take the bait. "You know what, I'm gonna get some coffee. You want a doughnut?"

It's obvious, what she's doing: sparing him the ordeal of going inside. Or perhaps sparing the other patrons the ordeal of dealing with him. "Fuck off."

"You used to be so much more creative with your insults. Profanity shows a lack of imagination, my dad always said. Honestly, Cyril, I worry you've lost your edge." She leans around him, beckoning the kids as the burly man on the motorcycle rumbles off. "Come pick your doughnuts, guys!"

Cyril stands there on the sidewalk as the kids barrel back to the window, stewing in his own bootless anger. He is supposed to be on the offensive. She is supposed to be the angry one. There has been a fundamental shift in their relationship, and he's not so willfully blind that he can't see what it is. It's not just that he's beholden to her for his freedom—that's merely an external expression of a far deeper alteration. Once, Tav's letters had been her road map; her compass; her northern star. She had read them nightly, until the printouts were worn past reading, but it didn't matter because she knew every word by heart.

And now she knows those words were his. He can deny it all he wants, but she knows she owns him, body and soul.

"That one!" Nora presses her face to the glass in front of a chocolate doughnut with rainbow sprinkles and chomps noisily on the fabric of her mask.

"Quit that." Robin gives her a thump on the side of the head. "Seth?"

He points to a bear claw, carefully not touching the glass.

She cocks an eyebrow at Cyril. He looks away. "George is in line, so I'm gonna be a minute. I need to talk to him about my trusses." As if he has the slightest fucking clue what trusses are. She leans into the glass door, bell clinking as she steps inside.

"Can we go to the plaza? Please?" Seth hops into view, front and center. He points to the corner. "Please?"

"Yeah!" Nora grabs his hand and drops, hanging dead-weight from his arm.

"Why not." With one quick jerk, he heaves Nora upward, letting go at the apogee just long enough to sweep his arm under her bum. She squeals—first in outrage, and then in terror as he shrugs and drops her, though only a few inches. Her arms cinch tight around his neck, and the shriek becomes a breathy giggle.

"Again!" she demands, kicking her heels against him. "Again!"

Kids are easy.

Kitty-corner to the end of the block sits a mist-shrouded park of towering redwoods, damp grass, and looping concrete paths. There's a gazebo on the near side, a rectangular water fountain in

the center, and a few pedestrians with coffee maintaining appropriate social distance while waiting for their dogs to crap.

He hesitates. Overwhelmed, suddenly, by the oppressive
certainty that even crossing the street on his own initiative will
be met with immediate discipline. He is out. Free. He wants
nothing more than to box up the past five years and stick them
on a shelf somewhere in the recesses of his mind. But apparently it's going to take time to get prison out of his head.

Warm, not-quite-sticky fingers press themselves into his palm.
Nine years seems plenty old enough to cross the street alone—
but when Cyril looks down, Seth's eyes telegraph the shy smile
hidden by his mask. Cyril gives the hand a quick squeeze.
Together, they step off the curb.

The instant they hit the plaza, Nora wiggles out of his grasp,
pom-pom pigtails bouncing as she charges off toward the gazebo.

The boy remains.

"Will you teach me?" he asks. "To play Dragons?"

"You have the ears of a bat." How much has the boy overheard? He sighs. "Look. First of all, you gotta have at least a
couple people to make up a party. But—I mean, I dunno, kid. I
don't know how long I'm gonna—"

"You're gonna leave us," Seth says.

The way he says it—not a question, but a conclusion—slices,
razor-like, through this asshole's thick hide. "Jesus." He grabs the
kid's head and pulls him close. The boy sinks into him, all bones
and angles now. Cyril is used to thinking of Seth as the exuber-
antly reactive four-year-old he once was, blissfully unaware that
adults possessed any greater emotional depth than simple doglike
adoration. The boy is capable now not only of thinking ahead, but
of detecting the raw tension between Cyril and his mother. How
much has Robin told him?

"I'm not—" Cyril sighs. What the hell is he supposed to tell
this kid, when he himself knows nothing? "Look, I can't sleep on
your couch forever." He knows that much is true. "So yeah, I'm

probably gonna find somewhere else to crash. But I'm not going away." He hasn't had a chance to think this far ahead, but as he says it, he knows it's true. "Not like before. I'll be around. For you. For as—well, as long as your mom wants me." He snorts. "Maybe even if she doesn't."

Seth leans back a little, tilting his face upward. "But she wants you to stay. In our house."

"She—" He opens his arms, letting the kid go. "She told you that?"

Seth shrugs. "Yeah. We talked about it." As if it's no big thing. "So will you?"

Suddenly, this asshole doesn't know what to do with his hands. He needs something to hold, or grip, or—something. He's slimmer than he used to be, but not slim, and he can only get one hand into a pocket at a time, leaning to the left or right. He tugs his mask off and rubs a palm over the stubble on his face. "Shit, kid, I—"

"You." This word, sudden and vehement, comes from a white guy in a polo shirt and neatly pressed cargo shorts, a half-assed handkerchief covering his face, standing roughly ten yards to the left. Glaring. "I knew it. It *is* you."

"Do I know you?" Cyril puts a hand flat on Seth's chest, moving him back and out of the way.

"No. But I know who you are."

Apparently, this is going to be a confrontation. He, Cyril, glances down at Seth and nods toward Nora, now playing by the fountain. Seth, fortunately, is smarter than his father ever was: he takes the hint and jogs off. "Congratulations on owning a television," Cyril tells the stranger.

"My brother was on the ground in Afghanistan when you pulled your little publicity stunt. His company had to pack up and retreat, and they were the lucky ones. You should be ashamed of yourself, you—" The man glances around, and, seeing that most of the other pedestrians have made themselves scarce, tugs the handkerchief down to his chin. "You fucking *traitor*."

"Is that all?" Cyril stifles a yawn as he slips his mask back on. "I usually prefer more specificity. Duplicitous, back-stabbing murderer, for instance. Or cowardly, gutless snitch." He pats his stomach. "Although that one's not strictly accurate. Let's see... Turncoat, sympathizer, Judas, provocateur—that's a good one— squealer, Benedict Arnold, reprobate—"

"You—" The man stalks a couple of paces forward, holding an index finger erect as he attempts an interjection. "You fat son of a—"

"Yes, yes." Cyril nods wearily. "We'll get to the fat jokes, too. Just—hold on." He lifts his own index finger. "I need a minute to catch my breath. Because I'm fat. Get it?"

At some point during this exchange, Robin has appeared. She hands Cyril a white paper bag, tugs her mask down to her chin, and then just stands at his elbow, sipping coffee and staring at the outraged interloper as he fumbles for his phone.

The guy's hands are shaking as he swipes on the camera. "I know the chief of police, you asshole, and he'll—he'll fucking—"

"What, arrest me because he saw a shaky-cam video of some jackass harassing a guy minding his own business on public property? I did my time, Einstein. But by all means, post it to Twitter. Let's go viral!"

"Her," Robin says.

Cyril and the amateur videographer both look at her.

"The chief of police." She takes a sip of coffee. "Is a woman. Which apparently neither of you knew. Janet Molina is aware that Cyril is in town."

The man's eyes dart between them. His mouth opens, like he's hoping something clever will pop out. Then he shoves the phone into his pocket and stalks off, yanking the handkerchief back up over his nose.

"Moron," Cyril growls.

"Give the guy a little credit; he didn't call me a bitch. Or, you know, other things." Robin lifts her cup, gesturing to a nearby park bench. "So you're famous now."

"And just when I'd perfected my fat joke repertoire." He follows her, yawning for real this time. It's still too goddamn early. "Gonna have to revise my entire routine to placate the traitorous scum stans."

She takes another sip of coffee. "Some people think you're a hero, you know."

He looks at her. She looks back over the top of the plastic coffee lid, cool as a cucumber, and for an instant he imagines knocking the cup aside and sweeping her into his arms. It's what Tavis would have done. Instead, he backs up and plants his fat ass on the park bench. It's damp. "Lot of good it did," he says, shifting in a vain attempt to get comfortable on cast iron. "Spend a decade exposing corruption, the surveillance state, and abuse of military power, and what's the public's response? Hey, I know! Let's elect an illiterate authoritarian plutocrat!" His real mistake wasn't letting himself get caught. It was assuming anyone would care. "Turns out Americans like getting fucked in the ass."

"Now *there's* the eloquent a-hole I remember."

He nods over her shoulder. "Incoming."

Nora barrels into her mother's legs. "Doughnut!"

Seth is right behind her. Both kids are sweaty and flushed. "Mom, I'm *so* hungry."

"Well, good, because I got breakfast. Such as it is." Robin brushes flecks of coffee from her arm before producing a tiny bottle of hand sanitizer.

"Where were you keeping that, your bra?"

"Hush." The kids hand her their masks, which she loops over one wrist, and dutifully hold out their hands for a couple of squirts before turning to look expectantly at Cyril.

"Your mom first." He pulls a cinnamon roll out of the paper bag and hands it over their heads. As he pulls out Seth's bear claw, Nora jams her hand into the bag, insisting loudly that she needs no help, and then promptly bursts into tears when she fumbles her "sprinkly" and drops it on the wet grass, face down.

Robin sighs. "Sweetie, this is why you need to wait your—"

"Hold on," Cyril says. "There's one more." He reaches into the bag and pulls out a fourth doughnut—another chocolate with sprinkles.

Seth gapes at his mother, aghast. "You got her *two?*"

"That one's for Cyril," she informs him.

Cyril hands Nora the doughnut. "Problem solved."

She snatches it from his hand and darts away, like a feral cat.

"Nora," Robin chides. "What do you say?"

"Fank you." She says it begrudgingly, around a mouthful of cakey goodness. Sprinkles stick to her lips.

"So much for natural consequences," Robin says.

Cyril cocks an eyebrow. "I think you mean 'just desserts.'"

She snorts. "Yeah, that's more like it." She balances her roll on her coffee cup and pulls her phone out to check the time. "All right, we'd better head back and get you guys to Greta's before my—" She sighs as Seth rockets toward the corner. "Wait for us to cross! And put your mask on!"

Cyril would be lying if he said he isn't hoping she'll turn and hurry after the kids to he can pick up the other doughnut, the one currently being investigated by a small black-and-red beetle. Even face down on the ground, it's more sanitary than most of the things he's eaten in the past five years. But she waits, so he heaves himself to his feet. "What's Greta, your babysitter?"

"Teacher. She coaches basketball at the high school, or at least she did until COVID. The kids go to her house for distance learning. I pay her back in remodel."

"They could stay with me, you know. I mean," he amends, quickly, when her eyebrows slide up. "As long as I'm sleeping on your couch."

"So... you're staying?"

"No. I mean—I don't—God damn it." She's got him completely tied in knots. "I'm not agreeing to shit. But it's not like I have anywhere else to go. Yet."

She laughs. "Okay. Well, I may have other uses for you. Let's see how things go."

At the corner, Seth seizes one of Cyril's hands and Nora claims the other. They cross, and once again the kids are off and gone.

"So what do you need to take care of today?" Robin hands him the remainder of her cinnamon roll. "I gotta swing by a client's house for inspection, but after that I'm all yours."

He scowls at the proffered pastry. "I don't need your—"

"Oh my God, just *take* it."

———

THE LAWYER NEEDS CYRIL TO SIGN SOME PAPERWORK to release what remains of his assets, which can be done easily enough via email. First, however, he'll need access to his bank account, and that requires identification. His license is expired, so stop number one needs to be the DMV.

"Fun," Robin says, rummaging in her purse to make sure she has whatever she needs to have when she leaves the house. "Nearest one's in Santa Rosa. We can go after lunch."

The other thing he needs is a computer.

She looks at him for a moment, lips pressed into a thin line of skepticism. Then she sighs and disappears into her bedroom, returning with a laptop tucked under one arm. "If I give you this, are you going to get into trouble?"

It's not a question of if, but when. Just looking at the slim silver case makes his fingers itch. Five years without access. He has no idea of the lay of the land. Assuming the FBI's keeping an eye on him—and they are—he'll need to start over with a fresh alias. He might be able to leak his identity to a key player or two, but reputation and trust will take time to rebuild. "Not for... a while."

"I guess that's as much as I can expect. Have fun digging up my dirt." She tilts her head back. "Come on guys, let's go!"

And then he's alone.

In a rare exercise of self-restraint, he places the laptop on the couch and sits, listening to the silence. It's been a long time since he was truly alone. He's not sure whether solitude is a relief or a burden, but he uses the opportunity to jerk off.

If she thinks acknowledging the fact that he's going to violate her privacy will prevent him from doing it, she's wrong. But it's not the computer he goes for, first; after washing his hands, he lumbers into her bedroom. There's not even a lock on the door.

Her bed, a spacious California king, is rumpled and unmade. She's far tidier than he is, but not a neat freak, and most unkempt in her private spaces. She used to keep printouts of his letters—when she thought they came from Tavis—in boxes under the bed. By this asshole's conservative estimate, there were roughly two thousand, in the end. And that's not even counting the hundreds he wrote and never sent. He finds only dust bunnies, now. When he hauls himself back up from his hands and knees, he sits on the edge of the mattress, pressing her comforter to his nose.

Her underwear drawer contains no secrets; only a vibrator, some batteries, and a couple of silicone bra inserts. He fingers them. In her last year of college, when Tavis—or, rather, Cyril— had encouraged her to pursue her passion for craftsmanship, she'd traded makeup and business heels for the comfort of jeans and a clean face. Not long after, she'd stopped straightening her hair and gone in for "the big chop." But, to his knowledge, she has never been self-conscious about her smaller-than-average bust.

The wave of rage is so sudden and overwhelming that he slams the drawer shut, rattling the empty water glass on her bedside table.

The inserts, the bed, her coyness about his presence here—she is seeing someone. That is this asshole's conclusion, instant and incontrovertible. Who or when or how many he does not know, or care. He does not even care that she is toying with him. Whoever they are, they've made her feel the need to be something other than her perfect self, and he will destroy them.

He can pretend his feelings for his best friend's wife are altruistic; that what he did to her was his unselfish—if misguided—attempt to give her the best in life, no matter the personal cost. But in moments like these, the pretense is stripped away.

She belongs to him. Not Tavis. He made her. He owns her, and he will have her at any cost.

I want you to stay.

She lied about his release. The inserts are a lie. Her words are lies. She is *lying*.

Why else would she let him suffer in silence for five years, let him believe she was gone for good—and then not only advocate for his release, but welcome him into her home? It's all a ruse. Payback. She's doing to him what he has done to her. He's not stupid.

But to involve her kids—

Five years is a long time. She's obviously changed. Maybe she's not as protective of her children as she used to be, when they were small. Maybe bringing a felon into her home is a risk she's willing to take for a little petty revenge.

There's a desk in the corner, papers piled around an empty spot the size of her laptop. No longer trying to conceal his intrusion, he paws through lumber yard receipts and design sketches, pulls out the drawer, looks under the lid of her printer-scanner. Nothing.

Her closet, almost deep enough to qualify as a walk-in, is in a state of organized disarray. Shoving aside winter coats and spare quilts reveals a space heater and a stack of plastic storage bins stuffed with kids' schoolwork and art. On top sits a handcrafted wooden box, which, upon opening, he finds sectioned into a grid of small compartments. He fingers through agate and mother-of-pearl, remembering the occasions that prompted the gifting of each piece of jewelry. Tavis had presented her with the matching earrings and necklace for their first wedding anniversary. The pendant rimmed in gold was an apology for his second deployment. When she wears jewelry—which is not often—she looks like a queen.

He digs through the upper shelves, finding only more blankets and a thick folder with legal documents pertaining to the purchase of the house he is standing in. No letters. No lies.

He ends his search where he ought to have begun: her computer. That's where his talents lie, and it's there he'll find the evidence to corroborate her deceit.

She's logged out of Gmail, but her password is saved in the browser, so he doesn't even have to do any real hacking. He braces himself for the inevitable note from a lover, but her inbox, like her text history, is mundane. Work. More work. Emails from the school district and the kids' teachers. A few notes from Cooke's wife: What would Seth like for his birthday, will Nora eat butternut squash, and so on. Robin has always been a bit of a loner, but her inbox suggests she's given up on cultivating a social life entirely.

Her browser history is equally bland. DIY YouTube videos, bookmarks of several Pinterest pages but no account of her own, online banking... nothing but the essentials. Her Facebook account still exists, but it's been deactivated for five years. She has no Instagram or Twitter presence; no Tinder or Snapchat or whatever the cool kids are using these days. It's as if, in his absence, she's erased herself from the internet. He can't say he blames her; when he'd dumped the classified intel and made Tav's death national news, the press had descended upon Robin *en masse*. To protect herself and, more importantly, her children, she'd had to shut down every public aspect of her life. And had decided, apparently, never to risk opening herself up to such scrutiny again.

The groceries arrive. He waits until the delivery woman returns to her car, then opens the door, lugs the bags inside, and assembles a platter of BLT's. Food prep drains the reservoir of his frustration, and when he installs himself on the couch with a full plate, he makes the magnanimous decision to let Robin's private life remain private, at least for the time being.

Instead, he Googles himself. The top result is a Wikipedia page, followed by a few articles about his impending trial, and then his plea bargain and sentencing. He sorts by "news" and "most recent." There are a few stories about his release, but they are perfunctory at best, buried in the general deluge of current events. In 2020, he simply isn't headline news. Good.

Browsing his usual online haunts is not as simple or mindless as it once was. He's managed to keep up with major world events by word-of-mouth and television, but his knowledge is shallow, lacking nuance or detail. The internet is alive, ever-changing, and without having been immersed in its flow, the current has passed him by. Jokes, memes, opinion pieces, even the way people use emojis and punctuation—all of it has continued to evolve in his absence, and now feels as though it's written in a dialect tantalizingly close to his own.

When he wearies of tumbling down rabbit holes of outdated information, he redirects to practical matters: resetting passwords and reactivating accounts, where he can remember. He regrets not having left himself an encrypted document with these details organized in spreadsheet form; he had always relied on his own memory to serve as his most secure vault, but at some point, his brain had decided to prioritize the orchestration of dungeon crawls to keep himself sane. He doesn't feel compromised, but five years baking in a central California sauna has doubtless blunted his edge.

He checks the time, then takes his empty plate back to the

kitchen, setting Robin's laptop on the dining table as he passes. He's loading the plate again when the light from a stained-glass window, flecking his arm with blue and green, brings his thoughts to a halt. He'd seen nothing in Robin's inbox from her mother. Nor on her phone. Were they on the rocks again? The prominent display of the older woman's artwork in the kitchen windows suggests not.

He returns to the dining table, opens Robin's email, and searches for "Glennis."

He is staring at a chain of emails from a funeral home director when Robin shoves in the front door. "Hey," she says, clomping past him into the kitchen. With her comes the scent of fir and fresh soil. "Oh—good, I was hoping you'd have something ready." She comes back, stuffing a triangle of sandwich into her mouth, and stops behind the dining chair. "Find anything juicy?"

After Tav's death, Cyril had tripped the breaker on a chain of events leading inevitably to prison in the confidence that Robin would be better off in his absence. He hadn't thought of it as deserting her; it was absurd that she'd decided to look to him for comfort in the first place. She was a survivor, and she'd had her mother to lean on. But the emails on Robin's laptop are four and a half years old.

Robin leans forward, squinting at the screen he hasn't bothered to hide. A crumb tumbles down over his shoulder. "Oh. Yeah. Between you and her, that was a pretty crappy year. Not that the one before it wasn't. Or the one after."

"What happened?" Glennis was old, but not ancient, and had always seemed energetic.

"Stroke, they think. She was driving on that oceanside stretch between Ventura and Santa Barbara, hit the median and rolled. Nobody else hurt, thank God." Her words are clipped and firm, suggesting frequent recitation of this story has blunted the raw edge of grief. "I was up here with the kids, working on Cooke's place, and Greta, she—" Her narrative cracks slightly as she reaches the end and extemporizes. "She's not the most touchy-feely person, but she kind of took me under her wing. Her husband says she lost a daughter, a long time ago, and... well. When this wreck went up for sale, I decided to stay."

"All a part of God's plan, I'm sure." He says it, with quietly devastating sarcasm, not because he believes it, but because it was what Glennis had written to her daughter not long after Tavis died—which Cyril knew, of course, because he read Robin's email. The woman had loved her daughter more than life itself, but nobody had ever claimed tact was her forte. Robin had shed furious tears for hours.

She does not cry now. For a moment she is still, and he listens to her carefully controlled breath in his ear. Then she straightens. "Must be so satisfying to be you," she says, to his back. "Do whatever you want, say whatever stupid shit comes into your head, and damn the consequences. I mean, people fantasize about that, and here you are living the dream."

"Yeah, it's worked out beautifully."

"Is it worth it?"

Worth five years in prison? Maybe. Worth his best friend's life? He doesn't look at her. "It's not that I want to be this way, Chica. It's just pointless to pretend I'm not."

———

EVEN WITH SIGNS MANDATING MASKS AND LINES marked out in six-foot sections, the DMV somehow manages to remain the same as it always was. Cyril, as much as he'd like to pretend otherwise, is not.

After half an hour in a line that winds around the block —"Hey, we're making good time," Robin says—and a temperature check, they're finally granted access to the building. Robin points to a kiosk in the corner, then takes the liberty of pushing the button and tearing off the number it dispenses. "You need what, a renewal?" When he doesn't answer, she leaves him standing in the foyer to go hunt for the correct paperwork. "Found your line," she says, when she reappears. And then she takes his arm.

He jerks away. "Fuck off."

She lets out a short breath, puffing her mask out. "Fine. Follow me. Assuming you can manage that."

She pokes at her phone while they wait in the next interminable line, texting Greta to let her know they'll be late. He is stuck staring down the half-dozen pairs of eyes which have come to rest on his unwieldy mass. This used to be simple: if people stared at him in public, it was because of his size. He either ignored them, or, if they decided to get confrontational, demolished them with a few scathing words. In a battle of wits, he could always win. Now he can't tell whether it's his size that draws curious gazes, or if they're frowning at Cyril Blanchard, hacker and traitor. Probably both. Then a toddler in a stroller one line over starts bucking against her seatbelt and shrieking, and he is no longer the center of attention.

He shifts his bulk from one foot to the other, attempting to relieve the perpetual ache in his knees and lower back. Folding chairs line the edges of the room. Stepping out of the six-foot square he and Robin occupy to grab one would take ten, twenty seconds at most. He won't.

"Chill, big guy." She's checking her email, using a thumb to flip through coupons and back-to-school offers. "Nobody's gonna jump you."

"That's not—" He cuts himself off as heads turn, and forcibly lowers his voice to a hiss. "I'm not *that* fucked."

"I can literally feel you steaming." Robin glances up and, seeing his stormy glower, tucks her phone away. She folds her arms over her chest. "What's eating you? Wait—are you pissed at *me?*"

"Shouldn't I be?"

She blinks, slowly. "I literally got you released, Cyril. You're sleeping on my couch. And now I'm chauffeuring you around town, holding your hand through your prison PTSD or whatever the hell is wrong with you, and you still don't believe me when I say I want you to..." She hesitates. "Stay."

"That's *exactly* why I don't believe you." There's no rational reason for her to want this. Him. If that is, in fact, what she meant when she put her hand on his cheek. She only wants him to think that's what she means, so he'll say something stupid, and then she can laugh at his expense. He knows how this game is played. "This is bullshit."

She casts a helpless look around the DMV, as if trying to locate the source of his insanity, and then shrugs. "Look, I don't know what else to tell you, Cyril. You need evidence of my sincerity?" She cocks a suggestive eyebrow. "Happy to provide proof here and now, if you want it. Just say the word."

Do it, a part of him says. Call her bluff. Take this smug bitch for all she's worth and throw her away when, inevitably, it goes south.

He can't. He won't. Confessing his desire would require dismantling a part of his emotional armor he knows full well could never be rebuilt, and he will not let her break him.

He is already broken.

"No." Yes. Fuck. He is a goddamn fool. He puts out a hand to brace himself against the line marker, but the elastic ribbon gives in to his touch. There is nowhere to go. Everything in his peripheral vision melts into a pulsating haze. The only thing solid is her.

Then his number's up, and for the next thirty minutes he's filling in bubbles on a test so simple a baboon could ace it, reading off letters with one eye covered, taking a photo, and finally securing a printed-out provisional license.

"North Street," Robin says, when he needs to supply a residence. "Healdsburg, nine-five-four-four-eight."

Outside, clear of the building and other people, he yanks his mask off and wipes the dampness from his face. Robin stops beside him, using a hand to shade her eyes as she surveys the lot. In the courtyard behind them, a woman talks loudly on her phone, held out flat about six inches in front of her face, mask over her mouth but not her nose. The voice on the other end of the line chatters back.

"Tell me," Robin says, tucking her mask into her purse. "Why do you think I'm doing this? Taking you into my home, letting you hang out with my kids—what, exactly, do you think I'm lying about?"

"Well, for starters, whoever you've been fu—" He cuts himself off, too late, choking on the fury that rises into his throat. His hands are shaking. He clenches them, and then shoves the crumpled printout into a pocket. He will not look at her breasts. "Seeing."

Both of her eyebrows arch. She turns to face him, and the veil of caution which has heretofore masked their interactions falls away, revealing genuine surprise. "You—" She points an index finger at his face and then lets it drop, jabbing his belly. "You let me fuck a complete stranger for seven years—marry him—give birth to his children—and now you're jealous?" She lets out an incredulous laugh. "That's refreshingly cliché, Cyril."

"Tavis was not—"

"A stranger? Not to you, maybe. But I haven't a clue who my husband was, Cyril. Not a one."

"He—"

"No." She cuts him off with a shake of her head. "You don't get to tell me who he was. I'm willing to forgive, but that ship has sailed." Her hand flattens against him as she leans in. "I don't know what you think you saw in my email," she hisses, "but I've dated exactly two guys since Nora was born. Neither one made it past first base. The end."

He forces himself to look her in the eye. Five years isn't so long he can't still read her with a glance. She's not lying. Not this time. The woman in the courtyard, having concluded her phone call, gives Cyril a *you're in trouble now* look as she skirts around them to the parking lot.

"But you knew that," Robin says, giving him a little shove. "Because you know me. So what is it, Cyril? Seriously?"

He doesn't want this. Not here, not ever. He steps off the curb and starts across the asphalt alone, as if they're not going to end up crammed into the cab of her truck anyway. He hears the swift clump of her footsteps behind him, and then feels a tug as she grabs the back of his shirt.

He swings an arm back, freeing himself from her grasp without turning around.

It doesn't matter. In the end he reaches the rear bumper of her truck, and there's nowhere else to go. She stops behind him, and he hears her pull out her keys, but she doesn't move to open the cab door.

His sigh comes out a low growl. "It's not—What I did, I—" He shakes his head. Robin is attempting to go on with life as if nothing has happened, as if he hasn't fucked with her so thoroughly and for so long that she will never be able to untie all the knots; as if discovering the truth hadn't destroyed her; as if he weren't personally responsible for the death of the father of her children. Not for a moment does he believe Robin can turn her back on a thing like that. Not ever.

But it's not just that. It's that she reached out to free him, too.

"Look," he says, finally, turning to face her. "Either you're crazy, or this is a trick."

Robin lets out a bark of laughter. A man passing by on the other side of the row of cars looks their way, eyes crinkling above his paper mask as he mirrors her broad smile.

Cyril's blood boils. "You think this is funny? I'll show you—"

"Hey." She puts out a hand, stopping short of touching him

this time. "Just—" She shakes her head, eyes closed. "Cyril. You built your entire—" She searches for the word, then lifts her hands, shaping them as if gripping an imaginary basketball. "Your *everything* around the absolute certainty that I'd never, ever give you a shot. Now I'm offering you one, and you can't deal. I mean, come on." She grins. "It's either hilarious or tragic, and let me tell you, I'm fresh out of tears."

————

THE RIDE FROM THE DMV TO GRETA'S IS SILENT, BUT the kids inevitably break the tension and then it's a rush to get them home and into their uniforms for "socially distanced martial arts on the plaza"—yoga, basically, Robin admits, but it's better than nothing—except that the pants are in the dryer, she thinks, and the belts are in the closet, maybe, no, wait, hanging on the back of the bedroom door—and you can't wear long sleeves under your gi, Seth, you'll get sweaty; yes, I know you get sweaty anyway, but I don't want you to pass out or—you know what, never mind, do what you want, you're nine, but you're taking a shower when you get home. Then Nora lets out a long, low fart and runs away, cackling.

Cyril wants this. All of this. Deeply and desperately—even more so, knowing it will be lost. He hates her for dangling this illusory carrot, even if it's what he deserves. He can't have it. But he cannot refuse.

There are only two banks in Healdsburg, neither of which has his money, so she runs him south to Windsor after dropping the kids off, walking him into the lobby like he's her fucking third child. "I don't need you to—"

"Martial arts is only forty-five minutes," she says, "so let's make this quick."

He sits across from her in the waiting area, neither of them speaking, until a woman in a beige suit takes him to a desk once walled in by beige partitions, now rearranged to surround the entire area, like a castle wall. She balks at his provisional license, but checks in with her supervisor and gets the go-ahead. The details take five minutes at the most, and then he's done. It will be two-to-five business days before his card arrives in the mail, but they allow him to withdraw five hundred dollars in cash.

"That'll cover about two days of groceries," Robin notes, when he returns to the waiting area, shoving the wad of twenties into one pocket.

"Jesus Christ," he snaps. "Would you give it a rest?"

She rises and follows him out, pumping a dollop of hand sanitizer from the complimentary stand in the entryway and offering a nod to the bank employee who holds the door for them so they can leave without touching anything. "What, harassing you? I think I've earned the right."

"Pretending we're bosom buddies, or—whatever the hell you think we are. You're not fooling anyone."

The lot behind the bank is empty except for her truck. As they walk toward it together, Robin tugs her mask off, checks her phone for the time, and then tucks it back into her pocket. "I get that all of this seems sudden to you, but the world didn't stand still while you were gone. Believe me, I was angry. For a long time." She flashes a tight smile that only accentuates the pain in her eyes. "I could probably fill a book with all the ways I imagined killing you."

"And now?"

She seems to consider, then shrugs. "I let it go. Mostly."

"Why," he says. It's not even a question. Perhaps he should say *how*.

She stops, halfway across the lot, and glances up at his face. "I don't have time," she says, simply. "For holding grudges. That's why."

"Inviting me back into your house—your life—" God, her

kids' lives—"is a little more involved than letting go of a grudge."

She snorts. "I dunno if you've noticed, Cyril, but a hundred fifty thousand Americans have died this year, and it's only August. Before that, I lost my husband, and then my mom. Life is short. And it's not perfect. *You're* not perfect," she adds, before he can make the correction. "Here. Lemme show you something."

They come to the back of the pickup, and she props one foot on the rear bumper, tugging the leather laces of her work boots until her foot slides out. The boot drops, and she uses a thumb to pull her sock down to her heel, revealing the smooth, firm skin of her ankle.

The tattoo is a wobbly, lopsided heart enclosing a smiley face with stick arms and legs jutting out of its vaguely circular head. Underneath, in equally shaky script, the artist's signature: Seth.

"What, putting it on the fridge for a couple days wasn't good enough? Jesus Christ, that's hideous."

Robin of five years past would have scowled and told him to shut up—but then, that Robin hadn't had the aplomb necessary to get a tattoo. This present Robin tugs her sock back up and straightens, studying his face as her toe feels its way back into the boot. She is, he realizes, filtering his words through the lens of Tav's letters. The ones she now knows were his. "It's cute," she pronounces, finally. As if certain he would agree, given privacy and a pen. "And you know it."

As if she has the first fucking clue who he is. "Two years from now you'll be covering it with band aids."

"Thanks, Mom." She waves him toward the passenger side. "I mean, that's kind of the point."

When he opens the door, she is climbing into the driver's seat. He watches as she props her foot agains the center console to lace her boot. "You might have to unpack that a little," he says, "because *whoosh.*" He grips the door frame and heaves himself into the passenger seat.

"I," she says, giving her laces one final tug, "have wanted a tattoo since I was eight. You know what I wanted?" She uses a finger to trace circles around the circumference of her arm, shoulder to wrist. "A big Asian-style dragon wrapped around, like this." She laughs and sticks her keys into the ignition, pausing to slather her hands with sanitizer and pass him the bottle before starting the engine. "I thought that would be so cool. Oh," she adds, as he sucks in his gut to fasten the belt, "I ordered some bigger clothes. Should be here Friday. Or Saturday, maybe. Mail's been running behind."

"Nobody asked you to—"

"You're welcome." She falls silent, briefly, as she looks over one shoulder to back out of the parking spot. "Anyway. Tattoo. Once I hit my teens and realized the whole dragon thing wasn't my aesthetic, I decided I wanted something decorative, like a feather or a dandelion, but my mom always insisted tattoos weren't Biblical, and my dad backed her up. In spite of the eagle-and-anchor monstrosity he had on his shoulder. In college... I can't even remember. Some symbolic thing from a book I read in my lit course—"

"Windmill," he supplies. She had seen in the character of Don Quixote not a mirror of herself but an ally; an earnest—if slightly pompous—reminder that not all was what it seemed, at first glance.

She levels a finger at him. "Yes! You know me better than I do, you creep. A windmill, symbolizing... Uh. Maybe you remember, because I don't." She laughs again, affectionately, at the earnest idealism of the girl she once was. "Then, once I realized woodworking had become my career, not just a hobby, I thought about getting a tattoo of my dad's old block plane, right here along my forearm." She glances at him. "Do you remem—"

He nods. She had obsessed about it for months, and even contacted a couple of artists.

"Course you do. But I never went through with it. I'm sure you can tell me why."

He rolls his eyes. "You were afraid you'd regret it."

"Exactly. Ten, twenty years from now. Who knows, you know, if I'd even be alive, but—oh no, what if there was something on my body I didn't like? What if I committed to that, no turning back, and then realized it was a huge mistake?" She shakes her head. "The day of the funeral—Mom's funeral, I mean, God, I hate that I have to specify—Seth drew a picture to make me feel better." She tosses a thumb over one shoulder, indicating the cramped extended cab. "Right back there, while we were driving from the church to the cemetery. I stuck it on the dash. Two days later I had to drive in to Santa Rosa to deal with her bank stuff. Passed a tattoo shop. Walked in and paid the first apprentice available to slap it on."

"You're... not really making this sound less crazy. Just FYI."

They're on the freeway now, heading back to Healdsburg, and she turns the blinker on, shifting left into the fast lane. There's traffic, and she ends up sitting with her hands at ten and two, frowning at the tractor trailer in front of them.

Her voice, when she speaks, is low. "When Tavis died, and then I found out that you—" She casts a quick glance his way. "Well. After all that, I spent a lot of time feeling like a failure. Feeling like an idiot for trusting him. And you. God. How could I ever—" She squeezes her eyes shut, just for a moment, and then strikes the steering wheel with the heel of her palm. "So *stupid.*"

"None of that was your—"

She holds her hand up. "I know. I know. You two assholes are the ones to blame. But that's exactly what I'm saying—in the end, I don't regret my choices. I don't regret trusting Tavis. How can I? I don't regret our kids, or my life. I tell Seth and Nora all the time that there's no learning without failure. You gotta take risks. For yourself. For love. You're not always gonna make the right decisions, and even when you do, the people you love will fail, too.

Spectacularly. And... that's okay. I mean, it's not *okay* okay, but if you waste your one precious life trying to avoid regret, you'll just end up regretting all the things you never did. I got the tattoo to remind me that risking disaster is what it means to be alive." Traffic shifts, finally, and the truck rolls forward as she lifts her foot off the brake. "There's no shame in a shitty tattoo."

"So, in the current scenario... I'm the shitty tattoo?"

She laughs. "Maybe? I dunno, I'm the one who thought a windmill would be profound. I guess what I mean is that now, the tattoo is just... a part of me. It's not good or bad, it's just me." She shrugs. "A whole lot of who I am, whether I like it or not— and I don't—is thanks to you. And... I like myself, Cyril." She shrugs. "Who knows? Maybe I can like you, too."

She sounds so fucking sincere. Jesus. He has to remind himself that this is the woman who neglected to mention the death of her own mother and showed up at his release acting like it was a surprise—not world-shaking elisions, no, but not things she could have omitted, before. Not without betraying herself with a guilty look, and then beating herself up for days afterward.

Maybe it's not a boyfriend. Maybe she's not even lying, in the most technical sense. But she's hiding something. Still. He can feel it.

So he falls back on that which has served him best, or at least most often: anger. "Listen to yourself." He uses his fingers to make air quotes as he mocks her voice. "Tolerating the asshole who fucked up my life might be marginally better than being on my own! Let's give it a whirl!" Maybe she can learn to live with him—but she can't seriously *want* him. "Nobody's that desperate, Chica. Nobody."

"Maybe you're right," she allows. "Maybe this will be a huge disaster. It's entirely possible I'll regret ever speaking to you again. Probable, even, knowing you. But I've had a lot of time to be honest with myself, and the truth is that it wasn't Tavis I fell for. It was the guy who poured his heart out on every page he wrote. And I can't—" She takes one hand off the wheel and rests it on the center console, palm up. Fingers open. An invitation. "I can't move on until I give him a chance."

He looks at her hand but does not touch it. "He doesn't exist. He never did."

"Not in the way I thought. But he's part of you."

He shifts his bulk to look out the passenger window. "I'm thirty-seven years old, Chica. If this caterpillar was gonna turn into a butterfly, it would've happened by now."

She places her hand back on the wheel. "I'm not expecting miracles. But we got along all right after Nora was born, didn't we? You were..." She hesitates, and when she speaks again her voice was soft. "Sweet."

He snorts. "That is the first time anyone has *ever* used that adjective to describe me."

"Fine. You're a big fat horrible nasty monster. But really, what does it cost me to give it a shot? I already know I can live without you."

————

AFTER SWINGING BY THE PLAZA TO PICK UP THE KIDS, they go home and she tells him, playfully, to get his butt in the kitchen and start dinner, because what is he good for if not food, right? And suddenly it hits him that his culinary options are no longer limited to packets of ketchup and ramen seasoning. Robin has an entire shelf of cookbooks and a drawer full of spices, and just like that he is lost in a cacophony of aroma. Nora follows him back and forth across the plywood floor, begging for one snack after another. Robin leans in long enough to say, "Wait for dinner," but he sneaks the kid a couple of chocolate chips from the bag in the pantry.

Nora is less pleased with his creamed spinach and linguine. "I wanted cheese!"

"The noodles are drenched in alfredo sauce, kiddo. Literally melted cheese." The pasta is a little under-done and over-salted, but neither of these flaws ought to be game-changing for an unrepentant booger connoisseur.

Robin sighs and grabs the Kraft parmesan from the fridge. Cyril makes a mental note to order a block to grate. He's no master chef, but fresh ingredients are enough to fool most palates.

Seth tells them about a television show he's invented, entitled "Invincible Block and Normal Shield," relating the plot of episode four in excruciating detail as Robin, catching Cyril's eye across the table, bites her lips to check her laughter. Seth had been unusually fixated on geometry as a toddler—preferring objects with interesting shapes and textures to anything with a face—and it's clear that he still views the world through a lens of complex mathematical relationships.

"I've missed your cooking," Robin says, savoring a bite with eyes closed.

"Your standards have really taken a nosedive."

"I'm a single parent in the time of quarantine, Cyril. If we only have chicken dinosaurs twice a week, I call it a win."

Then it's time to get the kids to bed, which is another exercise in chaos. Nora, informed that Seth will be having stories with Cyril, bursts into tears and proceeds to throw a tantrum. Not that she's got any idea what she's missing—it's only that her brother is apparently the recipient of a special treat, and she's not. Robin heaves the child over one shoulder and carts her into the kids' room, kicking and screaming.

Seth dismisses the incident with a fatalistic shrug, as if to say, "Sisters—what can you do?" Then he flops down on the couch next to Cyril and looks up at him. Expectant.

"Hey, kid." He is keenly aware, since this morning's walk to the plaza, that Seth is now more or less a complete person. Little kids are simple, like puppies: hungry and endlessly forgiving. Meaningful person-to-person communication? Yeah, this is where he fucks it up. "How's it going?"

"I dunno," Seth says, running the words together so it sounds like *iunno*.

Well. That's enough small talk. Cyril rocks himself forward and up, with a grunt, and goes to the bookshelf by the entryway. "Let's see. What should we read tonight?"

Five years do not seem to have altered Robin's reading habits significantly. She gravitates toward trade magazines and instructional handbooks—there's an actual Chilton's manual for her pickup truck wedged in horizontally on an upper shelf, as if she's referenced it recently. Her shelves are not entirely devoid of literature, however, and although most of it consists of true crime and nonfiction travel narratives, she has a few holdovers from her college lit courses. He walks his fingers over the spines, hesitating at *Don Quixote*.

"I want dragons," Seth informs him.

"Dragons?" Cyril skips past Jane Eyre and Alice in Wonderland and tugs out a thick volume. "You ever read *The Odyssey*, kid? It's got some good monsters."

Seth frowns at the cover, which is a uniform white with black lettering. "Not *that* kind of dragons."

"Oh," Cyril realizes. "You mean *Dungeons and Dragons?*"

Seth perks up, nodding.

"Okay, well, it's not really a book, per se. There's manuals, I guess, but they're not stories. It's a game. Right?"

Seth just blinks at him, bright-eyed and eager.

Cyril sighs. "You got some paper?"

Seth leaps to his feet and books it to the kitchen, where he yanks a drawer out so far the slides screech, and pulls out a yellow legal pad. Cyril takes a seat at the dining table and Seth drags a second chair around, jamming it right up against Cyril's thigh. He sits on his knees, leaning over Cyril's arm to see the page.

"Kid. I can't see with your head in the way." Seth sinks back a couple of inches and watches Cyril sketch out a character sheet. He's done it so many times he doesn't have to think about which boxes go where—in his head, he's already churning through potential storylines, shifting from one scenario to the other depending on the choices his players make, thinking about how Romero will inevitably Leeroy Jenkins the shit out of any battle scenario, so he'll have to keep the guy occupied with a puzzle only his character can solve while the rest of his party puts their heads together to come up with an attack plan that won't get them all killed—

Seth giggles. "Who's Braddeus the Bald?"

And this asshole looks down at the paper in front of him and sees he's already filled in half the stats for his dwarven cleric, except it's not June in Taft and he's not sitting on the edge of an aluminum bunk drenched in his own sweat trying to ignore the sound of Alder beating the shit out of that poor little bastard Mc-Cury on the other side of the room because it's not happening, not anymore. Or, rather, it is still happening, only he's not there. He's here. With this boy who has his mother's eyes in his father's face.

Seth waves a hand in front of him. "Are you okay? Should I get Mom?"

"No, uh—" Cyril flips the pencil over to erase the name and stats of his prison comrade except it's not a pencil, it's a pen, and the force of the blunt end tears a hole in the paper. He drops the pen and rips the entire sheet off the legal pad, wads it up, and pitches it toward the garbage can in the kitchen. "I'm fine. I just, uh." He clears his throat. "I used to play this with—with your dad." Not technically a lie, but nonetheless a lie. "You're a lot like him, and it just—brought back some memories."

"Oh," Seth says, quietly, imbuing that single round word with a world of meaning. This child, who has lost both father and grandmother, understands the weight of grief. He sits back in his own chair, suddenly a decade older, and places an earnest hand on Cyril's shoulder. "It's okay," he says, lowering his voice to a conspiratorial whisper. "Mom told me what you did."

That catches him off guard. "Really," he says. And wants to add, did she tell you I wrote the letters that made her fall in love with your dad? Or did she tell you I was the one who got him killed? Yeah, probably not. But if not that, then what? "You might have to be a little more specific, kid. I've done... a lot of things." Most of them to Robin.

Seth whispers: "How you saved Shafik."

He exhales a dry laugh of relief. Of course—Robin had told him about the little Afghan kid who was, back then, about the same age that Seth is now. The one who followed Tavis around the base like a little shadow, and in return for his company received packages Robin filled with batteries and candy. Tavis had done a lot of things in the name of God and country that kept him up at night, but when Shafik had vanished, he couldn't let it go. But he couldn't do it alone. "Did your mom tell you I broke a bunch of laws to do it?"

Seth nods. "That's why you went to jail."

"Prison. But yeah, same difference."

"And why Daddy died."

This, right here, is how myths get started; how guys with guns blowing people's brains out become exalted saints. Mommy looks at her kid and can't bring herself to tell him Daddy's job was killing people—or, in this case, mostly patching up the people who killed people—so she tells him the good part, the noble part. She simplifies. Because that part's there, too, sure, but it's complicated and all tangled together and it's impossible to say, "Well, Daddy did something wrong," without also answering, "What did he do?" Well, Daddy disobeyed the chain of command, because Shafik went missing, so it was okay that he broke the rules, sort of, but also it wasn't okay because that was what he signed up for and he knew exactly what the consequences might be and—and at that point Mommy's either lost her nine-year-old completely, or she's convinced him that his father was a monster. So instead she tells him the abridged, bowdlerized version of the story, which is that Daddy sacrificed his life to save a little kid.

And Cyril can hardly blame Robin because, looking into Seth's earnest eyes, he can't bring himself to tell him any different. "Yeah," he says. "Yeah, kid, that's what happened."

Seth smiles like he's been let in on a special secret. His eager face says he wants more—details, anecdotes about his father, whatever.

Hard pass.

Cyril runs a hand over his face. "Let's do this before it gets too late." He picks up the pen again and draws a rectangle at the top of a new page. "First thing you gotta do is make a character." And for the love of God, please don't let him ask what character his dad played. Bad enough Tavis is dead; if the kid wants to revive his childhood D&D character, Cyril is going to lose his shit.

Seth bounces on his knees, abruptly switching back to goofy-kid mode. "I wanna be a dragon."

Cyril taps the pen against the legal pad. "That's not one of the standard character races," he explains. Seth would need to choose a race, like human or elf, although the fourth edition of D&D had introduced dragonborn—not dragons, per se; more like lizard people, without wings or tails. If Seth wanted his character to fly, a better option would be to choose a class—the character's job, essentially—such as druid, which would allow him to shape-shift into various animals. "You couldn't take dragon form right away, but if you level up enough you could gain that power."

"Both," Seth says, with a decisive nod. "I want both."

Cyril talks him through the process of creating a backstory for this dragonborn druid, hastily named "Dragondude," and then pauses to dig through the board games on the bookshelf until he finds a pack of cards, sorting out two suits so Seth can "roll" for ability scores. It's hard to tell, honestly, if the kid is even listening to half of what he says. He slides back and forth on his chair, falls off a couple of times, but always scrambles back up, eagerly. Gradually he gets his wiggles worked out and settles in close, head pillowed on Cyril's shoulder as they work through Dragondude's stats.

"And that's it," Cyril tells him, finally. "Good job."

Seth lifts his head, looking confused. "That's... the game?"

Cyril chuckles. "No, that's all we can do to prep. To play the game, you need a party. A group of players. Like I said, it doesn't work with just one."

"Oh." Seth sits back, deflated.

"Well, I could give you a sample battle. You wanna fight some goblins?"

Of course he wants to fight goblins. Dragondude, however, has rolled a two for strength, so it doesn't go as well as the kid hopes. He dies, actually, but when Robin pops her head in to tell them to wrap it up, Cyril finesses the outcome so it's more of a close shave. The goblins aren't too sharp, in any case, and spend most of the fight arguing amongst themselves. When Cyril awards Seth a couple of experience points and declares the session over, he whines in protest.

"Gimme a break, kid, my voice is going out." Goblins are rough on the vocal cords. He pushes his chair back from the table. "Did you brush your teeth and pee?"

Seth looks at him like he's lost his mind. "Yeah?"

"Right—you're not four anymore." He ruffles the exuberant orange fro and nods to the hall. "Off you go."

Seth is gone just long enough for Cyril to slide his chair back from the table. "Kid," he says, turning as the boy's footsteps trot back out, "if you keep stalling, your Mom's not gonna—"

"Just one thing!" He hugs a tablet to his chest. "Here."

Cyril takes the device as it's thrust at his face. "Is this—" It's protected by a chunky sleeve of green foam, but he pries back one corner and finds that, yes, "This is the one I gave you."

The kid nods enthusiastically, tapping and then swiping to bring the screen to life. After five years, it's got plenty of scratches and a crack in one corner. "I'll go to bed, I promise. I just want to log into Minecraft so you can see my world."

"You play Minecraft on *this?*" The kid has a Nintendo Switch hooked up to the television. "You know there's a Switch version, right?"

Seth shrugs. "Yeah, I know."

"You want me to set you up? It'd be easier to see your stuff if you played on the TV."

Seth studies his face with almost comical gravity, and Cyril realizes he's considering not the question itself so much as whether his reply will hurt Cyril's feelings. Finally, he seems to decide honesty is best, and shakes his head. "I like the pad."

"Why? I mean, it's fine. I'm just curious."

"Because you gave it to me." *Obviously*, his expression adds.

Cyril is not expecting this answer—though he should have—and all he can do is grab the kid's head and press him tight against his chest until he can breathe again.

Seth's arms encircle his neck. "I missed you," he whispers.

Cyril would do anything for this kid. Fuck. "Yeah. Me too."

———

HE IS WANDERING THROUGH THE DIGITAL LANDSCAPE of Seth's imagination, blunting his emotions with an ice cream sandwich, when Robin wanders out of the hall and turns left into the kitchen. He ignores her.

Touches of humor—blue sheep, fields of wheat carefully shaped into smiley faces—grace skillfully constructed farms, houses, rivers, castles, cathedrals, giant cathedrals, and underground caverns, all in crude voxel-block detail. Seth's current project appears to be an amusement park for chickens. About twenty of them are stuck on a looped minecart rollercoaster, clucking incessantly as they are whisked round and round. Minecraft is meant to be played as a survival game, but Seth clearly prefers to spend most of his time in the peaceful "creative mode." He prefers building. Creating. Like his mother.

The microwave hums, and a minute later he hears vigorous popping. The scent of artificial butter follows, and then a telltale ping.

Robin shakes the steaming paper bag as she carries it into the living room, holding it by the corners. She stops in front of the couch, looking down at him, her bathrobe open to reveal her usual bedtime attire of jogging shorts and a tank top.

"So," she says, pulling the corners of the popcorn bag to release steam. "You're still here. Which I'm going to take as some kind of yes." She uses her knee to give his knee a shove, which sends a ripple through his belly. "Move."

She waits, teasing out the first few piping hot pieces of popcorn, as he sets the iPad aside and grabs one arm of the couch, rocking himself to the right. The back of his shirt rides up and he twists, awkwardly, trying to tug it down over the exposed roll of flesh.

"I'm gonna sit next to you," she informs him, munching an exploded kernel. "And we're probably gonna touch."

It is not a question: she hands off the bag of popcorn before planting herself next to him, then tucks her legs up and reaches for the remote. "I figure we've both got about five years of quality entertainment to catch up on," she says, flipping to the Netflix dashboard. And then she passes the remote to him. "You pick. Something we'll both like. I mean, as much as you like anything."

He tosses the crumpled ice cream sandwich wrapper toward

the coffee table. It bounces and lands on the floor. "I'm not a fucking mind reader."

"Not," she adds, stretching for the bottle of lotion on the end table, "something you think Tavis would think I'd like."

He is not interested in playing stupid games. Nevertheless, he scrolls through the menu, willfully ignoring her as she pumps cocoa butter into one hand, rubs her palms together, and runs a hand down the length of each bronze arm. Netflix's recommendations, based on what she's previously watched, contain mostly documentaries. Not interested. *Orange is the New Black* seems a little too on the nose. *Chapelle,* likely too coarse even for Robin. He pauses, finally, on *Jessica Jones.* He looks to her for an opinion, but cannot stop his eyes from flickering downward, to the hand now smoothing lotion over her bare leg.

She lifts the bottle by the neck, letting it swing toward him. "You wanna do it?"

"No."

She grins and gives him a nudge with her knee. "Liar."

When *isn't* he lying? "Look, do you wanna watch the goddamn show, or—"

"Yeah." She returns the bottle to the end table. "Go for it."

He presses play, and the intro begins with a slow, drunken stumble of notes. Robin helps herself to some popcorn. He tries to hand her the bag, but instead of taking it she scoots closer. They watch the goddamn show.

At some point, the knee touching the side of his belly becomes a leg, and then an arm. He reaches into the bag, not for the first time, but the popcorn is gone.

She rests the flat of her hand on his stomach, smoothing his shirt, and leans her head on his shoulder. He smells the tang of panic in his own perspiration.

"No," he says.

She sits up. Hits pause. "No... what?"

He shakes his head. "I can't." No rationale, no explanation. He just—can't.

Her lower lip disappears between her teeth. "We'll take it slow."

He looks down at the vast, pooling spread of his stomach. At the absolute mess he has made of himself, because he did not think he would ever be here. Does not belong here. He heaves all six-foot-five, four-hundred-fifty pounds of himself to his feet and lumbers into the kitchen, out of breath by the time he gets there not only because he's huge but because he's about to lose his shit.

"Is... this about Tavis?" Her voice, in the living room, is uncharacteristically small.

He laughs, bitterly. "No," he says, but with a sarcastic twist he knows she will assume means *yes*. This is how he does things. How he held her captive for seven years without so much as penning a single untruth. It's all in the implication. The omission. The blanks he knows she will fill. Even now, knowing what he did to her, what he is capable of, still she does not see.

She does not *want* to see.

What she wants is to feel sorry for him. She wants to believe that between the two of them, he and Tavis, they had managed to cobble together Robin's ideal husband. That Tavis hadn't been content with that. That he'd wanted to prove himself a hero in Robin's eyes, to have her for himself. Cyril wasn't getting anything out of the deal—except freedom, maybe—but for the sake of his friend he'd helped try and save the kid. And now here he is, the lonely, broken remainder of one functional human being. So sad. Right?

Right.

Or maybe the tortured survivor narrative is just the story he, Cyril, wants Robin to believe.

Maybe none of this was a mistake.

Maybe everything went according to plan.

He takes the leftover linguine out of the refrigerator, pulls back the plastic wrap, and makes it disappear. A tub of potato salad is next.

"Bring it in here, if you want," she says.

He ignores her. This is not about Tavis at all. At least, not the way she thinks.

When that kid went missing, two weeks before the end of Tav's last tour? The idea of saving Shafik hadn't come from Tavis, even if he would have sworn it had. Let's not be coy—Cyril is nothing if not a master manipulator. He knows perfectly well how to say exactly the right thing at precisely the wrong time. All he had to do was leave this sentence unfinished, or ask that rhetorical question. Maybe he'd known exactly how Tavis would fill in the blanks.

It's possible that all he'd intended, at the outset, was to convince Tavis to re-up just one more last time. To maintain the status quo for just a little longer, because Cyril needed time to let go of the woman who was never really his. Sure. Anything's possible. Maybe he never meant to put something into motion which, once begun, he couldn't stop.

Who knows—maybe it was all about the score. The high of teasing passwords from the people with the right clearances at Cooke's company; of talking Tavis through linking a laptop to the air gapped network on the ground in Afghanistan, cracking the system wide open. The rush of swimming through oceans of raw data, letting it sift through his fingers like glittering jewels. Maybe, just then, he hadn't cared about Tavis or Robin or anyone at all.

Maybe it was only once he'd begun to digest the forbidden intel, as the million and one pinpoints of data had begun to arrange and sort themselves in his mind's eye, that everything had come into sudden sharp focus. He'd seen all the moving parts and understood, with crystal clarity, how the machine worked. Shafik was one small sacrificial pawn in a much broader strategy to maintain stability in the region, preserving resources and saving American lives. And he'd understood, without a shadow of a doubt, exactly how far those in leadership would be willing to go to protect that plan.

He should've told Tavis to pull out. Should've stopped him from recording interviews with locals on his downtime, trying to trace the breadcrumbs leading to the child's whereabouts. Scrub the whole operation and suffer the consequences, if he was caught.

But he hadn't.

"You coming?" Robin still sits on the couch where he left her; the actress on the television screen is frozen, her mouth open in a silent "o" of understanding.

He tosses the empty tub of potato salad into the sink and reaches into the fridge. Breakfast sausages? He'd cooked them all this morning, with the intent to reheat them for the kids' breakfasts. It'll do.

Robin waits for him. Fucking *waits* for him to eat.

And—Jesus Christ, when he can stomach no more, he brings her a cookie.

"Thanks."

He sits. It hurts. After five years of relative abstinence, his body has grown unaccustomed to this abuse.

"Look," she says, "you don't have to do anything. Okay? Just... be."

She touches his arm. He doesn't move. She slides her hand under the sagging flap of flesh that contains his elbow and settles against him. Fresh and clean and warm.

"No," he whispers, or thinks he does.

Get away, he wants to warn her. Danger, Robin Matheson. For the love of God, *run*.

If she gets too close—if he touches her—not even the inertia of his mass will be enough to protect her from harm.

Robin presses play.

Here is the truth: for five days Cyril sat on that horde of data, while Tavis continued to snoop around on the ground in Afghanistan. For five days, Cyril peered through the keyhole window of his monitor as the buzzards circled. Emails flew. Tav's command realized they had been compromised. That someone had accessed the system. And then they went dark. Mostly. Cyril had retained backdoor access to a few key email accounts—and he was sitting at his computer, fingers deep in the digital cookie jar, at the exact moment that the commanding officer of Tav's commanding officer delivered the order that would remove Tavis from his normal detail and put him in a certain tank on a certain deserted road at a very certain time. "That should take care of our problem," the officer had written.

Cyril had stared at the text on that bright white screen until the words had burned themselves onto his retinas. And then, for the first time in a very long while, he shut off his computer and hauled his massive ass out of his apartment—to go for a walk.

Four blocks, from his house to hers. Slow going, back then, for a guy who had to take a breather in the way to his own mail-box. He stopped on the sidewalk outside the big picture window in front. It was evening, and the curtains were drawn, Robin and Seth illuminated like shadow puppets by the light that shone from within. He stood there, watching, for a long time.

And then he went home. He composed a warning to Tavis.

By the time he hit send, he already knew it was too late.

Robin snorts and laughs at something on-screen. She glances at him to share the moment, and realizes he is somewhere else. Her smile fades. "Hey, big guy," she says softly, putting a hand on his chest. "It's okay."

He is breathing hard.

CHAPTER 8

Cyril is whipping up a second round of bacon and eggs the following morning when Robin appears in the doorway. She tilts her head to one side, using an old t-shirt to pat her hair dry. Behind her, in the dining room, the kids are squabbling over the ketchup bottle. "Morning," she says, and offers a sympathetic smile. "You sleep all right?"

After having what was essentially a fucking panic attack? "Yeah. Fine." He keeps his eyes on the pan. "I need your computer again."

"Oh?" She wads the t-shirt into a ball and chucks it toward the laundry room. It lands with a soft plop on the plywood floor. "Miss something the first time?"

He uses the spatula to tick items off his fingers. "Phone. Car. Apartment."

"Oh." She glances over her shoulder, just long enough to say, "Guys, that's enough." The kids keep arguing, and she steps into the kitchen, around him, so his mass eclipses her view of the children. There's a plate on the counter and she picks it up, holding it out for two eggs over easy. "That's it, then? We're done?"

"Pretty much."

"Bacon!" Nora shouts. "I need more bacon!"

Robin nods to the plate in her hand, and Cyril loads it up with four sizzling strips. She starts to turn away, and then stops. "Look." He feels the breath of her words on his arm. "Don't... feel like you have to rush out of here. Wait until you get your feet under you. Cook. Clean. Have fun with the kids." She holds up the plate, forcing a bittersweet smile. "I mean, really, go to town."

Playing house. Like he had before the feds caught up with him and sent him to prison. Back when, as far as she knew, they were merely friends. "No." He can't go back. But there's no forward, either. "I mean—I will. I just." He rubs his forehead with the back of a hand, leaving a streak of bacon grease. "Shit." What he needs is to get out.

She tugs a dish towel from the oven handle and offers it. "It's okay. Not what I was hoping for, but... I understand."

"Right." Because she was *so* hoping he'd sleep on her couch forever.

Unfortunately, there's no swift route to extricating himself from Robin's life. Not unless he wants to hemorrhage money on takeout and motel rooms, anyway—and even finding an apartment is no guarantee of success. His house had been auctioned off to pay for trial fees and prison commissary, and the twenty K he's got left in the bank is going to evaporate quickly if he doesn't get off his ass and find some steady work, and soon.

So, step one: over the course of the following days, Cyril begins the slow, tedious task of performing an update on his professional life. The postal system is taking its sweet time with his bank card, but now that he has access to his account, he can link it to PayPal. He considers purchasing a laptop, but it would only be a stopgap measure; any employment he manages to secure will require a far more robust desktop system. His finances being what they are, he selects a refurbished Android phone with a shitty data plan and a pay-per-day option for establishing a mobile hotspot. Not having to use Robin's computer for internet access is at least one small step towards emancipation.

After dispensing with the necessities, he establishes an anonymizing VPN and dives deep. He spends hours catching up on current events in tech, trying to trace the subtle undercurrent of Anonymous as it springs up, seemingly at random, to shift the course of the political stream. Waves of opinion form, crash, and re-form as he encounters some new nugget of information. He loses himself upon a vast shoreline of ever-shifting sand.

After two or perhaps three days, surfacing only to cook and play Minecraft with the kids, his unsavory little corner of the internet begins to feel less alien. Still, he can't escape the feeling that there's been a fundamental shift. Hacker culture has never been wholesome, at least not where Anonymous and its various splinter groups are concerned, but during his forced sabbatical things seem to have taken a particularly antagonistic turn. His go-to securities forums are overrun with trolls and shitposters, and even in the more moderate communities, "edgy" humor has given way to explicit racism and jingoistic insanity. Marching on Wall Street hadn't upended the world, so all the young, unlanded knights had exchanged their Guy Fawkes masks for swastikas. Russian bots proliferate, with only the barest pretense of passing for something other than what they are. Disruption, not persuasion, is the tactic of choice. It's not entirely a surprise; the CIA had expended so much effort quashing domestic leakers and whistleblowers back in the Occupy Wall Street days, it hadn't stopped to think about what might rush to fill the void. Better the hacker you know.

He considers letting a few old contacts know he's looking for work, but decides to hold off while he's still living under Robin's roof. His release is public record, but his location isn't, and the last thing he wants is a bunch of news vans camped out on Robin's lawn. Instead, he ferrets out a closed message board that seems promising and jumps through the hoops required to prove he's worthy of an invite. He's approved, and after scrolling through the most recent posts he searches the archives for his name. There are several massive threads devoted to analyzing his exploits, and he clicks on the most recent one. There has always been a large "fuck the man" component to his hacktivism, so the anger and vitriol from his erstwhile fans is expected. What he doesn't expect is to see himself heralded as a hero of white supremacy. Apparently because... he's white? And his face has been used in some alt-right memes?

Once, this asshole existed on the hazy borders of legality and morality; he has not moved, but the world has shifted around him, and he finds himself become moderate. He feels old.

Robin leaves him alone, or at least doesn't insist on watching any more television, but at some point—the kids are running out the door with backpacks, so, morning—she informs him that he has a choice between taking a shower or relocating to the barn. She leaves to ferry the kids to Greta's house and he showers, wrapping himself in a sheet afterward because her towels aren't big enough and the entirety of his limited wardrobe is, as Nora put it, "super smelly." He starts the wash, tossing in the kids' martial arts uniforms to pad out the load. Nora had also extracted a promise of chocolate chip cookies, so he pulls out the ingredients and gets the first batch into the oven before returning to Robin's laptop at the dining table.

His initial Craigslist search had revealed that Healdsburg rents are off the charts; he's studying a studio listing in neighboring Windsor when a voice says, "Nice toga."

He jerks backward. "Fuck!"

Robin laughs, long and loud. "I was not being quiet," she says, rattling her tool belt to illustrate the point. She gives his bare shoulder a smack with the back of her hand. "You were really in the zone. What're you doing, reading my email again?" She leans over his shoulder and sees the apartment photos. "Oh."

He is not sure whether he imagines the hint of disappointment in her tone. "Cyril, before you—"

The oven timer beeps. He shuts the laptop and shoves himself to his feet, gathering the corners of the bedsheet with one hand. Not that it matters—at his size, nothing really conceals. "Don't you have somewhere to be?" He works his free hand into an oven mitt.

She sighs faintly, letting go of whatever it was she had been about to say. "Nope. Got my last job wrapped up yesterday." In one swift stroke she slides the hammer out of her toolbelt and uses it to point at the boarded-up stairwell and, by extension, the skeletal second floor. "Priority numero uno is getting this place buttoned up before first rain."

"Good luck with that." He doesn't need to be a carpenter to know the house is a wreck.

"Thanks for your vote of confidence." She holsters the hammer. "How about you give me a hand?"

"A hand?" he echoes, and then, realizing she's serious: "Uh, no." He trades the mitt for a spatula and begins transferring cookies from the sheet to a cooling rack. They're flat and slightly crisp, but it's not like the kids will mind. He startles slightly as Robin's hand snakes under his arm to grab one. "You're gonna—"

"Ow!"

"—get burned."

She passes the cookie, hot-potato-style, from one hand to the other, and then nibbles gingerly, pulling her lips back into a grimace. "Mmm. Worth it." She eats the rest slowly, savoring every bite.

He swallows, though his throat is bone dry.

She yanks the fridge open and pulls out a gallon of milk. "You're an ungrateful son of a bitch, Cyril, but as long as you're sleeping on my couch and eating my food, I think you can probably manage to help me out for a couple hours."

Does she think he's an idiot? "Five years on your own and suddenly the damsel needs my help? That's some grade-A bullshit, Chica."

She rolls her eyes. "I don't *need* you. But setting up the scaffolding'll take half the time if I have a second pair of hands." She chugs directly from the carton. "We both know your idea of a workout is hauling your ass off the couch, Cyril. Seriously, all you gotta do is stand and hold."

He considers this. Fuck her, but the fact remains that he's a guest in her house. "Fine."

———

ROBIN FAILED TO MENTION THAT STEP ONE IS dragging eight steel frames up the hill from the garage. Two trips down and back and this asshole is drenched. He pulls his shirt off over one shoulder, wads it into a ball, and uses it to sponge his armpits and other crevices. (If he were going to be self-conscious about showing skin in her presence, he'd have made better life choices.) "You said this wasn't going to be a workout."

"Did I?" She's sweating freely, but still fresh and filled with energy. She grins. "Because I don't think I did."

"So. This is who you are now? A duplicitous bitch?"

She shrugs. "You manipulate people to get what you want. Why shouldn't I manipulate you?" She waves him toward the half-completed back porch. It covers a dip in the terrain, with steps on the left and a ramp on the right that extends to the sidewalk. The unfinished edge, looking out over the hill to the barn, drops off sharply. "Have a seat. I'll—holy crap, what *happened?*"

He follows her stricken expression downward, toward the left side of his lower back. "Oh. Right." He can't see what she sees, but he stretches a hand back to finger the puckered crater of a scar. "Not as bad as it looks—prison docs are not exactly known for their sewing skills."

Her hand hovers over the spot for a moment, not quite touching. "Have you actually seen it? Because it looks pretty bad." She tugs her phone out, snaps a photo, and offers it up for inspection.

He shades the screen with a hand. She's right—it's a botched job, even by prison standards. "Well. The other guy looked worse." Cyril had slammed the attacker's head against a table, ending the fight with a couple of broken teeth. Nobody had touched him, after that.

She laughs. "You couldn't even keep your trap shut in prison. What did you say to make someone *that* mad?"

He shrugs. "Fuck if I know." Instead of taking a spot on the porch, he mounts the steps and lets himself into the kitchen. After drinking half a gallon direct from the tap, he fills two plastic tumblers with ice and water and slaps together a pair of sandwiches. When he steps back outside, Robin is just propping the last scaffolding frame against the house. She dusts her hands off on her jeans, then takes one of the tumblers and a turkey on rye. "Thanks." She seats herself on the top step, all the way to the left, and pats the redwood plank on her right.

He lowers his bulk to the second step down, though the top step digs into his back, so he's not looming over her. The sun is on the other side of the house now, and there's a bit of a breeze, so the shade at least is nice. "What's the deal with the ramp?"

"Oh—Greta's husband. You remember—"

"Do I remember the little prick whose company's military contract I hacked to gain access to the data for which I went to prison? Yeah, I actually do kinda remember him." Cyril had been the one to suggest Robin when the guy needed someone to renovate his condo. "He spends a lot of time at your place?"

She laughs. "He's actually never been here. But he cosigned my loan, so it seemed kind of rude to remodel the place without giving him access. Plus?" She tosses a thumb at the back door. "It makes moving appliances a cinch." She takes a bite of her sand-

wich, and then uses the remainder to sketch a rough outline in
the air. "My plan is to build a big deck out over the hill. Maybe
sink a hot tub over there, trellis with some planters or something
on that side to block the street. Dunno if I'll get to it, though."

"Before what, you sell the place?"

"Before I run out of money and have to go back to work,
before the market picks up, before..." She sighs. "Well. Lots of
things." She polishes off the last crust of rye and takes a long
drink of water before speaking again. "So." She glances at him.
"What's your plan? In terms of, uh, moving out?"

"Now that I'm a felon? I'm sure there's at least one slumlord
willing to look the other way in exchange for cash." Finding a
place isn't what worries him—it's getting enough work to keep it.
Living in the granny unit behind the house he'd inherited from
his mother had allowed him to exist on what he made renting it
out, plus whatever odd securities jobs piqued his interest, but the
money left over from its sale, after legal bills, wasn't even enough
for a down payment on a port-a-potty, in California. For the first
time in his life, he would need to actually hold down a steady
job.

"No, I mean, were you... Are you planning to head back down
south?"

He'd forgotten he'd only discussed sticking close with Seth. "I
was thinking I might stay, uh, nearby." He shrugs off her look of
surprise. "An air-conditioned room with a computer is the same
up here as it is in SoCal, and, you know, it would be nice to see
the kids." Like he has some sort of visitation rights. "Assuming
that's okay with you."

She puts her hand on his arm, and when she speaks, her voice
is full. "I'd love that, Cyril."

He doesn't want to look at her, but he does anyway, and in
that split second glance he takes in the fullness of her lips, the
wetness in her eyes. Why does she have to—God *damn* it.

Abruptly, she shifts back into her own space, picking up the glass to take another long drink. Then she twists to look at the tray sitting behind them. "Did you not bring any cookies?" With a grunt of exasperation, she gets to her feet and clomps into the house.

He lifts his elbows, letting his pits air-dry in the breeze.

"Here." She hands two chocolate chip cookies over his shoulder and drops back down onto the steps. "I'll ask around. About housing, I mean." She nods toward town. "The way zoning works here, something like every five acres of vineyard is permitted a barn or a farmhouse, so there's a lot of little places sitting around gathering dust. George, from the donut shop? Oh —right, you didn't come in." She waves a hand in dismissal. "George hired me to shore up one of his barns, and when he took me out there, I opened up these big old just-about-falling-off doors, and there's—I am not a-kidding you—a vintage nineteen fifty-seven Chevrolet Bel Aire sitting there like it just drove off the lot."

Her speech becomes less precise as she relates the anecdote, sinking comfortably back into the colloquial patterns inherited from her father. Her hands move with her lips, providing punctuation and emphasis. She is radiant.

He could spoil this with sarcasm. Would have, in times past, lest she suspect he felt anything for her other than unadulterated disdain. Even now, he shuffles through half a dozen possible insults in his head—but this time, he chokes them down. Because he doesn't have to keep up the pretense of hating her, anymore. All he has to do is keep his goddamn mouth shut, and he can just sit here and watch her glow.

She shakes her head in remembered disbelief. "Fifty thousand miles, Cyril. I'm like, what the hell, George, and he says, oh, this old thing? I drove it around when I was in high school. Turns out whenever he gets a new car, he just parks the old one in a barn somewhere. There's antiques and who knows what else just boxed away in attics and barns and spare rooms all over around here. It's crazy. Anyway." She slaps his knee. "I'll see if someone's got anything without rats."

"I can live with rats. What I really need is fiber optic cable." Although, if his tenancy happens to be off the books, so much the better.

"No promises. I'll see what I can do."

The cookies are gone and his shirt seems not-completely-soaked, so he finds the neck hole and drops it back over his head. As he feels for the armholes, Robin reaches to pull the rumpled cotton down over his back.

"I missed this," she says.

"What, helping a fat guy get dressed?"

She rolls her eyes. "No."

"Homemade cookies?"

"Warmer."

"My B.O.?"

She snaps and points at him. "Yes! Definitely that." She shakes her head. "You know. Just—having someone to talk to."

Five fucking years she could have visited, or called, or sent a letter, or—no. He has no right to blame her for that. Not really. "You have people," he says. "Cooke's wife, apparently, and this guy George—"

"You know what I mean."

"Do I?" He absolutely does not.

"I don't have to explain anything to you. My life was—is—complicated. Even more so now that everyone thinks they've seen the truth on the news. You get it, because you were there."

He had almost entirely forgotten about the public aspect of his arrest, or the effect that scrutiny might have on Robin's life after the initial uproar. None of that mattered, in prison. "Maybe you forgot, but I was there because I'm the one who made that shit *happen*."

She shrugs.

"Seriously?"

"You saved a kid, Cyril. You want me to condemn you for that?"

"Tavis. Saved a kid." As if that one tiny pearl in the giant pile of pig shit could possibly redeem everything else. Jesus. "You're nursing a serious case of Stockholm syndrome, Chica, you know that?"

She leans back to look up at him for one long, cool moment. He has the sense that she is reevaluating him, somehow. "I wonder," she says, finally. "Who do you lie to more? Me, or yourself?"

———

THE SOUND OF THE REFRIGERATOR OPENING IS WHAT wakes him, next morning. And then: "Well, bust my buttons, there's food in here! You might not bankrupt me after all."

He manages a grunt. Then he lifts a hand to rub his face. "Oh." His biceps are on fire. "Oh, God."

Robin saunters into the living room, holding an eight-ounce cup of yogurt. She looks down at him as she spoons a bite into her mouth. "You fell asleep while I was putting Nora to bed last night."

And apparently hasn't moved in the twelve hours since. He grabs the arm of the couch, and for one terrifying moment he can't get up. But then he rocks forward, gritting his teeth, and staggers to his feet. Everything hurts. " 'Give me a hand,' my ass."

She licks the spoon and uses it to tap his shoulder as he hobbles past. "You'll live."

"Not sure I want to. God. I'm not getting the kids ready for school."

"Neither am I. It's Saturday."

One long, hot shower later, he emerges to find the kids at the table, dousing pancakes in syrup. A Costco-sized box of Bisquick sits open on the counter.

"Cyril!" Nora says, brightening. "I want *Cyril* pancakes!"

Robin plops another fluffy golden disc onto her plate. "You will eat Mommy's pancakes or no pancakes at all." She tosses another plate onto the table and waves Cyril toward it. "I don't know what makes yours so much better, anyway."

He can answer that one: "Butter. Lots and lots of butter."

After breakfast the kids claim their right to cartoons, so he shares the couch and they introduce him to *The Dragon Prince*. Robin clomps through in her boots, says, "I'm gonna work for a little while," and a few minutes later he hears the table saw's long, low whine.

Two episodes in, the mail-person knocks. She's gone, walking swiftly down the sidewalk, before the kids have time to scramble to the front door. Along with a handful of junk mail, there are two packages. The one addressed to Cyril contains his phone—his first taste of true freedom. With this small black brick, he can do whatever the hell he wants without worrying about how it's going to affect Robin.

The other package has Robin's name on it, but he opens it anyway. This action becomes significantly less transgressive when he pulls out the clothing she ordered for him. More sweats and t-shirts, several sizes larger than the ones she had picked up the night he got out—and a button-up Hawaiian shirt in garish reds and blues.

"Oooh, pretty," Nora says, leaning over his arm.

The back door opens and slams, and Robin walks through the dining room with a hammer in one hand and a drill in the other. Cyril holds up the shirt. "What the—heck—is this?"

She laughs. "I dunno, I thought it was cute!" She sinks the hammer claw into the plywood blocking off the stairwell and yanks a nail out with a sharp squeak.

The kids, realizing she is about to unlock a heretofore unexplored terrain, bombard her with questions about how long it's going to take the sheet of plywood off until she tells them that if they don't back off and give her some space she's going to nail it back on again. When the stairwell is open, finally, they rush upward, shrieking.

For the next hour, as Cyril sets up his phone, he can hear them dashing back and forth over the upper floor. Robin's voice chimes in now and then with a warning, indistinct but probably "be careful." Or maybe "don't jump out the windows."

While the phone isn't the latest model, it's not five years old, so relatively speaking it feels like an upgrade. Settling for slightly out of date tech also makes it easier to jailbreak. That done, he downloads his usual array of anonymizing and recording apps, including the companion to the surveillance tracker he'd installed on Robin's phone. He thumbs through it briefly, familiarizing himself with the control interface. It displays her texts, her call log—all things he recognizes firsthand. She's allowed him unfettered access to both her phone and her laptop thus far, but it might be useful to keep tabs on who she's talking to, once he moves out.

While the communications log downloads everything saved in her phone, the tracking function logs its own geographical data, so it only has the information it's collected since he installed the app. The map controls could use a UI overhaul, but he experiments with backstepping through her timeline. Dropping off the kids daily at Greta's, running between martial arts and the bank, their trip to the DMV earlier that same day, and finally—

Cyril refreshes the display, but the information doesn't change. He frowns.

————

THE KIDS' BEDTIME ROUTINE CONSISTS OF EVEN MORE cartoons. When Robin insists it's time for sleep, really, no, seriously, they are less than thrilled. There is a lot of screaming and, eventually, muffled tears.

"That's always fun." Robin lets out a puff of air as she comes back into the living room, where Cyril is flipping through the Netflix menu from the couch. She stoops to pick up a couple of Legos. "Planning on passing out early again, or should I lock the fridge?"

He holds up his phone. "What the fuck is this?"

She blinks. "Uh... your phone?" She tosses the Legos onto the coffee table and comes to look, first squinting at the screen and then taking it from him, using a thumb and forefinger to zoom in on the map. "What is this?" she asks, obviously confused. She gets that he expects her to know what he's looking at, but she doesn't.

And then she does.

He'd installed the tracking app on Thursday morning, right before they'd walked to the plaza for doughnuts. Healdsburg has no buildings tall enough to impede transmission, so their route is traced perfectly, down to the side of the street they'd been walking on. After that, she'd had to run to a client's house for a final inspection. That's what she'd told him, anyway.

The map says different. Unless her "client" happened to be Kaiser Permanente Medical Center. Not here in town, but in Santa Rosa, half an hour away. She'd parked in the lot, entered the building, and stayed inside for over an hour. Visiting a patient? Seeing a doctor? She could have said, "Hey, I need to go in for my annual checkup," and he wouldn't have batted an eye. But she hadn't said that. She had lied.

She lets out a long, slow breath. "Why do you have to be *such* a prick?"

"You know what I am."

She tosses the phone onto his stomach and then just stands there, looking down at him, hands limp at her sides. Then, without comment, she turns and walks into the kitchen and opens the refrigerator door. She stands there staring into the cold light, long enough that he returns his attention to his phone, before saying, finally, "You want one of these?"

He glances up to see her holding a beer—a green bottle, not her usual golden Corona. "You know I don't fucking drink." He doesn't do well with moderation. If he'd ever bothered to cultivate a taste for alcohol, he'd have been long dead by now.

"It's non-alcoholic. But whatever." She slams the fridge door. "Get off your ass and follow me."

"Pass." Something hard hits his chest like a brick. "Fuck! What the—" It's a can of root beer.

"We need to talk."

Something in her voice makes him swallow his pithy comeback. "Fine." He hauls himself off the couch, gritting his teeth against the pain in his lower back, and turns to follow—only to see her jog up the stairwell. At the top, she puts a shoulder to a plywood hatch on hinges, newly installed to keep the kids out while she's not working, and steps through. Her boots tromp away somewhere over his head.

Thirteen steps, no railing, no landing. He tackles them one at a time, wincing as the ancient wood groans beneath him. He pauses twice to breathe, and by the time he reaches the summit he's not sure he's not having a heart attack. Is that what she wants? Maybe it's exactly what she wants.

"Over here."

She stands at the front of the house, one foot propped up on the sill of the big picture window, framed by a forest of two-by-fours and trees. The gaps between the bare studs are too narrow to squeeze, so he takes the long way around what will eventually be a hall. The scaffolding they'd erected hugs the exterior wall on his right.

"This is why you picked me up from prison? So you could fucking kill me?"

She looks up as he hobbles in. "I insulated the crap out of

these floors. It's the one place we're safe from little ears. Here."
She sets her beer on the window ledge, lifts a circular saw off a
scrap wood step stool, and kicks it in his direction.

It's low and too small for even half his ass, but he hands her
the can of root beer and spreads his legs, squatting like he's
taking a shit. It's not comfortable, but he manages to get himself
settled, back braced against a couple of framing studs.

She cracks the tab on the root beer, holding it out the window
as it spews. When the foam tapers off, she hands it back, shaking
the last drops of fizzy liquid from her fingertips before wiping her
hand on her thigh. She retrieves her beer and straddles the
window ledge, one leg swinging over the side.

"Can you... not do that?" He does not want his last memory of
her to be her brains on the sidewalk.

"What? Oh." She leans further out the window. "If this makes
you nervous, wait til I get up on the scaffolding. The porch roof's
out here, though. I'm good." She stomps to demonstrate, then
turns anyway and plants both feet firmly on the sub-floor,
dangling the green bottle between her knees.

They drink, in silence, as the sun slips between the trees.

"So," he says. "The view's nice, but I'm not getting any
younger here, so—"

"Cyril. Can you not..." She pinches the bridge of her nose and
lets out a long, heavy sigh. "Okay. Yeah." She tosses back the last
of the faux beer and stands, setting the bottle on the nearest horizontal stud. She squares her shoulders, facing him, and then, just
as suddenly, seems to deflate. She turns away, gazing out the
window.

"Well, that was anticlimactic."

She exhales a hiss of frustration. "Just—give me a second to
pick my words, okay? I didn't—I didn't want to do it like this. I
mean, you're just out of prison, you need time to—" She abandons the sentence with a shake of the head, passing a hand over
her brow. The sunset's orange glow transforms her into a slender

silhouette. "I wanted time to figure this out." She waves a hand at him and then herself. "To figure *us* out. Without you feeling, I don't know, obligated."

He snorts. "Us. Right."

She turns on him. "Oh, screw it, Cyril. I have cancer."

STAGE 3

BARGAINING

CHAPTER 9

This asshole doesn't believe, as Robin does, that there is any kind of divine order to the universe, any reciprocity or justice in the end. Still, it's all too much. Tavis, dead, and then her mother. Prison. All of this in addition to the broader catastrophe of COVID and distance learning and climate change and politics and whatever fresh horrors have dropped today in the endlessly rolling apocalypse which is 2020. And now—cancer? "No," he says. As if he can stop, rewind the words that have just come out of her mouth. Make it all un-happen.

She jams a hand down the front of her tank top. Two quick yanks and her breasts lie, little half-shells, between them on the floor. Her chest is flat. Her face is hard.

He rises, putting out a hand to support himself against the nearest stud. The empty soda can clatters to the plywood floor. His first impulse is to wrap his arms around her—to stop the pieces of her from falling apart. But he doesn't. "No," he says again. It's all that will come.

"What, you need to see my scars?"

He's close enough to catch her wrist before she can yank the neck of her shirt down, hard. For a moment they stand like that, her arm pinned across her chest, fingers clenched into a fist.

Then she steps back, jerking out of his grasp. "Don't look at me like that."

"When—" The shock is starting to wear off, and questions rush in.

"I found a lump three years ago. Just on the left, but it turns out I have the gene, so I had them take both." She crosses her arms over her chest, shoulders hunched. "Not like there was much there to begin with, and I'm done having kids, so." This is how she handles hard things: instead of emotion, she focuses on facts. "It's why we decided to stay in town. Partly. It was just—my mom died the summer I was working on Cooke's place, and after that job wrapped George offered to let us crash in one of his barns while I converted it into a duplex. When I got the biopsy results, Greta basically insisted we move in with them during treatment. That was the same year as the Tubbs fire, and this area was hurting so bad for carpenters I could quit everything on Friday and have three jobs lined up by Monday morning. Then this dump hit the market, and Seth had already made a bunch of friends at school, so... here we are."

The circular saw that had been on the step stool is attached to an orange extension cord. She bends, yanks the plug out, and begins winding the cord, elbow to palm. Waiting, he realizes, for him to do the math. "If that was three years ago—"

"I've been taking Tamoxifen. It's a hormone drug that inhibits the type of cancer I had. But it also ups your chances of getting uterine cancer. And..." She shrugs. "I got lucky. So now I have to do the whole miserable thing all over again." She loops the end of the cord through itself and drops the roll next to the stool. "I'm having a—oh, I forget what it's called. Basically a hysterectomy. Uterus, ovaries, everything. Plus chemo and radiation."

He shifts, pushing away from the stud. "When?"

"Surgery's on Wednesday."

"Wednesday. Like—"

"Like four days from now, yeah. Chemo starts two or three weeks after. So life's gonna be crappy for a while." She stoops, briefly, to pick up a couple of pieces of scrap wood, tossing them toward a pile of garbage that's collected in one corner. "Greta's already invited us to move in with them again, if we need to, so don't worry about—I mean, not that you—" For the briefest moment, her lips quiver, but she presses them together and clears her throat. Her eyes are dry. "If you want to leave, you should go. Soon."

"Uh, no. I'm not going anywhere."

She stops, half-bent for another piece of scrap, and straightens slowly. "Are you—"

"Of course I'm fucking sure." What other answer can he possibly give? She had sprung him from prison early, offered him everything she thought he wanted—*her*—to persuade him to be here for her kids, in her own home, when all she'd had to do was tell him the goddamn truth. Not that he can blame her for thinking manipulation is the most effective way to communicate with him.

She studies him for a long, level moment. "And that's it. No snarky comeback? No clever insult?"

"Christ, Robin, you have—I'm not gonna—" He gestures, wordlessly, and lets out an exasperated breath. "Jesus, even I have limits."

"Limits? You?" She laughs, with bitter disbelief. "All this time, I just had to get cancer?"

This is what he's done to her. "Well, it's not like you're getting a free pass, here." He pushes away thoughts of what's to come. "Uterine cancer buys you maybe, I dunno, five minutes of civility? Come back when you've got an inoperable brain tumor or bone cancer—then we'll talk."

She lets out a bark of laughter and socks him in the arm, hard.

"I hate you, you colossal jerk." Sudden tears carve tracks down her cheeks.

"Hey—no. Shit. Come here." He opens his arms, and she falls into his heavy embrace. He must smell like a locker room, but she gathers his sweat-dampened shirt in her fists, pressing her face into his chest, and sobs.

There's a limit to how long a person can cry. He's pushed her there, before. But not tonight. Eventually she sniffs, wiping her nose on the back of her wrist and then his shirt. She breathes deeply, stretching her arms as far around his middle as they will go. "I didn't want you to think this was why I decided to forgive you."

"Isn't it, though?" As much of a survivor as Robin is, she's obviously scared to be alone again, sick again, with her kids. Despite the many reasons this asshole given her to hate him, he would never do anything to hurt her kids—which was why, for Seth's sake, she had grudgingly tolerated his presence even after Tavis died. It's no surprise to discover she's willing to exonerate him for their benefit a second time. Why hadn't she just *told* him?

To her great credit, she doesn't protest. She goes still, listening to his heartbeat or his breath. He feels her swallow. "It's... like when Tav died," she says, voice low. "For a while, everything was about his death. But... that didn't make any of it less true."

Death. Prison. Cancer. He doesn't want any of the things that led to this moment. But he would give anything to stand like this forever. He lowers his chin, slightly, to smell her hair.

She lets out a long breath, and every muscle in her body seems to relax. Her arms squeeze him, gently. "Thank you."

"Don't."

She lifts her head, pulling back to look up at his face. "Hm?"

He takes her shoulders. He wants to shake, but he just grips her, hard. "Don't thank me. Don't—don't ever thank me. For anything." It makes him sick to think she'd felt the need to offer him anything, let alone the possibility of a relationship. He could spend the rest of his life trying to pay for what he's already done, and never make a dent in his debt to her. She owes him nothing, least of all her gratitude. Whatever she asks of him is owed. "Ever."

Robin takes a moment to absorb this. Then she nods. "Yeah. Okay."

She steps back and he lets her go, reaching to pull his shirt back down over his gut. She beats him to it, giving his belly a friendly pat.

He doesn't know how to respond to that, so he just stands there, staring at her like an idiot.

"Think we still have time for a TV show? I promise I'll keep my hands to myself."

He clears his throat. "You're the one with a job. Well. Sort of."

She holds an arm out toward the stairwell. "Felons first. I'll close up."

He turns, and nearly steps on her bra inserts. Not, as it turned out, meant to beguile some undisclosed lover, but him. "Don't forget your, uh."

"Oh shoot, my boobs."

CHAPTER 10

Long after she's gone to bed and he has thoroughly gutted the fridge, he digs a pen and two yellow legal pads out of the kitchen drawer and sits down to speak to her in the only way he has ever known how. No email, no pigmented pixels on a glowing screen. Just ink and onion skin.

He will tell her everything. He will explain the depth of his friendship with Tavis. How he thought he knew what love meant, until he saw her give birth. His devotion to her children, of which she is already well aware. Most importantly, he will tell her about her husband's death. He will not prevaricate. He will give her the unvarnished truth, and, with it, his soul. If they are to exist together under one roof, let it be with her complete knowledge and willing consent.

He spends a good twenty minutes hovering over that first blank page. And then, finally, in curt, compact script, he writes: *I loved you first.*

He looks at the words. Idiotic. Growling under his breath, he scratches them out.

Funny, isn't it? I thought Tav's death would set me free.

He crumples the page and begins again. This time, he forces

himself to write without thinking, without reflection. He fills one page and then another with half-formulated sentences, entire paragraphs written and then crossed out, ball-point pen pressed so hard it scores the pages beneath.

Lies, all of it. Nothing but lies.

He burns the first page over the stove, but he can't torch the rest without setting fire to the house, or at least tripping the smoke alarm. He rips the pages instead, and then douses them with water. The ink blurs and runs, shedding black tears.

None of this is a surprise. Don't think, after all these years, that this is the first time he has resolved to confess, to disgorge his heart of hearts and beg forgiveness for it all.

This asshole has never won a battle against himself. But he tries. Oh, he fucking tries.

He has vomited half his rancid soul onto the second legal pad when the lamp over the dining table is eclipsed by the rosy-fingered glow of dawn. His second attempt is no better than the first. Desperate now, he flips the pages over and scrawls on the back, but it makes no difference.

It's not her. He may like to shift the blame—but he has known that much, deep down, for a good long while. It is not that she is intimidating, or beautiful, or overwhelmingly angelic. She is every bit as flawed as any other ordinary mortal. No. It is not her. It is that he cannot face himself. That great and powerful *I*.

———

A PHONE TRILLS.

He jerks upright, grimacing as a bolt of sunlight pierces his vision, and rubs the cheek that has been flattened against the dining table, marinating in saliva. He blinks, and three bowls of mostly-eaten cereal come into focus. Three glasses once filled with orange juice. A children's Bible, forgotten. Sunday. While he's been playing Goldilocks, they've up and gone to... church? During a pandemic? Robin's mother might have been that zealous, but not her practical, level-headed daughter.

The phone rings for a third or fourth time, buzzing against his thigh. He digs it out and squints at the name on the screen. Her. "What?"

"Oh good, you're alive. I knew you were a deep sleeper, but I've never seen anyone sleep through Nora eating breakfast. Come down here and give me a hand."

To the barn, she means. "Now?"

"I mean, you could shower, but you're gonna end up covered in dust."

The line goes silent, and he consults the phone again to see that it's well after noon.

And then—he remembers. Cancer. His letter. He puts his hands on the table, as if the lacquered hardwood could be concealing his words. "Fuck," he breathes. She has taken the pages. Read? His gut clenches.

The pages from the first legal pad are still soaking in a pot of water on the stove. God, was he completely out of his mind? He pours off the grey water into the sink and then dumps the pulpy remainder into the garbage can.

The Sunday silence is cut by the sudden shriek of a miter saw. "Fuck," he says again.

Outside, the air is thankfully crisp and cool, tinged with a faint smoky scent which might, with equal likelihood, be attributed to a newly lit fireplace or a wildfire just beyond the horizon. He makes his way down the path worn through dry weeds to the ramshackle barn at the bottom of the property. One of two big doors has been pushed open, scoring a track in the dirt, an open portal to an interior which is warm and well lit. Small hand tools hang in neat rows on the wall, larger power tools racked in custom-built shelving. A layer of fragrant sawdust frosts the dirt-packed floor. Sunlight streaks in through gaps in the walls, illuminating a galaxy of dust motes drifting through the air.

Robin looks up from the workbench, no doubt alerted to his presence by the sound of labored breathing. A narrow shaft of light glances across the angles of her cheeks and nose. "You can say no," she says, mildly.

He yanks his shirt down. "You fucking know I can't." Not to anything she asks.

She pencils a measurement onto a piece of scrap plywood, the sketch so abstract he can't tell what it represents. "'Won't' is not the same as 'can't.'"

"Oh, you do not want to play semantics with me, Chica." He steps over the threshold. "Kids?"

"Lunch at Greta's. We watch the sermon at their house, and Greta does a little Sunday school lesson. They used to take the kids out to eat after church, but now..." She completes the sentence with a shrug.

Which means they're alone. "Did you fucking read it?"

"Read what? Oh—your long-ass letter?" She straightens and turns, tucking the flat carpenter's pencil into the lavender kerchief knotted around her hair. "Nope. Just filed it with all the others."

This is how stupid she makes him: his heart lurches. The others. She kept them.

Then his eyes follow the arc of her cocked thumb to a battered aluminum garbage can.

The ashes are still warm.

A fraction of a second earlier, he'd been worried she'd read the steaming pile of manure he'd produced the night before. Now he turns on her, hands in fists. "You—" In his mind, he grabs her throat and slams her head against the wall. Picks up the iron rake leaning in the corner and uses it to clear her workbench, smash her immaculately organized wall of tools, her truck—

"No more bullshit, Cyril." She leans her rear against the workbench, crossing her arms over her chest. Her flat chest, he realizes. "I'm not playing your games. You have something to say, say it to my face."

"I can't," he snarls, so close she winces at his sour breath. She knows he can't. He's a fucking coward. "Look, you called me down here to work, so either we do it or—"

She laughs, sharp and loud. "Are you actually opting to do manual labor instead of running your mouth? Maybe prison's changed you after all."

"Fuck off."

She ducks around him and crosses to the table saw, set up in the center of the open floor. "Don't try to guide it; just support the weight and let me do the rest. You can handle that, right?"

He watches, seething for no damn good reason at all, as she adjusts the guide on the table saw and then hefts a full-size sheet of plywood from a stack in the corner. Is it prison that persuades him not to set fire to the rickety footbridge spanning the distance between them? Or cancer? He would not be here, in her life, were it not for prison. But cancer is why he will pull his punches and stay. Cancer is a dense, massive body which warps the space around it, drawing all things toward its center. He is not altered; it is the world itself which is no longer the same.

She hits a button under the saw and it whirrs to life, buzzing noisily as it chews through the first sheet. He stands to one side, supporting the board as she guides it into the blade, and abruptly finds himself holding two awkwardly large pieces of wood.

"Over there!" She shouts over the noise, gesturing. "Against the bench!"

He leans them against her workbench and shuffles back into place to catch the second set. They do this five times, and then pause while she turns the saw off and adjusts the width of the guide, sighting down the table carefully. His ears are ringing. "Shouldn't you be wearing hearing protection?"

She lifts her head to look at him. "What?"

"Shouldn't you—" He starts to repeat, but then she catches his eye and winks. "Damn it."

"You used to be faster on the uptake, big guy." She nods toward the pair of blue plastic earmuffs sitting on the workbench. "If I put those on, I'd miss out on your charming conversation." She nods. "Two more, hot dog this time."

"Hot dog?" he echoes.

"Yeah. Like, hot dog, hamburger?" She saws the air with her hand, first longways and then crossways over the sheet of plywood. "That's how they tell the kids which direction to fold their paper at school."

"You have spent way the hell too much time with children."

She grins as she thumbs the red button and the saw spins to life. "And whose fault is that?"

He shakes his head, backing up as the long slab of plywood becomes two. As the pieces come off the end of the table, he shifts to get a better grip and stumbles back a step, ramming his rear into the far wall. His stumble is punctuated by a discordant clang—her father's old upright, shrouded in a canvas drop cloth.

"Crap." Robin jams a thumb into the off switch and comes around the end of the table, brushing sawdust off her shirt and pants before pulling back the paint-spattered cloth. "Seth must have been fooling with it again, because I did not leave the fallboard up." She runs a hand over the keys. "No harm done."

Robin does not play. To her, the piano is not an instrument; it is a work of art, a totem of familial affection. A well-worn castoff when it became her grandmother's prized possession, the wood had been restored to better-than-original glory by her father's expert hand. Once upon a time it had been the focal point of her living room, where Tavis, a competent pianist, would pound out her father's favorite ragtime melodies. Which Cyril knew not only because the letters he traded with Robin had given him a window into every aspect of her personal life, but because he was the one who had taught Tavis to play piano.

Cyril tries a couple of chords. "It's out of tune." Badly.

"Well, if it wasn't before, it certainly is now you sat on it." She steps back, evaluating the finish with a practiced eye, and sighs. "I need to get it back into the house before it rains, but there's just so many things that need to get—oh, shoot." She pats her back pocket and pulls out her phone, clicking it once to display the time. "I gotta pick up the kids. I told Greta—"

He cuts off her social niceties with a wave toward the truck. "Go."

She reaches into her tool belt and comes up empty. "Crap. I left the keys in the kitchen." Before he can reply she is off, belt jangling as she jogs up the hill.

Had the few identifiable chunks of Tavis Matheson's body not been buried six feet beneath the ground, the man would have immediately searched the garage for a couple of dollies and a rope and dragged the piano up to the house. Cyril knows this without a shadow of a doubt, because it is exactly what he would have told his friend to do.

He, on the other hand, reaches under the piano, pulls out the bench, and sits his fat ass down. His skin is slick with sweat and sawdust.

Five years since he touched a piano. This piano, specifically. There used to be sheet music in the bench, but he doesn't check. Music was his gateway to coding; in many ways his native tongue. So, without rehearsal or warmup, he simply puts his fingers to the keys and begins to play. The off-kilter calliope twang feels like early Cat Stevens, and he allows "Sad Lisa" to frame the path he wanders through a forest of dark and angry chords.

He plays prison, bitter and discordant and small. He plays Tav's death, and all he'd give to take back the choices he made. He plays Seth and Nora, light and joyful, grown so big it hurts. The time he's lost, notes tumbling down and away. And her. Oh, God, her.

The day he first saw her. Not in the campus study hall, but months before. Her laughter, so solid and fresh it felt like a slap in the face. Tavis, begging for help to make her his. Her tears. Her eyes, the look on her face the moment she learned the truth.

He plays cancer—but it doesn't fit.

How can it? This was never part of the song. There was no prelude; no hint of this melody in the overture. Cancer is a chance interloper, a colossal jumping of the shark. She has suffered so much already; she doesn't also deserve to be the victim of the whims of an indifferent universe. Her story ought, at least, to make sense.

When he's all played out, he stretches his fingers and puts the fall board down.

"See?" says a quiet voice. "That wasn't so hard to say."

He turns, just far enough to see her leaning against the barn door. "What the fuck."

She crooks a thumb over one shoulder. "Greta was out front with the kids when I got to the house. I put on some Pokémon." She crosses the barn floor, kicking tracks through the sawdust, and squats next to the piano. She snakes a hand around the back and yanks out a dolly made of scrap wood with a carpet sample stapled on top. "Let's move it."

He groans. "Now?" He should have gone straight back up the hill to the house.

She pops back to her feet, like a spring. "Look, Cyril, if you're going to stay—"

He lifts his hands in surrender. "Yeah, yeah. Your house, your rules. No time like the present."

She studies him a moment, as if trying to gauge the level of his sincerity. Then she gives a curt nod. "There's a hand truck and some straps back there somewhere. I'll get the truck."

When she's gone, he puts a hand on the end of the piano and heaves himself to his feet, taking a heavy couple of steps as his back and knees let him know how much happier they were sitting down. But he locates the pale green hand truck and shifts boxes until there's space enough to wheel it out. The rumble of Robin's truck is close and he can hear wheels spinning in gravel, so he steps outside and signals as she backs down the steep hill until the truck bed is halfway into the barn.

She kills the engine, hops out of the cab, and then eyeballs the piano. "I think we're gonna have to take off the camper shell."

"Course we are." He drops the tailgate and starts unloading the bed.

"Oh," she says, when he yanks out a small green tackle box. "Guess I can take that back up to the house." It rattles as she takes it from him and stows it in the cab.

The contents of the box could be virtually anything—nuts and bolts, beads, loose screws—but the truth solidifies like a marble in his stomach. Pills. "What, you thought I was gonna steal your meds?"

She clambers into the back of the truck and grunts as she pushes a box of spring clamps toward the tailgate. "I mean, you are a hardened criminal."

"You think you're joking, but I actually did—"

"Ransack my medicine cabinet. I know. But I figure even you aren't low enough to steal a cancer patient's pills."

"A stirring vote of confidence."

"Well, I mean, they're not gonna do much for you, unless you're into constipation and hot flashes. Wait til after my surgery if you want the hard stuff." She drops back to the ground. "I'll get the rest of this. Were there any moving pads back there with the hand truck?"

"I'll get them."

Once the truck bed is empty, Robin eyeballs the camper shell and the piano and decides that, actually, if they angle it just right, they might be able to make it work. Cyril contemplates tapping out about sixteen times in the process of loading the piano into the bed, but he settles for a few choice expletives and, with a lot of sweat, a few moving blankets, and a little leverage, they ease it in with about two centimeters to spare. They pile into the cab, and at the top of the hill he gets out and motions her into position as she backs up to the ramp leading to the back door.

By this point the kids have realized that something more exciting than Pokémon is happening, and they're running around, begging to be allowed to get into the bed of the truck and they promise they'll be good and not touch anything except for maybe a couple of piano keys just to see if it'll play on its side, wouldn't that be cool, and finally Robin steps between them and the truck and points to the door. "Cookies," she says. "You may each have one cookie. If and only if you go inside and stay out of the way. If you can do that, you will each get a second cookie. And then you can play with the piano. Understood?"

"Yeah!" Nora exclaims, as if this very thing was her goal all along.

"Aw, man," Seth whines, and dutifully plods into the house after her.

"God," says Robin, sighing.

"We could call it a day," Cyril suggests.

Robin yanks the tailgate down. "Oh, hell no."

They are easing the piano out of the truck bed when Robin says, "I need a favor."

"This—" Cyril grunts as he hefts the lower end of the piano, currently propped on one thigh—"this doesn't count?"

She hops out of the truck and positions the dolly underneath. "Down—little more—to your right—there." She grabs the base, steadying it as he lets the piano down with a whale-spout exhalation of air. "I want you to talk to the kids."

He tugs a shirtsleeve up to wipe his brow. "About what? Seth already knows I'm staying." In the area, at least, if not the house.

She sucks a breath in through her teeth. "Not... about that."

"About—" He drops his sleeve and, seeing her face, lowers his voice to a hiss. "You haven't told them you have cancer?"

"You'd have figured it out a lot sooner if I had."

"Are you fucking kidding me? *That's* why you didn't tell them?"

"Don't flatter yourself. They're kids, Cyril. I learned this the hard way, last time, but—they don't need time to process, or plan, or whatever." She crosses her arms over the top of the piano. "Nora doesn't even have a concept of time. Seth understands what it is, but he doesn't really feel it. If I'd told them when I found out—which was only like two weeks ago, by the way, so nice timing there—they'd have spent all this time freaking out. Which basically means getting into trouble and then screaming about the consequences because they're too young to understand how to process their feelings." She gives the polished oak two firm pats. "Better just to rip off that band-aid quick and fast."

So she'd been putting it off until right the fuck now, with fewer than three days left and both of them standing here covered in sweat. "And now you want me to do the ripping."

"It'll be fine. Just take them out for ice cream or something. You owe me. Plus?" She shrugs. "You're good with the kids."

Is she delusional? "You're literally their mother."

"I pack lunches, I do laundry, I drive." She waves toward the house at her back. "I put a roof over their head. You—I remember how you were with Seth. One time, he didn't understand why days were shorter in the winter. I'd have just told him that's how things work, but you sat down and explained the entire solar system in terms a four-year-old could grasp. You're good at... words."

"Says the woman who burns them. Just admit you're a fucking coward."

"Takes one to know one, asshole. Look, I just—God." She straightens and comes around the side of the piano, lifting her palms in surrender. "Honestly? I can't do this again. When Tavis died, I thought telling Seth was the hardest thing I'd ever have to do. If I could just make it through that—But then you—and my mom—and then—" She closes her eyes and takes a deep breath. "It's always just some damn other thing. Every time. You'd think I'd learn, but when I finished chemo, we threw a freaking party. And now—" Her voice cracks. "Now—"

"Yeah. Okay." It was so much easier to say no, from behind the safety of a keyboard. He didn't have to look her in the eye. "I'll do it."

She swallows and nods. They can hear the kids pounding back into the living room. When she speaks again, her voice is low. "But don't use the c-word, okay? Just tell them I'm gonna have surgery."

"Chica, I swear to God—"

"I'm not even staged yet, okay? They won't know how bad it is until they cut my uterus out and look. It could be basically nothing."

"I know shit about cancer," he hisses. "And even I know having it show up somewhere else in your body is bad fucking news."

And then she's crying. Again. Her hands hang limply at her sides, not even bothering to attempt staunching her tears. They just fall.

"No—Jesus." He gathers her into his arms. She used to be tougher than this. Or angrier. "I'll do it. Okay? However you want." Whatever she wants. As long as she stops crying. God.

"Cyril, I just—" She hiccoughs. "I'm just so tired of having to be strong."

"I know. I know." He sighs. "Look, don't worry about the kids. Okay? You take care of you. I'll take care of them. Let's just—" He takes her shoulders and stands her upright. "Get this goddamn piano into the house."

She manages a broken smile. "Will you play me a song?"

He puts his shoulder to the back of the piano and waits for her to take the front. "I will play you a fucking concerto."

She checks the wheels and the angle to the door. "Okay. We're good. One, two—"

Even on the dolly, the damn thing weighs a ton. "Jesus Christ," he grunts.

"See? Now you're glad I built the ramp."

CHAPTER 11

Cyril regrets his impulsive promise the instant he tries—and fails—to broach the subject of surgery with Seth. All he wanted was to stop Robin's tears, but the prospect of facing the children's is even less desirable. He gets why she doesn't want to be the bearer of bad news yet again, but the thing is, that's her problem, not his. He tells her as much on his fifth trip up the hill, hauling the plywood they'd cut the day before.

"You made a promise, asshole." She grips the top edge of the plywood and hoists it up to her perch on the scaffolding. Then she digs a hand into her toolbelt and chucks her keys in his direction. They land at his feet. "Pick them up. The kids, I mean. Don't come home until it's done."

"You really want me to fuck up your kids? Because I'm gonna fuck this up."

"No, you're not." Her grin is knowing, because she knows her kids are the one gaping vulnerability in his system.

He never fell for exploits like this sitting behind a screen. Or if he did, Tavis was the one who had to follow through. "This is bullshit." Nevertheless, he grips the scaffolding and bends to retrieve the keys before stalking off.

He's ridden shotgun in Robin's truck half a dozen times since he got out, but this is the first he's been behind the wheel. The drive through neighborhood streets to Greta's house, glancing down at the map on his phone, feels awkward and slow. His foot comes down heavy on the brake, and the truck jerks to a halt by the curb.

He's feeling for the button to release the seatbelt when the kids burst out the door and down the front steps. Greta appears only long enough to offer a nod and shut the door, which suits him just fine. She doesn't want to talk to him any more than he wants to talk to her.

It's been unseasonably warm since dawn, but when the kids open the passenger door a breath of hot wind gusts in like a furnace. Fire weather. "Holy crap." He reaches over the console and grabs the loop on the back of Nora's backpack, using it to help yank her up and into the cab. "Get in, guys, come on."

Seth follows, turning to wrestle the door shut with both hands. "Where's mom?"

"At home. She's fine, just busy working." Except she isn't fine, is she? And Seth's question is not simple curiosity, but the insecurity of a child who knows all too well that nothing in life—not his dad, not his grandmother, not even his mom—is guaranteed. "We're going—well, I was gonna take you guys to the park, but—"

"Yeah!" they chorus, as one.

"Guys, you'll have to wear your masks, and it's like a furnace out—"

"So?" Nora challenges.

"Okay. Fine."

He imagines he'll sit and supervise from the truck, AC blowing in his face, and once they've exhausted themselves, he'll go through the McDonald's drive-through and get them soft serve and they'll park somewhere shady and... talk it out. Or something.

What he ends up doing is spinning Nora on the giant tree-shaped merry-go-round before begging off to retreat to a picnic table under the trees, partially protected from both sun and wind. After half a day hauling plywood ("OSB," Robin had corrected) up the hill, the muscles in his back are staging a collective revolt, and now he's covered in sweat and a layer of fine dust kicked up by the wind. But Nora is persistent and, like her mother, impossible to refuse. At least the park is deserted, thanks to the weather, so they don't have to suffocate under masks, too.

Seth requests the keys to the truck—"What, you gonna take it for a spin?"—and returns with a plastic water bottle. He holds it out. "Here."

Nothing makes Cyril feel more like the piece of shit he is than the simple kindness of this child. In the time after Tav's death, Cyril enjoyed playing the hero the boy imagined him to be. Now, knowing what he's about to do to the kid, it's torture. Which is to say, exactly what he deserves. Is that why Robin has delegated this thankless task to him? "Thanks," he grunts. He cranks off the cap and chugs.

Seth stands there, watching. Then he takes a seat on the bench, facing outward with knees spread, mirroring Cyril.

"Oh, come on. You're nine." He gestures to Nora, now dashing up to the top of a slide. "Don't tell me you're already too cool for the park."

The boy wipes sandy grit out of the corners of his eyes. "You don't have to tell me."

"What?" Shit, had he overheard? That'll make his job a lot easier.

"I'm not stupid." His eyes grow dark. "You're leaving."

"Kid, I—" Cyril grabs Seth's arm the instant he bolts. Every muscle in his wiry little body is coiled tight.

"I knew you would," Seth says, hurling the words like shards of broken pottery.

"No," Cyril says, more sharply than he intends. "Hold on, kid. Just—siddown for a minute, will you?" He yanks Seth back, forcing him to plant his butt on the picnic table bench, and holds him there until his shoulders slump. "I'm not going anywhere. It's—" Jesus. If only it were as simple as that. "It's your mom."

Seth rubs his arm, not looking at him, taking a minute to absorb this information. He seems to fold in upon himself, growing suddenly smaller and more fragile. When he looks up at Cyril, tears fall in silent rivulets down his cheeks. "Is she gonna die?" he whispers.

Robin's mortality is not a thing Cyril has allowed himself to contemplate. But Seth has loosed the word into the world, and now he must answer. "Look," he starts, but the words desert him. He rubs the stubble on his face. "Shit." He glances at Seth. The pale outlines of his fingers still linger on the kid's biceps. "Sorry for—" He gestures. "Sorry if I hurt your arm."

Seth chews his lip. "It's okay."

Cyril sighs. "Your mom's not gonna—I mean, shit, kid, nobody lives forever. And I can't see the future. But as far as I know, she's not gonna—" Jesus. He can't even say it. "She's not going anywhere soon, okay?"

Seth nods, but his face doesn't look like he believes it.

"She needs surgery to take out her, uh, uterus. Do you know what—"

He nods again.

Well, at least Cyril doesn't have to explain all this *and* the birds and the bees. "Yeah. So. They don't know exactly what's up, but I guess they're gonna take it out and have a look inside. Okay?"

Seth swallows hard. Then he nods. "When?"

"Wednesday. And, uh." He shifts. "I guess the silver lining is,

I'm gonna keep crashing on your couch for now. Okay? For as long as your mom needs me."

Seth looks at the ground between his feet, rubbing his arm as he turns this information over in his mind. Finally, he lifts his head. "So... as long as she's sick, you'll stay?"

Even the nicest kids are egomaniacs. "How about we worry about what's in front of us right now? I want your mom to get better. I know you do, too. So let's help her do that and let the future worry about itself." He nudges the kid's shoulder. "Hm?"

Seth looks uncertain, but he nods.

"Good." One kid down, one to go. God, this is exhausting. He glances up to locate Nora and realizes, with a jolt of belated alarm, that he hasn't had visual contact with her since he started talking to Seth. Two kids are four times as complicated as one. "Shit. Where's your—oh." Nora dashes out of a tunnel made from old tires, a burrow that leads under the play structure, and heads for the climbing wall on the far side. "Kid!" Cyril raises a hand and motions for her to come. She gives him a pouting scowl, but hops her way to the edge of the wood chips and skips over to the bench.

"What are you gonna give me?" she demands.

"Excuse me?"

She puts her hands on her hips. "What's my snack?"

"I dunno," he says, "what did you bring?"

She looks outraged. "Nothing! That's your job!"

He snorts. "That's news to me." He pats the pockets of this sweatpants on the off chance he's forgotten a piece of candy or granola bar. "Sorry, kid. I got nothing. We can go grab a slurpee or something if you want."

She brightens immediately. "Yeah! That's what I was aspecting!"

"Super. How much money you got?"

Seth rolls his eyes. Nora totters somewhere between fury and tears. "I don't have any money!" she says, her voice whining upward in both pitch and volume. "I'm a *kid!*"

"Okay, okay. Chill." Cyril had only meant to tease her, not to get her all worked up before he'd even broken the news about her mom. He gives her a brief side-squeeze. "I'm just giving you a hard time. We'll get a snack in a minute, but we need to have a little talk, first."

"Mom's sick," Seth announces.

"I know," Nora shoots back.

"No you don't!" Seth retorts, anger flaring like a match. "I just told you!"

Cyril brings an arm down between them. "Cool it, guys. Seth, just—let me do the talking for a minute." He sucks in a breath. "Nora, what we mean is that your mom is going to have to go back to the hospital for a little while. On Wednesday." He holds up two fingers. "Two days from now."

She blinks at him. And then, suddenly, it seems to register. "Do we get to stay at Ms. Greta's?"

"I—no, you'll be at home with me. I think your mom might have to go alone, because of COVID. Or maybe Greta's going with her. I don't know. We can ask."

"Oh." She thinks this over a moment. "Ms. Greta has ice cream," she says.

He laughs. "We can have ice cream, too."

"Right now?"

"No, not—I mean—" Jesus Christ. "If you wanna get ice cream right now, we can do that. My treat. Or slurpees. But you gotta choose one."

She eyes him for a long moment, and he has the feeling she's contemplating whether crying might advance her agenda. Finally, she nods, pivots, and starts towards the truck. Seth dashes after her, not to be outrun by his little sister.

Cyril digs the key out of his pocket and hits the unlock button on the truck so they don't have to stand and wait in the wind while he heaves himself to his feet. They're climbing into the extended cab via the passenger side when he catches up.

"But I wanna go to Ms. Greta's," he hears Nora say, from inside.

"Trust me," Seth returns. "This is way better."

Cyril feels flattered for the half-second before Seth adds, "We'll get to play *so much* Minecraft!"

———

WHEN CYRIL LETS THE KIDS IN THE FRONT DOOR, Robin is sitting at the piano bench, a spray can of furniture polish in one hand. She opens her mouth, presumably to greet them, but all that comes out is a stuttering laugh.

"We got ice cream!" Seth informs her, helpfully. His shirt is streaked cotton candy blue.

"We got some for you!" Nora chimes in, offering her mother a very chocolate grin.

Cyril holds out a pint of mint chocolate chip. Her favorite.

"Uh—thanks." She rises, setting the polish and an old sock on the end table next to the couch. "Put it in the freezer, will you? I'll get these creatures into the shower. Wait." She presses two fingers to her forehead. "I feel like I'm forgetting something. Is it a martial arts night?"

"Yep." Cyril is not bad at this—the ordinary things. He can cook and clean and keep the kids' schedules straight in his head without effort. Systems and information are easy. People... well, they're easy too, so long as he doesn't care whether they hate him or not. He pulls his phone out. "Forty-five minutes."

She exhales. "Plenty of time. Into the shower, guys." She herds them into the hall, leveling a a finger at Seth as he begins to whine. "*Both* of you."

Cyril puts the ice cream away and then returns to the piano, which now gleams with a low luster. He touches a key—still out of tune—and then lifts the lid, finding a tuning hammer and a couple mutes clipped against the right inside panel. Robin might not care about the piano's practical function, but someone else certainly had. A careful application of force and a couple of bumps gets the front board free, and Cyril settles himself on the bench and begins to adjust the strings by ear. It's not perfect, but it's better than nothing.

He's about five notes into the midrange when he hears the kids bounding from the bathroom to the bedroom and then into the closet, on the other side of the wall at his back. A moment later, Robin joins him, sighing as she leans an elbow on the edge of the open piano top.

"I don't suppose they're hungry for dinner now," she says.

"That wasn't part of the deal."

"It's fine. I have to be a hard ass all the time, and Greta's more of a strict auntie. They need someone fun in their lives." She peers over the edge of the lid, watching as he hits F, bumps the hammer, hits F, bumps the hammer. "Where did you learn to do this?"

He contemplates a lie, then shrugs and offers the truth. "My mother was a piano tuner."

"Oh," she says, with a tinge of surprise. "I never knew that."

"No reason you should." No reason he'd ever voluntarily revisit all the summers he'd had to tag along with her, first because she couldn't afford childcare after his father took off and then because he never knew when she was going to have a breakdown and it was easier just to do her goddamn job for her than deal with the inevitable gossip. Not that it didn't happen anyway, but it was slightly easier to live down if it didn't happen in the middle of some client's living room.

"That sounds like a fun job," Robin muses. "Getting to see the inside of everyone else's houses."

Of course she would see it that way. All he remembers is the awkward stares from classmates asking "Mommy, what is *he* doing in our house?" The relief he felt when the list of the day's appointments contained only elderly widows. "So, I talked to the kids."

Robin gives him a quizzical look, then accepts the subject change with the arch of an eyebrow. "And?"

He pops the hammer off the pin and moves it to G, adjusting the mutes to damp two of the three strings. "Well, Nora's mainly concerned with what she's gonna get out of it."

"My little psychopath." Robin shakes her head. "This is all just her normal, unfortunately. Seth?"

"Yeah, he's pretty sure you're gonna die."

"You didn't—"

"Jesus, of course not."

"I told him you don't know how bad it is yet. Which—" He glances up. "Is the truth. Right?"

She blows her cheeks out with a breath. "I mean, they caught it early. My chances are good. For a metastasis. I guess." She runs a hand over her head. "Fuck."

"What are you guys doing?"

Robin straightens and turns. Nora stops between them, dressed in her little white gi, blinking curiously at the piano's guts.

"I'm tuning the piano," Cyril says, playing the G and bumping the hammer to demonstrate.

"Oh," she says, roundly, watching over her mother's shoulder as Robin kneels to knot the ties on her uniform pants and jacket. "So the music doesn't hurt."

He raises an eyebrow. Seth would not have noticed. But *hurt?* "Yeah. Exactly. Here. See this section?" He marks out the middle third. "Each note on the keyboard has three strings. And each of those strings has to be tightened until it's just right."

"Why?"

Robin presses her palm to his shoulder, briefly.

"I'm gonna check on Seth." He nods and she disappears into the back of the house.

"Why? Hm. Okay, let's see." He looks around the room for something string-like. His eyes land on the tie of her gi pants, which won't be useful, but the shoestring tie on his own sweat-pants isn't exactly getting any use. He fumbles under his stomach until he finds one loose end and pulls. It slides out. He stretches a three-foot section until it's taut. "Pluck that. Like you're playing a guitar."

Nora hooks an index finger over the string and pulls back, releasing it with a low, muffled twang.

"There," he says. "See how it goes back and forth?" He lets the string hang vertically and wiggles it back and forth, sending waves rippling down. "Like this, but faster. See the vibrations?" He swings the string in a slower arc, increasing the length of the waves. "This is how the piano—how sound—works. Shorter waves are higher notes, like your voice." He lets his voice dip down into his lowest range. "Longer waves, lower notes." He points to the open piano. "That's all this is. All you gotta do is get all the waves at the right lengths."

Nora says nothing, but she takes the string from him and flaps it up and down a few times. When he shrugs and returns to tuning the piano, she leans against him and watches as he works his way through another two notes. "I'm bored," she announces, finally.

"Feel free to do pretty much anything else, kid."

"I wanna play a song."

Of course. "Okay, I'll take a break." His arm is tired, anyway. He clips the hammer and mutes back into place, leaving the front board off. "Look, you can see how the keys work."

This is fascinating for about sixty seconds.

"Okay," he says, when her experimentation with the keys devolves into pounding, "you're gonna knock them all out of whack again." He puts a hand over hers to prevent her from slamming the keyboard. "You want to learn a real song?"

She looks up at him, and he can see the wheels turning behind her bright eyes as she contemplates doubling down on the pounding, and then, thankfully, decides to accept his offer. This kid's going places. She nods.

He can't really provide a lap, but he scoots the bench back and turns sideways so she can stand between his knees. "Okay," he says, clearing his throat to give himself a moment to think. "You, uh... you see the pattern here? The black keys? Three and two. Three and two." He rolls his knuckles over them to produce a simple tune.

Nora giggles. "Me!" she says, and instantly reproduces the pattern on a lower octave.

"Hey, you're a natural!" And he's not kidding—when he shows her middle C, she proceeds to pick out all the other Cs on the keyboard, leaning dramatically left and then right to reach. Within minutes, she's duplicating his fingering as he walks her through the chords of "Heart and Soul." When she gets it, he joins in with the melody. She giggles, dropping behind a few notes, and when he fills in her gaps she loses the thread entirely. He reaches around her on both sides and segues into "Everyday," dropping down an octave because his baritone can't match Buddy Holly's hiccoughing tenor.

Nora jumps when he belts out the first line, and then adds another little hop of delight, turning to stare at his mouth with an expression of pure wonder as he taps out the staccato notes. "More!" she cries, nearly drowning out his "a-hey-hey."

The chorus is all he remembers of the lyrics, so he cycles through that a few times and then hums the rest.

"More!" Nora shrieks again, grabbing his shirt and jumping. "Sing it again!"

He laughs as she knocks his arm and he loses the thread of the song. He ends it with a couple of sharp, final chords. "Give me a break, kid. I'm rusty." And out of breath. But it feels... good. Uncomplicated. He'd played music like this with Seth, what seems like a lifetime ago.

A movement at the corner of his eye catches his attention, and he glances up to see Robin standing in the dining room, phone held up to snap a photo. She slips the phone into a back pocket and mouths, silently, the two words he's forbidden her to say: *thank you.*

Seth saves him the necessity of a response by barreling out of the hallway behind her, yellow belt flying. "Ready!"

Nora looks up at Cyril, appealing to him with pleading eyes. "More! Please?"

Cyril scoots back and gives her bottom a swat. "Later, kiddo. Get your shoes."

Robin grabs her purse from the table, slinging it over one shoulder. "Flip flops and water bottles, guys. Truck's out in back."

Seth, who has already found his flip flops in the entry closet, skids to a halt in the kitchen. "Wait." He looks at the clock on the wall above the sink. "Does this mean we're not doing school?"

"You already did that, kid," Cyril says, heaving himself to his feet. "Martial arts, food, bed." Early. "Go on, follow your mom."

"No, for the thing—the thing with the teachers? And ice cream?"

Nora perks up. "I want ice cream!"

"Are you talking about Back-to-School Night?" Robin's brow contracts. "That's not tonight—"

"Oh," Seth says, looking confused. "I thought Ms. J said it was."

Cyril puts his hands on Robin's shoulders—sleeves, not bare skin—shifting her out of the doorway so he can pass into the kitchen. The calendar by the stove is empty, but he rifles through the stack of art and mail on the counter and finds the flyer he knows he's seen. "It's tonight, but it's on zoom. I figured you didn't care." Greta had seemed to be the one in charge of all things school.

Robin presses the bridge of her nose with a thumb and forefinger. "Why is this my life?" she whispers.

"I'll take the kids to martial arts," he says. "You do the school thing. Problem solved."

She pulls her phone out of her pocket and taps the email icon. "No, they just—I got an email a couple of days ago. Sonoma County just got bumped down to yellow tier, so they decided to do it in person, with some socially distanced thing for the kids outside. So they can actually meet their classmates." She sighs. "They sent the update out on Friday, and it just completely slipped my mind—"

"Skip it, then. Not the end of the world." She'll be having surgery the day after tomorrow. This is the least of her concerns.

She looks at him, over the kids' heads, and her eyes tell him everything she can't say in front of her children: they've already missed too much. Their father, obviously. And all the time she spent undergoing treatment the first time. Neither Seth nor Nora has played with another child in over six months. Cancer may take her health and literal pieces of her body, but she will be damned if it steals one more moment of joy from her kids.

"Uniforms off," Cyril announces. "I'll have dinner ready when you get back. Go on. Quickly."

Robin exhales, then looks down at her paint-spattered jeans and work boots. "Shoot, I need to change." She disappears after the kids, and he goes to the fridge to see what he can cobble together for dinner.

When she returns, she has breasts again.

"Oh," he says.

She joins him in looking down at her chest, and then reaches down the top of her silk shirt to adjust her bra. "Do I look all right?"

He snorts. "All right? Yeah. Yeah, you do." Strapless sandals with chunky cork heels, skin-tight jeans, a loose silk shirt, and the golden spiral earrings Tavis had given her for their fifth wedding anniversary. She's not even that dressed up, but it doesn't take much to make her look like royalty.

She looks pleased, or embarrassed, or some combination of the two. As if his opinion carries any weight. "Look," she says, glancing toward the hall to make sure the children aren't listening, "I need you to come."

"Uh, no." He feels like he's lived a lifetime in the past—what, nine days? Ten? But really, it's nothing. He can pretend everything's hunky-dory, but the truth is he's scarcely left the house since he got out of prison. "I'm not even sure I'm legally allowed to be on a grade school campus."

She rolls her eyes. "You're not *that* kind of offender. I asked your lawyer. I just—I need to talk to Nora's teacher about—" She cuts herself off as Seth materializes at Cyril's elbow. "Stuff."

He grins. "Nora's *bad*."

"She's not—" Robin puts a hand to her head. "Seth, this is none of your business. It's fine. I'll deal with it. Forget I asked. Nora?"

Robin's daughter scoots into the kitchen. She is wearing green corduroy pants and a ratty, stretched-out Minecraft shirt.

"Nora, that—" Robin shakes her head. "It's fine. It's fine. If I'm gonna make it to both of your classes, we need to get going." She nods to Cyril as she herds the kids out the back door. "See you in an hour or so."

"Wait." Seth looks from Cyril to his mother and back again. "Aren't you coming?" He looks genuinely crestfallen. "Who's gonna see my class?"

"Maybe next time, kid." He gives the kid a thump on the back. "I mean, I'm not exactly dressed for the occasion."

It's just an excuse, but Nora grins. "I know!" She dashes back toward the hall, neatly ducking her mother's intercept.

"Nora!" Robin shouts. "Not now! Seth, will you go get your sister and—"

Nora reappears, clutching the garish red-and-blue Hawaiian shirt that had been sitting, folded, on the bottom of the pile of clean laundry Cyril kept on a cabinet shelf in the bathroom.

Cyril laughs. "Thanks, kid, but it doesn't fit." He's embarrassed to admit he's even tried it on.

"What, really?" Robin, having apparently given up on getting out the door on time, takes the shirt from Nora and shakes it out, holding it open by the lapels. "Here. Put it on over your t-shirt."

"Fuck you" is what he would have said, were the kids not standing there looking at him expectantly. Instead, he rolls his eyes and thrusts his arms into the sleeves as she holds them out.

"Yeah. See?" Robin tugs his shirttails and adjusts the open collar. "It's casual. You don't have to button it."

Nora claps, delighted. "Pretty!"

He looks at Robin, who is studiously hiding her smile. Then he looks at Seth, which he should not have done. The kid's eyes shine with uninhibited hope.

"This is bullshit," he says.

CHAPTER 12

The line of masked parents waiting to get into the mission-style elementary school stretches down the block, six-foot segments marked out on the sidewalk in bright pink chalk. "Guess we're not late," Cyril says.

Robin finds a spot to park around the corner, and as soon as they cross the street the kids dash off to play under the maple trees lining the front of the building. Though she spent the drive lecturing them about maintaining six feet of distance between friends and making sure their masks cover mouths *and* noses, Robin still calls a reminder to keep their hands to themselves. She glances up at Cyril, flashing a tight, anxious smile.

"You sure about this?" About him, really.

She closes her eyes, and for a moment her soft black mask conforms to the contours of her nose and mouth as she inhales. Then she squares her shoulders and gives him a single firm nod.

He follows her lead as she steps off the red curb and into the street, striding past each and every person waiting in the lengthy line. Unsurprisingly, everyone but Robin is either white or Latinx. By the time they step into the first vacant chalk square at the end of the block, the attenuated crowd has gone unnaturally quiet. A woman two squares in front of them casts a hasty glance back and bends to whisper something in her wife's ear.

Cyril looks down at himself. The hot wind has dissipated, but the evening is still warm enough to make him regret the second layer of fabric in his armpits. "I knew this shirt was a mistake."

Robin laughs. "Yeah, *that's* what they're looking at."

A woman in a pencil skirt with a clipboard is working the line. She stops a few feet away from another chalk-boxed couple, engaging them in a chipper conversation about joining the PTA. Robin lifts a hand and offers a little wave. The woman turns her back slightly, clumsily pretending she hasn't seen. Bitch.

Cyril is used to attracting attention from strangers, though the disgusted looks and not-so-hushed whispers used to be about his size. Now it's a tossup between that, his face—splashed across national news for a couple of weeks back in the before-times—and the fact that he's showing up as Robin's plus one. Probably all of the above.

"Look," he says, "I can just, uh, wait in the car." No reason the stink of his reputation should rub off on her. Or the kids. "I'll think of something to tell Seth."

Robin looks startled. "What? No. Absolutely not."

How can she be so certain of him, when he is not? She hates these idiotic social functions—he knows she does, because over the seven years they corresponded she complained about every single event that involved mingling or small talk. She's here because, as a single black mother, thrust unwillingly into the public eye—thanks to him —she considers it her duty to dress up, show up, and advocate for her kids. As far as this asshole can see, his presence only complicates that objective. But for whatever reason, she has apparently decided that the potential benefit for her kids outweighs the risk of... him.

And so, to whatever degree it is within his power, he resolves —for whatever that is worth—not to give her cause to regret her choice.

When, eventually, they reach the head of the line, Robin calls the kids over for obligatory temp checks and the screening questions they've all heard five hundred times. Word of his identity has clearly reached the staff behind the folding table; they eye him warily, and the elderly volunteer who takes Cyril's temperature stumbles nervously over the questions.

"No," he says. "No to everything."

"I—I have to ask."

Robin and the kids wait on the other side of the table until he's cleared. But as they turn together toward the building's entrance, a mousy man in a brown suit (who has presumably drawn the short straw) steps forward and says, "Ah—excuse me, could you folks come over here for a quick chat?"

Cyril is tempted to tell him that no, they fucking can't, but he looks at the kids and keeps a lid on it. Still, he knows what's coming.

If Robin does, she doesn't show it. "What can we do for you, Mr. Tappin?"

The man in brown clears his throat. "We don't want to make a scene, but—"

"Then don't," Robin says, as if it were the simplest thing in the world.

A plump woman with thick black hair drawn up into a bun joins Tappin, presumably to lend moral support. "We're just not sure if it's a good idea for Mr., uh—Mr...."

Everybody looks at Cyril. But if he opens his mouth, he's gonna say something they'll all regret. So he doesn't. He just grits his teeth and stares.

"Blanchard," Robin supplies, quirking a questioning eyebrow at him. "His name is Cyril Blanchard." Like everybody doesn't already know. Like they're not standing here having this conversation because he's a troublemaker. A criminal. Because this is an elementary school, and he's been in prison.

"What's going on?" Seth pipes up, clueless but clearly able to read the room.

Nora's tiny hand pushes its way into Cyril's palm, forcing the fist of his right hand to relax.

"Nothing, Sweetie." Robin takes her son's hand and turns toward the building. "Let's go on in."

Tappin steps to the left, blocking her way. Cyril lifts his left hand, clenched, but before he can take a swing at the guy, the woman with the bun steps between them, completely oblivious to his intent.

"It's just that Mr. Blanchard is not a parent," she insists, looking slightly pained. As if she's not the one who makes the rules.

"Let the big guy in," someone calls from the back of the line. "Nobody cares."

Robin studies the woman for a moment, almost thoughtfully. "Pretty sure I saw Jeremy's grandmother go in ahead of us. Or do only blood relatives count?" She cranes her neck to look down the line of people behind them. "Dan, are you Freya's legal guardian?"

The man in question turns beet red. "I, um—no, I'm just—I mean, Brandi and I just started dating, I'm not—uh." He looks around. "Should I leave?"

"Chica," Cyril warns, directing a pointed glance at the kids.

She ignores him. "Maybe," she says, turning back to the woman with an air of cool vehemence, "if you'd stopped to consider that not every family has two parents, you'd have staggered the schedule so I don't have to be in two classrooms at the same time, and we'd have avoided this conversation altogether. But you didn't. So spare me your pearl-clutching."

The woman looks like she's been slapped—like she can't quite believe anyone, let alone Robin, would call her out on her bullshit. "I'm sorry," she says, not sorry but stiff with barely constrained tears. "Everything is challenging right now. We're doing our best."

"Yes," Robin agrees, with finality. "We all are." She nods to Cyril. "Including him."

Tappin touches the bun-lady's elbow, prompting her to step aside to confer. The woman seems particularly perturbed, gesturing at Cyril with agitation. Tappin shrugs and delivers a calmer response. Finally, they seem to reach an agreement, and it's Tappin who approaches them this time. "Ms. Matheson, your guest may enter the school as long as he agrees not to make any kind of disturbance or interruption."

"I assume that's the condition upon which *everyone* here enters the school, Harry. But sure. Yeah." She turns to Cyril. "You planning on punching people or flipping any tables?"

He doesn't know what she thinks she's doing, or why she has picked this hill to die on. (Him. He is the hill.) "Uh—*planning* on it? No." Nothing he does—or says—is ever really premeditated. That's kind of the issue.

"Great. Let's go." Robin turns and marches up the front steps, Seth still in hand. She stops, halfway up, to look back at Cyril. "Coming?"

He glances down at Nora, who blinks at him with saucer-round eyes. "Uh, after all that, I guess I better."

"Yeah, you *better*," Robin says under her breath, as he catches up.

The double doors are propped open, and the hallway inside feels like a wind tunnel, icy and loud with the thrum of two industrial-sized fans. Directly across from the entrance is an exit to the playground, and a young man waves to the kids and motions for them to come outside and "join the fun!"

As soon as the kids are gone, Cyril turns to Robin and says, "What the actual fuck was that?"

"You're asking me?" She shouts to make herself heard over

the fans. "I'm not the one who just stood there and swallowed that bullshit. When have you *ever* backed down from a fight?"

He dismisses her question with a wave of a hand. "It's a fucking elementary school. You knew they were gonna freak out."

She strides down the hall, far enough that the hum of the fans fades to a dull roar, then turns to face him. "Are you seriously defending them? You? Mr. All-Authority-is-Illegitimate?"

"No, I just—" He exhales. He'd thought this was a test. But apparently she'd expected him to come out swinging? "Look, I am *trying* not to embarrass you."

She laughs. "Oh, please. If I was worried about being embarrassed, you wouldn't be here." She offers a curt nod as the couple who had been behind them in line scoot past, giving them the widest possible berth in the corridor. "I am, like... *so* far beyond giving a shit what anyone else thinks."

"And the kids? Did you think about what's good for them?"

"Only every second of every day of my life." She exhales something between a laugh and a weary sigh. "Look. When they were little, they *needed* me. I was their universe. Even more so, after Tavis died. And for so long, I kept my mouth shut, even when I wanted to explode, because God forbid anything happen to me." She pushes away from the wall and starts down the corridor again, hesitating when they come to a split. She looks both right and left, frowns, and then reaches into her purse to consult her phone. "But I'm not the center of their universe anymore. I *can't* be. On Wednesday I'll be going to the hospital again, and—" She shakes her head as she scrolls through her email, tapping when she finds whatever information she's seeking. "Their circle has to be bigger than one."

"Yeah, I get it." He spreads his hands, palms upturned, to encompass the entire building. "Teachers. Friends. Parents." He lets his arms drop. "And you want to bring me in here to fuck it all up?"

She looks up from her phone, eyes wide. Then she snorts. "No? God, no, Cyril. They're not the circle. It's you."

So, she's lost her mind. "Why, so the other kids can point and laugh? So I can mortally offend their teachers, and—"

"They're black kids," she interrupts, with the sudden sharp impatience of someone who has had to explain the obvious one too many damn times. She waves her phone in the direction they've come, back toward the doors the kids took out to the playground. "They don't get to be swaddled in wide-eyed innocence until they're eighteen or twenty. The sooner they learn not to invest too much in what other people think of them, the better —because if they take every word these people say to heart, they'll find themselves shattered. I won't always be here to protect them, but I can show them how to speak up, and who they can trust to be in their corner." She drops her phone back into her purse and presses her palm to the pocket of his garish Hawaiian shirt. "That's you, Cyril. You. Are the guy. In the corner."

For about half a second, they look each other in the eye. And then he says, "Well, shit," because if she expects him to be touched, she should fucking know better. "Is that why I'm dressed like Dennis Nedry? If people are looking at me, maybe they won't notice your kids are brown?"

Robin's fingers contract, gripping the fabric of his shirt, and for a moment he wonders if she's going to punch him. A small, strangled sound comes from deep in her throat. Then her hand relaxes; she gives his chest a pat, and points to the hall on the left. "Seth's class is that way. Number fourteen. Try not to take this as license to make his teacher cry."

"Maybe a parent or two?"

She starts off to the right, waving a dismissal over one shoulder. "Acceptable."

———

SETH'S TEACHER IS TALL AND SLENDER, WITH COPPER
hair and skin like milk. A bombshell by any measure, and not
afraid to dress the part in a dark jade suit-dress, fishnet stockings,
and stiletto heels. Not exactly what he'd envisioned, but it means
everyone is staring at her—and not the enormous felon shuffling
his way to the back of the classroom. He stands by the bank of
open windows, six feet away from anyone else, because there is
no possible way he can seat himself in one of the diminutive
student chairs. He studies the linoleum flooring as she introduces
herself ("my pronouns are 'she' and 'her'") and talks about
distance learning strategies and engagement and fields questions
about the district's plans for re-opening. She concludes with a
smarmy riff on inclusiveness that feels like it's intended expressly
for the dozen curious eyes casting furtive glances in his
direction.

He's not sure he'll be able to resist saying something stupid
and cruel if she asks everyone to introduce themselves, but when
she tells them to "get up and stretch!" it's only to conclude the
meeting with an invitation to parade clockwise around the room,
so everyone can take turns looking at a selection of student
projects completed online but which she has printed out and
posted in a facsimile of normalcy. They all look the same to this
asshole, until he spots a wobbly MS Paint illustration of a block-
shaped superhero. He stops to admire Seth's attention to detail,
and the parent behind him stumbles into his backside.

"Oh. Gosh. I'm sorry, I, uh. Um. Guess I kind of failed at
social distancing, didn't I?"

Cyril ignores the man. Can't get in trouble if nobody else
exists. But the guy can't just let it go, can he? No. He leans
forward, waving a hand in Cyril's field of vision as they continue
to file around the room. Cyril looks at the appendage, noting the
professionally trimmed cuticles and plain gold wedding band,
before raising his eyes to the face which, were this prison, he
would simply have punched.

"Excuse me? Hi. I'm Jake's father."

Which means absolutely fuck-all to this asshole. "My condolences." He keeps walking, around the last corner and then out the door, into the hall.

The man—white, tastefully tanned, in a starched button-up which is clearly his "casual" wear—lets out a delighted (if slightly nervous) laugh that suggests Cyril has not only just met but exceeded his expectations. "Jake tells us you're putting together a Dungeons and Dragons group."

Seth. God damn it. "News to me."

"Oh!" Jake's father laughs again, more comfortably this time, and shakes his head. "Kids. Oh, uh, this way," he adds, pointing to the yellow arrows leading toward the back of the building. "All the hallways are one-way."

The arrows terminate at another set of double doors, propped open to the blacktop. A dry erase board propped on an easel instructs parents to wait for their child in the chalk circle marked with the number corresponding to their child's grade. Robin is absent from the one marked with a large purple K.

"Over here!" Jake's dad has already taken his place in the circle marked with a five, over by the empty tetherball poles.

His new best friend. Jesus. He shuffles into the circle. A teenager with a clipboard asks him for the name of his child. "Seth," he grunts.

"You know," the man continues, "if you do decide to give it a shot, I think Jake would get a real kick out of it. I used to play, as a kid." He hesitates. Though Cyril says nothing, he colors slightly, as though caught in a lie. "Well, kind of. A friend of mine had a, uh, what do you call it, a manual? When we were kids. We tried to play a few times, but we didn't really know what we were doing."

The man's voice trails off into an awkward silence which Cyril feels no compulsion to fill. The sense of unreality he experienced, waking up that first morning after getting out of Taft, descends again like a smoky haze. This conversation, such as it is, feels like something he's watching on television, or a dream. It is not the morbidly obese hacker or the felon standing here, having this conversation. He must have been unceremoniously dropped into someone else's life. Some other four-hundred-fifty-pound man.

"And, I mean, it's got such great educational qualities," Jake's dad adds, rushing to fill the dead air. "It's got all the STEM stuff —or STEAM, I guess it is now?" He ticks points off his fingers, gold ring glittering under the fluorescent lights. "Math, art, imagination, problem solving, teamwork—Oh! Anna—" He turns, holding out an arm to embrace a small woman with glasses and straight brown hair chopped off at the shoulders. "Anna, this is— Cyril, right? Yeah." That nervous laugh, again. "Of course."

Though Anna is as carefully groomed as her husband, the veins on the backs of her hands betray the fact that they are both at least a decade older than either Cyril or Robin. "I just wanted to meet you," she confesses, in a voice so soft it sounds incapable of expressing even the slightest irritation, "face to face, before we agreed to this." She gives him an anxious smile, as if to say, of course you understand.

Two weeks ago, his closest companions had been a drug dealer and a car thief, so, yeah, he understands. That these people are even talking to him is peak absurdity. They seem to think it's a thrill.

And then Seth thunders up, trailed by a smaller boy who is clearly the recipient of his father's compact physique and his mother's eyes. "So?" Seth demands. "Can we?"

Cyril raises an eyebrow. "Can we *what,* exactly?"

"Do D-and-D!" He casts a quick glance over one shoulder, but, not finding what he seeks, turns back. "Kai wants to come, too."

"Of course, it'll have to be on Zoom, for now," Anna interjects. "But maybe in the future..."

"Uh... yeah, I..." He meets Seth's eyes, round and wet with

longing. He sighs. "Sure. Little heads-up woulda been nice," he adds, as Seth bounds off.

"Can I ask you a question?" Jake's dad asks.

Cyril still doesn't see Robin. Not anywhere. "If I said no, would that stop you?"

"How does it work?" Apparently not. "Dungeons and Dragons, I mean. Like, is there a story already written out?"

He closes his eyes, attempting to summon the self-control necessary to answer without profanity, and then somehow twenty minutes have passed and he is surrounded by a ring of parents, writing on the whiteboard easel in the doorway by the light of one of the flickering solar lamps that dot the exterior of the building.

"Okay, hold on." Jake's dad flashes a hand. Again. He's seated on the edge of a planter in the long-neglected school garden, taking notes with a stylus on his phone. "The whole, uh, chaotic thing. Is that part of the character's abilities?"

"No. That's alignment." Cyril uses his forearm to wipe away half of the stat chart he's sketched. He draws a large tic-tac-toe board and fills in the left-hand column. "Good, neutral, evil." Then, left to right. "Lawful, neutral, chaotic."

"And do they roll the dice for that?" This follow-up question comes from Seth's teacher, Ms. Janusevskis, who had seen them out the classroom window and decided to join the fun. She lifts her phone to snap a photo of his chart.

Cyril shakes his head. "It's just a guide for how the character should be played. If a kid decides he wants to be a chaotic evil half-orc, he's probably not going to go around saving villagers. Unless," he adds, lowering his voice and pausing for dramatic effect, "he's saving them to eat."

Everyone laughs. They laugh because he is, when he wants to be, good at this. Humans. Manipulating them. Exploiting their most basic insecurities, their desire for acceptance and belonging. Even with those giant meaty brains, they are disappointingly simple. When he'd realized the military contract at Cooke's company offered an entry point into Tav's command, he hadn't even touched the software. He'd just flattered a couple of junior engineers with his attention, and then invented a pretext for needing access. He could just as easily select any one of the parents on the playground and, in the space of half a minute, humiliate them in front of their peers. He's done it dozens of times, to his own advantage, in the past five years. Anna, for example, is clearly self-conscious about the port-wine stain on the left side of her neck, still visible through a layer of concealer—

But then he glances to the right, and Robin is there. He does not know how long she has been leaning in the open doorway, arms crossed over her chest, but the cheeky glint in her eyes says long enough.

He pops the cap back onto the dry erase pen. "You want more, it'll cost you." Everybody thinks that's funny, too. The dozen parents who stayed "after hours," as it were, head out over the blacktop to collect their children, thanking him as they go. As if he has given them something of value.

When he turns to look for Robin, he finds Seth's teacher instead.

"Thank you so much for that," she says, pulling the double doors shut and securing the padlock. "You know, if you have any extra time, my class would absolutely love it if you wanted to do a Zoom lesson on character creation. I could incorporate dice into the math unit, and they could write stories using—"

"Not a single fucking chance."

She shrugs off the expletive, probably because he's spent the past half an hour putting on a good show of being human. "You know where to find me, if you change your mind." Invest five minutes in winning someone's trust, and they'd give you the benefit of the doubt for months.

Neither Robin nor the kids are anywhere to be seen on the

playground, though a few other adults and children remain. Behind him, Janusevskis clears her throat; when he looks at her, she points across the blacktop, indicating a second set of double doors which he recognizes as the ones the kids came through to get to the playground.

"Thanks," he mutters.

He finds Robin standing at the top of the steps in front of the building, watching the kids play in the dark under the trees. The screening table is gone, as are the administrators who had staffed it. She turns, tugging her mask down to her chin, as he comes out the entrance. "Well, *that* was not what I expected to find you doing."

He yanks a piece of yellow copy paper out of his pocket and shoves it at her with a growl. It contains the email addresses and phone numbers of interested parents. Anna had taken the liberty of writing everyone's information down. "Apparently I'm running an after-school D&D campaign now?"

Robin looks at him, eyes wide, and then abruptly throws her head back and laughs, long and loud. "Oh. Oh my God." She bends forward, holding her side. "Ow. Oh my God. Congratulations?" She snorts. "Good luck?"

"They *do* know who I am, right? Traitor? Felon? Fresh out of prison?"

"I can't imagine they don't." She hooks her arm through his, still grinning. "But you can be very charming, when you want to be."

He pulls away. "I realize I'm a phenomenally good liar, but Jesus, how stupid can people be?"

She cocks her head to one side, squinting in thought. "Is... that what you think you're doing when you're nice to people? Lying?"

"All social niceties are lies."

"So I should be flattered if you tell me this outfit makes me look fat?"

"No, it's just... better than the alternative." He hesitates. "But it, uh, doesn't."

"Thanks? I think." She jogs down the steps and waits, hands on hips, for him to follow. "Are you saying you'd rather I be brutally honest with you? Even if it hurts?"

"Doesn't matter." He grips the railing as he descends, suddenly conscious of how his gut sways with each step. "I already know this outfit makes me look fat."

Robin laughs, and they fall into step together, heading back toward the truck. "Look, you're not pulling the wool over anyone's eyes here. Even if people disagree with your methods, everyone knows you and Tavis did what you did to save a kid. So." Her earrings glint in the light of a streetlamp as she lifts a hand toward the mission-style building. "This right here is gonna be your most sympathetic demographic. Plus, I mean, how many people are on this list?" She tilts it toward the light. "Six? Of thirty. Twenty-four people probably hate your guts."

"If there'd been half that many kids who wanted to play nerd games when I was in grade school, I wouldn't've gotten the shit kicked out of me every week. Where are these people coming from?"

"Nerd stuff's enjoying a renaissance, haven't you heard?" She glances over a shoulder. "Seth! Nora! Let's go!"

"Star Wars, superheroes, sure. But D&D? I mean, that's pretty niche."

"There's a show." She moves her hand in a circle, attempting to jog the pistons of her memory. "Stranger Things. It's an eighties throwback about some kids who play D&D."

He snorts. "And now everyone's suddenly remembered how cool it is. Right."

"We're in the greater Bay Area." Robin spreads her arms. "Where geeks come to spawn. And you? You're basically every neo-libertarian tech-bro's patron saint."

That might have been flattering, five years ago. When he'd

gone to prison, the Bay Area had been the wild frontier of techno-
logical innovation, quirky startups crammed into every nook and
cranny of empty real estate. There'd been an unspoken code of
conduct; an understanding that everyone flourished when information was free. Google's motto had still been "don't be evil."
Now everything's been gobbled up by the many-headed hydra of
social media, and they've abandoned even the pretense of
collecting data in order to "provide a streamlined user experience." Manipulation has become breathtakingly overt as they've
followed the money straight to the lowest common denominator,
and the pioneers of free thought have gladly become autocrats,
granted enough power. "Tech-bros, or fascists? Because according
to the internet, I'm also popular with, like, actual Nazis?"

"Really?" She sucks air through her teeth. "That's par for the
course in 2020, so... I guess I shouldn't be surprised."

Cyril stops. "Five years is not a long time. What the fuck
happened to the world?"

"Honestly?" Robin shrugs. "Shit got weird."

————

IT TAKES ROBIN SO LONG TO GET NORA TO BED THAT
Seth doesn't even protest when it's his turn to switch off
Minecraft and hit the sack. Cyril tucks him in—Nora pops up to
give them a chipper hello—and then returns to the empty living
room, where he retrieves the tuning instruments from the case
inside the piano and seats himself at the bench. He's nearly
finished with the highest octave, plucking softly, when Robin
comes in with a glass of water and a handful of pills. She watches
him work as she swallows them, one by one.

"So, uh, how'd it go? With Nora's teacher?" Like he cares.

He does. He fucking cares.

Robin sets the empty glass on the coffee table and plops down
on the couch, back-to-back with the piano. "Well. It wasn't the

worst parent-teacher conference I've ever had. There's only so much trouble you can get into over Zoom." One small *plink* is followed by another: her earrings hitting the coffee table. "At least until she learns to spell. Which won't be long."

"She's bright." Satisfied with the last note, he plays a quick set of scales, *pianissimo,* before stowing the tools.

"She plays her cards so close to the chest, it's hard to tell. Seth's obsession with numbers tends to overshadow everything else. I think Nora got all the social skills. Or cunning, anyway." Springs creak as she changes position, and her feet pop into view as she props them over the left arm of the couch. She puts a toe to the opposite heel and one black dress shoe drops to the floor, followed a moment later by its mate. "Play me something."

"Uh, aren't the kids trying to—"

"Sleep?" She lets out an incredulous *ha.* "Not if they can help it. Play."

He shrugs and puts the front board back on—even if he doesn't have sheet music, somehow it helps to look at the flat, blank surface—before launching into some late Beethoven.

Robin raps the back of the piano. "Less depressing, please."

"I'm not your goddamn Pandora account."

"Clearly you've got skills, Cyril. Play me something like you played for Nora."

He considers treating her to some Chopin, but after herding the kids through their bath and bedtime routine, the last thing she needs is more childish pouting. He consults his mental catalogue and summons up a soporific Brahms instead.

"Oh. Yes. *So* much better."

He waits for the lull of the next whole rest to reply, on the beat: "Fuck you."

She laughs and exhales a noisy yawn, toes spreading as she stretches.

He plays a Mendelssohn solo after that, and one of Mozart's

less frenetic sonatas. His hands will give out long before he reaches the end of his mental archive, but he hits the damper pedal and lets the notes trail gently into silence. Robin says nothing.

If she's fallen asleep, he doesn't want to rouse her by getting up, so he waits, feeling his feet begin to tingle and go numb. The bench protests as he shifts, and he covers it with a few soft notes which, somehow, become Cat Stevens' *How Can I Tell You.* Which is not exactly what she asked for, but it's right.

Her feet disappear, and a moment later her head rises over the back of the piano, as she apparently kneels on the cushions to face him. Not asleep, after all. She folds her arms and rests her cheek on the back of one hand, eyes closed, feeling the chords vibrate through the polished wood. "Sing it," she whispers, when he reaches the end of the first verse.

"I don't... remember the words."

Her eyes open, and she looks at him, and they both know it's a lie. "Then tell me what you wrote," she says. "When you stayed up the other night. I promise I won't get mad."

"Like I give a shit about your feelings." He shoves himself away from the keyboard, though it's the piano and couch that move. "You wanted to know what I said, maybe think about that before you light shit on fire." He stomps into the kitchen, because this is what he does.

"Fine. You be mad." She is silent for a moment. And then: "Wanna watch a show?"

He ignores her. But when she spins up *Jessica Jones,* he returns to the couch with a package of Oreos.

"What the—" She pauses the TV and snatches one from his hand. "Where've you been hiding these?"

"White casserole dish."

"No wonder you haven't touched the ice cream." She gives him a sidelong glance. "How much junk food do you have stashed in my kitchen right now?"

He decides she's not asking for a complete inventory. "A lot." And not just in the kitchen.

"Is that a prison thing or a fat thing?"

"Both."

"Gimme another one."

It's not a happy episode. None of them get farther than dark, self-deprecating humor, really, but this one's all dark. When the end credits flash, Robin is curled up against his side, the Oreos are gone, and he's not quite sure how either one happened. He lifts his arm, but Robin doesn't move. He can't separate himself from her without physically shoving her away, so after a moment he places his arm back around her shoulders. She is warm.

"Tell me what you wrote," she whispers.

God. "Look, it was just—lies. All of it."

He feels her shoulders rise slightly as she inhales. "Was it, though?"

"You think you know me." Like the parents at school. She thinks if she understands the danger, it can't hurt her. "But you don't."

"Don't I?" She holds up an Oreo, which she had apparently saved, hidden in the palm of her hand. "I know the way to your heart."

She's joking, but he's actually offended. "I'm not Tavis in a fucking fat suit."

"Yeah, well." She twists the cookie open and licks the filling. "Turns out not even Tavis was Tavis in a Tavis suit."

———

HE DREAMS OF PRISON. CORRIDORS NARROWING steadily, looping in on themselves like a living Möbius. A feeling of oppressive, impending doom. The high-pitched wail of the unit alarm begins to sound, and somehow it's still prison, but also his childhood home, and he is trying desperately to shut out his mother's hysterical sobs.

A slight jolt brings him out of it, followed by footsteps across a wooden floor. He snorts and blinks, squinting in the morning light as his pounding heart slows to a steady thud. The wailing continues, only it's a child's reedy cry.

"What are you *doing?*" Robin's voice, enhanced by the echo of the bathroom. The toilet flushes. "No, I'm not—Seth, can you just—yes, I told you—okay! Nora—"

Seth shouts something incomprehensible and slams a door. Nora is crying unconsolably. She stops long enough to shriek, "I wanted to pee *first!*"

He, Cyril, is not in prison but on the couch, feet propped on the coffee table, partially covered by a blue duvet he recognizes from Robin's bed. His left arm bears the long imprint of a seam. When he puts a hand to the cushion next to him, he finds it still warm.

CHAPTER 13

Cyril feeds the kids breakfast while Robin showers, and then they switch; she runs them to Greta's, and by the time he's out of the shower she's already on the scaffolding outside, hammering plywood. Once he's dressed, he brings her coffee in her largest mug.

She drops to one knee and leans over the edge as he hands it up. "Mm. Just what the doctor ordered."

"You do realize you're having major surgery tomorrow morning."

She stands, balancing the mug carefully to avoid spilling the hot dark liquid. "Siding's gotta get done one way or another, and I'm gonna be out of commission for a while." She takes an experimental sip. "You wanna give me a—"

"No."

He has an excuse for not helping, this time, although he doesn't tell her that. Originally, he'd decided not to identify himself to any of his former associates while he was living in Robin's house, but cancer has tipped the balance on that equation. Crashing on her couch seems like it's going to be more long-term than temporary, and although she has implied financial stability, it's uncertain how long it will be until she's working again. In short: he needs money.

He'd reached out to a couple of his most reliable contacts—recruiters, essentially, who could connect him to nominally legal gigs that paid. Anonymously, of course, though he'd dropped enough identifying information that they, if not the FBI or the press, could ID him. All he wanted was some generic securities work, like he'd done off and on for Cooke's company, poking holes in the client's system to make sure it was hacker-proof before it went live. So far, he'd gotten just one response: an invitation to a private IRC. This time of day, he'd been told, was his best bet for finding it active.

His contact is not wrong. He drops into the chat, and, as an obvious noob, is immediately challenged. The irony of the dark web is how populated it is by people like him—which is to say, compulsive rule-breakers with authority issues—and yet how strictly it is governed by inane social protocol. They feel him out, and he lets them, putting up only as much fuss as is socially acceptable. The slightest misstep and his newly assumed persona will be shadowed by suspicion and distrust. The benefit of anonymity is that he can always try again, but the circles he runs in are necessarily small and wary.

It takes two hours for one of the obviously senior members of the chat to invite him to a private room.

Are you who I think you are?

Depends, he types back, *on who it is you think I am.*

One of my Boulder roomies? 07?

This, right here, is the real test. Cyril has never been out of the state of California, let alone Colorado. He did, however, perform a rather significant DDoS attack on a large banking system—known for its predatory loan practices—based in the city of Boulder. Three other hackers were involved. They were never caught, and the bank never made the attack public. But it wasn't in 2007. *Summer of 2009,* he types, *as I recall.*

His chat partner, who is currently using the name BSheezy, but whom Cyril still thinks of by his previous handle, FoShizz22, falls silent. Presumably running a hasty check on prison release records. And then: *Didn't realize you were out.*

It's no secret, but I'm keeping a low profile.

And yet here you are.

I need work.

BSheezy goes silent again. Cyril flips to his inbox. It contains a couple of automated emails from his bank, a request from the seller of his Android phone to review his customer service experience—and a group email from Anna, Jake's mom, which has ballooned to a chain of twenty-seven replies. She has taken it upon herself to be the official organizer of the whole kiddie D&D affair, which is apparently slated to commence the following week, assuming, of course, that Cyril is available. (Not that anyone's waited for him to reply.) If he doesn't want to make a complete ass of himself in front of a bunch of fourth graders, he'd better start prepping. Ordering manuals feels like a ridiculous luxury.

Just as he hits the Amazon purchase button, yet another new email winks into his inbox. Anna had shared the entire chain with Seth's teacher, who is now contacting him individually to beg him to let her submit a proposal on his behalf for their Friday enrichment program. He's not concerned with enriching children, but he would very much like to keep his own bank account in the red, and it sounds like they might be offering some green. Probably not much, but he can hardly afford to be picky. He sends a reply: *Is this a paid position?*

In response, his phone rings. "Aren't you supposed to be teaching right now?" He toggles back to the chat window. BSheezy still hasn't responded.

"The kids are working independently. If your proposal is accepted, and I very much think it would be, then, yes, you would be paid. Not a lot, but—"

"Having a criminal record seems fairly disqualifying."

"Nope. I checked." Of course she did. "Our enrichment program is contracted through a third-party provider, not the school district. As long as you're not a violent offender, you're good."

That seems like a hell of a loophole, but he's not going to object. "And you're taking care of the paperwork?"

"If you'd like me to, yes. There is one form you'll have to fill out first, which I can send over now—"

"Fine."

"Excellent! I'm so thrilled, and the kids—"

He ends the call.

"Was that your lawyer?" Robin had come into the house to use the bathroom on the tail end of the call.

He shakes his head without looking up from his laptop. "Seth's teacher. Wonder how she got my number?"

"Hm, it's a mystery." She grabs the bottle of lotion from the end table and rubs a drop into each elbow. The scent of cocoa butter fills the room. "What did she want?"

BSheezy has finally answered. *I'd legit like to help, but you're kind of risky. No offense.*

"She's trying to con me into a job." *Like I don't know how to keep a low profile,* he replies. He gets another inbox notification, and clicks open the promised document from Janusevskis.

"Oh, good." Robin gives his shoulder a patronizing pat as she passes the couch. "You can start paying for your own groceries."

Well, there was that one time, BSheezy replies.

They didn't find me. I outed myself, Cyril shoots back. Which BSheezy knew perfectly well. *Asshole,* he adds. "Take it out of my babysitting fund."

"Oh, you're hilarious." Robin starts up the stairs, and then jogs back down again. "Hey, do me a favor. Two favors, actually."

Honestly, it's... not really about that. Sorry. BSheezy drops out of the chat.

"Sure." Cyril clicks back to the group IRC. It's empty. He's been ghosted. "I... clearly have nothing going on here."

"One, make lunch. Two, pack the kids' stuff. Let's say three nights' worth—Greta can do laundry if it's more than that."

He twists to shoot her a confused frown.

"What, did you think the kids were gonna stay here with you?"

"I mean, after that whole speech about me being the guy in their corner? Uh, yeah."

"There's being in their corner, and then there's whether I trust you to keep them on a reasonable schedule and feed them three square meals for a week, and the answer is no." She grins. "I'm glad you like my offspring, but I need you to be here for me, now."

"I didn't even think anyone was allowed to have visitors right now."

"Yeah, no. I don't go to the hospital alone. Most of the time it's fine, but I'm not willing to risk landing some on-call doctor who thinks a black woman's pain is either drug use or all in her head. Fortunately, my surgeon went to bat for me."

He's not surprised she wants a chaperone, but he had accompanied her when Nora was born, so she already knows his bedside manner is less than superb. "You'd have better luck with Nurse Ratched."

"Greta?" Robin laughs. "This may come as a shock, but you're actually the better conversationalist. Seriously, though, she's already logged way too many hours in the hospital with her husband. She's in her fifties. She'd never admit it, but sleeping all night in a chair isn't exactly a walk in the park for her."

"Oh, but it's fine for me?"

"Cyril, I've seen you fall asleep sitting at the dining table." She turns, pointing. "This dining table, in fact."

"What—" He thinks she means the night he stayed up trying to write her a letter. Then he realizes she's thinking back to the weeks after Nora's birth. "Uh, yeah, because I was up all night with your little demon spawn so you could sleep!"

"What I'm hearing here is that you have the right experience for the job. Greta's got better things to do than sit by my bed twenty-four seven. You don't, so." She slaps a hand against a bare stud and she resumes her clomp upstairs. "Suck it up."

———

MIDNIGHT. ALONE, IN THE KITCHEN, SAVE FOR THE slabs of gouda and smoked ham he is slapping on sourdough. When he cooks for her, he tries. Alone, it's simple volume.

Behind him, he hears the hall door open, and the soft shuffle of bare feet.

"What's up, kid?" he asks, without turning around. Seth has already crept out twice tonight, first for water and then to pee. Those were his excuses, anyway. "Need a snack?"

"I'm supposed to be fasting," Robin says.

"Oh. Hey." He licks the mayonnaise off the butter knife and tosses it into the sink before turning. "Shouldn't you be—"

She's nude.

His mind says *what the fuck*, but the words never reach his mouth.

She just stands there, and he just stands there, silent, half-constructed sandwich balanced on the palm of one hand, because he can't not stare.

The first, most shocking thing—other than the nudity itself—is, of course, the horizontal fault lines which bisect each side of her chest. Shiny, puckered tallies of that which has already been lost.

"Jesus," he says, reflexively, "who'd they get to do your surgery, Dr. Frankenstein?"

She doesn't react. Her eyes are dark, and so deep he loses

himself. He can read nothing: neither desire nor despair. What does she want from him?

His eyes drop.

Her navel. The flesh of her belly two pregnancies loose, spiderwebbed with stretch marks like ice crystals edging a windowpane. And below, the small tangle of hair where her legs and torso meet. Too much. His eyes retreat to the sandwich in his hand, but he can't eat with his heart lodged in his throat.

Back to her legs. Strong, like two bronze columns, unshaven calves nearly thick as her thighs. Her feet: angular and long.

He swallows.

"Tomorrow," she says, drawing his eyes back to her face. "There will be less of me."

This is a truth both horrifying and utterly inevitable, and which he has, therefore, been trying to avoid thinking of at all. He ought to say something reassuring, but it is impossible to think with her pubic hair in front of him.

"I know this is a lot for you right now. But it's hard to remember what my body felt like, before—" Her hands come up, cupping air. "This. I didn't even think to take a picture."

He drops the sandwich on the counter and gropes for the phone in his pocket. His hands are shaking. "Do you want me to—"

Her fists sweep downward. "I want you to *remember*."

"Okay. Yeah. I can... definitely do that."

"I just—" She sucks in a breath and lets it out again, slowly. Her face softens. "I need someone to have seen me while there are pieces still left."

And then she turns and walks out of the kitchen. He follows her with his eyes, gaze fixed upon the twin dimples which mark the transition from the cello curve of her spine to her tight, muscular ass.

CHAPTER 14

There is no time for awkwardness in the morning. Only the rush of breakfast and getting the kids dressed and making sure they each have all the stuffed animals and clothes and toiletries they'll need for the next few days. At some point Robin tosses a bulging duffel at Cyril and tells him to "Add whatever you need. Including deodorant, please." Five minutes before distance learning starts, they're all piling into the truck. "Buckle up, guys!" Robin calls over one shoulder, peeling out of the drive.

His seatbelt won't reach.

"Well," she says, drily. "That didn't take long." At the next stop she leans over him, using an elbow to shove his belly out of her way, and pops open the glove compartment. In addition to a vehicle manual, napkins, and a tangle of electrical cords, it contains a seatbelt extension.

It's not new. "You *kept* this?"

"Guess I'm just sentimental like that."

At Greta's, Robin hops out and pops the driver's seat forward so the kids can squeeze out of the cab. Seth leans over the center console to throw his arms, awkwardly, around Cyril.

"You gonna be okay, kid?" The children had been surprised, but not crushed, by the news that they wouldn't be living it up bachelor-style with Cyril. Greta's house is familiar and secure, which Cyril has to concede is probably best for their emotional wellbeing right now.

"Yeah."

"Lemme out!" Nora gives her brother's rear a shove.

"Quit it!" The boy leans forward once more, quickly, to whisper into Cyril's ear. "Take care of Mom."

Cyril thumps him on the back. "I'll do my best." Hopefully, that will be enough.

Nora sticks her tongue out at him before following her brother out and up the front porch steps, where Greta waits to shoo them inside. "Log on," she says, brusquely. "You're already late." Robin follows, arms loaded with the kids' backpacks and travel bags. Greta hesitates, her gaze flicking to his window, and then shuts the door.

It opens again almost immediately.

"That was fast," Cyril says, as Robin climbs back into the cab.

"Morning meetings. They were distracted. Probably better that way." She offers Greta one last wave as she pulls away from the curb. "We're getting good at good-bye."

"Do their teachers know what's going on?"

She lifts one shoulder. "They'll figure it out."

She might not care what teachers or other parents think about her, but there is a kind of security in her indifference. Robin has always been a lone wolf, and nothing he's seen in the past two weeks tells him that's changed, but the network she's established here is strong enough that she can depend on others to fill in the gaps. She is seen.

She glances at him as she merges onto the freeway. He is already looking at her. Has been, for most of the morning.

"I know what you're doing," she says.

"What, picturing you naked? I mean, that's what you asked me to do."

"Is that what I said? I feel like I remember it a little differently."

He shrugs. "You don't want me to think about you being naked, don't show me your tits."

Her eyebrows go up. "My—"

"Figure of speech."

She levels a finger at him. "That was good," she says. "You almost got a rise out of me there."

———

"SAY YOU'RE GOING TO THE PHARMACY," ROBIN TELLS him, when they line up to enter the hospital.

"What? Why?"

"Trust me, it's easier. Oh, and give me the bag." She yanks her duffel out of his hands and slings it over one shoulder. "Holy cow, what did you put in here, bricks?"

"That's what I was going to ask you." Then they're at the table set up in the entryway. "Uh—pharmacy," he says, when the security guard asks whether he's had any symptoms in the past week and what he's doing there now. He follows the man's outstretched arm to the hallway on the right.

Robin catches up with him before he reaches his ostensible destination. "This way." She grabs his arm and leads him past the pharmacy to a lobby with three elevators, using a knuckle to push the "up" arrow before stepping into the first set of doors that slide open. "I cleared you with my surgeon, but they're not gonna know that at the front desk."

The elevator pings and opens into another broad lobby decorated in beiges and minty-greens. Every other chair in the waiting area has a laminated sign affixed to the seat warning patients to practice responsible social distancing. That doesn't seem hard, since there are only three other people in the room. All of them are alone. Robin hangs the duffel bag on his shoulder and nods to one of the upholstered benches lining the wall. "Have a seat."

He watches as she approaches the long front desk and waits in the designated spot until one of two women behind the plastic shield motions her forward. Rhinestones glued to the woman's long false nails flash as she accepts Robin's medical card through a slot, swipes the magnetic strip, and taps a few keys before printing out a plastic bracelet with a bar code. Robin slips her hand through the slot, and the glittering nails snap the band snugly around her wrist. The woman says something, eyes flickering over Robin's shoulder to Cyril.

Robin shakes her head and replies—not angry, but insistent. They exchange a few more words, and when Robin points to the phone on the woman's desk she rolls her eyes and picks up the receiver, using a knuckle to dial. She waits, speaks, and then listens for a minute before nodding and waving Robin toward the waiting area with a weary sigh.

Robin blows a breath out as she drops down next to him. "Well. That's taken care of. I think." She holds up a sticker that says "visitor" in big blue letters, then peels it off and slaps it on the front of his shirt. It has a barcode that looks like it matches the one on her bracelet. "I'll have to go in alone when they call me back, but then they'll call you in. Standard procedure in case I need to tell someone my boyfriend's been beating me."

It takes him a moment, mentally, to get past her casual drop of the word *boyfriend*, even if it is sarcastic. "And if you do?"

She considers a moment before shrugging. "Dunno. Let's test it out."

"While I'd love to get the hell out of here, I'd rather not do it in handcuffs."

"Here I thought that was your kink."

He gives her a long, half-lidded look. "What are you, fifteen?"

"Just messing with you. Which is my kink, by the way."

Nervous, is what she is. He gets it—bullshitting is better than crying. Maybe that's why she wanted him here: to keep her strong.

The door at the opposite end of the waiting area opens, and a woman in pink scrubs double-checks her clipboard. "Matheson?"

Robin touches his arm, briefly. "Also, you have to take a COVID test. See you soon!"

"Son of a—"

———

IT DOESN'T MATTER THAT HE'S ALREADY HAD IT. THERE are still too many unknowns. More importantly, it's hospital policy. So he grits his teeth and lets a nurse jam a swab up both sides of his nose. "When can I go back?" he asks, as she's slotting the extra-long cotton swab into a test tube and popping a cap on it. She shrugs. It's not her job.

The technician who calls him back, finally, instructs him to sanitize his hands to the elbows and put a hospital-issued mask on over his standard cloth variety. Only then is he permitted to follow the man down a wide corridor lined with gurneys and wheeled carts in a variety of dimensions. A brief word on an intercom gets them buzzed through a fire door, after which the tech makes a hard right, shoves in one half of a set of double doors, and stands back, waiting for Cyril to enter.

The pre-op holding area is a broad, oddly bare room with a nurse's station against one wall and a lengthy row of gurneys on the other, separated by thin curtains hanging on rails. Most are pulled back against the wall, revealing a room which is mostly empty.

Robin sits on the edge of the third gurney in a rough cotton hospital gown, one hand out-held for the muscular, tattooed nurse putting in her IV. "Hey," she says. "I didn't realize you'd have to wait so long. The anesthesiologist was already here when they brought me back, and she wanted to go over everything immediately so she could run back to her office for some—" She cuts herself off with a hiss of pain.

"There we go," the nurse says, clearly satisfied with his work as he tapes off the line snaking out of her hand.

Cyril dumps the duffel bag on the end of the gurney. "'There we go?' You fucking hurt her, asshole. Or are you stupid and deaf?"

The nurse kicks back on the rolling stool. "Well! You're every bit as spicy as she said you'd be." He casts a glance at Robin. "But I'm sorry if that hurt. I know it's uncomfortable, I was just glad I could get the line in your hand so we didn't have to stick you anywhere else."

"I know." Her eyes flicker to Cyril, but return to the nurse almost immediately, watching as he cleans plastic cannula wrappers off the bed and packs up his phlebotomy kit. The man's entire right arm is devoted to service—Marines, Operation Iraqi Freedom, the local fire department, even a memorial to his fucking bomb-sniffing dog. "Cyril, this is Pablo. I always ask if he's available because he's the best at finding my veins. Which are pretty shot at this point." She gives the nurse's hand a quick squeeze and a look of beatific gratitude that sears Cyril's guts with rage. "Thank you."

"My pleasure." Pablo offers a polite nod and turns to leave, pausing just long enough to meet Cyril with a cold, not-quite-unprofessional stare. "Be careful, my friend."

Cyril wants to follow the guy into the hall and punch his fucking lights out. He could, if he wanted; the nurse might be ripped, but he's got nothing on Cyril for sheer size. Throwing his weight around was something he'd learned in prison.

But he can't leave Robin.

"If you could not burn all my bridges while I'm in surgery," she says, "that would be great."

"I'm just—"

"Being an overprotective asshole, I know. Stop it. They will absolutely kick you out. I think Pablo's looking forward to it, actually." She gives the IV line a gentle shake to work out a kink before moving it out of the way. "I know these people, Cyril. They got me through this the first time. They're good at what they do."

"Apparently not good enough."

Her laugh trails off into a melancholy sigh. "Well. Yes. I am here again, so I'll grant you that." A sudden shudder runs down her spine, and she hugs her elbows, careful of the line in her hand.

He's an idiot. She is sitting there in nothing but a paper gown, five minutes shy of having some cocksure surgeon rifling through her guts. She doesn't need him marking his territory, or whatever it is he thinks he's doing. There is a starched blanket folded over the end of the gurney, and he lifts the duffel to pull it out.

She shakes her head. "It won't help." She taps the pole holding up her saline drip. "It's this. Chills me from the inside out."

He drops the blanket and glances down the sorry row of pre-op patients waiting for the privilege of vivisection. None of them have chaperones. There aren't even any chairs. "What the hell am I here for, then?"

She gives him a look that is equal parts irritation and amusement. "Cyril, I—" She struggles for words, then shakes her head, laughing softly, and extends a hand. "Here."

He looks at her open palm. What does she want, his phone?

She leans forward and snatches his fingers. "You are one seriously dense motherfucker, you know that?"

He looks at her hand, feeling the roughness of her palm in his, a strange contrast to the perfect sliced-almond ovals of her fingernails. "You just want me to... stand here."

"Yeah."

"And hold your hand."

"Yeah."

Like holding his clammy palm is a thing anyone could want. "Fine," he says, "I can do that."

So he stands there like an idiot, holding her hand. Nurses and doctors go by. Machines whirr and beep. One of the other patients is taken to the OR.

"I think I forgot to pack earplugs," Robin says.

"Do you want me to—"

"No." Her grip tightens. "If you leave, they won't let you back in again. And then—"

"I'm not going anywhere," he says. She's scared. She's good at holding herself together, but the cracks are starting to show.

A nurse from the station on the other side of the room approaches. "Dr. Effler is scrubbing in right now. We'll take you back in just a minute."

Robin nods, releasing Cyril's hand to scoot backward up onto the gurney. "I gave Greta your number. She'll probably text you tonight. She might want to know—"

"Look, I'll take care of it." His reply is more clipped than he intends. He shoulders the duffel and then her purse, when she lifts it off a hook on the back of the gurney and holds it out.

She slips her feet under the stiff cotton blanket. "Without being an asshole?"

He snorts. "Right."

Two men in scrubs—he can't tell if it's two nurses or two doctors or one of each—come through a set of double doors at the far end of the room, making a beeline for Robin. The one on the left says, "Robin Matheson? For your hysterectomy?"

Cyril turns. "How is that even a question?"

"They triple check everything." Robin holds her arm out toward the first man, who swipes a handheld barcode scanner across her bracelet like she's a goddamn piece of merchandise. "It's so nobody amputates the wrong leg. Chill."

The other guy slips behind the gurney and kicks a lever, releasing the wheels. "Ready?"

"Yeah." She lays back, not looking relaxed at all. "Let's do this."

"Chica—" Suddenly, there is a lump in his throat, but he is not going to lose his shit.

"Yeah?" She offers a hand. The nurses pause.

He gives her fingers one hard squeeze. He wants to yank her off the gurney, toss her over one shoulder, and get her the hell out of here before these butchers can do her any more harm. Instead he says, "Don't you fucking die on me."

She cocks an eyebrow. "What'll you give me to pull through?"

"I—what?"

"What's my motivation, here?"

"Like, aside from your children? Jesus, I dunno."

She studies his face, or whatever's visible of it above the double layer of masks. "Give me something, big guy."

"What do you want?" He knows exactly what she wants. It's written in her unflinching eyes.

The eyes crinkle, slightly, at the corners. "How stupid do you think I think you are?"

"I'm sorry," the guy at the foot of the gurney says. "We need to get going—"

"Shut the *fuck* up." He grits his teeth. "Chica, I—" Three words. That's all she wants. They both know it. And he can't even manage that. Even here and now, it would cost him too much. "I—"

She snorts. "Just say it, you incredible ass."

"Chica, don't—" Her hand slips from his grasp. The nurse, now in a hurry, starts pushing the gurney toward the doors at the end of the room. Robin, facing backward, fixes her eyes upon his. He shrugs. "Don't feel too bad about the tits. Your best asset was always your ass."

"Oh my God," she exclaims, with an incredulous laugh. The

head of the gurney bumps into the doors, pushing them open. "I'm gonna kill you, you—you ridiculous piece of—"

He raises a hand in farewell. "When you come out, Chica. Alive."

And then she is gone, and he stands there staring at the doors as they swing in shorter and shorter arcs and then stand still.

CHAPTER 15

Corresponding with Robin through Tavis had granted Cyril access to a relationship he'd never have had otherwise, even if only in his imagination. In prison, his ability to lose himself in alternate worlds had become a survival skill. Now, it's emotionally convenient to pull out his phone and slip into a parallel universe where Robin is not having her stomach sliced open. Or where he will not be spending the next day or two locked in a labyrinth of boxlike rooms and sterile halls which too-closely resemble prison.

Fortunately, the waiting room has decent wifi.

He'd hoped for a couple more responses from his old contacts, but his ProtonMail account is nothing but crickets. So much for legit work. It's not a surprise, but at least he can say he'd given it a shot.

Checking the handful of private forums where he's left a trail of breadcrumbs, on the other hand, yields a flood of messages. At least half of them come from angry users accusing him of being a poser and threatening to get him kicked off the platform (and, in fact, he has been booted entirely from one forum). There are also plenty convinced he's undercover FBI, which is hilarious. A handful of Alt-right shills and men's rights activists looking to recruit unsuspecting noobs, and... well, not much else.

It's tempting to out himself. Prior to prison, his reputation had always guaranteed him his pick of gigs, legal or otherwise. Now, it would also make him a target—if not for actual FBI securities agents, then for kids looking to earn a few bucks or a nasty reputation by stabbing him in the back.

Remaining anonymous is safer, but only just. Even if all he wants is greyhat work, rebuilding a rep from scratch means participating in shit he absolutely should not be doing.

That would not have given him the slightest pause in the before times, back when his "extracurricular" activities had been motivated by an idealistic moral imperative. He could have written an entire manifesto about the injustices of the corporate world and what needed to be done to take down the powers that be. But now? Now he's not so cocksure of his own inviolable rightness, or his power to effect change in the world. Now he knows exactly what a single slip-up might cost. And he's not so sure he's willing to risk his freedom just to make a quick buck.

But he's getting ahead of himself. Before he can even consider rejoining the bottom feeders running basic click farms and ransomware, he'll have to earn at least a scrap of trust from his peers. Which, even with his outsize skill set, takes time.

He mainlines IRC until his phone pings, tossing a text notification up in front of a heated discussion about TensorFlow implementations of GANs. The context switch derails him so abruptly that for a moment he cannot reconcile Robin in surgery with Robin sending a text. But Seth's teacher also has his number, and now, apparently, so does Cooke's wife, Greta.

Any news?

He punches in a curt *no*, resenting this woman for dragging him out of the abstract mental space where the real world ceases to exist. Somehow, he has made it past noon without feeling the slippage of time. He flips back to the discussion and tries to dive back in, but the flow is lost. The battery indicator on his phone is red. His stomach rumbles. Two techs chat as they push a cart down the hall.

With a snort of disgust, he pockets the phone and rises, performing his usual tug of pants and shirt, and turns to survey the ripple of disorder left in his wake: tangled earbud wires, empty snack wrappers, water bottle, Robin's bathrobe spilling out of the open duffel. He's shoving it all back into the bag when he realizes he is, of course, alone in the waiting room, and nobody working here is likely to make off with his shit. No need to act like a con.

He rummages in the bag for a power cord and plugs his phone into a nearby outlet before scouting out the hall. "Hey," he says to the nurse behind the desk. The man leans back in a rolling chair behind a plexiglass barrier, foot propped on one knee, tapping a pencil rhythmically against the edge of the chart he is studying. "Robin Matheson. Anything?"

The man raises his eyebrows, then seems to register Cyril's demand. His foot drops to the ground and he leans forward, using the pencil's eraser to tap a few keys on the station's keyboard. "Still in surgery."

Three hours. Is that short? Cyril hadn't asked how long this was supposed to last. And he's not going to betray his ignorance to this idiot. He'll look it up later. "Food?"

The guy cocks a thumb. "Cafeteria's that way. Normally I'd tell you to go out the Main Street entrance and turn right—there's a strip mall down on the next block—but if you leave, they won't let you back in."

Cyril heads for the cafeteria, stopping in at a bathroom along the way. Anything in the strip mall is doubtless superior to hospital grub, but even without COVID regulations he'd never have left this abattoir with Robin still under the knife.

He is right about the food, of course, but it doesn't matter; he's probably lucky the place is even open, with all the precautions they're taking. He loads a tray with prepackaged foods: chips, three individual servings of potato salad in plastic cups, and a ham sandwich wrapped in cellophane, bread visibly saturated with mayo. There's a sign taped to the checker's plexiglass shield that directs diners to an outdoor eating area, but he ignores it and takes the tray back to the empty waiting room. Nobody stops him.

Another hour passes, crawling this time. A cursory Google search for hysterectomy surgery times gives him an estimate of one to three hours, which Robin is already well past. He knows she's also having her ovaries removed, which the internet informs him is called a "bilateral salpingo-oophorectomy," but he doesn't know if it's laparoscopic or not, and by then he's reached the limit of his ability to stomach the thought of what's being done to Robin.

He locates a vending machine. A sign taped to the front informs him it's out of operation because of COVID-19. Under it is a map directing him back to the cafeteria. He leans a shoulder against the side of the big box and gives it a couple of good thumps, but nothing falls out.

The fifth time he paces down the hall, the nurse at the desk slips him a granola bar.

Another hour passes. He is on the verge of demanding to know what is taking so fucking long when the surgeon arrives. He's slight but compact, like a jockey, with a confident stride and half-rolled sleeves revealing arms covered in dark, wiry hair. Not everyone recognizes Cyril's ugly mug, especially hidden behind a mask, but this guy does—the jolt of shock might as well be written in sharpie on his brow. He recovers quickly, holding up a palm as he approaches Cyril. "Don't get up."

Like he was going to. "Well?"

"She's in the recovery room," the man says, clearly well versed in delivering the most vital piece of information first. He seats himself not in one of the twenty vacant chairs, but on the coffee table directly facing Cyril. "And she's stable."

He lets out a breath like a deflated balloon.

The surgeon extends his elbow, like a handshake but even more idiotic. "I'm Dr. Effler. You are...?"

"Not interested in your bedside-manner bullshit. And you fucking know who I am." What this surgeon thinks about Cyril's exploits or his prison sentence, he neither knows nor cares.

Effler lowers the elbow, and his face is carefully neutral when he replies: "Fair enough."

Cyril waits.

"We—" Effler shifts, leaning forward to prop his elbows on his knees. Like it's physically uncomfortable for him to maintain a distance of six feet. "Had some trouble controlling the bleeding once we removed the uterus, which is why the surgery took longer than expected. There was quite a bit of blood loss, which necessitated a transfusion."

"A—Jesus Christ." Cyril has been trying to hold himself together. Trying not to think too much about what's happening to Robin, or lose his cool, or do or say anything that might get him kicked out. But just hearing the words out of this asshole's mouth makes him feel like he's going to vomit. He looks at the floor between the surgeon's feet and breathes.

"It happens. Things might have been fine without one, but obviously it's better to play it safe. Fortunately, we were able to get the bleeding under control."

This smug, self-congratulatory asshole. It's not even personal, to him. Not Robin's uterus or surgery or blood. Just *the* uterus. *The* surgery. *The* bleeding. As if the body on his operating table wasn't the most important person in the world. "Her name," Cyril hisses, instead of throttling the man, "is Robin."

"Yes, I'm aware." The surgeon cocks his head, as if he's not quite sure what Cyril's getting at. "Is there anything else I can do for you, Mr. Blanchard?"

He doesn't want to know, not from this prick, but he can't not ask. "The cancer—"

Effler shakes his head before Cyril can finish the question. "That'll have to wait for pathology. Her oncologist will get the report."

His hands are fists. Soft, doughy fists, but there's bone underneath. "That's convenient. For you."

The surgeon shrugs. "It is what it is. Oh—and your COVID test came back negative, in case you were wondering. So you're cleared to—"

"I want to see her." Alive. Breathing.

The other man nods, once again the portrait of empathetic patience. "She'll be in the recovery room for a little while yet, but once we're sure she's stable we'll move her to a room, and you can see her there." His hand comes up, hovering for a moment, as if wishing he could lean across the distance between them and give Cyril's knee a comforting pat.

"If you touch me, I will break your fingers."

Effler laughs and slaps his own knee, as if he thinks Cyril is kidding. "Thanks for the reminder." He pauses to pump a glob of sanitizer into his palm on the way out.

———

BY THE TIME ROBIN IS RELEASED FROM THE RECOVERY ward, it's late afternoon and the nurse on duty outside the waiting room has gone off shift. A sixtyish woman in pink scrubs and compression stockings leads Cyril through a maze of backstage corridors and fire doors, up a gurney-sized elevator, and into a more polished hallway of closely spaced doors, numbered like hotel rooms. She strides past an unshaven elderly man with a walker and finally opens the door onto a room so small this asshole could reach out and touch both walls. A curtain hanging from a track on the ceiling blocks his view of the bed, but not the subtle dead-animal musk of dried blood.

"Jesus," he says. "I thought COVID rates were falling. This place must be bursting at the seams if you're putting patients in broom closets."

"This is a private room," the nurse says, as if the luxury ought to be obvious. She pumps hand sanitizer from a bottle on the wall. "We only have four."

"Lady, my prison cell was bigger than this." Bunk, technically, but same difference. He reaches around the nurse to slather his hands with the transparent gel.

A frown line appears between the woman's eyebrows. "Well," she says, clearing her throat. "Let's see how she's doing." The nurse peeks around the curtain. "Ms. Matheson, is it all right if I turn the light on?"

It is impossible to tell if the muffled groan means "yes" or "no."

Cyril shoves past the nurse and yanks the curtain aside.

He knew she would look like shit, but seeing Robin in the flesh hits him like a cattle gun to the skull. Every ounce of him rejects the hollow vacancy in her face, the terrible ash-gray tint to her skin. This should *not* be.

This asshole's gut reaction? Leave. Get out. Now.

No lie: he very nearly does.

"Chica." He chokes the word, and panic rushes in. He seizes her hand, the one without the wires and tubes. Presses it, too hard, between his palms. "Chica. Please."

She blinks—raising her eyelids seems to take effort—and her eyes roll, unfocused, in his direction. Her lips twitch. "Hey, asshole."

His laugh is rough. "Yeah. That's me."

The nurse pulls a keyboard down from the wall and uses a badge hung around her neck to log in. "She may be confused for a while," she tells him, glancing at the screen on one of the machines hooked up to Robin and entering the data into the computer. "That's normal."

"What can I—" He has never felt so fucking useless. "What do I do?"

She shrugs. "Just be here." She gestures to a rolling cart docked near the head of the bed, which holds a pitcher of water and a plastic cup with a straw. "She can have a few sips if her mouth is dry. No food yet. The on-duty nurse will check in every couple of hours. If you need someone, hit that button. She's still getting fluids and medication through her IV, so she shouldn't be in any pain."

And then the nurse just... leaves. Like it's okay that Robin is lying there, barely conscious, having come through major surgery, with no professional observation whatsoever.

Once, two weeks after Seth was born, Tavis brought the infant to this asshole's house, not specifically to meet Cyril but to give Robin a few hours of uninterrupted sleep. Cyril had scarcely laid eyes on the kid when Tavis got a call from a superior at the base, and he'd handed off the tightly-swaddled infant like a football and dashed outside for better reception. Cyril had been left on the couch, holding the tiniest, most fragile human he had ever encountered, not knowing what, if anything, he ought to do, or whether the wrong movement could irreparably damage this small, infinitely vulnerable creature.

That is how this asshole feels now. She looks—Jesus, she looks like death with a hangover, and he's just standing here, desperately palpating her hand. Surely she needs to be monitored by someone who knows what the hell they're doing.

One of the machines next to her bed emits an unobtrusive beep, followed by a kind of ratcheting pump. He follows the wires and tubes and realizes that it's a timed-release device, feeding into her IV. Narcotics?

"Are you—okay?" He releases her hand long enough to drop

the duffel bag and set her purse on the cart next to the pitcher of water. "Chica?"

She doesn't respond. He feels for her pulse in her wrist, but he can't tell whether it's there or only his imagination. He can't see her breathing.

Shit. *Shit.*

He's leaning over her to try to find a pulse in her neck when she sucks in a sudden, deep breath. And then lets it out again, nice and slow.

He breathes. Like an infant, it's impossible to tell whether she's dead or asleep. Well—he's not going to poke her again. He'll stand here. And watch.

His phone buzzes, and when he fishes it out of his pocket he finds five texts from Greta, all with increasingly insistent demands for information. He contemplates making her wait another hour or two before replying, but that wouldn't be fair to the kids.

She's out. Went long but doc says she's fine. Sleeping.

The "sent" notification under his text winks immediately to "read," but there are no ellipses to indicate that Greta is composing a reply. She has apparently decided to give him the silent treatment. Fine with him.

The only seat in the room, crammed into the corner not occupied by the bed, is a standard hospital-issue recliner which won't even come close to accommodating his doublewide rear. Fortunately, the arms of the chair are low, and layering the seat with extra blankets from a supply cart in the hall offers enough lift to wedge his ass into the rose-pink vinyl. When he leans back, popping out the footrest, the back of his head hits the wall.

———

"CYRIL?"

He has, miraculously, managed to fall at least partially asleep.

His name on her lips, albeit blurred and cottony, brings him back with a jerk. "Robin. Shit—" He can't get the chair back upright. He heaves himself forward, and then forward again.

"Cyril, I don... I don..." Her head rolls toward him in the dim light, her features contracted in a look that he recognizes instantly from Nora's infancy. He grabs the sick bag from the cart next to her bed and gets it to her mouth the instant before she retches. It's nothing but thin yellow bile. "Don' feel good," she finishes.

"I'll get a doctor." He uses the corner of the bedsheet to wipe her mouth.

She grimaces as the rough fabric and then swallows, with effort. "No. M'okay."

"You don't *look* okay. What do you need? Water?" He holds the plastic straw to her mouth, but she doesn't suck. Her lips are dry and cracked. Somewhere—he paws through her purse—yes. She always carries a tube of Blistex. Applying it to someone else's lips is trickier than he expects, and he squeezes out significantly more than necessary. He uses a finger to wipe off the excess, and then wipes his finger on his pants. "Is that, uh..."

"Hg," she says.

"What?" He leans closer.

She lifts her right arm, straight up, hand dangling loosely. "Hg."

"You want—a hug?"

"Mm." The arm drops onto his shoulder.

"Uh. Yeah. Okay." He leans over the bedrail, stooping to allow her arm to circle his neck. It starts to slide, and he catches it before it can flop back. "Here. Why don't you let me—" He wedges his hand under her ribcage and lifts, just slightly. She moans at the movement. "Wait, hold on." Carefully, he disengages himself, placing her arm at her side. He fiddles with the bedrail until it rotates down. There's just enough room to sit on the edge of the mattress, or at least lean a thigh, and he bends forward and manages to slip an arm around her neck without moving the rest of her. He gives her a light squeeze.

"Mm," she says, when he starts to pull away. This time it is a negative.

"Oh... kay." He plants his free hand on the other side of her body, to prevent himself from crushing her.

He is looming over her—like a vampire preparing to commence exsanguination—when a new nurse comes in for a check. "What—" The sudden arch of her eyebrows, visible even through her face shield, says she's two seconds from calling security. "Can I *help* you?"

"Fuck. No. I just—" He wiggles the fingers trapped under Robin's head. "Robin. I'm—gonna let go."

She doesn't object when he shoves himself upright, but her hand catches his arm as he pulls away. "Huuugs," she says, nuzzling the back of his hand. "Yer hugs're th'best. Skishy. Shish —" She frowns. "Shishy. Skish. *Squishy.*"

"Oh," the nurse says, her body relaxing slightly. "I see."

Cyril extracts his hand and kneads the kinks in the back of his neck. "She's... not gonna remember this, right?"

———

"Is it done?"

He looks up from the recliner, where he's idly playing a match-four game on his phone. "What?"

"Is it over? I had surgery?" She lifts the sheet up, presumably to examine her abdomen, and then immediately lets it drop, losing interest.

"Yeah. Like—" He clicks out of the game to check the time. Two in the morning. "Six hours ago." At this point, she's wandered in and out of consciousness half a dozen times.

She sighs. "Good. Did it go okay?"

"They had some trouble controlling the bleeding. You had to

have a transfusion. Otherwise I guess it was fine. No news on the cancer yet, but the meds are making you high as a kite."

"Oh," she says. "Yeah." She stares at the ceiling for long enough that he returns to his game before adding, "Oh no."

"Now what?"

"I have cancer?"

"Yep." He matches four tiles vertically and horizontally. The game congratulates him with a shower of confetti. "I mean, that's what I hear."

"I'm gonna die."

He blinks at her over his phone, then clicks off the screen and sets it aside. "Chica—"

She turns her head to look at him. "I don't wanna die." The way she says it is eerily flat; a simple statement of opinion. *I do not like pickles and jam.*

"Chica, you—" He sits forward, attempting to shove the footrest down in one swift move. It doesn't work. He tries again, and the chair jackknifes into the upright position with a thud. "Look, Chica, you aren't gonna—"

She interrupts him with a snort. And then a giggle.

"Jesus, now what?"

"You."

He looks down to find that his shirt has ridden up, exposing the vast white spread of his belly. "God damn it." He yanks the shirt back down. "This fucking chair—"

"You look like a s-s-stuffed sausage." She giggles like a child. Like Nora.

"That's flattering, thanks."

"No," she says, drawing out the word. "No... a cinnamon bun!"

"That—doesn't even make any sense, but... slightly better, I guess?"

"Oh, Cyril." She giggles again. "I love you."

———

IT'S TEMPTING TO IMAGINE THOSE THREE LITTLE words, like rocks in a riverbed, tumble over in his mind as he sits, staring at her profile through the remainder of that long, watchful night. Perhaps he plumbs each spoken syllable for nuance, or wonders whether her utterance represents her true thoughts, unfiltered, or if they are simply the product of a drug-addled, post-operative haze?

No. He does not.

He does not think of them at all. (Not because he is indifferent, though he pretends this is true, but because he is unwilling. Like all good things, he stuffs those words down as deep as they will go.)

What does he contemplate, then, as he watches her breathe?

This asshole thinks of how much better things were before.

Before cancer, or prison, or war. Back when Tavis was playing the part of husband, and Cyril the puppeteer. Back when he sat in the solitary safety of his own room, enjoying perfect *eu de Robin* filtered through glowing pixels on a screen. He hadn't gotten to fuck her, sure. But neither had he needed to deal with the gross corporeality of it all. And he's not fool enough to think that being present in the flesh means he's going to get a fuck, even now.

Especially now. Look at her. Carved up and stapled together like meat in a butcher shop. How the hell is he supposed to jerk off to that? And so he sits and watches her for the privilege of— what? Holding her hand?

He never signed up for this.

———

GRADUALLY, THEY TAPER OFF THE OPIATES, AND, gradually, her filter returns. With it comes pain.

"Oh, Cyril, I feel like shit."

"That's the most rational thing you've said since you came out of surgery." After another round of IRC networking, he's switched gears to D&D prep. Jake's mom, who has been anxious to nail down a weekly time-slot, has gotten wind of Robin's surgery and is now peppering him with emails offering to start a Meal Train or GoFundMe. Ignoring her seems like an invitation to disaster, so he replies with a firm negative and a Zoom invitation for one week out. Now he's skimming through an archive of bootlegged adventure guides.

Robin rubs her eye with a knuckle. "How long—"

He flicks the screen, then stops and marks a scenario that contains a dragon. If dragons are what Seth wants, then dragons Seth shall have. "Fourteen and a half hours. Your surgery went fine. You had a transfusion. No news on the cancer."

"I take it we've had this conversation before."

"Only about twenty times." He taps the screen, marking another dragon-centric scenario. "Also, yes, the kids are fine, they're asleep because it's five in the fucking morning, no, you did not wet the bed, the catheter just feels weird and they will remove it tomorrow. Scratch that, later today. Yes, I know this chair makes me look fat, yes, I can ask someone for another pillow but not-now-don't-leave, and yes, you will absolutely regret it if you try to raise the head of the bed."

"Good to know." She knuckles her eye again. "It smells like—"

"Burnt toast, yes, I know. Your sense of smell hasn't been damaged, I smell it too."

"Looks like we've covered a lot of ground. Have you been here this whole time?"

"Where else am I gonna go?" He glances up from his phone. She is looking at him. "Wait, are you actually lucid? Jesus, it's about time."

"I should've warned you. I'm sensitive to—well, everything, basically. Did I say anything crazy?"

"Not unless you count comparing me to a giant sausage about two seconds before declaring your undying love."

"Oh my God, I did *not*." She snorts, and then moans. "Oh, don't make me laugh. Ow."

CHAPTER 16

A stranger coming out of the elevator stops to hold the doors, offering Robin a sympathetic smile as an orderly maneuvers her blue hospital wheelchair inside. "Fuck off," Cyril growls, savoring the man's startled expression as the double doors slide shut. The orderly gives him a sidelong glance, but keeps his mouth shut as the elevator jerks and begins its slow descent.

"Feels empty," Robin says, quietly. She hugs her purse to her chest. "Going home without a baby in my arms."

Cyril could not have said whether they'd been in the hospital for forty-eight hours or seventy-two or something in between—time is a blur, and the dense haze of yellow smoke that greets them out the lobby windows doesn't help. He hefts the duffel bag higher onto his shoulder. "Listen," he says to the guy pushing the chair. "We both know hospital liability bullshit says you have to push her all the way outside. But I'm not gonna leave her sitting in that smoke while I get her vehicle, so you can either pretend you pushed her out and I brought her back in, or you can sit here and wait until I bring the truck around. Your choice." He leaves without looking back.

His cloth mask is no substitute for an N95 in fire weather, and by the time he locates Robin's truck he's wheezing. He switches the air intake to recirculate and turns the fan on high, then consults his phone for a map of California fires. There's a fresh blaze in the vineyards west of Healdsburg, but it would have to jump the freeway and tear through most of the downtown before it got to Robin's house. No roads blocked.

When he pulls into the loading zone outside the hospital entrance, he finds Robin and the wheelchair waiting on the curb. "Are you fucking kidding me?" he says, but the asshole order-ly isn't around to answer. He puts the parking brake on and climbs out of the cab. "Hey." Robin is staring into space. "Chica, are you okay?"

She blinks. "Yeah. Just... tired."

He grabs the bar on the back of the chair, which unlocks the wheels, and pushes her out to the passenger side of the truck. She hands him her purse and then grips the armrests, preparing to stand as he opens the door.

"Hold on," he says, chucking her purse into the extended cab. "I got you."

It's impossible to scoop her out of the chair without hurting her, but he figures it's better—and quicker—than her trying to stand up and climb into the cab. She wraps her arms around his neck and presses her face into his shoulder, muffling a whimper.

Once she's in, he tips her seat back forty-five degrees, then realizes he can't exactly buckle the belt across her abdomen. "Hold on," he repeats, and goes to the camper to grab one of the pillows they'd packed but failed to bring in. On second thought, he pulls her bath robe out of the duffel bag, too. He places the pillow on her stomach before buckling her in—she winces—and uses the robe to fill the gap between the seat and the door.

"Didn't know you were that strong," she murmurs, tugging her mask off as he wedges himself behind the wheel.

"Didn't know you were that light." He attaches the belt extension and then buckles himself in.

"Well, I did just lose a pound of flesh." She licks her lips and swallows, with effort. "You work out in prison?"

He hands her a water bottle from the pocket of the driver's side door. "Once or twice." He couldn't be DMing or in the kitchen all the time, and there was fuck-all else to do other than sit with his own thoughts.

She smiles as she sips. Like he's been holding out, and she's caught him red-handed.

"Don't worry, it won't happen again."

She closes her eyes and rests her head against the window, but the smile is still there. "We'll see."

———

HE PARKS ON THE STREET OUTSIDE THE HOUSE AND lets the engine idle, watching the cadence of her slow, steady almost-snore. Then a trio of pedestrians in N95 masks go by, chatting as if nothing whatsoever is amiss, and the rhythm is broken. She clears her throat, swallows, and lifts her head. He shuts off the engine and sets the parking brake as if they've just arrived.

Getting her inside, even via the ramp in back, is a slow, painful process that ends with her on the couch, tears leaking out the side of eyes squeezed tight, sucking in quick, ragged hitches of air. He makes a rapid circuit of the house, double checking to make sure all the windows and doors are sealed, and then uses a roll of duct tape she left in the kitchen to seal off the hatch to the second floor. When the house is as smoke-proof as it can get, he brings her pillows, a glass of water, and her duvet from the bedroom. Then it's time for her to take some more painkillers so he helps her sit up enough to choke them down.

"There's a hot water bottle in the hall closet—"

There's a pile of blankets in the closet, too, and grabs one from the top, tucking it under his arm as he fills the water bottle in the bathroom sink. When he brings her the warm rubber bladder, she attempts to apply it directly to her stomach before hissing *shit* and handing it back.

"Cold. I think."

He refills the bottle with ice cold water, which is apparently the correct choice, and then covers her with the duvet and the extra blanket. "I can turn on the TV, or—"

"No." Her sigh is more of a shudder. "I... kinda just want to lay here and moan."

So he parks himself at the dining table with her laptop, where he orders groceries and pretends he's not watching her to make sure she's okay until the meds hit her system.

When she dozes, finally, he grabs a Tupperware full of stale oatmeal raisin cookies Seth requested but didn't like and shuts himself in the laundry room to stuff his face because he is *angry*.

Angry at the doctors who cut her open. Angry at the hospital for sending her home like this, so weak and fragile she can barely move. Angry at her, most irrationally, for having cancer to begin with. Every time she whimpers, all he wants to do is tell her to shut up, and he must mentally check the urge to grab her and shake when she moans in pain. He just wants it to stop. To be over with. For her to be herself again, so he doesn't have to fucking *care*. It's exhausting.

When the tub is empty, he belches, shifts the laundry from the washer to the dryer, and goes to check on her again. She is still sleeping—deeply enough that she doesn't stir when the delivery person rings the doorbell.

He cooks.

When she wakes, he brings her lunch, but she closes her eyes and turns her face away from the tray. "I can't."

"I'm not your babysitter," he says, "so I'm not saying

I'm gonna make you eat, but I'm also not going to haul your ass back to the hospital." He sets the tray on the coffee table and uses a shin to push it flush with the edge of the couch. "Your choice."

She winces, then opens her eyes. "What—" she looks up at him, articulating the remainder of the question with her eyes. It is not the kind of thing he usually makes.

"The Percocet's gonna make you constipated," he tells her. "When you finally take a shit, this'll help." Pumpkin soup. Asparagus. Papaya.

She struggles to rise on one elbow, sucking in a breath as her abs flex. "How do you know all this?"

He hauls her up by the armpits, stuffing accent pillows behind her back. "Maybe you haven't heard, but there's this new thing? It's called the internet." The discharge nurse had also printed out about a ream of aftercare instructions, but Robin had been understandably preoccupied with more immediate agonies.

She dips a finger into the soup and puts it into her mouth. Her eyebrows go up. "A girl could get used to this," she says. "If I asked for a little background music, would you tell me to fuck off?"

He almost does. But why the hell not. He seats himself at the piano bench and plays a few light, tinkling melodies before wandering into Cat Stevens. Somehow it's always Stevens, with her.

She eats less than half the meal before pushing it away. "Cyril?"

He lifts his hands and releases the damper, silencing *Tuesday's Dead* mid-chord. "Yeah?"

"I gotta pee."

"Are you sure?" The nurses had helped her with the first agonizing trips to the bathroom, and he's not eager to experience it firsthand. "I could bring you a bucket."

"Now," she says. Not angry, but urgent.

"Yeah, okay." He closes the fallboard and comes around the end of the couch. "Maybe I should carry you."

"No, I—I think I'm okay."

"'Drugged' is not the same thing as 'okay.' Here." He hooks his hands under her armpits and lifts, gently. She whimpers. "Are you—"

"Keep going," she breathes. "Yeah. Just—oh God. Right there."

He lifts. Very slowly. She clutches his arms, pressing her face into his chest as she lets out a mewl. Her legs slide off the couch and then she is upright, hunched over and still clinging to his arms. He walks backward, leading her into the hall and then the bathroom. When he lets her down on the toilet seat, her face is streaked with tears.

"Do you want me to—"

She starts to pee.

He backs out, leaving the door open a few inches, and studies the picture of her parents in the hall while she does her business. In the bathroom, she is weeping, though her sobs are strangled by her attempts to minimize movement of her abdominal muscles.

His arms, where she gripped him, burn like fire. Ordinarily her touch—once, years ago, she'd stumbled and caught him by the elbow for support—would be an event he'd review, catalogue, and pore over for weeks. Years. Now all he wants is for it to stop.

"Okay," she says, finally, her voice soggy with tears.

He lifts her off the toilet and half-carries her back to the couch. When he sets her down on the cushion, she doesn't let him go. "Everything hurts," she whispers.

He puts his arms around her shoulders and squeezes, gently. Her body relaxes into him.

She sighs. "You give the best hugs."

He had no idea how to respond to that the first time she said it; even less so now that she's lucid.

WHEN THEY REPEAT THE BATHROOM ROUTINE AGAIN after dinner, she's able to hobble with minimal support. Whether it's because she's healing quickly or the drugs he doesn't know, but he'll take it. Still, he waits outside the partially-open door. "Bed?" he asks, when she's done.

She rests her elbows on her knees, bending her head to run her hands through her short hair. "You know what I really want? A shower."

"Oh yeah, that sounds like a fantastic idea. How about I get you a washcloth and a tub of—"

"No, really. I'm feeling better. If I do it sitting, I think I'll be fine."

He spreads his hands. The aftercare instructions had suggested waiting a day or two, but it wasn't expressly forbidden. "Your call."

From the toilet seat, she directs him in lining up her hair and body products, a fresh bath robe and towel, her hair wrap, and one of his shirts, when he can't locate a nightgown. He sets her cell phone on the counter, in case she needs him, and then stands outside the closed door, listening as she disrobes, cursing softly, and the water comes on.

He folds a load of laundry from the dryer, puts the kids' clothes away, and is surveying the sink full of dirty plates and pots and pans when he realizes the shower is no longer running. He raps on the bathroom door. "Everything okay?"

She says something, so at least she's alive.

He cracks the door. "What?"

"I could use a little help."

He shoves the door in.

She sits on the granite shower seat where he left her, one hand propped against the wall, head bent, carefully breathing. Nude, of course, and soaking wet. Droplets of water glint like diamonds in her hair. "I just—I got tired out, I think." She lifts her head, a little sheepishly. "Can you get me the towel?"

He grabs it off the counter shakes it open, shouldering into the shower stall to drape it around her torso. She is shivering. He puts his hands on her shoulders and rubs her down like a newborn pup, using the towel to chafe her arms and back. Because she's seated, he ends up half-smashing her face into his gut.

"Not exactly how I imagined feeling you up." He says it in jest, mostly.

"Yeah. Me either."

Like she's imagined it at all.

He leaves the towel wrapped around her and uses a hand towel to pat-dry her hair before tossing one of his freshly laundered t-shirts over her head. It's long enough to reach her knees. "Come on." He puts a hand under her arm and lifts her to her feet. She stands, still shaky, and passes an arm around his middle as the towel slides to the shower floor. He uses a foot to spread it out over the wet tile.

"Bed?"

She nods. "I was feeling all right, but I got under that hot water, and it just—I dunno, took it all out of me."

"Give it a few days."

"I know." She shakes her head in frustration. "I should really know this by now."

"You always have been a little slow on the uptake."

She uses her free hand to give his belly a slap. "Hush."

He lets her down on the left side of the king bed, holding her arms as she leans back. "You need, like, underwear or something?"

"The incision's exactly where the elastic goes, so no." She pulls the duvet up over her bare legs. "Going commando for a while."

"Sexy."

"Nothing you haven't seen before."

"Oh, is that why you showed up naked in the kitchen?" He realizes, as the snarky words leave his mouth, that he's hit the painful truth. She'd exposed herself to him the night before her surgery because that was how she wanted him to remember her: strong and self-possessed. Not this frail, trembling assemblage of flesh and bone.

"Actually," she says. "Yeah." She shifts, wincing. "Pillows would be nice. And some fresh water. Oh, and turn the heater up."

He mimes doffing a cap. "Yes, milady."

"Thank you, sir neckbeard."

He takes the empty glass from her nightstand into the dining room. The thermostat's already at seventy, but he cranks it up another five degrees before heading out to the truck, shutting the sliding door between the kitchen and the laundry room like an airlock before stepping into the night. It's as warm outside as it is in, and he can't tell whether the air is smoky or just dark.

When he lets himself back into the bedroom, arms full of pillows and the duffel slung over one shoulder, she is asleep. She's kicked the duvet half off, probably because the house is now a sauna, so it covers only her torso. At least she's comfortable. He drops the baggage at the foot of the bed, then edges around her side to plug her phone into the charger on the nightstand and switch off the lamp.

As he turns to leave, navigating by the light from the hall, one of her feet slides off the edge of the mattress. He nudges it with a knee as he squeezes past, but she leaves it dangling. She shifts, letting out a faint moan, and moves a hand on the duvet, over her incision.

Which is when he remembers the dressing needs to be changed. Not only because of the shower, but because it's time. He taps the face of her phone to check the hour. Past time.

"Chica." He says it in a low voice, not sure if he hopes she wakes up or if he hopes she doesn't. "Chica, you—"

Fuck it. He's already seen her naked. Twice. More, if you counted Nora's birth. If she cared now, she'd be at Greta's house and the kids would be here with him. He bends, propping one hand on a bedpost, and shoves both her feet toward the center of the bed. When she still doesn't stir, he pushes again, clearing enough room to plant his massive ass on the edge of the mattress. Reaching back, he grabs the duffel and unzips the smaller compartment on the side, angling it to catch the light from the hall. He sorts through a collection of pill bottles, arranging them in a line on her bedside table, before pulling out gauze pads, tape, latex gloves, and a little bottle of sterile rinse. Then—

Then he lifts the duvet. And her shirt.

Touch her, his inner voice urges. She's right there. She can't stop him. Go ahead. Do it.

He clenches his fists and waits, staring at the dark crevasse between her legs, until the blood thundering in his ears dwindles to a dull roar. He is a colossal fuck-up. An enormously dysfunctional mess of a human being. But even he has limits. Maybe he isn't complete garbage after all.

Jesus, his bar is low.

His hands are shaking so badly it takes him a while to work his fingers into the gloves. Then, carefully, he peels back the existing dressing. The nurse had showed him how to loosen the tape with fluid, but the dampness from the shower has already done the job. It comes off easily.

He is rinsing the wound with a few teaspoons of the bottled solution when there is a change in her breathing. He pats the wound dry with a piece of gauze, and then covers it with a second.

She is crying.

Knock it off, he wants to say. Pull yourself together. Doesn't she know *he's* the fucked-up one? Putting herself through school after her father's death; raising Seth when Tavis deployed; Tav's death; Nora's birth; his sentencing. Through it all, she's always pulled herself together, always soldiered on.

But now he's sitting here taping gauze to her pelvis, listening to her strangled hiccoughs in the dark. He doesn't ask whether it's the physical pain, or the casual violation of his touch. Probably both. He finishes, quickly, and tugs the t-shirt down.

She fumbles in the dark, finds a pillow, and pulls it over her face. He doesn't know why he doesn't leave, then, but he doesn't. Inertia, maybe.

He pulls the gloves off and packs the supplies back in her bag. "Are you—do you want anything?" He's an idiot. And he forgot the fucking water.

There's a word, muffled by her pillow, but he's pretty sure it's "No."

"Okay, well, I'm gonna be in the living room." He leans forward, propping his hands on his knees to rise. "Your phone's here. Text me if—"

She moves; her fingers brush his hand, and then sink into his arm. "Don't."

Don't what, he always says. But he knows.

Don't leave me alone.

It's not as simple as sliding in. There's not enough room on her side, and he's not sure she could move even if he asked, so he gets up and goes around to the other side of the king-sized bed. He sits on the edge of the mattress, slipping his shoes off heel-to-toe, and then heaves himself backward. Shifts. Adjusts his belly. Works one leg up and then the other. Grabs the headboard and heaves himself toward the center of the bed again until, finally, he's close enough to touch her. It's a whole process, getting himself into bed, and at the end he's breathless and perspiring.

He leans his back against the headboard, blood pounding in his ears.

He's not sure what to do, then, but when he touches her shoulder, she reaches for him. He picks her up like a child, hands under her armpits, and helps her settle onto him. Even in the heat, she is shivering. He stretches, rocking his bulk slightly, and manages to snag the corner of the duvet. He pulls it over her shoulders.

Her arms spread wide over him, one ear pressed into the hollow between his sagging man-boobs. He feels her lips move against his shirt, damp with sweat and, now, her tears.

"I didn't even want another baby," she whispers. "But now I can't. And for some s-stupid reason that seems like the end of the world."

————

TOO EARLY THE NEXT MORNING, SHE WAKES HIM TO give her a boost out of bed. She sits on the edge of the mattress to take her pills and then makes the rest of the trip to the bathroom herself, shuffling out to the couch when she's done.

Getting himself out of bed is another ordeal—sitting with his back against the headboard all night hasn't done his back any favors, and his right leg, which she's been laying on for hours, has gone completely numb. When he plants his foot on the floor, the blood comes rushing back. His shoulders, his neck—everything feels like he's been hit by a truck. More so than usual. Her meds are tempting, but he leaves them alone, going into the bathroom to piss and choke down a handful of Aspirin.

"You okay?" she asks, when he limps out of the hall. "You snore like a chainsaw. It's kinda nice, actually. Like white noise."

"Fuck," he says, hobbling into the kitchen, "off." He puts the coffee on—for her, not him—and starts breakfast while he's waiting for the drugs to kick in.

Eventually, they do, and he brings her coffee, pills, and oatmeal waffles with strawberries on a tray. This time, she's able to sit up on her own, tray perched on her knees. "Can you turn the couch, like, ninety degrees? So I don't have to twist my neck to see the TV."

He eats four waffles, standing in the kitchen, while she flips through Netflix menus and finally settles on a subtitled police procedural which sounds Scandinavian. He could go for another, but he'll stop there. He's fine. It's enough. He skipped his habitual mortification in the hospital, and here, last night. Not to mention the last five years. He doesn't need to gorge himself while she's sitting there in the next room, because as easy as it is to muster the necessary self-loathing, he doesn't want her to see him stretched to his limit, gasping for breath.

Oh, as if she could possibly have forgotten the past. Like the time she'd had to pick gravel out of his arm because he couldn't reach his own elbow. Or how about when Seth had insisted on inviting him to his fourth birthday, and he couldn't fit into a booth at the ice cream parlor? Even if she wanted to wipe that incident from her memory (and she undoubtedly does), the photographic evidence is tacked to her kid's wall. And who could forget the time he'd made the mistake of forgetting to adjust his clothing before sitting down on her living room couch, and his belly had spilled out of his pants, and he was so big he hadn't been able to reach his own waistband and (oh God) she had reached over and pulled his pants back up over his gut? He certainly never will.

Which is substantially different from getting into her bed... how, exactly? Or climbing the stairs? Or walking downtown? Or what about the massive shits he takes, which no amount of air freshener could possibly hope to cover? His dignity, if he ever had any, is long gone. Look at him. Just *look* at him.

And if more proof is necessary: Last night? Holding her as she fell apart?

Best fucking night of his life.

He inhales another waffle.

"Hey, can I get some more orange juice?"

He knows what she's doing. Trying to distract him. To make *him* feel better, when he should be the one taking care of her.

The television goes silent. "Cyril—"

"Shut the fuck up!" It's half growl, half gasp.

The house is silent. And then, a moment later, the TV goes back on.

He has no shame. He is disgusting. Robin's in the next room, suffering, through no fault of her own. She deserves love and sympathy, or at the very least, a caretaker who is an even slightly functional human being. And still, he does this to himself. He knows what kind of sick fuck that makes him.

But he keeps shoving carbs into his mouth—"eating his feelings," as his mother had so often quipped—until there's no doubt in his mind that one more bite will make him vomit. And he refuses to push himself that far, because he's not going to absolve himself of the consequences of his depredation. No. He deserves to carry this weight in full.

When he is able, he pushes himself away from the counter and lumbers into the dining room, willing her to do them both a favor and just pretend he doesn't exist.

"Hey," she says, hitting pause as he reaches for her laptop. "Sit with me." She pulls her feet back from the end of the couch.

He pulls a chair out from the table but doesn't sit. He's not sure he can. "I'll block your view."

"Nah. Come on. Keep my feet warm."

Her voice is gentle. Because, of course, she knows what he's been doing. The recursive loop of insanity that spins inside his head. He wants to scream at her: yes, she knows. He knows. Does she think he doesn't fucking *know*?

But he does as she asks, pushing the foot of the couch back

slightly so she doesn't have to try to see around his head. He sets the laptop on the end table before backing up to the cushion and letting himself drop with a heavy, breathy grunt. He spreads his knees, attempting to accommodate his bloated belly, but any way he sits it fucking hurts. Good.

"Sexy," she says. Dishing out leftovers of his sarcastic comment the night before. She wedges her feet under his thigh, hits *play,* and takes a sip of orange juice. The glass is half-empty.

———

WHEN SHE'S NOT NAPPING, ROBIN SPENDS MOST OF the next two days binge-watching the procedural, which, it turns out, is Icelandic. He fetches food, water, washcloth, socks, air purifier, phone, laptop, magazines, pillows, blankets, and whatever else she needs to remain parked on the couch. Not without complaint. He is one hundred percent committed to this fiction of not giving a fuck.

And then, on the third day, the sun doesn't rise. This is not a metaphor. He is still asleep when Robin's hand rests on his shoulder, shaking gently. He blinks and asks, "What? Are you okay?"

She stands at the end of the couch, looking from him to the window. The curtains are open. "It's nine A.M." she says, and he snorts because it's quite obviously still pitch black outside. In a quiet, uncertain voice she says, "Check your phone."

"Holy shit." She's right. He gets up and goes to the window to peer out. The world is black, although in the place that ought to be the horizon there is a disc of dull red. "Okay. Um. Get your meds together. I'll pack some shit and pick up the kids—your friends, too, if they want—and we'll go."

But there's nowhere to run. The fires are everywhere, from Los Angeles to Oregon. The smoke column extends eastward as far as Colorado. They could drive for days and still not find fresh air. Robin texts furiously with Greta. The kids are fine. She and her husband are fine. Thanks to Robin's handiwork, their house is essentially airtight and filtered. The kids are already in school.

Robin turns on the television and they eat breakfast sitting on the couch, watching the world burn.

CHAPTER 17

ight returns the next day, though the sun is still no more than a smoldering red circle through the haze. Robin showers without assistance and gets up from the couch once or twice to putter around the room, saying "I just need to move" when he tells her to sit the fuck back down. She's obviously feeling much better, but he resists the temptation to pretend it's all sunshine and rainbows from now on. The fires still burn. There's still chemo to come.

When she muses, "I miss the kids," he looks up from her laptop long enough to say, "No."

She wiggles her toes against his thigh. "No? No what?"

"No, they can't come home yet."

"Who said it's up to you?"

He looks at her again, and then closes the laptop and balances it on the arm of the couch. "If they come home, you'll be running around trying to get them dressed or feed them or whatever. And they'll jump on you and beg you to play or get them a cup of water and you'll do it."

"That's what you're for, big guy."

"But will you let me?"

Her eyes widen, all innocence. "Yes?"

"You're a shit liar."

She clicks the television off. "Cyril, I am *so* bored. I need some snuggles from my little guys."

"Consider a hobby." Everything she enjoys is in some way physical. "Read a book? Knit?"

She sticks out her tongue. "Seriously, though. This is the longest I've ever been away from them since—" She stops.

Since the last time she had cancer. "Yeah. I know."

"I just need to hug them and know they're safe."

"They're safe where they are. Probably safer." The walls of the ramshackle old Victorian are more like semi-permeable membranes, and even with the doors and windows shut the smell of smoke permeates everything. "Honestly, if you wanted to make an argument in favor of joining them at Greta's, I'd be more inclined to agree."

She chews thoughtfully on her upper lip. "What if—what if they just came over for dinner?"

He sighs, elaborately. "Fine."

———

GRETA'S FRONT DOOR OPENS THE INSTANT BEFORE HE can knock—but only a crack. The half of her face he can see hisses "Quiet," before she steps back to let the door swing in.

He steps over the threshold and she shuts the door behind him, twisting the knob carefully so the latch doesn't snap. He sucks in a lungful of crisp, fresh, filtered air.

It's rare to find himself eye-to-eye with a woman, but Greta nearly manages it. She is both muscular and slightly overweight, though the latter would not be so immediately apparent were her narrow leather belt not cinched two notches too tight over pleated old lady jeans. Her expression, as she turns to look him over, is one of bitter distaste, as if she's just bitten into a square of baking chocolate.

"*Don't* wake him," she warns, eyes flicking to the room on his right. "I'll get the kids."

As she leaves, he turns, wincing as the floorboards creak, and finds himself in a cozy formal living room, a wool lap blanket folded neatly over the nearest floral-print rocking chair. A worn leather armchair and a matching ottoman sit next to a gas fireplace, the face of which is eclipsed by a humidifier gamely puffing out a stream of fine mist. Facing the fireplace is a couch, and when Cyril comes around the end of it, he finds the cushions occupied by a sleeping man.

Cyril had met Cooke in person only once prior to becoming his employee, and then only briefly; since that initial consult, their interactions have been conducted exclusively online. He knew the guy was disabled—carbon-fiber elbow crutches propped against the far end of the couch confirm nothing's changed there —but he hadn't remembered him being so small. The sallow face is all angles, and a hand draped over his narrow chest is nothing but translucent skin and bone. His knees, drawn up in a pyramid, are half-covered by a blanket identical to the one on the rocking chair. Cooke looks like a desiccated rat.

Cyril uses a knee to give the arm of the couch a good thump. "Hey. Wake the fuck up."

Cooke's eyebrows arch before his lids snap open, and his eyes dart around in bleary, unseeing confusion before landing on Cyril and snapping into sudden focus. "Oh. I was wondering when you'd show up." Cooke pushes himself up on one elbow, running a hand through short salt-and-pepper hair. "So," he says, in conversational singsong, "how was prison?"

Nervy little fucker. "I need work."

He clears his throat with a laugh. "Your breviloquence is refreshing, as always."

"While you manage to be even more pretentious than I remember." Cooke's confidence in his own intellectual superiority had permeated his company, leaving less confident underlings ripe for exploitation. As the guy hired specifically to find holes that needed plugging, Cyril obviously had an unfair advantage, but he'd been hired to test the code, not the employees. With zero access to anything classified, it had taken him less than a week to find a sucker with clearance willing to let him hop on his laptop for a sec. It wasn't logged in, right? His machine was at the other end of the building and he just needed to hop on and fiddle with one line of code. Five minutes and a rootkit and the USMC server in Afghanistan was his. "Which, honestly, I didn't think was possible."

"Heaven forbid I disappoint." Cooke tucks a hand under one knee and, with a quick, practiced tug, drops one foot and then the other to the floor. Seated upright, he makes a few careful adjustments to the sleeves and collar of his button-down shirt. He looks abruptly younger, more animated—a puppet master well versed in crafting the illusion of life.

"Well?"

He exhales another dry laugh. "Blanchard, it's taken five years to repair the damage you did to my company in a single day. We'll never get another government contract again. You may have my political sympathies, but if you think I can possibly justify hiring—"

"Not you, fucktard. You have contacts. Friends."

Cooke's left eyebrow slides upward. "For the sake of argument, we'll assume I haven't already called in every favor I could in the process of resuscitating my business. What makes you think any of my 'friends' will hire you?"

Is he playing stupid? "You know what I can do." If there were vulnerabilities in a system, no matter how small or Byzantine, he would find them. Work that took most securities firms weeks and a team of personnel, Cyril could accomplish in days. After exposing the most glaring oversights, he'd often be called back months later to test the revised system. One job for the price of two. Hackers didn't even bother trying to infiltrate systems they knew he'd worked on because his fixes were considered so impenetrable.

"Oh, better than anyone." Cooke leans forward, over his knees, and snags a corner of the blanket, which had fallen to the ground. His brow contracts as he pulls it, end over end, into his lap. "But at some point, being good just isn't... good enough."

Cyril senses an awareness in those words—not that Cooke is privy to the dismissive responses Cyril has elicited when reaching out online, but as if he can easily guess. "What the hell does that mean?"

Cooke's cool blue eyes meet Cyril's. Searching. Then he sighs. "Nobody's told you."

"I'm not playing your fucking games, you little—"

"Look up the Castro Valley shooting." Cooke shoos him with a flick of his fingers. "Leave, unless you want my wife to—mm. Too late."

"The fuck?" He has no idea what to make of Cooke's words, but Greta's firm footsteps sound in the hall, and he looks up as she rounds the corner into the living room. Her eyes go first to her husband; she places one large hand on his shoulder, as if reassuring herself that he is there, and whole. Cooke puts his hand on hers, giving it a little squeeze. And then she raises her eyes to Cyril.

He expects fury; a tongue-lashing, at the very least. But the expression on her face is not anger. It's exhaustion. As if she can't summon the emotional energy necessary to chew him out. Instead, they share—something. A look. A fleeting moment of mutual understanding. She, too, knows the special desperation of loving someone who may, in an instant, wink out like a star.

But it's not like that, with Robin. She'll be fine. Of course she will.

Cooke clears his throat, and Greta's face shutters. Whatever it

was, as far as she's concerned, it never happened. She lifts her
other arm, hefting two child-sized backpacks straining at the
zippers, and motions Cyril toward the front door. "They're
playing out back. We'll go through the gate." She shakes her head
when he opens his mouth to protest. "Don't worry, they have
masks. They needed to burn off some energy. Desperately. You—"
This last is directed at her husband, with irritation.

"Will stay put. Yes, yes." He waves her away, as if dismissing a
servant. "Go on."

Her frown says she will deal with her husband's nonsense
later. Outside, Cyril takes the backpacks, waiting as she turns to
shut the door. "What are these for?"

She tugs a rumpled N95 mask out of one pocket and slides it
over her face. "You need to take them."

"The backpacks or the kids?" He doesn't bother with his
mask; cotton's not going to do shit for smoke.

"Both."

"Oh. Great. You just decided this?" He follows her down a
ramp which leads from the porch to the side of the garage—it's
such a natural extension that he doesn't immediately realize it's
sloped. Robin's handiwork. As is the side-yard gate that Greta
pauses to unlatch. He runs a hand over the top of the fence.
"Your husband—"

"He's fine." Her clipped reply bears the edge of something
deep and raw. "Just—tired. How is Robin?"

"Fine," he says, tossing the word back with a sneer. "Just
'tired.'"

If looks could kill, the one she levels at him might have
reduced an entire town to ash.

This is when it occurs to him, belatedly, that the disdain writ
so plainly on her face is not secondary, on Robin's behalf, or even
banal physical revulsion. She hates him because of what he's
done to her—and, more specifically, her husband. Obviously,
there was fallout from hacking Cooke's company, but he, Cyril, is

used to thinking of his exploits in broad, corporate terms. It's always been about challenging the system, for him; nothing personal. Cooke still seems reasonably well-off, but who knew what he'd gone through to preserve his comfortable upper-middle-class lifestyle? Maybe he'd had to sell his condo down south; restructure and downsize his company; lay off employees he considered friends.

This asshole's not going to apologize, but maybe he doesn't have to be a complete tool. "She's in pain," he admits. "But better. I've been trying to keep her off her feet."

"Trying." The word is flat. Heavy with disapproval.

"Well, I tried tying her to the bed, but the screaming got on my nerves."

Greta exhales a sigh of weighty disapproval. She steps through the gate and, leaving it open, heads down a concrete path toward the back yard. Halfway along the length of the garage she stops, so abruptly that Cyril, following, nearly runs into her.

"Uh—"

"His respiratory system is compromised," she announces, without turning around. "My husband. The smoke doesn't help."

"Oh," Cyril says. "Uh. Okay."

She keeps walking.

The kids don't notice their entry into the back yard. They're too busy cavorting in what is apparently this sour shrew's personal fantasy fairy garden. At least, it would be, on a sunny day. The smoke reduces the variegated colors to rusty reds and browns. Seth sits on a swing suspended from an orange tree in the back corner; it's obviously not made for more than swaying, but he's doggedly pumping it as high as it'll go. The lower half of his face is covered with a close-fitting black neoprene mask, with circular discs on either side for replaceable filters. "Wow," Cyril says, "you have some sort of black market contact?"

"A friend at the hospital. I put a couple of N95's in Seth's bag."

"Nice." It takes him another moment to spot Nora. Instead of steps, the ends of the L-shaped back deck curve out and down in a gentle oval, meeting at a wrought iron table in the center of the garden. Artistic, but also accessible; Robin's work again. Nora, masked in pink with hair done up in braids fastened with translucent jewel-toned balls, crouches beside the table, half-under a bush bursting with red flowers. Her fingers manipulate a couple of slender blossoms which are clearly engaged in deep conversation.

"Robin has done a lot for us." Greta bends, plucking a tiny weed from a barrel of begonias or pansies or whatever. "And she can take care of herself. But if you—"

"If I hurt her, I'll be swallowing the business end of your shotgun. Got it, thanks."

She treats him to another long, withering stare. Then she turns, shaking her head in disgust, and pulls a couple of loops of garden hose from the coil hanging on the fence.

"Look, lady—believe it or not, I've spent my entire adult life trying to make her happy."

"Then you've done a piss-poor job, haven't you." This is not a question.

He shrugs. Even if she's right, he owes this woman nothing, least of all explanations.

She points the muzzle of the sprayer at his chest. "Do better."

He snorts. "Why do you think I'm still here?"

She turns the sprayer on the barrels by the fence, not bothering to hide her eye-roll. "You're a man and she's an attractive woman. I know exactly why you're here."

"Hope springs eternal." He delivers the line with snide sarcasm, but it's not a lie. That this woman can even consider his potential for intimacy with Robin buoys him up like a balloon. Or maybe it's that the unfiltered smoke is starting to make him light-headed. Either way, her next comment catches him off guard:

"I can see why she likes you."

"You can?" It's easy to convince himself that Robin is manipulating him; much harder to imagine this woman fibbing on her behalf.

"No."

This is the moment at which Seth notices them, shrieks "Cyril!" and goes hurtling off the end of the swing. He lands with a thump next to Nora, showering her with loamy soil. Her response is an inarticulate screech. Then she looks down at her flowers, tiny trumpet bells now filled with dirt, and bursts into tears.

Greta sighs, cranks the spigot off, and wades into the mess: pulling Seth to his feet, giving him a quick dusting-off, and then dropping to one knee to help Nora restore her fairy circle and clear the dirt from her blossom-dolls.

"Sorry," Seth says, without prompting. He darts an anxious, apologetic glance at Cyril.

"Come here, kid."

Seth gallops over. "Is Mom better?"

"Not all the way. But she misses you. You ready to come home?"

The brilliance of Seth's smile could light up a black hole. He collapses against Cyril, head buried in his stomach, arms stretched wide.

Greta enters the house through one of the sliding doors on the back deck and returns with a paper bag, which Nora loads up with her flower collection, plus the few she plucks as she wanders toward the gate. Eventually, she is persuaded to join Seth in the truck.

After belts are buckled, Cyril shuts the passenger door. Greta follows him around the front of the vehicle. When he reaches for the handle, she places a hand, palm flat, against the door.

"Am I being detained, officer?"

Her face is dead-serious. "You don't have much longer."

"The fuck is that supposed to mean?"

Greta steps back. "She waited five years. If you think you've got another five to get your act together, you're kidding yourself."

"Waited?" He snorts. "Trust me, she hasn't been—"

Greta exhales disgust. But there is a little bit of disappointment, too. "You're even stupider than you look."

Jesus. "Lady, there are so many comebacks to that line, I can't even pick."

CHAPTER 18

Cyril snags an arm from each child as they drop their backpacks and attempt to rush the couch. "Hold it, guys."

Seth stops and redirects his attention; Nora wriggles and screeches, then falls limp in Cyril's grasp.

"There will be no jumping on your mother. Okay? She's still healing. So be"—he edits out the word *fucking*—"careful. Got it?"

Seth nods; Cyril lets him go.

Nora scowls, crossing her arms and giving him a pouty *hmph*. But when she sees Robin embrace her brother, she flails her arms and whines, "I'm careful! Lemme go!"

He walks her to the couch and sits her down next to Robin before releasing her arm. She's exactly like Seth was, when he was little: sincere as sunshine, with the attention span of a gnat.

Robin hugs the girl, tight to her chest, and then leans back, running a hand over the braids sprouting from her daughter's head like so many antennae. "Hey, cutie. Did you have fun at Greta's house? She sure is getting good at doing your hair."

Nora bobs her head to one side and then the other, listening to the clack of the plastic balls at the ends of her braids. "Yep!"

"She dumped her milk all over the table," Seth announces.

"Seth," Robin warns, reaching out to give his arm a gentle squeeze. It's as if she hasn't seen her children in years; she can't stop touching them. "Let her talk."

"That's what I *wanted* to do," Nora says.

Robin frowns. "You spilled your milk on purpose?"

"No you didn't!" Seth interjects, unable to contain himself. "It was totally an accident!"

Nora sticks her chin out, doubling down. "I wanted to see my milk on the floor!"

Seth is outraged. "You're *lying!*"

"Hey." Cyril, halfway to the hall with the kids' bags slung over his arms, drops them beside the dining table and motions to Seth. "Come give me a hand in the kitchen." They may not be jumping on Robin like a trampoline, but she doesn't need them playing verbal ping-pong for her attention.

Seth looks stricken. "But—"

"You'll get your turn. Come on." Cyril raises his eyebrows to indicate he's not fucking around, and the boy dutifully rises and plods after him into the kitchen. "Here." He opens the cabinet above the fridge and hands down a quick-prep box of mac and cheese. "You're gonna need a pot."

"*I'm* making this?" Seth is incredulous.

Cyril pulls salmon and asparagus from the fridge. "Are your fingers broken?"

Seth rolls his eyes—an unusually tweenagey reaction, from him—but squats down affably to hunt through the pots and pans in the cabinet to the left of the stove. "Nora really did spill the milk on accident."

"I believe you." Since he's at the fridge anyway, Cyril does the kid a favor and pulls out the milk and butter, lining them up on the counter next to the stove.

"She always does stuff and then says she meant to. Or she'll just, like, make up stuff that didn't even happen. She lies *all* the time."

"I think your sister's idea of reality is just a little more... malleable than yours."

Seth rises, pot in hand, and squints at him. "What's that?"

"Malleable? It means she's five and she doesn't understand the difference between reality and fiction. Even her own."

"How does that even make sense?"

"I dunno, kid, but I think most kids are like that." Seth had always been an exceptionally literal child—on one of the many occasions he'd tagged along with Tavis to visit this asshole, he'd entertained himself by crawling around the granny unit on all fours, barking. When Cyril had inquired whether the doggy would like a doggy treat, Seth had sat up on his three-year-old haunches, frowned in a way that suggested deep concern for Cyril's mental health, and said, "No. I boy. Just pretend!"

"Were you?" Seth's question pierces the memory like a pin.

"Was I... what? Lost in my own little fantasy world?" If only. That particular talent had taken him years to develop. "I... don't remember. Look, first you gotta fill the pot with water."

Dinner is salmon for Robin, macaroni and cheese for the kids, and both for him, with an asparagus risotto on the side. Nora loves asparagus, it turns out, and Seth insists she's going to have stinky pee ("It's true! Really! I'm not kidding!") until she shrieks and bursts into tears. Robin looks across the table at Cyril, and although she does not say the words, gratitude is written in her eyes.

Then she notices the kids' backpacks, still lying where he tossed them in the corner. "Why—"

"They're staying," Cyril confirms. "Surprise."

Her face brightens. "Seriously? You changed your mind?"

"Not my choice." He shrugs. "Greta had their stuff packed and ready to go."

"Oh?" The delight on her face gives way to concern. "Is everything okay? She didn't text me."

"She said her husband wasn't feeling great because of—"

"Oh, the smoke," Robin finishes, punctuating the air with her fork. "Right. I completely forgot. The last fire season just about killed him." She spears a chunk of salmon.

Seth breaks from the conversation he's having with Nora long enough to interject: "He was coughing a bunch."

"Mm." Robin swallows. "First big project I did was to install vapor barriers in the attic and under the house. Then I replaced the entire ventilation system. It's all HEPA certified. But you still gotta open a door now and then."

More often with kids, Cyril guessed. "Well, the guy looked like death warmed over."

"Oh, he always looks like he's about to croak." She laughs. "He's probably fine. Greta's just paranoid. I mean, justifiably. But COVID's sorta tuned it up to a whole 'nother level. I'll text her." Robin reaches for a back pocket that doesn't exist, since she's still wearing nothing but the shirt that looks, on her, like a dress. "Uh, my phone—"

"Stay put." He shoves back from the table. The kids' plates are fairly well picked over. "Guys, it's time to—"

"No!" Seth and Nora whine in unison.

"Please?" Seth adds. "Just a little longer?"

Cyril had been about to say that it was time to clean up, but he's not one to pass up an opportunity for leverage. He holds up a finger. "One, you guys help me clean up the kitchen. Two, your mom goes back to the couch. Three, you guys brush your teeth and get your pajamas on and I will read you one and only one bedtime story. And *then* it will be bedtime. Deal?"

"Deal!" Seth shouts.

Nora bolts for the hall.

"Hey!" her brother calls. "Where are you going?"

"Pajamas!"

Seth pounds after her. "That's step three! You can't do that first—"

"I wanna!"

Cyril runs a hand over his eyes. "Oh my God."

"Two kids, four times the work." Robin sits forward slightly, brushing crumbs off her shirt. "I've been a parent for almost a decade and I still don't understand how it's possible to love them so much when all they do is make me want to scream."

"They're fucking exhausting." He circles the table and gets a hand under her arm as she stands.

"But everything seems empty when they're gone." She leans against him for a moment, exhaling a tired sigh before letting him help her back to the couch. By the time he gets her settled, wrapped snugly in a blanket, the kids are back, in pajamas now, still arguing. This time it's about which bedtime story he's going to read.

He hands Robin her phone. "I told you guys, your mom—"

"Is going to read the story," Robin interrupts. "Seth, go get the next *Three Investigators* book."

Cyril gives her a disapproving frown as the kids thunder back out of the room. "You said you were gonna let me—"

"You were about to snap." She holds up two fingers, pointing at her own eyes. "I could see it. It's fine; I want to. When I was going through my mom's stuff, I found a box of my favorite books from when I was Seth's age. We started going through them together the last time I was in chemo, so it's kind of our thing. I can read. *You* can wrangle them to bed."

So in the end, he's the one left cleaning the kitchen while Robin snuggles up with the kids on the couch to read from a small hardback book with a once-brightly-colored cover now worn to shades of brown. As it should be. When he's done, he grabs the laptop which seems to have become his by default and parks himself at the kitchen table, close enough to intervene if the kids get out of hand.

It's the first opportunity he's had to access the internet since his brief conversation with Cooke, but he checks his email before Googling the Castro Valley shooting. It can't be anything good. If his email somehow contains a lead on a job, he'll be able to jump on that and avoid the inevitable for just a little longer. But there's nothing.

He glances at Robin. Her face is Madonna-like as she reads, glowing with a perfect balance between serenity and exhaustion. He makes a note of the time so he can shoo the kids off to bed before she wears herself out completely.

Then he clicks over to his incognito browser, hesitates, and finally types in the requisite phrase.

As one of the smaller of the dozens of mass shootings that had occurred while he was in prison, the Castro Valley shooting hadn't even made a blip on his radar. White male walks into a Denny's just after midnight and opens fire. Six dead. Two of the victims are children. But what the hell does that have to do with this asshole?

It takes him a while to find the connection, mostly because the fringe communities who once congregated on unindexed forums have migrated towards more ephemeral channels on Discord and Telegram—but also because news agencies are getting slightly better at not obsessing over the shooter in excruciating existential detail until the next nutcase decides it's his turn to get famous. But he finds it. The guy's manifesto is fifty rambling, handwritten pages long, and in that space, he manages to drop the name Cyril Blanchard about two hundred times.

Once he knows what he's looking for, it's everywhere. Hundred-page 8kun threads that begin with tongue-in-cheek memes mocking the shooter for his bizarre fixation on the comically obese hacker slowly morph into conspiracy-laden analyses connecting Cyril to the shooter and their supposedly shared ideology. Cyril Blanchard is a hero. A true citizen. His data leak exposed the rotting underbelly of a government corrupted by

Jews and Blacks who want to take away the white man's agency and make sure he never gets laid.

Jesus Christ. No wonder this asshole can't find anyone to hire him; if he believed even half the shit that's being attributed to his name, he'd be the bastard stepchild of David Duke and Jeffrey Epstein.

He'd like to shrug it off. What has he to do with the actions of a lunatic wielding a gun? The guy would have snapped regardless; Cyril was simply in the public eye at the wrong time. And it is, obviously, lunacy. Shooting up a restaurant full of people is definitional.

And yet. Lodged beneath every half-coherent declaration of outrage is a seed of truth.

Here was how he'd justified his hacktivism, back before it had cost Tavis his life: he was fringe, yes. Radical, absolutely. But his flagrant, willful disregard of the law provided the essential function of keeping the balance of power in check. His exploits—the lulz—were a bulwark against the slow erosion of digital and intellectual liberty. You want to regulate an idea? Yeah, go ahead and try.

Except that wreaking digital havoc in the name of liberty was necessary only so long as he was in the minority; a trivial faction railing hopelessly against a monolith to compel at least some level of accountability. A man tilting at windmills never plans for victory.

It's not his fault the world turned out to be full of vulnerable idiots who couldn't tell the difference between targeted misinformation and news. Or, worse, didn't care. He'd been part of the effort to inoculate the world against targeted misinformation—and instead he'd become a vector for disease.

Still—that's how these things work, right? In the mind of a lunatic, the kernel of truth gets warped. That didn't make the truth less pure or right.

Oh, but he'd watered those seeds.

He clicks on a link and reads the obituary of a three-year-old victim. And he looks at Seth and Nora. And he wonders how the truth he clung to so fervently could possibly be worth the lives of two innocent children.

Robin glances up, catching his eye as she turns a page, and he looks away, reflexively, because he doesn't want her to see what's on the screen reflected in his face.

He closes the open browser tabs. He visits each forum and systematically deletes each of his newly opened accounts. He uninstalls his IRC client and Tor. Then he closes Robin's laptop.

And he does not open it again.

———

ROBIN IS NO LONGER ON THE COUCH WHEN CYRIL finishes putting Seth and Nora to bed. He ducks into the bathroom, thinking perhaps she's stranded herself in the shower again, and finds the sink littered with medical detritus—latex gloves, plastic wrappers, and a bloody swatch of gauze.

She is in bed. "Did you fucking change your own—"

"I know, I know." She drapes an elbow over her eyes. "I have regrets."

He jerks up the bottom of her (his) shirt, revealing a pair of pale pink underwear.

"Disappointed?"

The dressing is messy, but it looks all right. No swelling or discoloration that he can see, although he obviously didn't get a look under the gauze. He pulls the shirt back down. "What am I even here for, if you're not gonna—"

"I *know*," she moans again.

"Fucking send you back to Kathy Bates," he mutters, covering her with the duvet and using his fingers to tuck it in around her, tightly. "Let *her* take care of you."

"Oh, cut Greta some slack." She lifts the arm off of her face.

"You don't survive a quarter century in the public school system without getting a little rough around the edges."

"Yeah? She should give prison a try." He turns on the bedside lamp and takes her empty water glass, flicking off the overhead light as he exits the room.

After he fills a clean glass, he starts the dishwasher and then the washing machine. She seems to be asleep when he returns, but when he reaches for the chain to turn off the lamp she says, "Took you long enough."

"Well *someone's* gotta keep this household running." That gets him a smile. He sets the new glass of water on her nightstand and turns to leave.

"Wait," she says, like it's the beginning of a sentence that hangs, incomplete.

"Those dishes aren't going to wash themselves," he replies, with chipper, housewifely sarcasm. Like they both don't know he's on his way to toss a frozen pizza into the oven.

She stretches an arm out, patting the empty side of the bed.

Like, what, she's doing him a favor? "Give me a fucking break."

"Binge in the morning, whatever. Can you just—" She sighs. "I just hate sleeping on my back, okay? I haven't been able to get comfortable since that first night. You know, when you—"

"Are you serious?"

She rolls her eyes. "Yes, I am serious."

He is forced to admit she might be telling the truth. "Fine. Gimme a minute, I gotta piss first." While he's at it, he brushes his teeth, too. No particular reason.

She is watching, this time, when he heaves himself onto the mattress. "That's, uh, quite the workout for you," she observes, and then thrusts her arms out.

He ignores her while he stuffs all the pillows within reach behind his back. He sleeps half-sitting on the couch anyway, but he's not interested in enduring another night with the headboard gouging his spine. Once he's situated, he pulls her—gently—onto his chest.

She sighs as she settles in, using a hand to smooth his shirt down over the curve of his side. "Hey," she says. "Thanks for handling the kids. They drive me nuts, but when they're gone I miss them."

"Figured I'd better, after what you said the other night about having babies."

She *tsks* annoyance. "Apparently not having ovaries means dealing with some weird emotional swings. I *definitely* do not want any more kids."

"If you say so."

"It's weird because I never like... seriously identified as female? I mean, I'm a woman, I'm not saying I ever wanted to be something else—it just wasn't that important to me. But now that I'm kind of androgynous, I—"

He clears his throat. "You're, uh, definitely not androgynous."

"You're just saying that because you want to fuck me."

"If I were going to lie to get into your pants, Chica, I'd think of something better than 'Hey, you don't look like a dude.'"

"Point." She hesitates. "I mean, you do, though. Right?"

He lifts an eyebrow. "Lie? Yes."

"No, do you want to—" She lifts a hand. "Never mind. You'll just say something to piss me off. Here." She shifts, letting out a grunt of discomfort, and stretches a hand back toward the night-stand. Her fingers fall a few inches short.

"What do you want?" He puts one hand on her back, holding her securely against him, and uses the other to tap the glass. "Water?"

"No, the—yeah," she says, as he touches the rolled-up maga-zine sticking out of the nightstand drawer. "Read to me."

"From..." He tugs it out, letting the pages flop open on the bed. "Architectural Digest?"

"I just like the sound of your voice. Very... soporific."

"I'm flattered." He tosses the magazine aside and pulls out his phone. He's already got the Project Gutenberg app installed, and he flips through the "classics" menu briefly before landing on *Don Quixote*. Robin wasn't a consistent reader, but about once a year she'd get sucked into something big and heavy and be unable to think of anything else until she'd devoured it whole. In college, *Don Quixote* had struck her as both hilarious and remarkably contemporary in its worldview, and quotes from Cervantes had peppered her emails for months.

He thumbs through the table of contents, the introduction, and the sonnets, then clears his throat and speaks from his lungs: "Somewhere in La Mancha, in a place whose name I do not care to remember—"

Robin laughs. "Ow."

"Are you—"

"I'm fine. I'm fine. Keep going."

He works his way through paragraphs detailing Don Quixote's attire, estate, and favorite books and is starting to regret his choice about halfway through the lunatic's deliberations over the name of his horse—Rocinante—when Robin lets out a long sigh.

He pauses. "Are you—"

Her body jerks slightly. "Uh?"

"Oh." She'd been halfway asleep. "Sorry. I'll keep going."

"Mm. No. That's good." She stretches her neck, yawns loudly, and settles back into him. "You're *so* comfortable," she sighs.

He sets the book aside and clicks off the bedside lamp. "Is that all I am to you? A giant pillow?"

Her arms contract, briefly, squeezing him. "I was imagining a teddy bear, but yeah. Sure."

Something—something about the simple, unguarded affection in her voice when she says this—gets to him. He cannot pretend there is even a shadow of a lie.

It is, quite literally, the first time in this asshole's miserable life that he has ever been forced to consider the possibility, however remote, that his physical presence might be anything other than repulsive. Even this ghost of a thought makes him want to shove her away, roll out of bed, and flee. But he can't. She is holding him.

He squeezes back, ever so slightly, and suddenly finds himself fighting the urge to exert the full force of his strength. She exhales a small *mm* of contentment, and he feels her relax into sleep.

Comfortable.

He sits, carefully holding but not crushing her, awake to the realization that he is being pulled inextricably in. No; it's far later than that. He'd thought the escape hatch was open. Told himself that if this were a trap, he could always turn and leave. But that was a lie. If there was a threshold, he hadn't seen it—but he is inside. The door is locked, and he's lost the key.

"CYRIL, WAKE UP. SHIT. CYRIL."

"What—" He grabs the fist she is drumming against his chest and releases it again when she yelps in pain. "What the—what's wrong?" Mentally, he's already leaping into action: Keys? His pocket. Her insurance card is in her wallet, in her purse, on the kitchen counter. He can get her to the hospital in less than—

"It's raining."

He reaches into the darkness, fumbling for the lamp chain, and finally clicks the light on so he can get a good look at her face. "Come again?"

Her eyes are wide with panic. "It's *raining*."

He listens, and does indeed detect a telltale patter on the window. "Well, that should improve air quality." And hopefully put out the fires. He taps his phone. "It's also two in the morning. Are there any other interesting facts you'd like to—"

"Upstairs, Cyril." Her hands sink into his stomach as she tries to push herself up and away from him. "The roof's on, but everything else is open."

Oh. Now he gets it. "Okay, okay. Chill." He grabs her by the shoulders and props her against the head of the bed. "What do we need to do?"

She massages the palm of the hand he grabbed. "Um, okay, well, first I need to get my tools out of there."

"*I* will get your tools." He pockets his phone and heaves himself to the edge of the bed. "You stay here."

"I put a hinge and a latch on the top of the stairs, so you're gonna have to—"

"I'll figure it out." He rocks forward once more, gets his feet on the floor, and stands. "Go back to sleep. Or at least pretend."

Dutifully, she shuts her eyes.

———

TAVIS WOULD HAVE KNOWN EXACTLY WHAT TO DO IN this situation.

This asshole can't even figure out how to get upstairs. The hatch she's installed over the top of the stairwell is battened down tight, and even using his phone as a flashlight he can't figure out the latch. He starts back down the stairs, realizes there's no way in hell he's about to drag Robin up here, and finally puts a shoulder to the plywood and rips it off its hinges. Good thing both the kids sleep like the dead.

The rain is light but steady, sheeting in through the open window frames as the wind whips around the house. Holding his cell phone out like a dowsing rod, he finds his way into the central room. Tavis would have been able to effectively triage the tools, but since this asshole knows nothing he grabs whatever he can carry from the wettest area, near the big picture window.

It takes four trips to get all the crap—cords, drill, circular saw, boxes of screws and nails and whatever the hell else—down to the bottom of the stairs. Tavis would have made an effort, at least, to put the plywood back in place, but Cyril's knees are killing him and he's slick with rain and sweat. It's not raining hard enough to flood the first floor, and the stairwell climbs through the center of the house—though there's definitely a draft. He leaves it open.

He visits the bathroom to towel off his face and armpits before opening the bedroom door. "You're not even pretending," he says.

Robin looks up from the glowing rectangle of her phone. "Thought I'd better be on hand to call an ambulance if you had a heart attack. Did you get everything?"

"Yeah. I think."

She lets out a long sigh of relief. "Good. Okay, so, there's a big roll of Tyvek down in the barn. You're not gonna be able to get the whole thing up the hill, so get the sheetrock knife out of my tool belt and—"

He lifts a hand to stop her words. "Hold up. What?"

"I need you to seal off the windows." She holds up her phone. "The forecast says it'll be raining for at least two more days."

———

"MOMMY! MOMMY?"

He feels Robin move against him. She groans, expressing his sentiments exactly. Whatever time it is, it's too early. "What do you need, sweetie?" she mumbles.

"I'm *hungry!*"

Cyril blinks and uses a thumb and forefinger to clear the sleep from his eyes. Nora stands in the open doorway of Robin's bedroom, arms akimbo. The toilet flushes and Seth appears behind his sister, tugging his pants up.

"Me too," he says. "Also, don't we have school?"

"Oh *shoot,*" Robin says, although this is clearly a substitution for a different word. Her attempt to push herself up lands an elbow in his ribs.

"Ow! Fu—ow. Will you stop?" He moves her aside. "Stay put. I'll take care of it."

Thoughts which run through his head as the kids watch him rock his bulk to the edge of their mother's bed: Do they think this asshole and their mom are having sex? Does a five-year-old even know what that means? Probably not. But nine—definitely. Or is it assuming too much to imagine Seth would entertain the thought of his mom sleeping with anyone other than his dad? And since they're definitely *not* sleeping together—in the metaphoric sense, if not the literal—why is he even worrying about this? Why does he give a fuck?

Because they're kids, that's why. They don't deserve to be caught in the backwash of adult drama from which they have no escape.

They trail him like ducklings into the kitchen. Neither one seems particularly concerned about the fact that they're already late for their morning meetings on Zoom. "Can we read this?" Seth asks, holding up the book his mother had been reading the previous night. The cover of *The Three Investigators in the Mystery of the Flaming Footprints* features a pulp-style illustration of three teenage boys. The one in the foreground, extinguishing the titular pair of flaming footprints, is a fat kid in a Hawaiian shirt.

"What? Now? You're already late for school. Go find your bag and get your laptop out."

"You smell bad," Nora informs him.

"Okay, look. I can either make breakfast or take a shower right now, kid. Pick one." Although now that he looks down at himself in the daylight, he realizes it's not just dried sweat and rain. The roll of Tyvek had apparently been sitting for some time down in the barn, and his arms are streaked with dirt and sawdust, so thick in places it's crumbling off in brown eggshell flakes. The bedclothes are going to need washing. Robin will have to shower, too, probably. Why hadn't she said anything?

Nora thinks about this as he flips the water on and uses dish soap to give his hands and forearms a good scrub. Finally, she nods. "Breakfast."

"Good choice. Eggs or pancakes?"

"Greta made us French toast."

"Okay, I can do that. Is that what you want?"

"With coconut."

"It was crunchy," Seth chimes in. He has not made a move toward finding his bag. He holds the book open, flipping pages as he reads to himself.

This asshole is too exhausted to deal with this shit. "See, now, neither of those things was a direct answer. Any chance I could get a yes or no?"

Seth shrugs. "Sure." He is already drifting out of the kitchen, reading as he walks.

"Again, not a yes or a no, but I'll take it."

"I want a doughnut," Nora decides.

———

THERE ARE FIVE PILLS ARRANGED IN A LINE ON ROBIN'S bedside table. She places the first on the back of her tongue and downs it with a gulp of water. "What's Nora crying about?"

"I made French toast."

"You're a monster."

"I'm gonna shower. I told the kids not to bother you, but—" He points to the doorknob and then turns the lock. "I'm locking this just in case."

"Wait—don't they have school?"

"Turns out it's Sunday."

CHAPTER 19

Cyril slams Robin's lunch down on her bedside table. The glass of orange juice rattles. "It's a fucking *abomination*."

"What," she says, looking up from the clipboard where she's sketching cabinet designs, "did you think Zoom school was gonna be a walk in the park?"

He'd thought he knew how to use a computer, is what he'd thought. He'd thought he could be fun, and about ten times as useful as "Ms. Greta." Maybe show the kids a few shortcuts or tricks. "Seth is limited to four open tabs—*four*—and Nora's teacher had to restart their interface and spent over an hour trying to walk fifteen kindergarteners through *logging in*."

"Welcome to distance learning."

"Pull them. They'll learn more reading and playing Lego."

"Can't." She flips her pencil over to erase a line. "Healdsburg doesn't have enough room for all of its students. If we leave, their spots get filled and then I have to spend the next six years driving them to Windsor. Just do what you can. And mute yourself if you feel like yelling at a teacher."

"When can Greta take them back?"

Robin looks up, surprised, and laughs. "I told her you were taking over."

"You—*what?*"

"You offered to, didn't you? She's had them for long enough already. And her husband's not exactly what you'd call a kid person. Speaking of which, Greta was gonna drive me to my post-op appointment this afternoon, but he's still not feeling great, so we're all gonna have to get in the car and—"

"This is it," Cyril says. "This is why you got me out of jail."

"You got me. Children are the best revenge." She looks up as Seth appears in the doorway, open laptop balanced in the crook of one arm. "What do you need, sweetie?"

"What?" Seth says, looking from his mother to Cyril and back again. "What does that mean? How is a kid revenge?"

Cyril ruffles his halo of red hair. "Inside joke, kid."

"What's that?"

"What's... what? An inside joke?"

"Yeah."

Nora's footsteps come pounding in. "I want one! Give me one too!"

———

NOBODY BUT ROBIN IS PERMITTED INTO THE OFFICE building adjacent to the hospital. Cyril pulls into the roundabout, turns the truck off, and fetches one of the hospital's blue patient wheelchairs. "I've got it from here," she says, when he parks her at the back of the line to get into the building.

"But—"

"Get back to the kids before someone calls the cops. Take them to the park on Second Street." She waves him off. "It'll be fine."

It is not fine. It is raining. Not a gentle sprinkle, like when they left the house, but a downpour.

He takes the kids to the park anyway, because the other option is to let them destroy the inside of the truck, and within two minutes Seth has stomped a puddle about two inches deeper than the top of the tennis shoes he wore because his feet were too big for his rain boots and Nora has slipped and fallen and is screaming bloody murder, not because she's hurt but because her precious yellow rain jacket is now smeared with mud.

A stranger walking his dachshund stops, tugging his mask down to pop a stick of gum into his mouth as he surveys the scene. When Cyril shoots him a glare, he says, "Still better than fire," tugs his mask back up, and keeps moving.

Cyril gets Seth to sit down long enough to take his shoes off —"socks too, if you're gonna run around some more"—when he feels the phone vibrate in his pocket. But his hands are smeared with rain and mud, so he takes Seth's things back to the truck, using the kid's socks to wipe his hands before tugging his phone out of his pants. There's a one-word text from Robin: *Done!*

"Guys. Hey." He tosses Seth's shoes and socks into the back of the cab, fishes an umbrella out of the center console, and wades back into the soupy grass. "Seth. Nora. Your mom's ready. Come on."

"Awww," Seth whines. He is shirtless now, drenched and panting with exhilaration. "I just—"

"I know. Come on. She's waiting."

Nora has to be dragged to the truck, kicking and screaming.

———

IT'S HALF AN HOUR BACK TO HEALDSBURG ON A CLEAR day, but nothing slows traffic in California like precipitation. After the first two times Robin asks the kids to tone it down—they're screeching at each other in the back of the cab—she flicks on the radio and cranks the volume up. "Sometimes I play this game," she tells Cyril, raising her voice above the cacophony, "where I just keep turning it up every time they get louder. Just to see how long it takes for them to notice."

"Do they?"

She shakes her head. "Not a-once. Although Seth sometimes asks me to turn it down because he can't hear himself talking."

Cyril chuckles. "Poor kid."

"Poor kid? Poor *me!*"

"Well, that goes without—" He cuts himself off as the noise reaches a crescendo. "That goes with—That—Oh my *God,*" he roars, finally, killing the radio with a jab of a thumb. "Will you two just *shut up?*"

The truck goes dead silent.

"Sorry," he growls, glancing at Robin. "Sorry, I just—"

Nora giggles.

"Sorry," Seth says, in an unapologetic singsong.

"Christ," Cyril mutters, under his breath.

Robin bites her upper lip, concealing a smile.

He turns the radio on again, quieter this time. "Seriously, though, these two have got to blow off some steam." They've been trapped inside for days thanks to smoke, and thanks to COVID there's nowhere else to go. But if he takes them back to the house, they're going to tear it down to the foundation. "Isn't there, like, a mall or something around here? But not a mall, obviously, because COVID." There's just no way out.

Robin shrugs. "We could drive into the woods and set them free. Oh—wait!" Robin flaps her hand at the windshield, indicating the exit on the right. "Get off here! Turn under the freeway."

Seth leans forward, poking his head between their two seats. "Yeah!" he exclaims. "Ice skating!"

"The rink's not open, bud. But there's benches and that big overhang to play under. Maybe the museum will be open. We can check."

Cyril follows Robin's directions to a parking lot behind two

Swiss-chalet-inspired buildings encrusted with gingerbread trim. A five-foot tall statue of Snoopy stands in the manicured garden patio out front. "Well this is adorable," he says.

"You should see inside. This is Charles Schulz's place—the guy who did the Peanuts comic strip? He lived in the area. And he really liked ice skating, apparently, so here we are." She laughs as Cyril parks next to one of only two other cars in the lot: a canary yellow Chevrolet pickup with a black zigzag stripe down the side. "Looks like someone from the family's here, anyway."

The rain has tapered to a light drizzle. Cyril exits the cab, and since there seems to be no imminent danger of anybody getting run over, he pops the driver's seat forward to let the kids out before going around to help Robin. When she's standing, hand on the open door, he stoops to pick her up.

"What are you—no." She smacks his hand away. "I can walk."

Seth appears in the passenger seat. "Shoes?"

Robin looks down at his bare feet and laughs. "There you go. Carry him. Where's—oh." Nora is already streaking across the lot towards the garden in front of the building. "I've got her."

"Be care—*oof!*" Cyril stumbles, catching himself against the side of the truck as Seth leaps from the cab onto his back. He makes a grab for the kid over one shoulder, but Seth, having not quite made it to Cyril's neck, slides down to the ground. "Okay," Cyril growls, "shall we try that again?"

The patio outside the entrance to Snoopy's Home Ice is composed of smooth, multicolored pebbles. Nora, having abandoned her yellow boots by the Snoopy statue, is now sliding her bare feet up and down the walk, protected from the drizzle by a broad overhang. Cyril lets Seth down and bends to pick up the boots before joining Robin, sitting on a bench by the entrance. She slides over to make room for him. Whether by chance or some unseen observer, Peanuts movie music tinkles from speakers overhead.

They sit there, blessedly silent, watching the kids cavort for a good ten minutes before he finally asks what he must: "How was, uh, the appointment?"

"Doc said everything looks good." She glances up at him. "Or do you mean when's the chemo? Still a couple weeks out. She wants me healed up before they start injecting poison." She sighs. "Again."

"So—how's this go? You gonna go bald and puke a bunch?"

Robin snorts. "Sounds simple, when you put it like that. But yeah."

Silence again. Then the clack of the release bar on a door. He and Robin look toward the entrance as a slender young woman in a sequined skating leotard steps out of the building. Her thick brown hair is slicked back into a tight ponytail, long enough that it falls to her elbows when she reaches back and runs it through one hand.

"A *princess!*" Nora gasps.

The girl breaks into a dimpled grin. "Thank you, sweetie," she says, hurriedly pulling a mask out of her canvas shoulder bag and slipping it on as Nora runs up to greet her. She looks from Nora to Robin, obviously flattered but confused. "You know the rink is closed, right?"

Robin offers a brief wave of greeting. "Just trying to find somewhere the kids can let off steam. They've been cooped up in the house too long, and... we have a lot of happy memories here."

"Me too." The girl looks down as Nora slips a hand into hers, and then lifts her eyes to acknowledge Seth, hanging back a bit less enthusiastically. "Do you two like to skate?"

"Yes!" Nora declares.

Seth rolls his eyes. "She just likes to be pushed around in a chair."

The girl laughs. "Well, who wouldn't?" She chats with the kids for another minute, bending down to open her bag and show Nora her skates before checking her phone. "I'm sorry, I have to get going, but hold on one second." She stands, shouldering her bag, and raps a knuckle on the glass door before opening it and leaning in to talk to someone. "You're cleared!" she announces, tossing the kids a wave as she dashes off toward the parking lot. "Enjoy!"

Cyril looks at Robin, who shrugs. Before either of them can act, the door opens again. "I was told there were two little ice skaters out here!" says a petite woman with head of carefully coiffed burgundy curls. A sky-blue mask printed with flock of yellow Woodstocks covers most of her face, though her reedy voice and lined eyes say she's at least seventy. She waves them toward the open door with one gnarled hand. "Come on in. The rink's all yours."

"I—what?" Robin looks at Cyril, and then at the woman again. "I thought you were closed—"

"For public skate, yes. But we still accept private bookings so our athletes can practice. Sarah just got called back in to work, so the next two hours are free."

Robin uses Cyril's shoulder to help herself to her feet. "I don't —I honestly don't even know what to say."

"Yes, I hope!"

The kids don't need a second invitation. They scoot past the little woman, who steps out onto the patio and holds the door wide for Robin and Cyril. Inside the lobby, the kids are already measuring their bare feet against outlines on a big brown mat to find their correct skate size.

"Look," Cyril mutters, watching the woman vanish into a hallway and reappear behind the ice skate counter with a box of multicolored socks, "There's no fucking way I'm getting out there and—"

Robin interrupts him with a snort. "No," she says, "you are not."

"And I'm not letting you—"

"Relax, big guy." She gestures towards the double doors

leading into the rink. "They have chairs. You know, for kids who can't skate? All Nora wants is to be pushed around."

"Wow, lazy."

"You should talk."

The kids approach the high counter, where the little woman asks them their sizes—Twelve? Are you sure? Better check twice! —and produces a pair of worn brown skates for each of them. "I know these don't look as pretty, but I promise they fit better when they're broken in."

Robin steps up to the counter to sign as the woman holds out a pen and two waivers. "How much do I—"

"Oh! Honey, no. No, no. Please. My treat." The woman waves a hand in front of her face, like she's swatting a fly, and then pops back around the hallway and into the lobby. "You said you've been here before?" She pauses for Robin's nod. "You know where to go, then. I need to take care of some things upstairs, but when you're done just put your skates here and let yourselves out. My next booking is at"—she checks her wristwatch—"three o'clock. So let's say two forty-five?"

Robin finally seems to start back to life, reaching out a hand as the woman turns to go. "Thank you. Really. I just—Thank you so much. If you knew what these kids have been through—"

Above the mask, the woman's eyes crinkle. "I know," she says, softly. "We've all been through the wringer these past few years. Try and steal a little joy."

"Are you gonna cry?" Cyril asks, when the woman has gone.

Robin smacks his arm with the back of her hand. "Shut up."

They follow the kids through a set of heavy wooden doors into the rink. "Oh my God," he sighs, as the kids take off running. It's like walking into a meat locker. Which is to say, amazing.

Robin cocks an eyebrow.

"I could live here." He could *sleep* here.

The kids rush back, having realized that the skates need to be on their feet before they can go on the ice. Robin directs them around the curve of the rink to a staging area filled with low benches and lockers. "You're gonna have to do the skates," she tells him.

"Yeah. Okay." Cyril manages to lower himself onto a bench which is no more than twelve inches off the floor and pulls Nora's foot onto his knee.

"Tight around the ankles," Robin says. "Tighter than you think. Or she'll be wobbling all over the place."

"Yeah. I know. I haven't—" He pulls the waxed laces taut, passes the long ends twice around her ankle, and ties a double knot. "—Always been this fat."

"Yeah, but you've never *not* been a killjoy, so."

He swaps Nora's left foot for her right, laces her up, and then motions for Seth to scoot into her place. Robin stands, arms folded over her chest, watching until he pats Seth's foot and says, "Go get 'em, kid."

"Please," Robin adds, "don't get too crazy with your sister, okay? No spinning."

"Aw," Seth moans. "Just *some* spinning? I'll be careful."

Robin sighs. "A *little* spinning. But don't think I won't pull you off the ice if I have to. Here. Let me have your masks." She tucks the kids' masks into the pocket of her hoodie, sighing as she watches them clomp off toward the rink. "We're gonna have to pull him off the ice. It's inevitable. He just gets carried away and forgets everything else." She looks down at Cyril, still seated on the bench. "You stuck?"

"Maybe I'll just hang out here until it's time to go."

She laughs and holds out a hand, but he shakes his head. Leaning forward, he gets a grip on the nearest bank of lockers and uses the leverage to get himself up. He yanks his shirt down, hikes his pants up, and then follows her to the plexiglass half-wall bordering the ice. Robin leans on the rail, and they watch Seth flounder until he gets Nora's chair up to speed. Inertia's a bitch.

Cyril nods at the kids. "They gonna be warm enough out there?"

"Even if we'd brought their jackets in, they'd be off in ten minutes. Tav's kids run hot." She shifts, wincing, and puts a hand to her stomach. "I need to sit down before I pop a stitch."

He nods to the café adjacent to the lobby. Its windows look out over one end of the rink, and in the back there's a massive open fireplace with a few small flames licking at a single log. "There?"

She gives him an appraising look, as if suspicious of an offer so obviously intended only for her benefit. "Maybe later." She loops a hand through his arm and nods to the auditorium seating on the other side of the rink. "How about there?"

"Yeah. Sure." He could argue about the distance, but the longer they stand here the less time she spends sitting down. He walks her around the edge of the rink, past the windowed-off café. Robin takes it slow, but she seems otherwise all right.

Three steps up separate the rink from the bleachers. "You're not going to fit," she realizes, looking at the antiquated theatre seats, each with fixed armrests.

"No, but you will." Which is the point.

A little further down the side of the rink, there's a wooden bench situated at ground level next to a square marked out for wheelchairs. "Over there," she says.

"Or we could go back to the café."

"So overprotective!" She sits on one end of the bench—carefully—and pats the empty space beside her. "I'll admit I was not expecting that."

He sits. "Yeah, well, if you didn't want me to be overprotective maybe don't get your guts cut open."

"I'll try to remember that next time I get cancer."

"Don't—" He cuts himself off.

"Don't what? Say *cancer*?" She laughs and lifts her chin to shout: "Cancer, cancer, cancer!" The call echoes back and forth across the ice, rendered almost instantly incomprehensible. She shrugs. "It's like Tav's name. I used to have a hard time saying it, after he was gone, but I couldn't avoid it, and after a while—well, you hear it often enough, and it kind of loses its power." Seth staggers past, skates clacking loudly as he pushes his sister across the ice, and Robin lifts a hand to wave. Seth yells, but his words, too, fold back upon themselves. Robin gives him two thumbs up and nods. "At some point, you realize none of the words matter. We're all just living on borrowed time."

A loud click sounds overhead, and then a disembodied voice: "Would my skaters like some music?"

They look up, instinctively, and spot the little woman in an office window overlooking the rink from the second floor. She waves before reaching toward a desk filled with electronic equipment. The opening chords of the Peanuts Theme, rendered slightly scratchy by the sound system, blare out over the rink.

Robin waves back, calling "Thank you!" though she must know she can't be heard. A shudder rattles down her spine as she lowers her arm.

"Café," he says. "Now."

Before he can get to his feet, she grabs his hand, scoots in close, and pulls his arm around her shoulders like a heavy shawl. "There."

He sighs. "Chica, I don't—"

"Yeah. I know. Hush."

They watch the kids go around and around, apparently unaware that their solo skating status means they can crisscross the ice however they like. When the Peanuts Theme is finished playing, the loudspeakers continue to pipe in music from what he assumes, based on the lyrics and chipper voices, are winter-themed kids' movies. After several rounds, Seth manages to pull Nora's chair to a stop on the other side of the plexiglass divider and yells something they figure out, after several repetitions and some hand gestures, is "Take a picture!"

Robin fishes her phone from her purse, taps on it, and hands it to Cyril.

Seth and Nora strike goofy poses and demonstrate some fancy "moves" that can in no way be captured by a static image. Finally, he hands the phone back to Robin and waves them on.

Robin flicks through the photos. He does not hear but feels her chuckle at a couple of the goofy poses. He has gone back to watching the kids, idly, when he realizes Robin is holding the phone out at arm's length. "Smile!"

"Wh—" The flash blinds him. "Jesus Christ."

She inspects the photo. "Wow, I look like shit."

"*That's* your takeaway? You might have some kind of body dysmorphia."

"Yeah, and you would know." Her laugh ends in a sigh. "A month from now I'll only wish I felt this good." She opens her cloud-based photo storage, using the dates on the sidebar to scroll back a couple of years. "Here." She taps an image to enlarge it, then hands him the phone. "I think that's the only photo I have of me from—uh, last time."

Even as short as her hair is now, Robin's baldness is a shock. "Jesus," he mutters. The smile she is forcing, in the photo, is made terrible by the pain in her eyes. "You're a skeleton." She's in bed; not a hospital bed, but not one he recognizes, so probably a room in Greta's house. The grandmotherly quilt on the bed supports this hypothesis. The kids, three years younger, sit on either side of their mother, clutching her as if she might slip away at any—"Fuck," he whispers, pushing the phone back into her hand. "I can't even fucking look at that."

"Well, I hate to tell you this, but in a couple weeks—"

"That's—different." Mainly because it hasn't happened yet, so he can still pretend it won't.

"It's gonna be pretty bad, Cyril. But you know, the worst part? Was being alone."

"You had Greta, didn't you?"

"She's not—" Robin sighs. "It was so soon after mom died, and, yeah, Greta's wonderful. But she's not—well, she's just not my mom. You know? Mostly she was there for the kids. She has a huge heart for kids. And that was what I needed. To know they were safe and loved. But there was so much time where I was just... alone. There's only so many books you can read."

He's silent. He thinks of the million-and-one letters he composed and then discarded in his head, these past five years. The countless ways he's tried and failed to say he's sorry, to explain, to—no. He never put pen to paper because the words to make it right did not exist. But she—if only she'd *said* something. It didn't have to be a letter. She could have called. He'd had all the goddamn time in the world. If only he'd *known*.

"I know what you're thinking." She tucks the phone back into her purse. When she pulls her hand out again, she's holding a piece of paper folded into four quarters. It's worn, softened by the friction of the fabric inside the inner pocket of her purse. A flick of her wrist and it falls limply open.

He knows which photo this is even before she holds it up. Seth, eating ice cream. Sitting next to him. The two of them grinning like idiots.

"Really?" he says. "A million photos of Seth, and you choose *that* one?"

She doesn't answer. She doesn't have to.

A million photos of Seth. Only one of him.

"When you get chemo," she says, quietly, "each chair has a clipboard next to it, for your chart and notes or whatever. Every time I sat down to have that poison pumped into my veins, I clipped this picture to the board."

"Not gonna lie, Chica—that's kind of weird."

"At first, I just—" She lifts a clenched fist. "I would look at you and just *hate* you. For everything you took from me. From us. The lies you told. All the things you didn't say. And every time I started to feel like life was unbearable, I'd think, at least you had it worse. At least you were locked away, rotting in a cell." She twists her neck to look up at him, quirking a wry smile. "I imagined that spark of hope you must feel, no matter how you tried not to, every time they called your name for mail. I'd think about all the things I *could* write, if I wanted to. The things you must be hoping to hear from me. And then the disappointment—the rage —you would feel when it turned out to be just some paperwork from your lawyer. Or whatever. It felt good to think that, even doing absolutely nothing, I had that power over you." She lifts her eyebrows. "Did it work?"

He wants to hurt her. Call her terrible names. But there is nothing she has done which he has not deserved. He flexes a hand, carefully. "Yes."

"Good." She settles back into him. "There were a couple of weeks when I honestly wasn't sure I'd make it. I couldn't even fathom leaving the kids—couldn't even go there in my mind. But I fantasized about how it would be when you got out and realized I was gone. That I'd suffered and died alone, and that it was all your fault. I consoled myself with the knowledge that you'd never forgive yourself."

"That... is some fucked up kind of revenge."

"Isn't it?" Her fingers fold the photo and open it again with practiced familiarity. "Thing is, though, Seth—he's in this picture, too. God, look at him. I thought he was so big, then, and he was so small." The warmth in her voice is heavy and full. "I'd think about, like, folding it so I couldn't see him. So I could focus on how much I hated you. But I couldn't crop out my son. I mean, look at that happy little smile." In her hands, the photo folds and is unfolded again. "After a while, it got to be where it almost felt like the two of you were keeping me company. The nurses made a joke of it—they'd say, hi Robin, how are your boys today? And we'd laugh. And after a while, I stopped burning with rage every time someone said your name. It just... lost its power."

Like Tavis. And cancer. Live with a demon long enough, no matter how monstrous, and it becomes familiar as an old friend.

"And then—I didn't want to, but I couldn't help it—then I'd remember something you wrote. Something I thought Tavis wrote. And sometimes that thing was—" She makes a quick swipe at her eyes. Clears her throat. "Literally all that kept me going that day."

"You... do what you need to survive."

"That's what Greta's husband always says." She tucks the photo away. "At some point, I started to wonder if maybe part of what made me hate you so much was because I actually—"

And just like that, he can no longer bear her touch. He pulls away.

"Cyril, I—oh, shoot." Her attention flicks back to the ice. "Nora's trying to get off. Can you—"

"I got it," he growls, and stalks off around the rink. He wants to go bash his head against a brick wall until the memory of the words she nearly said is gone. Undone. He needs to leave. Now. But where is he going to go? He can't leave them here. Fuck this. Fuck cancer, fuck everything.

Nora shrieks.

So he goes to help the little girl.

———

"SHE HAD TO PEE?" ROBIN'S HANDS ARE CUPPED around a mug of hot cocoa.

"Yeah." He pulls out a chair and joins her at the little café table overlooking the rink. It's as far from the fireplace as it's possible to be, and it's still eighty-plus degrees. "She was fine going into the restroom by herself, just needed... reassurance, I guess?"

"Jean—I think she said that's her name—came down to chat for a minute." Robin lifts a napkin off a paper plate sitting in front of her and pushes two giant pretzels across the table. "She said these were all they had that didn't need cooking. Thought I was hungry but I'm not." She lifts the mug, pausing before taking a sip. "Okay, actually, I grabbed them both for you."

"Uh... thanks."

Out on the rink, the overhead lights dim, and then begin flashing in time with the music—red, blue, red, blue. An obviously pre-recorded voice comes on over the voice to announce that "It's tiiiiiime for the hooookey pokey!" Seth and Nora look up, confused.

"We had Seth's birthday here last year." Robin nods to the back of the café. "There's a party room back there."

He follows the tilt of her head, taking in the stained-glass windows depicting Snoopy characters, and grunts an acknowledgment. Suddenly, the pretzels are gone.

She gives him a searching look. "Had enough?"

She has no idea. There is not enough food in the world. "Why —why do you—" Fuck. He crumples the paper plate in one hand. He is sweating.

This asshole can't even ask the question. He can't even let himself *think* the question. Why, if she loves him—if she *thinks* she loves him, which she doesn't, because fuck, no, she cannot, then why—why would she just sit here and let him stuff his—

She touches his hand.

He jerks away. "Look, just—stop. Fucking—stop. Okay? I don't know what you think is going to happen here, but I am not going to—"

"Change. I got it. You keep telling me that."

"And you keep saying you believe me, but here we fucking are."

She licks her lips, and then presses them together. "I'd like to say a lot more."

"What's stopping you?"

She doesn't answer immediately, and for a moment he thinks the conversation is over. Then she draws in a breath. "The fact that any time I even come close to telling you how I feel, you punish yourself."

"You mean I stuff my fat fucking face until—"

"Yeah."

"So. You do care about—" He lifts his arms. "This."

"Of course I care." She uncrosses her legs and then crosses them again in the opposite direction. Takes a sip of cocoa. Looks out at the kids on the ice. "It's a nice little catch 22 you've set up," she says, almost to herself. "If I don't care about your size, it's proof I don't care about your health, ergo I'm just *pretending* to care about you. If I do care about your size, obviously I'm a superficial bitch who doesn't *really* care about *you*." Her eyes flicker toward him. She sets down the mug. "It's not the bingeing that bothers me, Cyril. I mean, you're not ever going to be skinny. Or, you know, *less* morbidly obese. I can live with that. What I'm having a hard time dealing with is knowing that showing even the slightest bit of human kindness causes you pain. That's—not something I know how to fix."

He is silent. Motionless. Stone. "You can't."

"I know." She offers him a slightly pained smile. "Shit-talking is fun, Cyril. But I'd like to say I love you now and then."

CHAPTER 20

He doesn't know why the fuck she's still wasting her time on him. Can she not see that this asshole is irredeemable? Yet here she is, continuing to make space for him in her life and in her mind. She can't change him. She knows that. All she's doing is giving this parasite the time and opportunity to infect her. What is she hoping for, here? A happy ending?

Fool.

He goes back to sleeping on the couch. She doesn't try to wheedle him back into her bed. Doesn't say a thing, actually, and now he knows it's because she knows her words will only make it worse, and she cares enough not to do him that much harm. Which only makes it worse.

Because apparently stuffing food in his face isn't masochistic enough, he Googles the Castro Valley shooting on his phone and forces himself to watch a press conference featuring the dead toddler's grief-stricken mother. Just so he's clear on what a piece of shit he is.

"Cyril," she says, once, when the kids are asleep.

"Don't," he snarls. It is not the same night he returned to the couch, though it might as well have been. He is still standing in front of the open fridge. "Just—don't."

He realizes it is not Robin only when the boy repeats his name. The way Seth says it, small and drawn out, sounds like the mispronounced approximation the boy had used as a toddler: "Cereal?"

Cyril closes his eyes, briefly, and then carefully places the butter dish back into the fridge, as if Seth has caught him in the process of putting it away. As if the loaf of bread he'd baked that day weren't sitting on the cutting board next to two thick, freshly cut slices. Not to mention the chimichanga wrappers in the trash. "What's up, kid?"

Seth yawns and mashes a fist into one eye. "I'm hungry."

The surge of panic that wells up inside this asshole manifests only as a dull stare. Naturally the kid is hungry; he'd only eaten about three bites of chicken cacciatore for dinner, even after his mother had warned there would be nothing more until morning. He's not here because he's caught on to what Cyril does at night, or because Cyril's presence has somehow infected the kid with his vices. You don't catch fucked-up like the flu.

Cyril turns, sighing, and pulls the butter back out of the fridge. He spreads it generously on both slices and hands one down to Seth. "Don't tell your mom."

Seth grins. "I love bread." The words are muffled by a mouthful of crumbs.

"Shocking." Cyril gets the kid a glass of milk, too, but he doesn't trust him to hold it in one hand without spilling, so he takes it to the table. If anything, the kid is too skinny, but he can't help issuing a word of warning. "Don't make this a habit, okay, kid? You don't wanna be like me."

"In jail?"

"No, like—" Seth is probably the only person in the universe who has never once judged him by his size. The kid's heart is pure, and even this asshole isn't asshole enough to shit on that. "Forget it."

The boy crashes into his chair, showering the seat with crumbs, and reorients himself long enough to take a sip of milk and swallow. "Mom says you eat your feelings."

Well, fuck. "That's one way to put it." Robin, apparently, had not been so delusional as to think a nine-year-old wouldn't notice they never actually ate the leftovers they packed into the fridge each night. This asshole pours himself a glass of milk and saws off another slice of bread before returning to the table and seating himself across from Seth. He'd hoped the boy would be finished eating by now, but he's taking slow, mouse-sized bites. Any excuse not to go back to bed.

"It's okay to have feelings," Seth says.

Cyril snorts. "Not when you have feelings like mine."

Seth blinks, and seems to take a moment to digest this. Then he nods. "I have bad feelings sometimes, too. That's why Mom makes me do martial arts."

"Kid, what could you *possibly* have to feel bad about?" This asshole regrets the question the instant it leaves his mouth— because, really, what *doesn't* this kid have on his plate? He hasn't even hit double digits and he's already had to survive his dad's death and his mom's cancer, not to mention a global pandemic and the threat of annual wildfires.

Seth shifts in his chair and looks elsewhere: his milk, the bread, his finger worrying a crack on the edge of the tabletop. "People," he admits at last, quietly. "I get scared about people... leaving."

So long ago it's scarcely worth remembering, Tavis Matheson's mother ran away with Cyril's old man. The day it happened —everyone knew—Tavis had looked at him across the third-grade classroom, and he had quickly looked away. When Seth looks at him now, it is with that same mixture of grief and anger and fear.

Dying, is what he doesn't have to say. His dad is dead, and he's scared his mom is dying, too.

"Come here." Cyril lifts his arm, and in a heartbeat, Seth is around the table, burying his head in this asshole's shoulder. He hugs the boy, too tight. "You shouldn't have to deal with any of this. I'm sorry. It's shit."

Seth empties his feelings onto Cyril's shirt, simple as that, and when he is done, he wipes his face on a kitchen towel, drinks the last of his milk, and allows Cyril to shepherd him back to bed.

After carefully closing the kids' bedroom door—the last thing he needs is Nora waking up—Cyril stands in the hall, staring at the string of portraits illuminated dimly by the nightlight in the bathroom. In the half-light, Seth's portrait could just as easily have been his father, at the same age. They are so alike.

At nine, Tavis had already been charming and athletic and possessed of a natural talent for anything he touched. He would not naturally have gravitated toward the sedentary, antisocial loner who spent recesses on a bench by himself, but that cataclysmic intersection of loss had lured him into Cyril's orbit.

"Hey," Tavis said, in the hall after school.

"Leave me alone," this asshole had replied, emphasizing the point with a shove. That was all he wanted, ever. To be left alone.

Nevertheless, they both ate school lunches, and there were not so many children that it was possible to ignore the fact that Tavis had begun to devour everything, including the disgusting slop not even the fat kid would touch. He pocketed soft red apples from the "share" bowl when he hoped nobody was looking.

"Goodness! You must be hitting a growth spurt," one of the lunch ladies joked. Cyril was not that stupid.

Once a week, he stayed late for science club. When he left, Tavis was often still out on the playground, kicking rocks or hanging upside down from the bars. Alone. Since apparently nobody else was going to do anything, Cyril finally walked over to the fence and said, "You can have dinner at my house."

Tavis let himself drop into the bark chips and dusted his knees. "Your mom won't mind?"

Cyril's mother had spent the better part of his short life pestering him to invite friends over, an annoyance which had gotten exponentially worse since his dad hit the road. She cried. He didn't exactly want to give her the satisfaction, but he also had an idea that bringing someone home would help take the focus off him.

It worked. She fawned over Tavis like a puppy, tousling his copper-penny hair and offering him firsts and then seconds of all her baked goods and asking him about his favorite subjects in school and laughing with delight as he described the antics which had earned him the scrapes on his elbows and knees and oh, Cyril, why don't *you* ever try things like that?

Even the revelation that Tavis was the son of the woman who had stolen her husband hadn't dulled his shine; in fact, she seemed to feel it was something they had in common. The second time Tavis came for dinner, she had reminisced about falling in love with Cyril's father, cried, and then pulled out her wedding album.

It was humiliating. But what was Tavis going to do? Blab? That Cyril's mother was a fat, hysterical mess was obvious to anyone with eyes. If Tavis wanted home-cooked meals—and for all her faults, Cyril's mother was an excellent cook—he'd keep his mouth shut.

The strange thing was that Tavis actually seemed to enjoy the attention. Whatever questions Cyril's mother posed, no matter how personal, he answered without hesitation, flushing a rosy red and grinning ear to ear as he happily disgorged his soul. Maybe if you hadn't spent your whole life being peppered with stupid questions, it was kind of nice. Or maybe Tavis didn't know that the confessions he made would be collected and sharpened into barbs that would, inevitably, be flung in his face next time she worked herself into a frenzy of fury and despair. Surely he could not be that naïve.

Whatever. What mattered was that it gave Cyril a chance to slip away into his room and play on his computer. Alone.

Until Tavis came in. He just stood there for a while, looking over Cyril's shoulder. But eventually he said, "Can I try?" and Cyril couldn't think of a reason to tell him no. As it turned out, Tavis barely even knew how to use a computer, so Cyril had to show him how to use the arrow keys and remind him over and over that Ctrl was fire, Alt was strafe, and space bar was use item. He got himself killed immediately, so Cyril had to restart the game, and then give him strategy tips in addition to constant keyboard reminders, and—it wasn't so bad. Actually, it was kind of fun.

By the time Cyril's mother knocked on the open door to say, "It's getting dark, boys," Tavis had gotten the hang of the game, leaning forward so his nose nearly touched the screen.

"Can I spend the night?" he asked, without even looking up.

The sheer audacity of the request—not even discussed with Cyril—was breathtaking. But Tavis hadn't seemed shy or self-conscious at all. Might as well try, his posture suggested; the worst she could do was say no.

Cyril's mother blushed. "Of course! We'd love to have you. I mean, if it's okay with your father. I'll give him a ring."

Tavis shrugged. "He won't care."

She went into the kitchen and came back a few minutes later, looking puzzled. "He wasn't there, but your sister said she'd let him know. I guess he can always come and pick you up." She grinned, clasping her hands together in exaggerated delight. "Oh, the two of you look so cute. Do you want some pajamas? You and Cyril are almost exactly the same size. You could be brothers!"

Same height, maybe, but Cyril outweighed him by at least thirty pounds. As Tavis hunched forward to cinch the waist of the oversized Garfield-print flannel pants, his shirt lifted to reveal the pale skin of his lower back.

"Wow," said Cyril, ogling the stripe of purple across his knobby spine. "What happened?"

Tavis glanced up long enough to see where Cyril was looking. "Got whupped."

"For what?" Cyril's dad hadn't been around much, even before he left, but at least he'd never done *that*. Cyril imagined Tavis must have done something nigh unforgivable.

"I dunno." He shrugged. "Talking back?"

Sometimes, Tavis stayed for days. Other times, he seemed to vanish for weeks at a stretch. The bottom drawer of Cyril's dresser was reserved for his clothing, composed of Cyril's castoffs and the odd jacket or pair of sneakers his mother picked up at a garage sale. Tavis witnessed more than one of her meltdowns, in which she railed at Cyril and his god-damn no-good father for having betrayed her and let her down. Sometimes, when her rage had collapsed into helpless sobs, Tavis crept softly into the living room to hold her hand.

Time passed. They went to junior high, and then high school. Though they operated within increasingly disparate spheres, Tavis and Cyril always made time to grab a couple of controllers and play a game. Having been royally fucked by their respective families, it was understood—never directly discussed—that they had formed a bond of their own.

When Cyril's mother died, Tavis was still there, holding her hand.

————

THE NEXT MORNING, COMING OUT OF THE BATHROOM, Robin stops him with a look of stern appraisal. "I don't know what the two of you talked about last night—"

"He had some worries. It's fine."

She opens the hall closet and yanks out a fresh towel. "I'll take your word for it," she says, squeezing past him into the bathroom. "But just so you know, if you mess this up today? I will gut you."

"Wait, what's today?" he asks, just to see the look on her face. With the increase in Robin's mobility and the decrease of the local COVID rate, plans for D&D had moved from Zoom to out-of-doors; specifically, the barn at the bottom of Robin's property. Her threats are unnecessary—as much as he may disappoint her, he will not fail the kids.

"Wow," she says, when she realizes he's joking. "I continue to be baffled that you didn't get yourself killed in prison."

Since acquiring the first Dungeon Master manual, he'd continued to place orders for items as they came to mind, accumulating a small collection dice, plastic figures, maps, and reference books. Now he retrieves his stash—kept in a plastic grocery bag in a spare cupboard in the kitchen—and heads down to the barn. Seth is so excited he runs down the hill and then up again, literally doing a lap around the outside of the house. How he can do this with a mask on and not pass out is a mystery.

Robin has already spent time describing the barn setup to the other parents on the chain of emails that has now moved to a never-ending group text, so all Cyril has to do is follow her outline: drag the barn doors out as far as they'll go, move her table saw out of the way, set up a grid of four sawhorses, and then cover them with a sheet of plywood and a canvas drop cloth. Seating hadn't come up for discussion, but he finds a couple of folding chairs tucked back behind the hand truck. He flags Seth down and sends him up to the house for more.

There are five kids in addition to Seth and Nora; as they arrive, Robin meets the parents on the deck outside the back door, presumably to assure them that at least one non-criminal adult will be present for the event, and possibly to keep as much distance between them and him as possible.

This asshole had imagined three hours would be more than enough time for the activity, and it is—for him. Thanks to COVID and wildfires, the kids haven't seen each other or been outside in an eternity, and they spend a good thirty minutes just running around the property screaming. Robin, apparently having sussed out at least one of Cyril's hiding spots, brings down a package of Oreos and some juice boxes, along with paper plates, wet wipes, and a pair of latex gloves with which to hand them out. She stays to make sure everyone is six feet apart before they remove their masks to eat.

And for one blessed moment, as they stuff Oreos into their mouths, the children are silent. Cyril rises, looming large over the ad hoc table, and waits until all eyes are on him before lifting a fist and bringing it down on the plywood with a crash—once, twice, and then three times. One of the kids lets out a yelp, spraying crumbs.

"Wake, strangers!" he booms, and pounds on the table again. "Wake, and come out to face Valnoth, the high cleric of Spinsel temple, and his holy acolytes! We know you have taken the scroll!"

For one long, gloriously silent moment, the kids just stare at him, eyes wide. A little wispy-haired waif, the only girl in the group besides Nora, looks like she might be about to burst into tears until Seth stifles a giggle. She looks at him, and her shoulders relax as she exhales.

He bangs again, loud enough to make her jump. "Miscreants! If you do not come out, we will come in and take the scroll by force!"

Now the kids trade looks with one another. They're so flummoxed—but also transfixed—that they don't even notice Robin as she circles the table, collecting napkins and empty juice boxes. Finally, a little towheaded boy summons the courage to say, "Um... what scroll?"

"Do not play the fool! The sacred scroll of Soleah, of course!

We know you travelers have taken it! The innkeeper has said you are the only outsiders to have frequented this establishment within the fortnight! Will you open the door, or shall I command my acolytes to sully their flaming axes?"

Seth can no longer contain himself. "I open the door!" he crows.

Cyril inclines his head toward the boy. "You have chosen wisely, young traveler." He lowers the volume of his voice and speaks as though narrating a documentary. "The seven of you file out into the main room of the inn. You find yourselves face to face with a scowling, broad-shouldered man in black robes. This is Valnoth, the high cleric of Spinsel. Behind him are his acolytes, dressed in red and gold, all six of them holding axes with gleaming golden blades." With a rough clearing of his throat, he extends a hand and switches back to Valnoth's growl. "The scroll. Now."

"But we don't have a scroll!" the little girl protests. She looks slightly panicked, as if she's forgotten her homework.

Cyril doesn't break character, but inwardly, he grins. They're getting the hang of it. "Exactly what a thief would claim. Identify yourselves, ruffians." He points to Seth. "You first!"

Thanks to a little pre-game coaching, Seth knows what to do. He holds up his character sheet and announces, "I am Dragondude, the dragonborn druid!"

The table descends into chaos as the kids demand to know what that means and to see what's written on his sheet. Cyril slides a blank character sheet towards each kid, withholding pens and pencils until he's had a chance to explain the races and classes they can choose from, along with the process of rolling dice for stats. None of them listens to anything he says to the others, so he's forced to explain the entire character creation process six separate times. One little punk, Kai, asks the same exact question three times in a row because he stops listening the instant Cyril begins to explain. He's about two seconds away from tearing up the kid's character sheet and kicking him out of the barn when Robin places her hands on his shoulders from behind, leans forward, and whispers, "They're having fun."

Her hands feel rougher than usual, and when he glances at her he realizes she is wearing leather work gloves. "What do you think you're doing?"

"Just tidying up." She waves his attention back to the kids.

He keeps one eye on her as the children assemble their ragtag band of adventurers, and Valnoth the high cleric renews his demands for the scroll of Soleah, threatening violence if the travelers don't submit to a search of their belongings. All but "Flamey the wood elf ranger" agree to the search, and Flamey's attempt to sneak out of the inn undetected fails when he rolls a measly 5 on his stealth check.

Robin sweeps off her workbench, uses a pocketknife to sharpen a couple of pencils, and then begins assessing her stock of wood, pulling out lengths of pre-primed trim and two-by-fours. She makes some notes for herself, writing directly on the barn wall, and then returns to sorting planks.

Valnoth is not thrilled when his search for the scroll turns up empty. He's contemplating carting the travelers off to the local dungeon to see if a little torture can convince them to give up the location of the scroll when one of the acolytes pipes up with a suggestion: "Wait, your holiness!" Cyril says, in a whiny falsetto, "While our fair city has surely never seen a more suspicious, dirty group of wanderers, it is possible that they may not be responsible for the stolen scroll!"

"We totally didn't do it!" Dragondude exclaims, echoed by Flamey and Prince Bubblehead.

"You question my judgment?" Valroth booms.

"No, your holiness! I only say it is *possible!* And since we cannot determine the truth, perhaps we could... motivate these ruffians to find the scroll *for* us."

Valroth strokes his long beard thoughtfully. "Yes. If they claim that the scroll is not in their possession, then they must find it for us!"

"Seriously?" says Prince Bubblehead. "How is this our problem?"

"The scroll," the acolyte informs him, "contains the spell which we use to bring water to this land. Without it, our city will be consumed by the desert which surrounds us. Without the scroll, none survive. Not us, and not you."

Cyril hasn't exactly left them much choice in the matter, so after a brief discussion, the adventurers agree to try and find the scroll for Valroth. Once they're out of the inn and wandering around the town square, however, they can't decide whether to start their search in town or follow the acolyte's suggestion to consult the soothsayer living in a tent outside the city walls. They organize a vote, but it's a tie, with three in favor of each option. When Nora—to whom Cyril has assigned the role of magical cat familiar—is designated tie breaker, the most specific answer they can get out of her is the declaration that she wants to be invisible and fly. Cyril is on the verge of roaring *it doesn't fucking matter what you pick, choice is an illusion and you're going to end up in the diamond minds either way,* when he looks out the barn door and see's Kai's mother pulling up next to the house.

Though all the parents show up promptly, it takes considerably longer to round up the children. Anna, Jake's mother, comes down the hill to thank Cyril profusely, confesses it's the first time Jake has been out of her sight since the lockdown in March, and begins to cry. He looks at Robin, who shrugs, declining to rescue him.

Finally, they're gone. Even Seth and Nora have made themselves scarce, apparently sensing that cleanup duty is imminent. Cyril plants his hands on the makeshift table, expelling a long breath as he shoves himself to his feet. "The collective noun for grade-schoolers should be 'an asylum.'"

Robin starts collecting character sheets, wincing as she squats to pick one up off the dirt floor.

"Don't do that. Come on." He snatches the papers from her hand, sorts them into a coherent order, and slips them into the Dungeon Master's manual along with the maps. Robin just stands there, watching him. "What?"

She shakes her head. "It blows my mind every time I see you do that."

"Do what?" He sweeps the dice off the edge of the table, tucking them into the pouch they came in, and helps himself to the last of the Oreos.

"You know. Transform. Into..." She waves her hand in a magician's flourish. "Some kind of medieval bard, or whatever. The story, the voices—every one of those kids was completely engaged. Even Kai"—she looks around to make sure neither of the kids is present—"who is a little asshole. Teachers would kill for that kind of focus."

"Well, maybe teachers should be better at their jobs." He tosses the rest of the figurines and tokens into the plastic shopping bag, helps Robin fold up the drop cloth, and props the sheet of plywood against the wall.

"Do me a favor," Robin says. "Get the kids in the shower before you give them lunch. They're filthy."

He hesitates. "You're not coming—"

"Just a couple more things I wanna do. I'll be up in a minute."

He falls for it, hook line and sinker. He's got the griddle on the stove, warming it up for grilled cheese, when he hears, in the distance, the air compressor's long, obnoxious *waaaaa*.

He rings her from the dining room, shutting the hall door to tone down the shrieks of the children spraying each other with the handheld attachment in the shower. "What do you think you're doing?"

"I told you. Just a little cleanup. Nothing big. I promise."

"I can hear your fucking nail gun."

"Okay, I'm doing a little light cabinetry."

"That is not—you know what, never mind. Just get your ass back up here."

She laughs. "Make me."

And then the line goes dead.

He scowls at his phone, then jams it back into his pocket and opens the hall door. "Wrap it up, guys!"

Seth is the first to emerge from the cloud of billowing steam, wrapped in one of Robin's plush green towels. Cyril hands him a pile of clothes. "Get dressed, go down the hill, and get your mom back up here ASAP."

He's flipping the third grilled cheese sandwich onto a plate when the back door opens and shuts again with a *thwack*.

It's just the kid.

"Mom said that's cheating," Seth informs him. "Can I have lunch now?"

"God damn it," he mutters, under his breath. He went up and down the hill in the back yard so many times the night it rained his legs still have PTSD. He slaps two grilled cheese sandwiches on plates, one for each of the kids, and takes the third for himself. "Get some apple juice for you and Nora," he tells Seth. "Try not to spill."

The sandwich is gone by the time he reaches the barn. "This —" He sucks in a deep breath and clears the phlegm from his throat before stepping through the open doors again. "This is not funny."

Robin props the butt of her nail gun on her shoulder. "I dunno, I mean, *I* think it's funny."

Jesus Christ. "You were bored. You wanted your kids back. I got them back. Now go fucking take care of yourself."

"What're you gonna give me, if I do?"

"No. I'm not doing this." He slices the air with a hand. "I'm not playing this game."

"Says the guy who started it. Fine." She sets the gun on her workbench with a thump. "Here's the deal. Take me to dinner."

He looks at her for a long moment. "Are you fucking kidding me."

"Answer me this, big guy. If—" She levels a finger at him, realizes her hands are coated with sawdust, and dusts them off brusquely. "If you're gonna punish yourself every time we get close, why can't I offer an alternate incentive?"

It takes a moment for him to fully comprehend her utter insanity. "You cannot fucking *bargain* with your body."

"Why not?" She picks up the nail gun again. "You do." She bends over a half-assembled cabinet and squeezes the trigger, popping off a line of nails.

"You're a goddamn lunatic," he says, shouting over the kickback.

She moves to the next joint and lays another row of nails. "Nothing fancy. Bear Republic has outdoor dining, if you're cool with burgers and beer. Greta said she's happy to come over and hang out for a couple hours." She shrugs. "Up to you."

CHAPTER 21

G reta sizes him up like spoiled leftovers. "This... is the best you could do?"

"Says the woman in a polo shirt and mom jeans." Cyril steps back, ushering Greta over the threshold with a sarcastic flourish of one hand. "I had about four hours' advance notice. What was I supposed to do?"

Her eyebrows arch. "You've had *years*."

"Oh, right, it's not my clothes, it's everything underneath."

"I was referring to your personality," she retorts, stiffly.

"Obviously. You'd never resort to body shaming. Glass houses and all—"

"I already have two kids," Robin says, sweeping into the living room. "I don't need two more."

They fall silent, but not because of her words. She'd assured him casual dress was fine—not that he owns anything else—and, in a technical sense, her attire meets that definition: a sleeveless linen shift accented with teardrop earrings and beaded sandals. But she is stunning.

Cyril looks down at his flip-flops and the garish Hawaiian

shirt she'd insisted he wear—again—and is forced to agree with
Greta: "This is fucking absurd."

The older woman's head swivels to give him a sharp look. "Is
that the language you use with the children?"

"I dunno, is that the *face* you use—"

"Would you stop?" Robin snatches her mask and purse off the
top off the piano, grabs Cyril's arm, and drags him toward the
door. "Greta, thank you so much, the kids are *supposed* to be in
the bathroom brushing their teeth."

Greta nods. "Have... fun," she says, though her tone says she
can't begin to fathom how that might be possible.

————

"Two," ROBIN SAYS, HOLDING UP THE CORRESPONDING
number of fingers.

The blue-masked host grabs a pair of menus and nods for
them to follow him across a square hillock of bright green grass.
Three of four sides are lined with rustic wooden booths that look
like they've been salvaged from an Irish pub, with the addition of
vinyl dividers on stakes stretched around each set of high-backed
benches to provide an extra measure of isolation. A chorus of
low *whomphs* sounds as a breeze gusts around the vinyl
partitions.

Cyril catches her wrist. "Do you eat at any restaurant that
doesn't have booths?" Months after Tav's death, he'd offered to
take her out to dinner for her birthday. They'd had to wait for one
of the few tables at the steakhouse to free up because the thought
of him squeezing into a booth had been utterly laughable.

"You'll fit," she says, pulling out of his grasp.

"The fuck I will," he growls, following her across the grass.
It's damp, and his feet sink into the soil. Last time they'd gone
out, he'd passed off the dinner invitation as a gesture of friendship. Tavis had always made a holiday of her birthday, and Cyril

had known the first year without him would be especially hard. Now she knows the truth. Oh, maybe she doesn't know it took him weeks to compose that idiotic little speech he'd had to read off a fucking piece of paper because he couldn't trust himself not to go off script, but she knows he was the one who had composed all the birthday cards and poems and jokes Tavis had presented her with over the years. She has to have realized it was never just dinner between friends, for him.

It's a squeeze, but, actually, he does fit. Robin lifts an I-told-you-so eyebrow.

"You think this is funny?" he demands, when the host has distributed menus and assured them that their waiter will be right along. Now that she knows how pathetic he is—how even after Tavis was dead and buried he just couldn't fucking let it go—does she get a kick out of making him squirm?

Robin tugs the table toward herself, giving him another inch or two of clearance. "Cyril, I can eyeball measurements to the quarter inch. Give me a little credit." She casts a glance at the menu and then flips it aside. "You're not nearly as big as you think you are."

"Oh, yes, because four hundred fifty is so much lighter than—"

"Six hundred?" She scoffs. "Yes. It really is. You're a *big* guy, Cyril. Six foot what, four?"

"Five."

"See?" She flutters a dismissive hand. "You can get away with a lot."

He plucks at the ridiculous Hawaiian shirt, unbuttoned out of necessity rather than choice. "It's the macaws. Everyone knows parrots are slimming."

She snorts. "Seriously, though. I don't know how you feel, but you look a lot more comfortable in your own skin than you did when you went to prison."

"Oh, is 'comfortable' the new euphemism for fat?"

She gives him a long, low-lidded look of disdain. Then she rolls her eyes upward and sighs. "Okay. I give up. What do I do when you hate on yourself? Is it better if I just ignore it?"

"Honestly?" He shrugs. "Doesn't matter." No matter what she says or doesn't say, his self-talk is louder than her voice can ever be. Just like no matter how much weight he sheds, he will always be that obscenely bloated loser playing pretend with his best friend's widow.

Robin studies his face, as if she's trying to figure out what's going on in his head. Then the waiter arrives, sparing him from further scrutiny. Robin waits politely as the young man recites the day's specials, then orders pulled pork sandwiches and house-brewed root beer for both of them.

"That's not what I wanted."

She hands their menus to the waiter, dismissing him with a nod. "Trust me, it is."

"You've been here?"

"Oh, all the time. Well—before COVID."

"With who?" He can't imagine her chilling at this hip brewery with Greta and her pocket-sized husband. Especially since the guy doesn't seem to go outside. And it's definitely too upscale for the kids.

She tugs at one earring, sliding the hook back and forth through the piercing in her earlobe. "Myself."

"That's not weird or anything."

"What? You know I've always liked solo dining. It's a forbidden pleasure when you've got two kids." Her eyes crinkle with humor. "Plus, I'm excellent company."

The waiter brings their drinks, and Cyril realizes the young man's chitchat is not just the simple politeness he had first assumed, but that in fact this nascent adult knows Robin well enough to comment on the fact that she hasn't ordered her usual non-alcoholic beer.

"Sometimes I just get tired of the fake stuff. Yours is the best, but still, why even pretend?" She tugs her mask off and samples the dark amber liquid from a glass beaded with condensation. "The root beer is excellent, though, thank you."

Cyril tosses his own mask aside and tries it. "Not bad." This is a massive understatement. But everything tastes fantastic after prison grub, so it's hard to know whether he's being objective.

Robin's phone pings; she pulls it out of her purse and laughs when she sees the message on the screen. "The kids are trying to convince Greta they should get Minecraft for bedtime stories. You've spoiled them." Smiling, she taps back a reply with her thumbs.

"I will never understand why the kids like her."

Robin snickers as she tucks the phone away. "Same reasons they like you, big guy." She holds up an index finger. "You're both fantastic cooks—"

"Bullshit."

"I admit Greta's more skilled, but she'd never make the kids jello and macaroni, so you each have your advantages." She lifts a second finger. "You both love kids—"

"I *hate* kids. I love two very specific people who also happen to be children."

A third finger goes up. "You're both wildly overprotective—"

"Look, we're both ugly as sin, I'll give you that." He sits back, lifting his arms out of the way as the waiter arrives with their meals. "Beyond that, I have nothing in common with Sue Sylvester. But we already know you're good at believing whatever the hell you want."

"If you—" Robin cuts herself off, nods a thank-you to the waiter as he retreats, and cocks her head to one side. "Okay, I have to ask. Sue Sylvester—you watch *Glee?*"

"Voluntarily? No. There was only one television, and I was not in charge of the remote."

She stares at him, unmoving, and then blinks, slowly. "I have so many questions."

"And none of them are going to be answered."

He eats. She talks. Mostly about frivolous, inconsequential bullshit. Clothes she needs to buy for the kids. Local businesses that have closed because of COVID. Her plans for what to tackle next on the house. When and if church might open for in-person services again. This is why he was never interested in relationships.

At some point, Robin catches on. She stops talking. Raises an eyebrow. "Am I boring you?"

"I don't know how to answer that in a way that won't offend you."

"So, yes. You're welcome to change the subject."

He shrugs. "We're just killing time until I fuck things up again."

She tilts her head back, casting a thoughtful look upward through the spindly tree branches to the sky. "I don't get it," she says. "You've spent years obsessing over me—we've written the equivalent of entire novels to each other. But now we're here, together, and you're not interested in conversation?" She shakes her head. "Why are you even here at all?"

"Because taking you to dinner was the only way you'd agree to rest before chemo—"

"You know what I mean. I assume there's *something* about me that you can't get from anyone else. I mean, there were plenty of hot women on campus back in college. You never came across like you had some weird black girl fetish. So why was it *me* when we met in the library that day? Was it just that I was there, and female?"

"That's not—" He stops. Looks at his plate. Shovels a few bites into his mouth.

She frowns. "This is gonna be one of those things where I wish I hadn't asked, isn't it."

"It's just—that's not where we met." Not the first time, anyway.

"Pretty sure I'd have remembered you and your big fat mouth."

He doesn't answer. She shrugs. They eat in silence. When she's cleared about two thirds of her meal, she lifts her plate and scrapes the remainder onto his. He finishes without comment.

She reaches for her purse, pulling out her mask and orienting it with the nose wire on top.

"It was outside the silo," he says. The lecture hall had earned its nickname because it looked, on the outside, like a giant tin can.

She puts the mask down.

"You were with a group of freshman girls, walking up the steps. White, suntanned, bleached-blond hair straight down to the middle of their backs. Your friends, I assume."

She snorts. "In my defense, my choices were limited."

"I don't know what you were talking about, but you were all laughing." This is a lie. He'd heard them loud and clear. The shortest one had been bitching about her father, painting him as an overprotective buffoon because he called her to check in every single night. When she'd neglected to return his calls over the weekend, he'd called the police—who had showed up with lights flashing, first thing Monday morning. "You made some excuse about having forgotten your notes. Then you ran back down the steps and ducked behind the bushes." There was a tiny clearing in the corner formed by the steps and the side of the building, and the horizontal branch of a California cypress provided a perfect seat. A seat which he himself had been occupying only a moment before. "For about five minutes, you just sat there and let the tears run down your face."

He'd had no idea she wept for her father, then. What had fascinated him was not that she cried, but the effortlessness of her tears. There was no attempt to stifle or subdue her grief; she simply let go. And when the storm had passed, she dried her face with the hem of her shirt, sniffed, and turned to leave.

She looks at him, now, with a puzzled expression. "I don't remember this at all."

Which is to say, she does not remember it in particular; there had been many days when she excused herself to cry. This was something he had discovered later, having made a study of her habits. She never made a scene, but if someone saw her, she didn't try to hide. She felt what she needed to feel, and moved on. "I doubt you saw me." Though he hadn't been quite so... memorable, back then. (Memorable being, in this case, a euphemism for "huge.")

"Were you, like... hiding back there?"

He eases himself out of the booth, pulling out his wallet to toss down a trio of twenties before looping his mask over his ears. "It was a good place to read between classes." Hanging out in public view tended to come with irritating interruptions.

"Why didn't you *say* something?"

"I did. I got as far as 'hey' before you shrieked and ran off." She is still seated, and he's just standing there beside the table like a dumbass. It occurs to him that maybe her incision is sore. He offers a hand.

"Wait." A crease appears between her eyebrows as she takes his hand and rises. "That," she says, "was you?" She tugs her hand away and uses it to give his shoulder a soft punch. "You scared the shit out of me!"

"I know. You mentioned it twice in emails to your mom."

She makes an exaggerated gagging noise. "Creep." And then she laughs. "You couldn't just introduce yourself, huh?" She tugs her mask into place, shoulders her purse, and starts for the exit, lifting a hand and calling out "thank you!" as they pass their waiter tending another table. Outside, she turns right.

"Uh." He points left. "Truck's that way."

"We're taking a stroll."

"That was not the deal."

"I'm altering the deal." She hooks her arm through his. "Come on. I'm supposed to be getting some light exercise. And it certainly wouldn't hurt you."

She leads him along the sidewalk parallel to the plaza, passing other masked pedestrians who either risk stepping into the street in an effort to maintain distance or hurry quickly by. Though a smattering of tourist boutiques have their doors propped gamely open with racks of merchandise displayed on the sidewalk, the handful of shoppers scurry in and out and back to their cars as if rushing to beat an impending storm. There is a collective awareness that this effort at maintaining some semblance of business-as-usual is only temporary. Winter looms on the horizon, bringing with it rising COVID rates and another wave of shutdowns.

Robin, seemingly unruffled by the general mood, stops to peer into the darkened window of a store which—as the sign on the door explains—repurposes vintage kimonos into dresses and handbags and shit.

"Isn't that, like, textbook appropriation?" he asks.

"Like you care. They're pretty."

"Not your style."

"No," she agrees, unbothered by his criticism. "But they remind me of my mom."

At the end of the block, they reach a bookstore, its open doors like a lighted beacon in the dark. Robin looks up at him, and he knows that behind her mask there's an expectant smile.

"Yeah, no." He's gotten through dinner without making a scene. No need to tempt fate by interacting with anymore humans right now. Although, as far as he can see, there's nobody inside.

She pulls her phone out to check the time. "Oh, look," she

says, with mock enthusiasm. "If we go home now, I have time to glue up some cabinet doors!"

"Fuck off."

This asshole had stopped going to bookstores well before he went to prison. Before he'd quit going out because of his size, even. He'd stopped when bookstores had replaced their science fiction and fantasy sections with fifteen shelves of Tolkien and a handful of recently released "high concept" titles which inevitably failed to deliver. Oh, and toys.

"You're such a snob," Robin says, when he relates this to her. "Copperfield's is different. They curate their selection. Go look in back."

"Of course it's in the back."

"The perfect place for antisocial assholes like you."

"Aisle's probably twelve inches wide."

She gives him a shove. "Go."

Not that he'll admit it, but she's right. It's one of those indie shops where shelves are embellished with employee recommendations handwritten on little three-by-five cards. Those he refuses to read, but he also finds a wealth of paperbacks new to him—no great shock after five years in lockup, but these are obviously the sort of niche, lesser-known titles that he'd normally only hear about online, and then only from other connoisseurs. The good stuff.

He's picked out a short story collection by Gene Wolfe and the first two books of VanderMeer's Southern Reach trilogy—which he'd owned but hadn't gotten around to reading when he went to prison—before an employee spots him. "Good evening! Do you need help finding anything?"

He spares only the briefest glance at the plump girl with colorfully tattooed arms and retro horn-rimmed glasses. "Fuck off."

"Who hurt you, Cyril?" Robin teases, coming around the

other end of the aisle. She has a stack of picture books tucked under one arm. "Who made you like this?"

He shoves the short story collection back onto the shelf—horizontally, on top of the other books. "Who didn't?"

She waits as he picks through the remainder of the selection, leaving the books in disarray, and then exhales a sigh. "Tavis," she says. "Tavis didn't." She shifts the picture books to her other arm. "Was that all it took to win your friendship? *Not* hurting you?"

"You make it sound easy." He takes the books from her. "Are you done?"

She nods, gesturing for him to precede her to the front of the store. "I don't think I've ever come out of here with less than five books for the kids."

He bought dinner, and now he buys the books, thumbing the crisp new twenties onto the counter. As if he's not the guy who's been mooching off of Robin since he got out of prison, utterly failing at every attempt to secure work. The bespectacled woman packs the books into a white paper bag with the store's logo stamped in red, eyes trained firmly upon the countertop.

"Don't worry," Robin tells her as she hands the bag around the plexiglass divide. "It's not you. It's definitely him."

When they cross at the corner, Robin steers him onto a sidewalk path that meanders diagonally through the deserted plaza, more or less in the direction of the truck. They pass a bronze statue of a boy holding a folded American flag to his chest, head bowed. The dedication at the base lists the names of local World War II veterans. Cyril snorts. "Could that possibly be any more saccharine?"

Robin releases his arm, hands him the bag, and plants a hand on the boy's head to steady herself as she bends. She scratches an itch on the ankle with the tattoo, and then slips her sandal off. "Apparently the source of a big political dustup here in town, actually."

"Who's going to object to *that*? Other than me, I mean."

"That's exactly what the city thought, so they let the Lions Club install the thing without bringing it up for a vote. Apparently they forgot a couple of names?" She laughs as she brushes off the insole of her sandal. "I dunno, small town drama."

"Jesus. And this is where you decide to raise the kids?"

Robin drops the sandal and steps back into it. "It's petty and inconsequential and... refreshing." She tugs her mask down to her chin. "To know that people can still disagree and not, you know—"

"Show up with an automatic and slaughter everyone?" Unlike the nutcase who shot up a Denny's in his honor.

The silence which follows is sharp. Her eyes flicker up, and he sees he sees that she knew about the shooting, of course. Everyone knew. And now she knows that he knows.

"It wasn't your fault," she says, finally. But she is looking at the ground. "A lot of things were your fault. But that wasn't one."

"Yeah, I'm sure my good intentions are a real comfort to those bereaved parents."

She chews her upper lip. "It's not that simple."

"Save one kid, two kids die. Seems like a pretty simple equation to me. You can stick your head in the sand all you want, but there's no reason it couldn't happen here." Particularly with him around.

She looks up. "Is that what you think I'm doing? Holing up in this idyllic little town so I can raise my kids and pretend the rest of the world isn't on fire?"

"I'm not blaming you." He tugs his own mask off and pockets it; there's no one around. "Cancer is a pretty good excuse to check out—"

She cuts him off with a snort. "I'm a black woman and a single mother, Cyril. I don't get the luxury of escape. You get to shut your laptop, and poof—" She makes a fist and then spreads her fingers. "Gone. Me? Last month, I had to tell George—the guy with the cars in the barns?—I had to tell him I wasn't gonna bring the kids over for cookies unless his wife put away her collection of damn mammy jars. I got the manager at the lumber yard to stop offering me discounts in return for a date, so now I get to listen to him joke with his buddies about how 'cold' it is every time I stop in. The week after I bought the house, I took a box of candy and my kids to the police station just to make sure they see my kids as *kids*. I could say fuck it and move to Oakland, but that's not better, it's just a different set of compromises. There's no winning move here. Not for me."

"So you've given up on trying to save the world, then."

She shakes her head. "You don't get it. I'll keep fighting until I take my last breath, Cyril." She pulls her cell phone out and clicks it on, showing him the background photo of her kids. "It's just that I've realized my kids are the world."

He blinks at the screen, and then at her face. "Is this where you start spouting bullshit about how every person is a universe?"

"Well, they sure as hell aren't equations. Look, you saved a kid's life. And maybe you share some responsibility for the deaths of some others. But if you're gonna reduce your worth to a formula, you have to add in everything. Playing the piano with Nora. Teaching Seth to make mac and cheese. You and Tavis were always so obsessed with fighting the giants outside the walls, you never understood that the real battle is here, inside. Wading through all the shit but existing anyway—being happy anyway—*loving* anyway—that's a revolutionary act, Cyril."

"Serious question: are you drunk? Because I would have sworn you had root beer with dinner."

She spreads her hands, expansively. "If ordinary life doesn't exist, there's nothing worth saving. There's no point in fighting the good fight if that's all you ever do."

They look at one another for a moment. Then she lets her

arms drop with a sigh, tucks her hand into the soft crease of his elbow, and tugs him off the path and into the soft, damp grass. With her free hand she fiddles with her earring and then, with a grimace of irritation, tugs one and then the other out of her ears. Lacking pockets, she starts to drop them into the open mouth of her purse, and then, on second thought, reaches for his shirt pocket.

"What are you—"

"If they go into my purse, one or both are never coming out." The button on his pocket flap is caught on a stray thread, and it takes her a moment to work it through the hole. "Do you remember our second anniversary? I mean, I know you wrote the damn card. But Tavis knew he'd be deployed, so he bought these like three months in advance and hid one in—" Her fingers stop.

"What?" As if he doesn't know.

She licks her lips, and then her eyes flicker up, all bittersweet and sad. "I'm an idiot."

"No more than anyone else."

Her hands fall away from his chest. "You." She cups the earrings in one upturned palm, letting the golden links twist in the moonlight. "Picked these out. Didn't you?"

He snorts. "Tavis bought them."

"That's not what I asked." She catches his arm, her grip tightening as he tries to turn away. "Answer me. Did you pick these earrings? Yes or no."

He shakes free of her hand and backtracks to the sidewalk path, taking the most direct route across the plaza toward the truck. But he is slow and quickly winded and as he passes the fountain at the center of the square, her swift footsteps overtake him. She hops up onto the broad concrete lip, trotting along the fountain's edge to keep pace and eye-level with him. "You picked out all of his gifts. And planned the surprises, too." Her path ends, abruptly, as the fountain makes a sharp ninety-degree turn.

She stands balanced at the corner, opening her fingers to look at the earrings again.

"I thought I had it figured," she says. Not to him, but to the earrings. "Thought I'd sorted the two of you out, column A and column B. But it's never over, is it?" She glances up. "There's always more."

He doesn't know what to say.

She holds her hand out over the water and lets the earrings fall. Plop, plop.

He turns away and keeps walking.

She drops back to the grass and follows, falling into step beside him. "Jesus, Cyril. You had me thinking it was just the letters, but he really outsourced everything but the sex, didn't he?"

A surge of anger. He knows what she's trying to do—pin the blame on Tavis. It's easy to blame a dead man. "That's not how it was," he growls.

"Wasn't it? All he had to do was give you friendship, and you would have done anything for him. Tell me I'm wrong."

"It's not that simple." He hadn't just swallowed his own desire because Tavis was his friend, and Tavis had wanted Robin. Tavis had *deserved* her. And she had deserved a partner who could love her like she deserved to be loved. Even if Cyril had attempted to woo her himself—and even if she had, for some insane reason, responded to his advances—he would eventually have ruined it by doing what he does best: using his words to make her feel small. She deserved more than that, then and now.

Robin dashes ahead, turning to walk hop-skip backward so he has no option but to speak to her face. "Tavis could have had any girl he wanted, Cyril. Ask yourself—why did it have to be *me?* You don't think he knew, in his heart of hearts, that I was the one you loved?"

"I'm not doing this."

"No, of course you're not. Because if you did, you might come to the conclusion that *he* wasn't the one being used." She stops, forcing him to pull up just short of barreling into her. "And if Tavis wasn't the victim?" She plants a finger on his chest. "That means the sucker was *you*."

He grabs her wrist, meaning to jerk her arm—and the rest of her—out of his way. But he hesitates, and in that moment they both look down at her hand. Her left hand.

She spreads her fingers, and the moonlight hits the diamond set in the thin gold band. "Did you—"

His silence is answer enough.

She turns away, tugging her hand from his grasp. The hunch of her shoulders makes him think she is crying, but then she shifts, slightly, and he sees she is using a thumb and forefinger to pry off her wedding band. It doesn't come easy.

"That—that—*fucker*."

"Chica—" He drops the bag of books and then lunges as she takes a long step toward the fountain, arm cocked back to hurl. He captures her wrist in time. "*Robin.*"

Her lips press into a hard line of indecision, and then, finally, she lowers her arm and tosses the ring at his chest. "Fine. Take it." It bounces off his shirt and slips through the fingers of his right hand, but he manages to trap it against his body with his left.

Lacking a better outlet for her anger, she kicks the leg of a park bench. Gently, since her sandals are open at the toe. "I can't believe I kept his name."

This asshole tucks the ring into his shirt pocket. "Chica—"

"Don't fucking try to tell me it was all your fault." Her hand flutters, indicating him. "You wrote letters. Okay? Tavis *fucked* me. I had his *children*. And he couldn't even pick out the goddamn wedding ring?" Her voice catches, and her eyes gleam with unshed tears. "How, Cyril? How could you love me, and let him do what he did?"

ROBIN DOESN'T WAIT FOR HIM TO GET OUT OF THE truck. She parks, climbs the front steps, and disappears. When he steps into the living room, her purse is where she dropped it, half open on the floor. The slam which comes from the back of the house is doubtless her bedroom door.

Greta looks up from the couch, where she is making notes in the margins of a Bible. "Dinner went well, I see."

AT LEAST SHE SLEEPS IN. ENDURING THE inevitable shitshow of dinner was worth it, if only for the sake of fulfilling his half of her ridiculous bargain.

That's his first thought, anyway. By mid-morning, his relief has given way to concern. It's like Nora's infancy, except instead of fretting that she's stopped breathing or choked on her own spit-up he worries about an accidental overdose or negative interactions between her medication. That and the fact that increased fatigue could indicate a resurgence of cancer.

Around eleven, long after he's fed the kids and set them up in their bedroom with school, Robin meanders in and flops down on the couch. She is dressed in shirt and jeans.

"Hungry?" he asks, half-expecting her to ignore him.

"Starving, actually." She yawns and shifts as she flicks the TV on. "I think my appetite's finally coming back."

He abandons the half-folded pile of laundry and is ten minutes into constructing eggs benedict from a recipe on his phone when he glances into the living room and realizes the couch is vacant. The TV is still on. He lurches into the dining room. "What are you—" She's halfway up the stairs. "Jesus. Would you come back—" He starts forward, realizes the slotted spoon in his hand is dripping hollandaise, and rushes back to the kitchen. "Damn it." The sauce is turning into runny scrambled eggs. He yanks the bowl off the pot of boiling water and drops it into the sink. Probably a loss anyway.

By the time he gets back to the bottom of the stairs, she's gone.

"Your breakfast is fucked!" he shouts up the stairwell.

The only answer he gets is the kickback of her staple gun.

"God damn it."

Upstairs, he finds her in one of the two smaller bedrooms at the back of the house, lavender kerchief knotted around her hair, stapling gaps in the Tyvek he put over the windows. There are more than a few, because he nailed it up in the dark in the rain in the middle of the fucking night. His back is killing him and he's out of breath so instead of arguing he walks up to her and yanks the staple gun out of her hand.

"Hey—!"

She makes a lunge for the tool, but he holds it up over her head, beyond her reach. "We had a deal, Chica."

She glowers. "Fuck your deal."

"I was joking when I told Greta I tied you to the bed—"

"You *what?*" Her laugh is incredulous.

"But I swear, Chica. I swear to God I will fucking do it." He pops the rechargeable battery out of the gun, shoves it through the gap in the Tyvek, and lets it drop to the yard below.

She turns on him with fire in her eyes. "You." She slices the air in front of him with an index finger, as if to send him flying out the window after the battery cell. "Do *not* fuck with my tools."

"Your tools can be replaced. *That*—" he uses the gun to gesture, vaguely, at her torso—"seems like it might be worth, oh, I dunno, *slightly* more."

The fire dims. She goes to the window, pops a corner of the Tyvek off with a couple bumps of her fist, and stares, chewing her lip, at the ground below. She plucks at her shirt with a little sigh.

"This temple's already wrecked, Cyril." She shakes her head. "I won't let my house fall apart, too."

"It's—you're—" Her casual dismissal of the frame he's so pathetically abased himself to preserve makes him feel oddly defensive. "You're not wrecked. Not even close."

"Says the guy who won't even sleep in my bed."

"I—you fucking know that's not why."

"Explain, then."

Explain that he's so fucked in the head that the slightest touch of her hand makes him want to put her nail gun to his head and blow his brains out? She already knows, and nothing either one of them says is going to fix it. "No." This is just a distraction. *"You* explain *this*. Why are you up here? Working? This old hulk is a disaster, but it's not going to collapse if you neglect it for a few weeks. I realize laying around on the couch is boring as shit, but you have *kids*. You can't just—"

"I already told you." She looks out the window, shaking her head. "Everything I do is for them."

"How does that make any sense?"

"Because—" She turns to face him, finally, pulling the kerchief off her head as she looks up, meeting his eyes. "Because this is how I want them to remember me."

For one vertiginous moment, he thinks she means the unthinkable: that this is the end. That she is actually going to die. But no; it's only the fear of the thing. She's already come face-to-face with her own mortality, and she's terrified she might not survive a second encounter. Life has taught her to expect the worst-case scenario.

"Chica," he says. He looks for somewhere to set the gun down and, finally, stoops slightly and lets it drop to the floor. "That's not—that's not how it's going to end." He steps forward, but she doesn't move toward him, and he doesn't reach out. Not quite. "Look, I—" He rubs his forehead and looks at the floor. "I know I'm completely fucking everything up, but—you do the radiation and the chemo and whatever the hell else—you *fight,* Chica, and I swear to God I will be here. For—" He swallows. "For whatever you need."

And she laughs. Softly. Sadly. The look she gives him says, *surely you already know.*

"What?"

"Cyril, there's... not going to be any chemo."

STAGE 4

DEPRESSION

CHAPTER 22

"I don't understand."

She offers him a small, knowing smile. "You did, a minute ago."

He's been patient. Played by her rules. He made a fool of himself playing nanny, nurse, and even boyfriend on her stupid fucking date—and still, she's jerking him around. He steps toward her, head lowered and shoulders squared in a way that every prisoner would immediately recognize as trouble. His fingers close around her bicep, hard. "I am done with your games."

Robin doesn't even flinch. She just sighs, as if disappointed in him for making her explain. "It metastasized. I've been holding the line at stage four for... a while."

"A *while*? Stage four? What the fuck does that even mean?"

"Oh, come on." She shrugs out of his grasp. "Don't pretend you didn't google uterine cancer and oophorectomy and whatever else." She stoops, wincing a little, to pick up the staple gun. "If it was only my uterus they wanted, they could've gone in laparoscopically. They didn't need to cut me open for that." She checks the tool over, like she's worried he might have damaged it, like that's something that even matters, and then crosses the floor to tuck it into the dry bones of an interior wall. "It's everywhere, Cyril. They cut out what they could get. It'll buy me a few more months, maybe a year, but—"

"No," he says.

"But I'm done with treatment. I'm not gonna spend my last months in a hospital shooting up poison and puking. I'm gonna be here. Doing what I love. With my kids."

"How—" But he can't even speak the words. Everything has stopped. "How long have you—"

"What, known that I'm dying?" She steps around him, leaving the upstairs bedroom. He follows her past the stairwell—he can hear one of the kids talking on Zoom, downstairs—and into the big room at the front of the house. She turns, seating herself on the second rung of a stepladder, and lifts a hand to examine her nails. "Depends on how you look at it." She picks at a ragged nail. "I went into remission a couple of times after my mastectomy, but it never lasted long. I got into a couple of different drug trials that helped, but never permanently. I mean, I could keep hitting it with chemo and radiation, but at this point it's just a matter of time."

"Why—why would you—" Why would she do this to him? Or, more specifically, why, in the face of her impending mortality, would she waste even a second of her time on this worthless asshole? Why pick him up from prison? Why bring him to her home, let him sleep on her couch, reconnect with her— "Oh," he exhales, as it hits him like a wall of water. "Oh. Fuck." He tries to suck the air back in. Pain radiates through his chest. "The kids. You want me to take the—"

She laughs. Not unkindly. "No. Greta's adopting them."

Which was why she'd been sending the kids to Greta's while she was in the hospital, instead of leaving them with him. Why they went to her house for school. To ease the transition. It was also why she'd wanted them back as soon as possible, surgery be damned. Because—oh, fuck. Fuck. She didn't have much time left with them. But then, why bother with him? "I don't understand," he says.

But oh, he does.

"You knew this was a trap," she says, and looks up, finally. Watching his face as the realization sinks in. "Didn't you? You've been looking for the catch. Well, here it is." She shrugs. "You thought you could have the best of both worlds—a marriage of minds, without all the messy parts like mortgage payments and morning sickness and fights over who left the fridge open. But that's not how it works, Cyril. You don't get to turn a relationship on and off like a power switch. When Tavis died, it destroyed me. You know, because you watched it happen. So now it's your turn. The body of the man I love is gone, but not his soul. You made me love you, Cyril. For better or worse. And now you're gonna learn what it means to love someone 'til death do us part."

He's got nothing. Nothing whatsoever. He just stands there, utterly bereft, watching her gnaw on a cuticle.

She gives up on the nail with a sigh of frustration, uncrosses her legs, and stands. "That's my revenge, Cyril." She spreads her hands. "I brought you home to help me die."

CHAPTER 23

Later, when he tries to recall what he said, what he did after she spoke those words, there is nothing. Only a haze of blind fury. Directed not toward fate, or whatever insensate rubric of chaos and chance governs the universe—but toward Robin.

This—all of this—is her fault. For hiding her diagnosis, for dangling the irresistible prospect of time with her when she knew there was none. And before that, for letting him into her home after Tavis died. For allowing him to fall in love with her children. And even before that, for tolerating his friendship with her husband. For failing to see the lie behind his letters. For being impossible not to love.

For all of this, he hates her.

And yet he does not. Not really. Cannot. Will never.

He finds himself on the sidewalk in front of the doughnut shop, exhausted and pungent with sweat. The light outside is dim, but he cannot tell whether it is dusk or dawn. He looks in through the window at the empty baking racks.

She cannot do this to him. He will not let her. That's what he keeps thinking, though he knows it's irrational. The thing is already done.

What can he *do?* Nothing.

Nothing but watch the only person who has ever made life tolerable suffer slowly and die.

He wants to die. Perhaps he is already dead. Perhaps this is hell.

No. This is just a prelude. Hell is what comes next.

The cowbell clinks. "You hungry?"

He blinks, and the baking racks are full. Morning, then. "What?"

A wiry old woman with faded strawberry blonde hair swept back in a hairnet leans out the door, releasing a waft of sugar and warm dough. "You hungry?"

He is starving. This is how he knows he's still alive.

She wrestles the door open with one foot, dragging a sandwich board out onto the sidewalk. "Don't worry if you can't pay," she says, trundling past him to prop it open on the curb. A crude shelter of two-by-fours and corrugated steel roofing now spans the four parking spaces in front of the shop. Pandemic architecture. "Nobody leaves my place with an empty belly."

"Lady, do I look like I need an extra meal?"

She shrugs. "Ain't always about the food, honey. Up to you." With another clink of the cowbell, the door swings shut.

He continues to stand there, mostly because he doesn't see any point in moving, as the old woman continues bustling in and out of the shop, bringing a box of napkin-wrapped utensils to set out on the tables under the shelter, and then a tray of heavy brown mugs. An ancient Chevy rumbles up to the nearest empty parking spot. The man behind the wheel is so old and brittle a puff of wind could blow him away, and it takes him a good five minutes to fumble a paper mask over his ears and ease himself out of the truck. He checks himself in the side mirror, using a gnarled thumb to slick down his wiry eyebrows, and gives Cyril a skeptical once-over as he hobbles up the curb and then down again, into the makeshift dining area. "Hey, darlin!" he says, too loudly, as the woman from the shop comes out again with a steaming pot of coffee. "Fill 'er up!"

A few yards down the sidewalk, in front of a little drug store, there's a bank of empty newspaper dispensers, a public telephone with no receiver, and a cast iron bench with about sixty coats of flaking green paint. This asshole takes a seat and, mostly out of habit, pulls out his phone. He clicks the home screen on, and then stares at the background—a photo of Seth and Nora eating chocolate chip cookies—until it goes dark.

More trucks and an old diesel BMW putter into the lot. Five o'clock in the morning on a weekday is apparently meetup time for bowlegged old farmers in white Stetsons, snakeskin boots, and Levi jeans. The grizzled old guy who'd entertained the kids with his magic tricks the morning after Cyril's release arrives on his grumbling Harley.

A leaner motorcycle slides by out on the otherwise deserted street, stopping briefly at the corner. The black-jacketed rider plants a boot on the ground, and his helmet turns to look at the diners. Or Cyril. Perhaps both. The rider pulls his leg up, seems to hesitate as he rolls through the intersection, and then makes a U-turn through the parking lot, coasting to a stop next to the Harley. He pulls his helmet off.

It's Greta. Riding a motorcycle. Because of course she does.

She swings a leg over the back, dismounting it like a horse, and leaves her helmet balanced on the vacated seat.

He doesn't tell her to fuck off when she stops beside the bench. He meets her gaze evenly. Not angrily. Just... empty.

"She told you," Greta observes. Her voice is muffled slightly by the black cloth mask layered over a disposable paper one.

Because of course she knew. "Fuck off."

Greta lets out a short *hm,* as if his vitriol were a minor point of interest. She nods at the shanty. "I'll buy you breakfast."

"Why does everyone assume I'm broke?"

She shrugs. "You buy, then."

"Hard pass."

"You're remarkably blunt, for a man who supposedly trades in words."

"Yeah, I'm only eloquent in ink." He uses a hand to wave her away.

She doesn't move, and he feels her eyes on the back of his skull as he bends his attention pointedly to his phone.

"Cass," someone says, or something like that. It's a greeting.

"Morning, Joe. It's Cooke now."

"Right. Sorry. Old habits. Comin' in? Or out, I guess." A dry laugh.

"In a minute."

The cowbell clinks. The old woman comes out with a tray of food.

Greta is still there.

Cyril shifts. "Look, lady—"

"We're going to be seeing a lot of each other in the future," she says, "whether we like it or not. We might as well figure out how to tolerate one another."

"Good news—I don't plan on sticking around that long."

She is silent for a moment. And then: "I've been teaching for a long time, Mr. Blanchard. I've had plenty of students lose a parent." She punctuates her pause with a sigh. "I've seen a few lose both. Trust me when I say Robin's children don't need any more burdens to bear."

"Trust *me* when I say they're better off without me. It's not my fault she dragged me into this."

"In my experience, attempting to deal with the situation at hand is far more effective than resorting to hyperbole."

He sighs and clicks off his phone. "You're not going to leave me alone, are you."

"Mr. Blanchard, I absolutely cannot wait to leave you alone."

She unzips the front of her jacket, reaches inside, and pulls out a crisp new paper mask. "After breakfast."

"Jesus. Fine." He snatches the mask and puts it on. "Out here? With all your friends?"

She snorts. "The only option at this hour, unfortunately."

He hauls himself to his feet and follows her through the posts and lintel of two-by-fours. Two tables at the far end of the space have been claimed by the coalition early-morning elders, chairs spread out in a loose semicircle. A middle-aged man in a button-up shirt and tie sits alone at another small table, perusing a newspaper.

When Greta steps down off the curb and into the ad-hoc dining room, every face turns to look. A couple of hands toss casual waves. "Join us?"

"Not today." Greta gestures to a table up front, helping herself to a vinyl chair as Cyril does the same. Behind her, one of the old men says, in a too-loud whisper, something about Greta chewing up the big guy and spitting him out. She rolls her eyes and says, without turning around, "I can hear you, Rabbit."

There are guffaws, and then—when she shoots them a glare—hurried shushes. The waitress comes back out, walking around the outside of the shelter to deliver a couple of plates, and warns the old men to "behave" before making her way back around to the front. "Glad you decided to come on in. You need a menu, or—"

"I'll have my usual." Greta inclines her head toward Cyril. "Standard breakfast menu. What do you want?"

He clears his throat. "Two eggs over easy, hash browns, bacon. Sourdough toast."

The waitress raises her eyebrows over her notepad. "That all?"

"You expecting me to order the entire pig?"

"She's asking if you want a drink," Greta says, sourly. "Orange juice? Coffee?"

"Juice. Large."

The waitress tucks the notepad into her apron. "Bob'll have it whipped up in a second."

Greta nods. "Thank you."

They are alone, or at least as alone as they can be in a parking lot dining room frequented by Healdsburg's most proficient gossips.

"So," he says. "This your morning routine?"

She gestures at her motorcycle. "Going for a ride, yes. I don't always end up here."

"And your husband?"

She snorts. "He'll sleep til nine, if he can get away with it."

The idea of this woman—anyone, really—thinking of Cooke as a slacker is laughable. When Cyril had contracted for him, he'd not only answered messages at all hours, but had usually also been in the process of doing half the work himself. Or re-doing it, to his own exacting specifications. "And up past midnight, I assume."

She shrugs. "His life."

And then it hits this asshole, suddenly, that he's sitting here having this utterly pedestrian conversation, waiting for his breakfast to arrive, while cancer is eating Robin from the inside out. He rubs a hand over his face and mutters a soft expletive. "I need to piss."

Greta nods at the doughnut shop door. "All the way in back."

The bathroom, wedged around a corner at the back of a dining room about a quarter of the size of the one in the lot, is the size of a broom closet. Actually, it is a broom closet, plus a bucket and mop. He manages to empty his bladder and wash his face without getting stuck or breaking anything, though he wouldn't be sorry if he had.

Breakfast is waiting when he comes back out. The old codgers go quiet, watching with unrepentantly curious stares as he seats himself and begins to butter his toast. Greta casts a puzzled glance over one shoulder.

"Everyone's gotta watch the fat guy eat," he explains. They want to see him stuffing his face so they can reassure themselves they'll never end up like him. He downs half the orange juice. "They know who I am?"

"They watch Fox News. How much of their information is accurate, I don't know."

Nobody knows. The only people who understand what he did were the experts at the FBI. And maybe not even them, fully. But every asshole's got an opinion. "Let me guess—I'm either a vigilante hero or enemy of the state."

"Split was about forty-sixty, last I heard. Which was a while ago. The news cycle's long since moved on."

"Good. I guess." For Robin and the kids, anyway. The rest of the country might be better off if his early release still qualified as the worst thing on the news, but after five years in prison he's no longer particularly invested in the state of the nation.

They eat. The eggs are mediocre, the bacon greasy and limp. The biscuits and gravy on Greta's plate look significantly more palatable.

"Let's talk," she says.

"You don't have to convince me I have to do this for the kids. I fucking know."

"You're staying, then."

"I—don't know." Not even twenty minutes ago, it had seemed impossible that the universe could continue to function without Robin, and that was precisely why he hated her with every fiber of his being. And then this woman forced him to talk to her and now he's eating bacon. "None of this makes any fucking sense."

"Well." Greta uses a butter knife to saw off a quarter-sized hunk of biscuit. "You're going to be miserable whether you stay or go. But that's nothing new for you, is it?"

"Wow."

"The way I see it," Greta says.

"Here it comes."

"The way I see it," she repeats, sharply, "is that you've got a choice to make. You can be miserable alone, or you can be miserable with someone who loves you."

He snorts. "Lady, have you not been paying attention? Robin's spent the better part of five weeks trying to convince me she cares about me—just so that when she told me the truth, she could twist that knife extra hard. She doesn't love me. She hates my fucking guts."

Greta spears a bit of biscuit with her fork and sticks it neatly into her mouth, without touching her lips. "You of all people," she says, pausing to swallow, "should know that the heart has plenty of room for both."

"Does it matter? There's no carrot at the end of this fucking stick. She's dying. No matter what I do, I end up alone."

She sets her fork on the edge of her plate and looks at him for a long moment, steadily. "If you think the end goal of loving someone is what you get out of the bargain, you're beyond help. Everyone ends up alone. Eventually."

"And what really matters is the friends we made along the way? Don't trot out your fucking high school philosophy with me."

Greta tugs a paper napkin out of the dispenser in the middle of the table and wipes her fingers, almost thoughtfully, before picking up her mug of coffee. "A lesson from my own life, then: You can punish yourself, or you can love her as she deserves. You can't have both."

"If she can love me and hate me at the same time, I can sure fucking try."

She sips, then sets the mug down in exactly the spot she lifted it from, adjusting the handle so it's angled in precisely the same direction. "And how's that working out?"

"Jesus Christ." The woman treats everyone like a recalcitrant student—and she's not the slightest bit afraid of him. "Look, even if I wanted to—to *whatever*—"

"Forgive yourself?"

"I can't. I'm not—fixable. Trust me, I've tried."

Greta pulls her phone out of her jacket pocket, briefly, consulting the time. "I need to go. I told Robin I'd take the kids for school again." She zips her jacket up and stands.

"You're sticking me with the check?"

She looks down her nose at him. "I suggest you use this opportunity to figure out how you're going to tell them good-bye."

———

ROBIN IS ON THE ROOF.

He stands on the sidewalk and watches as she scoots butt-first down one of the valleys, squeezing goop from a caulking gun into the gaps under peeling shingles. Eventually, she lifts the gun to look at the business end, pumping the trigger in vain. "Shoot." Still crouched low, she pivots toward the ladder, and sees him. "Oh. Hey." She looks at the caulking gun, and then back at him. "Could you run down to the barn and grab me another tube? I mean, not *run*, obviously—"

"I was right," he says. "This whole time. You're a fucking liar."

"Yeah?" She sits, dangling a leg over the edge of the roof. "So are you."

"If you weren't dying," he says, the word like chalk on his tongue, "would you have picked me up from prison?"

She cocks her head. "If I told you I was dying, would you have gotten into my truck?"

"No."

"Then don't waste my time." She lifts the caulking gun. "You gonna get me the tube, or should I come down?"

He gets her the fucking tube. When he hands it up the ladder, she pops it into the gun, lops off the tip with a knife from her tool belt, and continues to work her way back up the next valley to the peak of the roof. Finally, after pressing down the nearest shingles one last time, she backs down the ladder, caulking gun held out so the gooey drippings land on the grass. On the ground, she fishes a screw from a can sitting on the porch and uses it to plug the end of the tube before letting it drop to the grass. "Roof needs replacing, but I'm not gonna get to it." She uses the back of one hand to wipe her eye, leaving a streak of black caulk across her cheek. "Hopefully that'll hold out another year or two."

"I can't do this," he says.

She squints up at him, and then shifts slightly to put her face in his shadow. "Do what?"

"Live. Without you."

Her smile is tinged with bitterness. "Sure you can," she says, quietly. "You've done it for years."

And suddenly, he's crying. Fucking *crying*. Not polite little sniffles, but full-on heaving, body-wracking sobs. Like he did only once, alone, when Tavis died. Except now he's standing on the sidewalk in front of her house, a spectacle for the whole world to see.

"Is everything... okay?" a man's voice asks, from a car. If it's someone Robin knows, this asshole can't tell through the haze of tears.

"No," says Robin. "But it's not an emergency."

The car leaves. A neighbor comes out onto their front porch and goes back inside again. Someone crosses to the other side of the street to avoid the drama. He is still crying.

At some point, through this ridiculous blubbering, this asshole manages to choke out the words: "I can't—I can't watch you die."

Robin waits, watching him, until, eventually, he simply runs out of tears.

He pulls the sleeve of his t-shirt up to wipe his face, though it accomplishes little more than smearing snot around. His throat is raw. His gut aches.

Robin is still standing there.

She takes his right hand in hers, and then reaches slightly to capture his left. They stand face-to-face, his belly pressed against her torso. "We can't have forever," she says. "We never did. All we've got is now."

"Fuck," he chokes. That's all he's got, in the end. "Fuck."

She squeezes his fingers. "Be with me, Cyril. While there's still time."

CHAPTER 24

"So here's the deal." Robin takes a swig from her half-frozen water bottle and hands it to him.

"Wait, there's a deal?" They're standing on the back porch, in the shade of the house. "I feel like you should have mentioned this before I spent the last three hours cutting your siding." He drinks, shakes the bottle to move the frozen core, and drinks again.

She draws a circle in the air, prompting him to turn around. "If you stay—"

He turns his back to her. "I thought I was the one doing *you* the favor here. Now there's conditions?"

"Just three." She brushes the sawdust off his backside with a few brisk strokes. "One, you help me finish the house. Like, for serious. Not just giving me a hand now and then."

He turns to face her again. "Chica, I know fuck-all about construction—"

"You have two hands and you can follow instructions." She turns on the ball of one foot to present her back, casting her words over one shoulder. "I'll take care of the rest."

He looks at her, and then up at the second story. He still

doesn't understand why she feels compelled to do any of this shit, but it's her life. Or lack thereof. "Fine." He brushes her off.

"Two, my time is limited. So I need what little I have left to not be about..." She uses both hands to mime an aura around him. "This."

"You just gestured to all of me."

"Yes. Exactly. I'm not going to waste my last months on earth trying to fix—whatever it is that's wrong with you." She takes the water bottle back. He hasn't left her much that's not ice, but she finishes it off and then presses the bottle, still beaded with condensation, against her forehead. "If you have issues with physical contact, or whatever the hell else you have issues with, just, you know, keep that shit to yourself. You want to eat yourself to death, be my guest. You'll still be here longer than me."

His mouth goes dry. His fingers contract into fists. He could hit her. He sees it in his mind's eye. All it would take is a couple of well-placed blows. She'll be dead soon anyway.

Jesus. What, in all she has said, could possibly justify his fury? Because she's right? Because she sees him for exactly what he is?

Is it really so terrible? To be seen?

"Cyril?"

"Yeah," he snaps, moving to open the back door. "Fine."

She plants a hand in the center of his stomach, stopping him. "I'm not done."

He brushes her arm aside and turns, taking the knob in one hand. "Maybe I better get some paper to write this down."

"Number three is easy."

He has one foot over the threshold. She can't stop him, but he stops. Half-turning to look at the hand she places on his arm. "What?"

"Kiss me."

Her eyes, when he looks at them, burn with a bright, feverish intensity.

It's not desire. He knows that. It's the sleep she hasn't been getting. The handful of pills she chokes down twice a day. The mounting panic as she watches the dregs of her life circle the drain.

Take it, the voice inside him says. Take it anyway.

"Be careful what you wish for, Chica," he growls.

She grabs his shirt with both hands and tries to yank him around. It doesn't work. She's strong, but not strong enough to move him. "What?" she says, giving him a shove instead. "You think you're gonna hurt me? I lost a husband, Cyril. My mom. Found out my entire life was your own personal RPG. I've been poked and poisoned and sliced up and stitched back together again. You think a couple bruises are gonna break me?" She snorts. "Go on, then. Do your worst. I can take a little roughing up."

He obliges. There is a brief tussle of muscle and cloth, and then his hands are on her wrists, and she's pinned against the side of the house.

She doesn't flinch. She just looks up at him, breath hot and close, one nostril curling in disgust. "See? You're all talk. You never *do* a goddamn thing."

He tightens his grip. His knuckles are white. "I swear to God, I'll—"

She interrupts him with a bitter laugh. "Look at you. You're shaking. You think you're some big scary monster? Like you're gonna hurt me if you don't hold back?" She jerks one arm free, and then the other. "Fuck, Cyril. The only person you scare is yourself."

How casually she strips him bare.

"Kiss me. Once. Is that really too much to ask?"

It's not love, either. It's pain and cancer and loneliness and all the pretty lies he wrote, once upon a time. "Yeah. Sure." He bends, hands propped against the house, and gives her a peck on the cheek.

She slaps him. Hard.

"Ow! What the—"

"Don't play stupid with me, asshole." And she slings and arm around his neck and presses her lips hard against his mouth.

Time freezes. He is suddenly conscious of the loudness of his own breath, exhaled through his nose. Blood, pounding in his ears. The slight friction of her shirt against his. A breeze ripples through the Tyvek covering the second-floor windows, like a handful of beads on a drum.

But this is not the first time they've kissed.

Each time the brain recalls a memory, it rewrites the experience anew. The memory of the memory replaces the original. A favorite moment may, in the course of a lifetime, be overwritten a thousand times. And because brains are meat, there's no backup to prevent data loss. Details slip. One color substituted for another. A word or phrase exchanged for one with a similar meaning. The edges blur. Eventually, even the most curated memory will become so distorted it bears only the slightest resemblance to the original event.

Perhaps that's why he's avoided thinking about the day he went to prison. The day she found out the letters were his. The day she kissed him good-bye. The feel of her hands on his body, the heat of her lips melting into his.

Not for love, but spite. Because she wanted him to spend every second of his sentence knowing exactly what he'd missed.

Then, like now, he didn't care.

Robin pulls back, slightly, and they breathe. Somehow, he is holding her. "I—" he begins, and she pulls him close again. Her lips part. They are both fragrant with sweat, and the taste of her is salty and sweet.

The memory of five years past is utterly overwritten.

When she steps back—or, rather, leans against the house—she sucks in a breath and runs a hand over her short hair. "Jesus," she exhales. "*Finally.*"

"Did I get it right? Or should I try kissing your ass next

time?" There's no negotiation between his brain and his mouth—the words just pop out.

She blinks, and for a moment he thinks she might slap him again. But then she gives an appreciative snort. "Boy, you don't miss a beat."

CHAPTER 25

So they kiss. And then what? The universe doesn't explode. This asshole doesn't turn into a handsome prince.

The clock begins to tick again.

He opens the door, starts to go into the house, then thinks he should maybe hold it open for her instead, backs up into her, and nearly knocks her off the porch. He mutters an incoherent apology and then realizes, what the fuck is he doing? He reverses course and steps inside.

He makes lunch. They eat. She leaves to get the kids. He makes dinner. They eat again.

He stares at her across the table. Her lips are moving. He hears no words, except this: he kissed her, and she is going to die.

No.

Yes.

"Cyril. Hey."

He is still sitting at the dining table. The kids are not. She is standing next to him. Her hand is on his arm. Shaking him. He feels nothing.

"When was the last time you slept?"

He says nothing, because he doesn't know.

"Where did you even go, last night?" When he doesn't answer, she grabs his arm and pulls. "Come on. The kids won't bother you in my bedroom."

———

HE KNOWS HE HAS SLEPT ONLY WHEN ROBIN CLICKS ON her bedside lamp, though not how long. She sits on the edge of the mattress, sipping water and taking pills. When she finishes, she pulls her feet up onto the bed and covers herself with the comforter, pulling it half off him. "I'm going to sleep. You gonna stay here or go ransack my kitchen?"

"Jesus. A little warning would be nice." He yanks his shirt down over his exposed belly and heaves his bulk toward the edge of the bed, walrus-like, letting out a stiff breath when his feet hit the floor. He has to piss, at the very least. Then he can decide if he's coming back to her bed.

She reaches for the lamp chain. "Just keep your hands off the avocados. I've been waiting for them to ripen all week."

He leans forward to stand, then eases back for just one moment more. His joints ache. His back hurts. Everything hurts. How long had he wandered, before washing up at the doughnut store? Not that walking is the problem. Like he doesn't know what causes this. He knows. He's up two sizes since his release, at the least. But he's still thinking about making a BLT. He rubs his temples with his hands. "Why?"

"Guacamole."

"No." He squeezes his eyes shut. "Why—me?"

The chain clinks softly against the lamp as she drops it, and at his back he hears her shift toward him. "What do you mean?"

"Why bother with—with my bullshit?" He'd agreed to keep it to himself, but they both know that's a promise he can't keep, no matter how hard he tries. He's filled with bullshit to the brim. Every time he moves, it spills. "Why not spend the time you've got with your kids?"

"You think I'm *not* spending time with them?" The vehemence of her reply catches him off guard. "They still have to go to school. Or do school from home. Or Greta's. Whatever. What do you expect me to do, spend the rest of my very short life sitting next to them in front of a screen, just so I can sacrifice myself upon the holy altar of motherhood?"

"Uh—no. That is not what I said." Though it was, honestly, kind of what he'd assumed. She'd always placed her children first before all else.

She lets out a huff of frustration. "I know. I just—I've already given them everything. You know that. From the day Seth popped out of me, my life belonged to him. And I'm not saying I regret that. I gave it willingly. But it's hard as hell, Cyril, especially on my own. The only way I've made it this far is reminding myself, day after day, that in ten years they'll be off to college. That as they become more independent, I become more of myself again. Except now I don't get that. Maybe it's selfish, but don't I deserve something, too?"

"And—what you want for yourself is..." He gestures to himself. "This?"

She props herself up on one elbow, and then, on second thought, sits up and knee-walks across the bed. "I married an imaginary man," she says. "Half that man was Tavis." She drapes her arms around him from behind, resting her chin on his shoulder, and holds out the hand which once held her wedding ring. (The ring she'd thrown at him, and which he'd quietly tucked back into her jewelry box when she wasn't looking.) "The other half was you." She studies the band of lighter skin as if admiring a gem, angling it back and forth, and then lets her hand drop with a sigh. "As much as I hate you, Cyril—I have to admit that I love you, too. Surely you can understand that."

He doesn't have to say *I do*.

She smooths his t-shirt over his shoulder before patting his forearm. "If this was forever, I'd cut my losses and look for someone less... abrasive. If I had another decade, I'd care that you're gonna die of a heart attack before you're forty. But I don't. All I've got is now. And right now? I hate you for what you did, but I also just... miss you."

He shrugs her off. "So I'm leftovers."

"Leftovers are all I've got, I'm afraid." She slides her bare feet over the edge of the mattress, sitting next to him, and leans her head on his shoulder. "You're... comfortable. You piss me the hell off, but when you hold me, I feel safe and warm. I could spend my last days on earth hating you, or I can forgive you and focus on the part of you I love. I choose love. Most days, anyway." She glances up, flashing her broad-toothed smile. "Plus, you know, you're cheaper than a hospice nurse."

He starts to cry. Again. He hides his face in his hands. God, this gigantic fucking baby.

"Oh. Sweetie." She wraps her arms around him, pressing her nose into the soft sandpaper stubble of his jaw. "Cyril. No."

He doesn't stop her. He doesn't push her away or get up and leave. She's the one who's dying, and this revolting tub of lard lets her waste her precious time and energy comforting *him*.

When his body stops shuddering, she tugs the bottom of his shirt up and uses it to wipe his face. "I like it when you cry."

He chokes a laugh. "Christ, you're brutal."

"I learned from the best." She pauses. "That's you, in case that wasn't obvious." She grins. "It's just nice to know the sweet, passionate soul who wrote me all those pretty words is still in there, somewhere." She gives his belly a gentle poke.

He yanks his shirt back down and stands. "I need to piss."

"Well, don't let me stand in your way." She pulls her legs up, hugging her knees to her chest to let him pass.

He relieves himself, and then splashes his face with ice cold water from the sink. As he dries his face (and the counter) with a hand towel, he forces himself to meet his reflection's eyes. He manages only a glance. "Get your shit together, asshole," he rasps. Looking at the floor. Coward.

He has no intention whatsoever of returning to Robin's bed. But when he opens the bathroom door, she is standing in the hall. "What—"

"I could go for a snack."

He looks at her for a long moment, first resisting the urge to shove her away, and then internally paging through all the crass replies that would send her back to her room, either in a huff or in tears.

"Hello?" she says, waving a hand in front of his face. "Earth to Cyril."

"Fine," he says, finally. "I was thinking BLTs."

She turns and leads the way into the kitchen. "Sounds good, assuming we have bacon."

"We have bacon."

It takes a few minutes to fry up. Robin sits on the counter next to the stove, prying apart a head of iceberg lettuce and dropping the leaves into a bowl.

"Do you think your letters are the only thing I liked about you?" she asks, apropos of absolutely nothing.

"I—" He stops. "Yes?" What else is there?

She sets the bowl aside. "Well, after Tavis died, you made me laugh again."

"Me?" He shakes his head. Even pretending he had nothing to do with Tav's death in the first place, he'd mostly just pissed her off. "Seth was the one who made you smile."

Her eyebrows furrow. "You—" Her head tilts to one side, and the look she gives him is almost a wince. "Cyril, his father had just died. I tried not to let my grief impact him, but I was totally checked out. I managed to drink enough beer to pass out. Twice. And that was before I found out I was pregnant with Nora. If Seth was happy—and he was—that was your doing."

The edges of the bacon are crisping, and he uses tongs to lay them out on a paper towel. "Yeah, well, he's easy to please."

Robin picks up a strip. "Ow." She sends a couple of puffs of air across one end and then bites, gingerly. "When I was doing my first round of chemo, I spent a lot of time trying to remember good things. And the place I kept going, in my head, was the time right after Nora was born, when you were staying with us. I don't think I realized it at the time, but I was happy, then. Content. I needed space, and you took all the burden of the kids. All I had to do was enjoy them. I never got that when Seth was born. Even when Tavis was home, he never took nights." She shifts, crossing her legs in the other direction. "And then, with you? I had so much wrapped up inside, and I knew I could say whatever came to mind without feeling judged. I didn't have to worry about doing grief right."

He snorts. "Yeah, because I didn't give a shit about profanity, and you didn't give a fuck about my opinion."

"That's what I thought, yeah." She eats the entire piece of bacon, thoughtfully. "Later I realized it was because, deep down, I know there's nothing I can say that will ever change how you feel about me. There's a freedom in that." She tips her head toward him. "That was you. Not letter-you. *This* you."

"Right. So... Swearing and babysitting. That's a real winning—"

"No." She holds a hand up in front of her face, palm out. "Nuh-uh."

"What?"

"There's a thing I tell the kids, whenever they say 'I'm stupid' or something like that. I say, kiddo, I wouldn't let anybody else say that about you, so why would I let you say it about yourself?"

"Stating the facts is not—"

"You care for my kids, Cyril, and I don't mean making sure

they do their schoolwork and eat their veggies. That's not a small thing." She hops down from the counter. "I'm done listening to you belittle yourself. You're allowed to take up space."

"What, are you my fucking therapist now?"

The look she gives him says no, but he seriously *needs* one. She's not wrong. "Come here," she says, grabbing his arm. He bends, and she plants a firm kiss on his cheek. "Thanks for the bacon. Enjoy your BLT. See you in the morning."

——————

SETH IS THE FIRST ONE OUT OF BED THE NEXT DAY, unless Cyril passing out on the couch counts as never having gone to bed at all. He is half-awake when the boy's footsteps pad softly into the bathroom and then the hall, so he does not jerk in alarm when Seth climbs onto the couch and settles into him.

Cyril lets his arm slide down around the boy's shoulders. "Hey, kid. What's up?"

"Nothin'."

The sun peeks in around the edges of the drapes. Every single bird on the block decides, in unison, that it's time to let the world know they're awake. Someone slams a car door.

The boy says nothing, still, but his inarticulate *need* is palpable. What is he looking for?

Seth had been in his room doing school when Robin had told Cyril she was going to die, and he had simply walked downstairs and out of the house—what had Robin offered by way of explanation? Had he heard about Cyril's public breakdown out on the sidewalk? Or has he sensed something amiss with his mother? Perhaps it's something more banal, like a tiff with a classmate in one of their Minecraft worlds. It had been so much easier when he was small and blurted out every thought that came to mind. The world would be a better place if everyone were even half as honest as a four-year-old. But Seth's old enough now to understand that people expect him to filter his words, so as not to hurt or shock or offend. His peers have surely taught him that exposing the true depth of his feelings invites only mockery and scorn. So he hides.

It's better this way. Better that Seth not end up at odds with the world. Like him.

"Mom's working on the house again."

It clicks. The boy knows his mom is recovering from surgery. He does not want to express disappointment about this, but he is also keenly aware that Cyril had only promised to stay so long as his mother needed him around. Now that his mom is back on her feet, he's worried Cyril is going to leave. Again.

If only that were the worst-case scenario.

Seth looks up at him with a question in his eyes, and Cyril realizes he's squeezing the kid, tight. He forces himself to loosen his grip. "Hey... kid?"

"Yeah?" Filter or no, Seth can't stop his face from radiating hope. It's his natural state.

"I was thinking I might stick around, if that's okay with you. Like, permanently."

Seth's smile is the sun coming up all over again.

CHAPTER 26

Like time-lapse photography, individual moments crystallize into what seems, in retrospect, like a too-swift tumble of hours and days. Suns rise and set while Robin is curled up next to him on the couch, or, occasionally, in her bed. He lifts and carries and cuts and hauls, though not without complaint. There is a lot of grunting and swearing involved. A few pulled muscles. She brings in an electrician—"I don't mess with current," she says—but takes care of the rest herself. They get the windows in upstairs before the first torrential downpour, and after that the house seems far less permeable. He sweats. A lot.

Autumn days give way to rainy winter nights. COVID numbers soar; Greta locks down her household again, and the kids celebrate birthdays and attend school in their pajamas on the couch. Thanksgiving and Christmas come and go, and with them the circumference of his waistline waxes and wanes like the phases of the moon. Bit by bit, the world contracts, until the perimeter of Robin's property seems to be the end of it all.

Spring brings rain (though not enough) and the promise of vaccines.

Once, this asshole had counted the days until the end of each of Tav's deployments, when his freedom to write what and when he wished to Robin would come to a temporary end, or at least be significantly curtailed. After Tav's death, he'd numbered each hour until, inevitably, the Feds came to take him away. And then, when Robin had welcomed him into her home, he had marked the time until sentencing. And then, of course, there was prison.

Now he counts the days until she dies.

"I know what you're doing," she says, one Saturday morning (because she works fucking Saturdays, too). "I see you watching me."

Waiting for the first symptoms of decline. Fatigue. Loss of appetite. Headaches. Twice in the past ten days, she's begged off work to stay in bed, citing "hormonal" issues. The calls she's placed to her doctor—from the barn, when he's occupied with the kids—prove that's a lie. "Yeah? And what the hell else am I supposed to do?"

A stack of sheetrock two feet tall sits in the center of the upstairs master bedroom. She is measuring and scoring the top sheet with a knife. He's just standing there, waiting to help with the heavy lifting.

She finishes popping out the rectangle she's cut to accommodate an outlet, thumbing the knife back into its sheath before slipping it into her belt. As she straightens, she gestures for him to grab the far end. "I dunno, just—enjoy the moment?"

He gets his fingers under the edge of the sheetrock and lifts, tilting it upright. Robin grabs the other end and nods to a wall. As he maneuvers around the remaining sheetrock, his toe catches on the corner of the pile. "Wow," he grunts, recovering with an awkward lunge, "yeah, this moment is the best."

She grins. "You know, the upside to dying is that it allows you to just—let go. Stuff that annoyed the crap out of me before now just seems kind of... sweet. Like Nora screeching, or Seth's endless Minecraft monologues, or—"

"Me?"

She laughs. "Yeah. You." They ease the sheetrock into place, and she uses her hammer to bump the edge until it's perfectly lined up with the electrical box. "I dunno, it's weird. Everything sparkles a little more when you know it might be the last time." Her hand dips into her tool belt and she drops to one knee, sowing a line of drywall nails down the edge of the sheetrock so swiftly it looks mechanical, two perfect hits to each head. "Although," she says, shifting to the next stud as her hand reaches into the nail pouch again, "I guess you guys aren't the temporary ones. It's me." She nails two more rows and then stands, slotting her hammer back into its loop. "In the long run, it doesn't matter. There is no long run. It's just now."

"Easy for you to say. You're not the one left behind."

"Oh yeah. Dying. So easy." She returns to the pile of sheetrock, crouching to get her fingers under the next piece. And then she stops. She straightens and turns to look at him. "You know what? You're right. I'm here today. And I feel great." Her hand unbuckles her belt, and it drops to the floor. "Let's go do something fun."

"You're admitting that hanging sheetrock isn't a blast?"

"It might not be the most fun I've ever had." She looks out the window. "It's a beautiful day."

"It's a fucking sauna." In Healdsburg, like most of inland California, spring isn't a gradual increase in warm days so much as it is alternating rain and sun. Today is sun. Though, admittedly, it's far worse in the unventilated second floor.

"Let's go to the park."

———

It's eleven, so he packs a picnic lunch while she changes into shorts and sandals and wrangles the kids. It takes her the entire time he's assembling sandwiches and slicing apples to pry them away from the television, get them dressed, and herd them to the truck. And then they spend the entire five-minute drive whining.

"Holy cow, you guys," Robin says. "Minecraft will be there when you get back. I promise." She thumbs the driver's side window down and sticks an arm out, letting her hand sail on the breeze. "The sun is out right now."

"The sun's up every day," Seth points out. From any other kid, this would be snarky petulance; Seth is primarily concerned with the facts, ma'am.

"Yeah, but you can't always see it, can you? You've been stuck inside with nothing *but* Minecraft for months!"

"I like inside!" Nora declares.

"Yeah," Seth agrees, emboldened by his sister's moxie. "We want Minecraft!"

They don't know their mother has an expiration date, so it's not fair to expect them to treasure every moment with her—but Cyril still wants to reach back and wring their scrawny little necks.

Before he can snap at them, Robin puts a hand on his arm. Her fingers slide down into his palm. She squeezes, briefly, before returning her hand to the wheel. "You'd have to stop playing to eat lunch, anyway. Let's eat at the park, and then if you guys are still bored, we can go home. Okay?" She shoots him a knowing look; once the kids are at the park, they'll never want to leave.

Robin skips the left-hand turn that would take them to the familiar Georgie Park. Instead, she turns right and drives down a series of winding, shady roads descending into a neighborhood on the south end of town, down by the base of the largest geological formation in the area. She nods to it and says, "Fitch Mountain." It's more of a large hill.

"It looks like a hat!" Nora pipes up, the previous moments' complaints apparently forgotten.

Cyril ducks his head slightly to squint up at the ridgeline. "Looks more like a snake that swallowed an elephant, to me."

"It totally does!" Seth exclaims.

Cyril manages to twist himself far enough to glimpse the kid over one shoulder. "You remember?" *The Little Prince* was one of many books he'd read to Seth, back when Seth was four.

"It's one of his favorite books," Robin explains. "He's only read it about fifty times."

"Mom won't read it," Seth informs him. "It makes her cry. A *lot*."

"Really appreciate you sharing that info, buddy."

"Mom," he says, gently chiding. "It's okay to cry."

At the park, Robin parks in front of a fenced-in dog run where an elderly man throws a tennis ball for a terrier that looks like Toto from *The Wizard of Oz*. She is barely out of the truck before the kids are squeezing past her, ignoring the dog entirely as they rush for the play structure. "Masks!" she shouts.

Cyril eases his bulk out of the cab and goes around back, where Robin is hauling the cooler out of the truck bed. He takes it from her. "Shoulda bought a house down here."

"Yeah, it's a lot cooler, isn't it?" She points across the grassy field beyond the play structure, bordered by trees covered in ivy in a green so deep it looks black. "River's right through there." She pulls out a paper grocery bag with napkins and utensils and then shuts and locks the camper shell. "Great in the summer, but about every fifth spring the neighborhood floods."

"And you know that how?" She talks like she's been here forever. Like she owns the place, or it owns her.

Robin cocks an eyebrow. "You'd be surprised how much you can learn from sitting around listening to old farmers complain."

"The doughnut shop?" There are three picnic tables under the tree beside the playground, and they all look about a hundred years old, splintered and honeycombed with beetle boreholes. He sets the cooler on the end of the nearest and tests the bench with a foot. It creaks.

"Yup." Robin bends, scoping out the underside of the table, then points to the righthand bench. "This one's good." She turns, shading her eyes with a hand. "Kids aren't gonna want to eat, now."

He slides one leg under the table and straddles the bench, facing the yard. "More for us."

She climbs onto the table, planting her feet on the bench in front of him, and unwraps the sandwich he hands her. "This park's smaller than Georgie, obviously, and older, but we used to come here a lot right after Nora learned to walk." She nods to the low chain link fence that encircles the play area. "She's a runner. Not so much anymore, thank God. Once, when she was three, Seth left the front door open after he got the mail and she just walked right out. Cops found her halfway to the plaza. Thank goodness I'd already made friends with the chief." She cocks a half-smile. "At the doughnut shop."

They watch the kids play. They're the only kids present, so when Seth asks if they *have* to wear masks Robin sighs and says she guesses not. She collects them from both children and tucks them into a pocket.

Cyril's sandwich is gone, so he starts on the apples, being careful to reserve exactly three quarters for his companions. Another car pulls into the lot, and when its driver opens the door a large poodle clambers out, barking as it bounds toward the field.

"I thought about getting the kids a puppy," Robin muses.

"Seriously? You don't have enough on your plate?"

"I know. I was just thinking about, you know, getting one now. So that when I..." She lets her words trail off. "So they'd have something."

"Nothing's gonna make it easier for them," Cyril says. "You know that."

"Yeah. I know." She crumples the saran wrap around the crust of her sandwich. "Plus, now they've got you."

He senses this is the lead-in to a conversation about breaking the news to the kids. It's a conversation he doesn't want to have. Not now. Maybe not ever. "Is that supposed to be a compliment?" he says, making it flippant instead.

Robin grins, and he can see, in her eyes, as she decides to let it go. For now. Then the grin becomes a yawn that she attempts, unsuccessfully, to stifle. "Ugh," she says, shaking her head. "I need more coffee."

"Maybe if you took a fucking break now and then."

She gives him a wide-eyed, innocent look. "Is that not what I'm doing?"

"Mom! Mommy!" Nora trots up to the table. She accepts the half-sandwich Cyril holds out to her and uses it to point across the field. "I wanna go to *that* structure!"

Robin's brow furrows. "Sweetie, that's not a—"

But Nora is already out of the gate and dashing across the field. Robin sighs and gets to her feet. "Seth! We're heading that way!" She glances at Cyril. "You coming?"

"Yeah. Why not." He takes the other sandwich half for Seth, slides a bottle of water into one pocket, and flips the cooler lid shut.

Robin is right, of course. The "play structure" is some kind of above-ground water junction, with six-inch pipes painted red and blue. The kids stand in front of it, munching thoughtfully on their PB&Js, perhaps trying to decide whether this development is more interesting or disappointing. Then Nora says, "Look! A path! I'm gonna find treasure!" and dashes off into the trees.

"Sweetie, I don't think that's a trail!" Robin calls. "Come on back!"

Seth follows his sister into the brush. "It is, Mom! There's steps and everything!"

Robin looks down at her sandals and Cyril's flip-flops. "We're not exactly wearing appropriate footwear here."

"Do we have a choice?" The kids are gone.

"Damn it." Robin takes off at a half-jog into the woods.

Cyril tromps down after her into a tangle of ivy, decaying wood, and damp, sandy soil. Though the entire area has obviously been recently underwater, the ivy is already hard at work covering the detritus with a blanket of thick foliage. The river comes into sight just through the first phalanx of trees, broad and fast and grey-brown, churning under the flat surface.

"Guys!" Robin shouts from up ahead, jogging down a series of four-by-fours lodged into the hill as rudimentary steps. "Guys, slow down!"

Cyril follows more slowly. On the far side of the river, there's a gravel plant, dredging the river bottom and *chu-chunk*ing perfect little kernels of rock. Downriver, at the bend, is the perfunctory little bridge that leads into town. Close to the waterline the trees thin out, and it's easy to see the kids scrambling along the top of a steeply eroded bank.

Robin catches up with them, finally, not so far ahead of him that he can't hear her say, "Guys, look at the water." She points down. "See how fast it's moving? If you fall in, you'll be swept away."

"Oh," Seth says.

Nora says nothing, which suggests she might be taking her mother's warning as an invitation to adventure. But then Seth picks up a pebble and throws it, and soon they're taking turns chucking rocks and sticks into the water, seeing how far they can throw and which objects sink or get swept away.

As Cyril emerges from the thickest underbrush, Robin backtracks a few paces up the bank to join him. "Hey," she says, smiling. "Look at you."

"Fuck off," he growls, low enough the kids don't hear. But she's right. He doesn't feel like shit. He isn't gasping for breath.

He has absolutely not lost weight (or not much, anyway), but it's possible he's traded some fraction of fat for muscle and stamina. He's tried to avoid thinking about that. Allowing himself even the slightest sense of accomplishment is the first domino in a cascade failure of self-loathing and masochism.

Abruptly, rock-throwing ends and the kids dash further on down the path.

"Jesus, are they communicating telepathically?" He moves to follow, but Robin shakes her head.

"Where are they gonna go?" She points upriver. The path is visible from their vantage point, and the bank much more gradually sloped. "If one of them falls in, they'll float this way."

He shrugs, and they stand together on the little rise and watch, half-hypnotized by the water's flow.

Robin's fingers find their way into his hand.

He squeezes. Gently.

She squeezes back.

If he could stop time, he would do it here. All those days in prison, one exactly like the next. All those nights he spent getting up to no good on the internet. All of them worthless. Here—this day, this moment—is the one he would choose to repeat again and again.

"This could be nice," she says, softly. Not looking at him. "Right?"

"It could've been." But now it's gone. Whisked away like a leaf on the river.

She leans away from him, slightly, to look up at his face. "You're stuck on a point in the future, but you wouldn't even be standing here if I hadn't told you what was coming. Would you?"

They both know the answer is no. Were this anything but his last possible chance with her, he'd never have allowed her to get this close. It would have always been not now, not yet, maybe next time. Someday. When he was good enough. "Is this part of your revenge? To—" his voice catches, but he forces the words out. "To show me what I could have had, before it's gone?"

She pulls him to a log at the edge of the bank. She steps up onto it, so she's nearly at his eye level. "You *can* have it, you idiot," she says. "Now." And she takes his head in her hands and presses his lips to his.

This time, he doesn't resist.

"Mom?"

Both the kids are standing there, mouths open.

Cyril shoves her away. Not hard, but hard enough to throw her off balance, and although he makes a grab for her, he's too late. She lands on her rear in the sandy soil. "Shit—"

"I'm good, I'm good!" She's laughing, stretching out a hand to be pulled back to her feet. He obliges, and she dusts the sand off the back of her shorts.

Seth's freckled face is crimson.

Nora looks between them, wide-eyed. "Are you guys gonna marry?"

"No," Cyril snaps.

Robin laughs again. "Don't worry about it, baby." She grabs Cyril's hand, lacing their fingers together, and gives his knuckles a quick peck. "Let's head back to the playground."

Nora shrugs and skips off; Seth darts a quick glance at them and then hurries past, as if he can't get out of there quickly enough.

The path is too narrow to allow them to walk side by side—his arms are striated with scratches he'd acquired on the way in—but Robin doesn't drop his hand. She goes first, pulling him along behind. Her pace is faster than he's used to, and it's a gentle slope upward all the way, but when his breaths become audible, she glances back and then stops, turning to face him. He pulls the water bottle out of his pocket, empties half of it into his gullet, and then hands the remainder to her.

"I need you to do something." She takes a sip and then offers it back to him—holding onto it when he takes it from her until he looks up, meeting her eyes. "For me."

"Shit." She's gonna force the issue. Right here, right now. This is where she asks him to tell the kids, or maybe be there when she tells them, and he doesn't know how he can possibly bear to watch that realization dawn in her children's eyes. He also can't tell her no. He takes another swig. "If you're gonna ask me to haul your ashes to Antarctica or some shit like—"

"Fuck me."

He laughs, short and sharp. "What?"

Her gaze does not waver. "You heard what I said."

He snorts, then laughs and shakes his head. "No." He caps the bottle and slips it back into his pocket. "You don't—Jesus, no." He laughs again, and the sound is harsh and dry. "You don't want that."

"You don't get to tell me what I want, Cyril. Not anymore. I make my own decisions now."

"Oh my God, you're crazy." He shoves past her and doesn't look back until he gets to the truck.

————

THE RIDE HOME IS SILENT. HE LOSES HIMSELF IN prepping dinner. The kids log onto Minecraft in the living room, and Robin goes down to the barn to work on... whatever. He doesn't care. Dinner is nearly ready when she comes back, walking past him without acknowledging his presence but stopping to grab a beer from the fridge, and tells the kids, curtly, that it's time to turn off screens.

Seth comes into the kitchen. "Not now, kid," he says, and Seth reads the room for once and leaves.

Not five minutes later, Cyril hears the kids head upstairs to bother their mother. He considers stopping them, but that's her problem, not his.

Dinner comes off the stove, and instead of plopping the pan of pasta in the center of the table he serves up individual portions on plates, sets the table, and gets drinks. When there's nothing more he can do he goes to the bottom of the stairwell, listening to the thunder of little feet over head.

"This one's mine!" Seth's voice declares. It's clear as a bell because the second floor is still a blank canvas of sheetrock and plywood flooring. Everything echoes.

Robin laughs. "Who says you get to choose? You guys are pretty good at sharing. I think—"

"No!" shouts Nora. "I want my own room!"

"You said!" Seth protests. "You said we—"

"Okay, okay, chill. I'm teasing. Yes, you get your own rooms. But there's just two to pick from, so you have to agree."

The kids discuss the benefits and drawbacks of each room for a while, in a surprisingly civilized fashion. How long will they get to enjoy their own spaces before they're gone again?

And then the obvious conclusion dawns on him: the kids aren't moving. When Robin is gone, Greta and her husband will move in. Now the ramp makes perfect sense. They'll occupy the downstairs bed and bath and office, while the kids will have their own space, unaltered, upstairs.

And where is he supposed to go? It doesn't matter. Nothing matters, after she's gone.

"Think about where the sun rises and sets," Robin tells the kids. "That way's east, so this one's gonna be light first thing in the morning."

The food is getting cold. He considers yelling up the stairwell. Then he sighs and starts up the steps instead.

Nora hears him first. "Is it dinner?" she demands, and when he says "on the table" she squeezes past him and dashes downstairs. Seth at least waits until he's finished coming up the stairs before following his sister.

Robin doesn't appear in the hall. He finds her in the eastern bedroom. "So the Cookes are moving in," he says, keeping his voice low.

She turns to look at him, her face registering confusion. "What?"

"Here. I mean, you said the kids could choose their rooms—"

"No? The Cookes are perfectly happy in their own home. And the second floor is hardly accessible. Although," she adds, thoughtfully, "I have considered installing an elevator in the laundry room. Remodeling their place really sold me on universal design."

He couldn't care less about Cooke or the accessibility of his house. "Then you're just—fucking with the kids? Let them have new rooms for a couple of months and then have it all ripped away when you—" He can't say it. This fucking coward.

"No," she says, slowly. Her confusion grows deeper. "I figured they could come stay here whenever they want. Weekends or holidays or whatever works out."

"How?"

She cocks her head, giving him a puzzled—if slightly irritated —grin. "Are you being intentionally obtuse? I thought the plus-size bathroom remodel made it pretty obvious. Or, like, the fact that I made all the doorways four feet wide and seven feet tall."

He stares.

"Mommy!" Nora calls, drawing the word out. "Mommy! I need ketchup!"

Robin shrugs, turns, and jogs down the stairs.

———

THE CHILDREN ARE NEARLY FINISHED WITH DINNER when he comes downstairs again. Seth says something, but he doesn't answer, and when he lets himself out the front door he hears Robin telling the kids not to follow.

He doesn't leave. He can't. He's not sure, now, if he ever really could.

He just needs to be alone. He sits on the front porch steps, which only this week he'd helped Robin rebuild, and holds his head in his hands. He's tired. Exhausted in a way that has nothing to do with flesh or bone.

Inside, as Robin herds the kids to bed, there are more footsteps; more laughter; more screams. No matter what their—*her*—children do, it's loud. And there is always more laughter than tears.

A few dog walkers pass, casting curious glances at him from behind masks. The sun sets. The house is, finally, still.

The front door opens. Her bare footsteps pad across the porch, and then she is standing beside him. Something cold touches his shoulder, and he looks up to find her handing him a can of root beer. He takes it. She sits. Pops the cap off a green bottle of non-alcoholic beer.

"Why are you doing this?" Trying to give him her house, her kids, her everything?

"I think the bigger questions is, why can't you accept it?" She upends the bottle, briefly, taking a swig. She grimaces and lets out a grunt of disgust. "I always think this stuff is gonna be better than it is."

They watch the stars come out. She finishes off her not-quite-beer. The root beer sits next to him on the porch rail, unopened.

"Look." She puts a hand on his arm. "Right now? I feel good. And I know, like, for sure, that this is the best I'm ever going to feel again. Top of the roller coaster. I can't afford to sit around anymore and wait while you mope or self-flagellate or whatever the hell it is you do. Honestly? This is not even about you. It's—"

"About you? Wanting"—he grabs a handful of flesh from his belly and gives it a savage shake—"this?"

"Is that really so hard to believe?"

"Disgusting," he hisses. "Is the word you used to describe me, five years ago. Don't pretend you've suddenly developed a taste for ass cracks and cellulite."

"I'm not pretending anything," she says. "But I'm also not who I was, five years ago." She leans back, hands on knees, looking up at the rafter they'd sistered under the porch roof, and lets out a slow breath. "I guess... I've gotten used to you."

"Oh, well, in that case, yes, absolutely, let's fuck." He puts a hand on the railing and heaves himself to his feet, stooping to pick up her empty green bottle as he climbs the steps.

She catches the door as it swings shut between them. "You think blind lust is the only legitimate basis for having sex? News flash, Cyril. Tavis was objectively hot, but he was not actually my type. But I sure as hell fucked him, didn't I? You made damn sure of that."

He collects the dinner plates from the table, stacking his own on top, and eats cold corn on the cob as he files the dirty plates into the dishwasher. She stands in the middle of the kitchen, hands propped on hips, watching him. He squirts dish soap onto the dirty nonstick pans in the sink and runs the water hot.

Finally, she lets out a huff of breath, lets her arms drop to her sides, and yanks the fridge open. She pulls out another non-alcoholic beer and uses the hem of her shirt to twist off the cap. "Seriously, though, are you really that scared of me seeing your cock?"

He plunges his hands into the hot, soapy water.

She leans a hip against the counter and uses the butt of the beer bottle to poke his gut. "Is it hideously deformed? Did it fall off?"

"Dunno," he growls. The first pot comes clean, and he reaches for the dish towel to swipe it dry. "Haven't seen it in about a decade."

She snorts laughter. "Well, I know you've touched it." She makes exaggerated huffing noises. "You breathe like a walrus having an asthma attack, you think I can't hear you in the bathroom?"

"Fuck." He slaps the towel down on the counter. "Off."

She follows him down the hall and into the bedroom. *His* bedroom, he realizes. With the Cal king bed and the double-plus-sized bathroom on the other side of the wall. The room now serving as the kids' bedroom will be his office, so he doesn't have to climb the stairs when, inevitably, he balloons back to six hundred pounds. (Because what else is he gonna do, when she's gone?) What he had assumed was the upstairs master bedroom is a combined play area, filled with the kids' books and electronics. Two smaller bedrooms, one for each kid, so they can come and visit the home their mother built and play with the toys she gave them and talk to the man who worshipped her and lie in the beds where she used to tuck them in and feel, as they sleep, that she might be just around the corner.

She means him to be the keeper of her mausoleum.

He yanks open the closet door, where she's already cleared him his own space inside, moving herself out of the picture foot by square foot. Tav's old canvas seabag is crammed into a high shelf; this asshole gives it a rough shake and begins stuffing it with the shirts and sweatpants he pulls off the shelves.

"You need me to say it, Cyril?" she says, so close he can feel her breath on his neck. "You're not anywhere near as hot as Tavis. But am I physically attracted to you? Yes. Would I have been, under ideal circumstances? Probably not. Doesn't matter. Everything in my life is a compromise."

He turns, forcing her to back up a step.

She spreads her palms. "What is your hang-up? Isn't this exactly what you've always wanted?"

He shoulders past her without meeting her eyes. "I want *you*. Not your body. Not—not that. Not unless it's real."

Behind him, as he leaves the bedroom, she chokes out a high, disbelieving laugh. "Real? *Real?* You want real, honest-to-goodness fairytale magical true love for ever and ever, or nothing at all?" She laughs again. "When did you ever offer me that choice?"

"I never asked you for anything."

"Oh, but you'd sure as hell take it from me, wouldn't you?"

He glances at the kids' bedroom door. "Jesus Christ, you're gonna wake—"

"Don't you fucking lecture me about my own goddamn kids."

He retreats to the kitchen, where the pots are still soaking in sudsy dishwater. Why won't she just leave him alone? "Look," he says, opening a cupboard. He pulls out a package of Double-Stuf Oreos. "I'm gonna spend the night in the barn." There's a folding cot in the back about the size of his prison bunk. "Tomorrow I'll—"

"What, leave? Run and hide?" She spits the words. "Fucking coward."

He lets himself through the laundry room and out the back door. The screen door slams behind him, and then immediately screeches open again.

"I don't care what you want," she calls after him, as he plods down the hill. "Or whatever the hell you're afraid of. You fucking *owe* me."

———

HE IS BACK WITHIN THE HOUR. NOT TO APOLOGIZE OR capitulate, or even because all the Oreos are gone (though they are), but for the most infuriatingly banal reason in the world: he needs to take a shit. Fortunately, she doesn't burst out of the bedroom to renew the confrontation. As he does his business, occupying himself with a game on his phone, there is a small, regular noise in the background which he assumes to be produced by the water heater in the hall. She'd replaced it a month past, but the new unit had been making ticking noises at odd hours. But as he steps out of the bathroom, the flush of the toilet fading away, he realizes that what he has been listening to are her muffled sobs.

Is she an idiot? He knows she is not. But he is not worth even a fraction of this melodrama. Never before, and certainly not now. "Shut the fuck up," is what he wants to tell her. Instead, he stands motionless in the hall outside her door.

Abruptly, she falls silent. Having realized, perhaps, that his footsteps have not plodded back outside. Waiting.

"I don't deserve to be loved," he says.

Her voice, when she answers, is bitter: "But I do."

———

WHAT HE SPENDS THE NEXT HOUR DOING, BEFORE HE returns to the barn, is so patently obvious it's not worth record-ing. (Hint: it involves the fridge.) It doesn't help. It never does. It is only ever a momentary distraction, a temporary anesthetic. But if it's any consolation, this time he doesn't even achieve that much relief.

Fuck her. It's what she thinks she wants, isn't it? Just fuck her, and get it over with. She'll realize it was a huge fucking mistake, and that will be that.

He can't.

What he did to her before was bad enough. She was completely ignorant. He took advantage of her. And now—now she thinks she *knows*. She thinks she understands what he did and who he is and what she wants. But she doesn't. Not really. She doesn't know all he has thought and done. All that he has wanted to do. The things he didn't say. And if she was vulnerable then...?

She's twice a mother now. A widow, now. She is *dying*, now.

And it's not just about letters, this time. Not just mental

manipulation, as bad as that was. No. Doing what she thinks she wants—what he has *made* her want—would be rape in every sense of the word.

It is, perhaps, a very fine an arbitrary line.

But it is a line. And it is one he will not cross.

So he does what he has always done. He hides. He eats.

And he writes. Not pretty. Not persuasive. But as much of the garbage piled inside his head as he can bear to disgorge. All of these stupid fucking words. He tries to tell the truth.

~~If, somehow, she can read this, and still claim to want this asshole in her~~

No. Damn it. Get it right, for fucking once.

Robin. If you read this, and still claim to want me in your bed—

What am I supposed to do? I could never tell you no.

CHAPTER 27

ROBIN

J esus Christ, Cyril.
    Christ.
    I don't even know where to begin. I mean, I knew you were
    fucked in the head, but reading this is like looking at you through
coke-bottle glasses or in some kind of warped funhouse mirror.

Let's just get this out of the way first, so we're 100% clear:

You are fat. Yes. I am aware. Oh my God, am I aware. Thank you.

But if I can get my breasts cut off and still be sexy, guess what? You can
be fat and attractive, too. You have goddamn dimples when you smile. (Not
the smirk. Your real smile.) Do you know how many guys can pull off that
half-assed perpetual 5 o'clock shadow? I love how your face is soft and
scratchy at the same time. (Yes: because you are fat.)

Your hugs. God. You know who hugs like that? My dad. After he died, I
had these dreams where he was hugging me again. I'd wake up crying,
because even in my dreams I knew he was gone. Remember after Tavis died,
when you came with me to Nora's ultrasound and I broke down? You
hugged me then, and even though I hated you somehow it still felt like
going home. After you went to prison, the dreams started again, but it
wasn't my dad anymore. It was you.

And your voice. Oh my God, Cyril, your voice is like whiskey. Sometimes when you read bedtime stories to the kids I just sit in the other room, listening. Why do you think I'm always asking you to sing when you play the piano? Complete fucking turn-on.

There. Now it's in ink, so you can't edit it out or twist it around later.

You know, I think the only completely honest thing contained in this flaming dumpster fire of self-deception is the fact that you lie best by omission. Here's the thing, though, Cyril: You're no longer living by proxy. You're here, with me, and I have eyes and ears. So let me fill in a few blanks.

How about teaching my son to make macaroni? You skipped right over that scene, didn't you? Let me tell you how it went. He got frustrated and angry and tried to quit, but you stuck with him. You talked him through every step. You made jokes, and he laughed. And when he sat down to dinner—dinner that he made himself—oh my God, his smile. Did you legit not notice me trying not to cry?

I haven't seen my son smile like that since you went to prison. He wasn't old enough to understand why you left. And then his grandma died. And I got sick. And then fucking COVID cut him off from all his friends. He's so empathetic, so open to everything, everyone—he carried it like a backpack full of bricks. You lifted the weight of the world off of his little shoulders. Do you have any idea what that means to me? You helped him be a kid again.

And Nora. Daily meltdowns. Sometimes hourly. Neither Greta nor I could get her to sit down for more than ten seconds. Forget school. Then you come in and teach her how to play the piano. And don't give me that "oh she has natural talent" bullshit. Yeah, maybe, but she's also five. She can't even brush her teeth without running off halfway through. But she can play Hot Cross Buns and Twinkle Twinkle, because you sit with her at that bench every single day, redirecting her every ten seconds without ever losing your cool. Her confidence has skyrocketed. She's stopped crying at night. Hell, Cyril, she's even started eating her goddamn vegetables. Yeah, you're a monster, all right.

Then there's how you make everything a game for the kids, and make sure they're fed and dressed and bathed—pretty sure this is the cleanest my *kids have ever been—and really, truly play with them. You make sure each one of them gets a little one-on-one time with me every day, just like you always, always make sure I have a clean mask in the car and a fresh glass of water by the bed.*

That's a lot of fucking blanks, Cyril.

I can already hear the excuses you're making in your head. It's not you, it's just the kids naturally maturing. They're just excited because you're someone new. It could have been anyone. And even if it is your doing, none of it matters, because oh my God you killed your best friend.

Please.

Maybe I didn't know who Tavis truly was, but I lived with the man. He was nobody's fool. He was military, Cyril. Not just a grunt, but a Navy corpsman attached to Marines. He knew the risks he was taking far better than you possibly could. You sat behind a keyboard. He was living on the front lines.

Maybe you wished for his death. Maybe you could have done more to stop it from happening. But you did not get Tavis killed. That burden belongs to the Afghan who wired the bomb. It belongs to the officer who ordered Tavis to be in the wrong place at the right time. And it belongs to Tavis, who decided the life of a kid half a world away was the hill he was willing to die on. Don't dishonor his sacrifice by trying to rob him of his agency.

Here's a question. Tavis had everything—looks, friends, talent—and still called you his closest friend. Why? He never invited you out with the guys. Or to our house for dinner. Now that I think about it, did he ever even show himself in public with you, anywhere? No. He was happy to come to your place. Alone. I don't have a lot of friends, but even I know that's not how friendship works.

When I first met the two of you, you were a brilliant student with a smart mouth, if a little... rough around the edges. I resented you because you took Tav's time, but mostly? I was intimidated. Everyone assumed you'd end up in Silicon Valley making millions of dollars. But by the time Tavis died, you were a six-hundred-pound recluse. You don't get like that without someone to enable you.

Consider why you're so desperate to paint yourself the villain. Maybe it's because, deep down, you know that if you aren't the antagonist in this story, you're the tool.

Is that why you can't trust me? Are you afraid that I, too, might be manipulating you? Or have you just spent so much time lying to yourself that it's impossible to recognize the truth?

You're a liar, Cyril. But I'm not.

Believe me when I say I want you.

STAGE 5

ACCEPTANCE

CHAPTER 28

Reader, he fucks the girl.

If morbid curiosity demands to know how a four-hundred-fifty-pound guy with a gut like a half-inflated inner tube sticks his dick in a chick, feel free to consult Google for all the fat fetish porn nobody ever wanted to see.

> "You're terrible at this, you know
>   that?" she says, peering over his
>   shoulder as he types. "It was
>   warm. And comfortable. And
>   loving." She squeezes his arm.
>   "You were nervous."
> He. *He* was nervous.
> "Maybe you have issues acknowledging
>   your own feelings, but I'm not
>   obligated to sustain your clever
>   literary device. *You* were nervous.
>   You said a lot of stupid, vulgar
>   things. But you were funny, too.

```
        You listened, and you tried. You
        were good to me."
    Now who's a liar? It was like
        fucking a whale.
    "I like whales."
    The only reason he is still
        composing this absurd narrative is
        because she begged him to
        continue, so if she doesn't want
        him to delete the entire document,
        she had better quit reading over
        his fucking shoulder.
    "Fine, fine. I'm out."
    Jesus.
```

—————

THE MORNING AFTER. HE WAKES TO THE RHYTHMIC crunch of swinging pickaxes. It is Monday, and the kids are enjoying their twenty minutes of Minecraft before, from their perspective, breakfast magically materializes on the table. Next to him, Robin sleeps with mouth slightly open, one arm out-thrown over her head. Beneath the comforter, her toes curl against his calf. He watches her breathe, revisiting every curve of her body in his mind. She jerks, slightly, when the pickaxe *chunk* is drowned out by a cartoonish explosion and Nora's shriek of delight. The kids are detonating whatever they've built.

Tavis died with the roar of combusting ammonium nitrate in his ears so that five years later, his best friend could lie next to his wife, listening to his kids gleefully exclaim over laying waste to a world on a screen.

"Hey," she says, smiling sleepily. She stretches, groaning, and reaches for him.

If she thinks this monumental climax is a moment of transformation, of redemption, of transcendence for him—well, she hasn't been paying attention. Wishful thinking. Try again. Here is how this asshole responds, the morning after she's given herself to him: he grunts and rolls out of bed.

"Cyril?" Her fingers, as he shrugs away, trace soft tracks down his arm.

He grabs a change of clothes from the closet and leaves the room, pretending not to see the disappointment on her face. The hurt and hope deflated. But he sees. Oh, he absolutely does.

What does she expect? Consummation changes nothing. It's a moment in time, no less and no more. He showers and makes breakfast and runs the kids to Greta's and Robin goes to work upstairs and he puts the laundry in the dryer and life goes on just as it did before.

He doesn't call her to lunch, but she comes anyway. It is a silent meal.

"Cyril," she begins again, finally, inevitably. "I realize I project an aura of unassailable confidence, but we just did the most intimate thing two people can do and now you won't even look at me and I'm starting to feel just a *tad* insecure. Can you just—"

"Look, I did what you wanted. I didn't agree to massage your ego, too."

She just looks at him. Then she draws in a breath and lets out a heavy sigh.

"What? Did you think this *meant* something?"

She tosses her fork down onto the table and stands. "I know it did."

"You believe whatever you want to believe." She was an idiot to trust him. He's only giving her what she deserves.

"You realize this is completely transparent, right?" She stacks her cup on her plate and picks up both. "You're in love with me and you're terrified to admit it and last night you made yourself vulnerable for ten whole minutes and now you're scared of rejection so you're pushing me away."

He snorts. "Yeah... you know what?" He uses his fork to rearrange the potato salad on his plate before inserting it into his mouth. "I'm gonna do us both a favor here and be honest."

"Please do."

"It actually just wasn't that good."

———

SHE SPENDS THE NEXT WEEK METICULOUSLY replicating every detail of Victorian gingerbread trim from the lower half of the house to the upper exterior, hanging out of windows and clambering over scaffolding like she's actively trying to get herself killed. Outside of what's strictly necessary for the care and feeding of children, she does not speak to him, and he does not wait for her to ask him to move back to the couch.

It's not until the nine-day mark that Seth, bless his oblivious little heart, finally detects something amiss. "Hey," he says at bedtime, "is Mom mad at you?"

There's no real way around this question. "Yeah."

"Why?"

"Because I hurt her feelings."

"Can't you just say sorry?"

"I could, yeah." And she'd come running right back, because apparently there's nothing he can do or say that will convince her he's not worth her time.

"Why don't you?"

Because it's better this way. "Because I don't want to."

Seth's eyes get big. As if the idea of an adult being intentionally spiteful is a concept he has heretofore never dared consider.

———

"HEY. ASSHOLE."

He hits pause on Minecraft, which he's started playing even

when the kids are gone. Right now, they're doing school at Greta's, and he's sitting at the dining table with a bag of goldfish crackers. "Oh, are we back to that?" He prefers it, actually.

"Come upstairs."

"Not if it means—"

"It means if you want to keep living in my house you better mud some damn sheetrock."

And because he has no right to refuse her anything, even now, he grabs a handful of goldfish and trudges up the stairwell.

"I'll tape, you mud," she says, all business. She hands him a giant putty knife and an aluminum pan filled with goop.

"Yeah, uh, once again, I have no idea what we're doing, so you're gonna have to—"

"Look." Rather than explain, which she's terrible at even when she bothers, she takes back the pan and putty-spatula-thing and demonstrates, scooping gray goo and applying it to the crack between two pieces of drywall. She scrapes the spatula clean against the edge of the pan, then uses it to point down the length of the crack, all the way to the corner. "Just keep going. Bucket's over there when you need a refill."

It's comparable to icing a cake with Jiffy. His first few attempts are messy, and a glob lands on the subfloor, but then he catches the rhythm.

"Scrape your knife every time," she says, from behind him. "Otherwise, it'll dry and then I gotta scrub it with steel wool. And make sure the edges are smooth."

"Aren't the irregularities part of the character?"

"No. Oh, and don't go too wide."

He straightens to level a glare at her. "Look, you want help, or do you want to do this yourself?"

"What I want is to get this done quickly and not have to come back and redo your shitty-ass work."

He muds. Behind him, she dips long strips of white paper into a five-gallon bucket of water before applying it over the crack he's filled with mud. She's twice as quick as him, but each time she catches up to him with the tape she goes back and runs over their work with a wider spatula, smoothing tape into mud and mud into wall. When the sun hits the front window, she opens everything up and turns on her industrial floor fan, orienting it so the air flows straight through from one side of the house to the other. The windows, hallways, and rooms are all arranged for optimum air flow. He is still drenched in sweat.

Three rooms, a bathroom, and the hall. It takes four hours to work around to the spot where they'd begun. He scrapes the spatula one more time before dropping it into her bucket.

Robin looks down into the milky-white water. "What are you doing?"

"Does it not need to be washed?" He pulls up the bottom of his shirt to wipe his brow.

She bends, plunging her hand into the bucket, and pulls out the putty knife. She wipes the blade on her thigh before holding it out to him. When he takes it, she raises a finger to point at the ceiling.

He looks up and groans. *"Now?"*

"It's easier to blend if the mud on the walls hasn't set." She props her hands on her hips and takes stock of the room. "I know you can reach the ceiling, but you're gonna kill your back if you don't get up a little higher. Can you handle the stepladder?"

"A stepladder is not going to save my back."

"You wanna be out for a day or two or a month?" She shrugs. "Your choice."

As it turns out, the steps on the ladder offer a convenient place to lean his bulk—but mudding overhead is an entirely different animal. Two swipes and he gets an eyeful. "Fuck!"

She laughs. "Don't work directly overhead. Go left or right."

"That would have been helpful advice to have before I went blind." He drops the knife. "God *damn* it."

"Here. Here. Hold on." Aluminum rattles as she comes down

from her taller ladder, and then one of her hands is on his arm. The other pats his ass. "Left foot. Down. No, not the—yeah, right there. Okay? You got it."

Once grounded, he stoops, fumbling for her bucket, and uses his hands to splash his eyes, muttering profanities at the sting.

"Good thing I just changed out that water. You all right?"

"Oh, yeah, just peachy." He straightens, using his shirt to wipe his face again, though that accomplishes little more than smearing mud around. "Like you give a fuck."

"I did, remember?" She tugs the purple paisley kerchief off her head, stooping briefly to dunk it in the bucket and wring it out. When he takes it, she catches his hand and gives it a gentle squeeze. "I'd give a lot more, if you let me."

He tugs his hand away and wipes his cheeks and brow.

"I'm saying I'd have sex with you again. In case that wasn't clear."

"Jesus. Would you stop?" He balls up the handkerchief and chucks it into the bucket. It lands with a wet plop. "Who do you think you're fooling, here? With this—" He gestures at her, vaguely. "Whatever this is?"

She shrugs. "I dunno, I was about to ask you the same thing."

"I can't even—" He dusts off his sweatpants, for all the good it does, and heads for the stairs. "Two weeks ago, at least I could pretend you were better than this."

"Better than... wanting to have sex with you?" She laughs. "You know you're insane? And I don't mean that, like, hyperbolically. I mean you are genuinely mentally ill, and you need therapy and probably medication."

He stops. Turns, and stares her down, humorlessly, until her smile stiffens and fades. And then he speaks, slowly and deliberately, so there can be no room for misunderstanding: "I like you less for loving me."

"That's assuming I do actually love you, which I don't, even though I think I do. Did I get that right? God, your mental gymnastics are exhausting."

"Whatever. I'm done."

He's just reached the stairwell when something hits his back with a splat. At first he thinks it's her handkerchief, but when he reaches over one shoulder he comes away with a handful of mud. He turns to look at her in disbelief.

She cocks an eyebrow. "We're not done until I say we're done."

"You fucking—" He flings the glob back at her, hard.

She lifts her hands—palms out, fingers splayed—to block her eyes. It mostly works, but there are flecks of gray on her face, and, when she touches it gingerly, her hair. Her mouth opens in voiceless outrage. "Oh—oh, you did *not* just fuck with my hair—"

And then, faster than he can react, she grabs the taping knife from the tray on the floor and flicks her wrist, slinging a fist-sized clump of mud directly at his chest.

The entire bucket of mud sits open in the corner opposite the ladder. He lunges toward it, filling both hands. He fires, one-two, but she ducks and both projectiles miss, spattering the ladder and the wall.

"Cyril!" she wails. "No!"

But then she's running away from him, shrieking with laughter, and he is lurching after her, and there is no way he can catch up except that she slips and catches herself against the wall and she still tries to beat him to the stairs but he catches her shirt in one muddy fist and stuffs a handful down the back of her neck and then they are stumbling down the stairwell, grunting and shrieking and panting as they smear mud on each other's hair and faces and arms and clothes.

And then she's shoving her tongue down his throat and it's chalky and bitter and he stumbles into the dining table and falls hard, taking her with him, and she lands half on top of him and instead of pulling away she straddles his belly and kisses him again, and when she pulls back to breathe her hands crawl up inside his shirt and she whispers, "Fuck me, Cyril, fuck me now."

———

THIS—

When they are lying half-naked on the dining room floor and she says, "don't make me wait so long next time" and he wants to offer a pithy retort but can't, because he's still trying to catch his breath—

When she springs to her feet and stands over him, hands propped on hips, and says, "I'm gonna go up and fix the wall," and he closes his eyes and nods—

When her footsteps fade and he hears the ladder judder across the floor overhead and it's his turn to roll onto his side and begin the process of getting himself to his feet and, in the echoey emptiness of the upstairs bedroom, she begins to whistle a wandering rendition of *Rubylove*—

When, finally, he stumbles to the bathroom and struggles out of his shirt before sitting down on the granite shower bench with a grunt, and his hand reaches to crank the water on and his mind attempts, as always, to construct a highly convincing rationale for her actions which do not involve actual feelings for him—

This—not the first, but the second time—is when it becomes real.

Because no matter how he twists and turns that Rubik's cube, this is what it comes to: she only needed to fuck him once. If she secretly found him disgusting and this were all a trick, a ploy to lure him into a vulnerable position before stabbing him in the back, once was enough. If she were crazy, or deluded enough to think she loved him, or hoping to make herself love him in spite of all evidence to the contrary—once would have been enough to dispel that fantasy.

Pinpoints of scalding water hit his face, and a wave of euphoria crashes over him, so intense he must will himself to breathe. She loves him. She loves him? Somehow, she loves him. And then, the inevitable undertow: No. He is trash. No. He cannot let her. No. This cannot be.

The shower door opens, and she joins him, lifting her face to the shower-head. Rivulets of water carry streaks of gray-white down over her body. He watches the dirty water circle the drain.

"Hey. Scoot over." She squeezes in next to him. "You okay?"

"No." He expects something acerbic to follow, but nothing does. He is drowning.

She looks at him, then presses her lips to his bare shoulder. "Talk to me."

"No," he says, knowing full well he is going to talk all the same. "I just—" He exhales a growl and shakes his head. Reaches for the washcloth hanging on the door handle and uses it to scrub his face. He cannot speak—or even acknowledge—the sinkhole of self-loathing. "I can think of plenty of reasons why you'd fuck me once. Not good ones, but—I can think of them. But I don't— there's just no rational reason why you'd do it again."

"Oh, gosh, Cyril, I dunno." She takes the washcloth from him, wrings it out, and begins to wipe the mud off his neck and back. "Could it be because I wanted to?"

He has tried so many ways to convince her not to care for him, but, in the end, it's just one more way he's failed. He looks down at his hands. "I never wanted to love you." He thought it would pass. It was just supposed to be a joke. He was doing it for Tavis. And then—

"I know."

He has spent half his life running from this thing. Denying it, stuffing it down as far as it will go—and now it has overtaken him. She has gotten inside. Peeled back his skin and stripped him clean to the bone. Whether or not he can accept it, he must admit defeat. "I don't want to hurt you."

"You have, and you will." She stands, lifting the shower-head from its holder, and rotates the dial to a gentler stream. She holds it over his head, running one hand through his hair, and then rinses his shoulders and back and belly. "I don't know if you can hear this, Cyril," she says, slotting the shower head back in place. "But I'm gonna say it anyway. I don't love you in spite of what you did, or because I don't have time to move on. I love you now because you are the one I have loved all along."

She is right. He cannot hear it. Maybe someday, but not today. "Chica," he says, "you are very committed to this shitty tattoo."

She laughs. And then she puts one hand on each of his shoulders and bends, touching her forehead to his. "Yes. Yes I am."

CHAPTER 29

This asshole lays hardwood like there's no tomorrow. She works next to him—so close he can smell her—until he's got the rhythm of laying down the boards, and then she starts on baseboard. He says something stupid. She smiles. Her hand, as she gets to her feet, rests briefly on his thigh.

What he wants to do is touch her. All the time.

Not fuck her, mind you—though he wants that, too. No; he wants to feel her skin beneath his fingers, to know the constant assurance of her steady pulse. His desire for her is so intense, he wants to crawl inside her skin. For the time being, he'll settle for a staple gun and a good view of her ass.

"Damn it," she says, from the next room.

He is dripping sweat. "Which finger did you cut off this time?"

She releases a flat *ha*. "I think—" The window squeaks open. "Yeah. I'm having a hot flash." She vocalizes disgust. "Of all the things on my bucket list, going through menopause was not one of the things I wanted to do before I die."

———

"SO. WHAT *IS* ON YOUR BUCKET LIST?"

She is sitting on the front porch steps, fanning herself with one hand. "I honestly haven't given it much thought." She laughs, almost sadly. "You, I guess."

"Well, check that one off." He hands down a glass of iced tea.

"Oh—I shouldn't—"

"It's decaf." He'd finally read through the stack of printouts she'd collected every time she saw her doctor or went to the hospital. Removal of her ovaries triggered menopause, which meant hot flashes, exacerbated by heat, stress, alcohol, and caffeine. Most of the medication that would have relieved the symptoms also accelerated the growth of cancer.

She sips, thoughtfully, and then nods upward. "This house, I guess. Though in retrospect, I should have prioritized the AC." She glances over one shoulder, at the empty porch. "Or a damn bench." Her laugh is wistful. "There are so many things."

"Really?" He lowers himself, in careful stages, to the step next to her. Flooring's hard on the knees. "That's all you got? The house?"

"I dunno. I mean, none of the things I really want are attainable. Seeing the kids graduate, get married, have—" Her voice catches. She shakes her head. "I dunno. There's nowhere I want to go. Nothing I want to do, really. I just want to be. Here, with you. With them. For as long as I can."

"Damn. I was hoping for something actionable."

"Like parachuting off the Eiffel Tower?" She clutches his arm and flutters her eyelids. "Oh, Cyril, would you do that for me?"

He is not sure how he got from blubbering on her bed to chuckling when she jokes about her impending mortality. But here they are. "Uh, no. Not that. But, you know, *something*."

"Such as?"

He shrugs. "Cake?"

She laughs. "Cyril, I will absolutely take cake."

———

THEY MAKE IT HALFWAY BACK UP THE STAIRS BEFORE Robin stops, hesitates with her hand on the rail, and then shakes her head with a sigh. "Nope. I gotta lay down."

"Oh." It's not the first time. Panic rises like bile in the back of his throat, but he chokes it down and gets her a glass of cold water, pushing the coffee table close to the couch so she can reach it easily. Then he opens the windows and lugs her big industrial floor fan down the stairs and sets it up in the kitchen to speed up air flow.

She requests her clipboard of sketches, and when he brings it, she holds up her phone. "Cooke's getting his second shot today. That'll be a big load off Greta's mind."

The fuck if he cares. Greta's husband is fine? Meanwhile Robin's laying here, happy for him as she spirals into a slow decline. That gimpy little prick will outlive her—how is that fair? "Great," he mutters, and heads into the kitchen.

He makes sandwiches, but when he brings the food into the living room, he finds her asleep, clipboard face-down on her chest. He sets the tray on the dining table and stands at the end of the couch, eating lunch as he watches her sleep. Memorizing her, because the memories they make now are going to have to last a lot longer than five years. It feels as though he ought to stand here for as long as he can, until she wakes, but after he finishes his sandwich (and hers) his mind begins to wander. He turns back to the kitchen to do what he always does, knowing this is just one more moment he'll look back on and regret forever.

At the threshold, he stops. He turns to look at her. Then looks through the doorway into the kitchen again.

"Fuck," he says, and goes upstairs.

———

THE FLOORS WERE MOSTLY FINISHED ANYWAY. WHEN he comes back down, an hour later, she's still—somehow, even with all the nailing he's done—asleep. Her phone, sitting face-up on the coffee table, is flashing with a string of silent text notifications. He picks it up, and when he sees it's Greta texting about the kids, punches the security code into the lock screen.

He glances up when Robin yawns and stretches, rubbing her eyes with one hand.

"Sorry," he says. "If I woke you."

She pushes the clipboard aside—it falls to the floor—and reaches for the glass of water. "Out for two minutes and you're already in my phone?"

"Try two hours." He pulls out the piano bench to sit as he taps a reply. "Greta's taking the kids to the park. She'll drop them off around dinner time." He glances up, though he can no longer see her from his seat. "How are you feeling?"

"Ew." Her head pops up over the back of the piano, nose wrinkled. "Don't start that."

"Guess I won't ask if you want me to get you anything, then."

"You're good where you are. But I'll take my phone."

As he rises slightly to slide it over the top of the piano—her hand flashes up to catch it—his belly brushes the keys, sounding a soft, off-kilter chord. He covers it with a one-handed arpeggio and then, getting comfortable on the bench, begins to play George Fischoff's "Little Ballerina Blue."

"What?" Robin exclaims, four bars in. She gets up and comes around the end of the piano, standing at his shoulder and watching his hands as he plays to the end. "How did you know —" She shakes her head, dumbfounded. "This was bumper music on the Art Bell show in the eighties. My dad loved it, so my mom tracked down a copy. I used to lay in the sunshine on Saturday mornings while my mom practiced, and she'd always end with that because it was my favorite."

He hadn't known, of course; not really. While rooting around in the barn for the cot the night he'd stormed out, he'd unearthed a box full of old sheet music, much of it with penciled annotations in her mother's handwriting. The sheet with "Little Ballerina Blue" was as thin and yellowed as onion skin. This is how hacking works. A little bit of guess, a little bit of luck.

"That's... actually impressive," she says, when he explains. She nudges his shoulder. "Again."

"Just like your daughter," he growls. But he does play it again. The third time around, he lets the bittersweet tune carry him away, segueing into one improvised variation after another until he's arrived at another place entirely. Before he quite knows what's happening, he's playing the race of his heart when she walked into the bedroom and disrobed. Her skin like velvet beneath his hands and the lamp's soft glow. The shame and desire and apprehension all wrapped into one, and then the act itself, hesitant and awkward and fumbling at first, and then needy and urgent and at last hot and heavy and slow.

Robin's fingers dig into his shoulder. She shifts, as if to lean against him.

"I'm covered in sweat," he says, by way of warning.

"A little sweat never bothered me." Robin's arms fall around his shoulders from behind. She presses her nose into the hair on the back of his neck. He feels her body tense. "Oh. Wow. You are... *really* covered in sweat."

"I told you."

"What have you been doing?"

"What do you think? Finishing the floors."

She straightens. "Wait, really?"

"Wasn't that the fucking deal?"

SHE MEETS HIM AT THE BATHROOM DOOR AS HE'S
coming out of the shower, purse slung over one shoulder. "Hug,"
she orders, as if it's her right, and it is. He wraps his arms around
her, and she sinks into him. "Floors look good," she adds, which,
when it concerns construction, is about as complimentary as she
gets. "Last row's a little wonky, but it's an easy fix."

"Good to know."

"I'm gonna head over to the park and meet up with Greta and
the—" She stops. Sniffs, noisily, at his shirt. "Okay. I have to ask.
What is that smell? And no, I don't mean your B.O. After you
shower. You always smell a little bit like my dad, but—"

He lifts his arms, releasing her. "Why the fuck would I smell
like your father?"

"Your deodorant and aftershave." She hikes up her purse
strap. "It's the same scent."

The deodorant and aftershave she had stocked the bathroom
with. Not just now, but after Nora was born, when he'd come to
stay with them. "And I thought *I* had issues."

She grabs his arm and leans in, sniffing again. "Seriously, what
is it? It's so familiar."

He rolls his eyes and sighs. "Talcum."

"Baby powder?" She laughs. "That's totally it. But why do
you—"

"It helps," he growls, brushing past her. "With... chafing."

She giggles all the way out the front door.

He sighs, and then turns toward the kitchen. If he doesn't
have dinner ready by the time she gets home with the kids,
they'll eat him alive. He's pulling chicken and broccoli out of the
fridge when he stops—pauses—and then puts them away.

Instead, he gets out a mixing bowl and starts to bake.

———

A LITTLE OVER TWO HOURS LATER, THE FRONT DOOR bangs against the wall. "What smells good?" Seth asks. Nora gallops into the kitchen, skidding to a stop at the sight of the cake. The chocolate frosting, hastily but generously slathered on, glistens a deep, dark brown.

"Don't touch," Robin warns, dumping her purse on the dining table as she follows on her daughter's heels. "How on earth are we gonna get them to eat dinner now they've seen—"

"This *is* dinner." He opens a cabinet and pulls out four salad plates.

The look she gives him is a mixture of amusement and dismay.

He shrugs. "It's not gonna kill them—or you—to have dessert first once in a while." Using his foot, he pulls open one of the lower drawers, stuffed with miscellaneous cooking and baking implements.

"It might kill *you*." She steps around him and bends, pulling out a cake knife and server. "Here."

He looks at the utensils she hands him. Both are engraved with her and Tav's names and wedding date. "Awkward."

"Like everything else isn't?" Her head swivels. "Nora, I told you—"

"I didn't touch!" Her eyes are wide and innocent, but she has a smear of frosting on her cheek.

"She stuck her finger in," Seth volunteers. "Right here."

"Girl knows what she wants." Cyril makes a cut on either side of the mark and slides the slice onto a plate. "Have a blast, kiddo."

Nora sits on her knees at the dining table, putting a protective arm down around her plate as she digs in. With her mouth.

"Gross," Seth says.

Cyril snorts. "Like you were any better at this age."

"Like he's any better *now*." Robin leans over the table and nabs the second slice.

"Hey!" Seth protests. Not objecting to the commentary on his dining habits, but because he expects to be served before the adults.

"Hold on, kid. Lemme get some milk."

Robin makes an elaborate show of inserting the first bite into her mouth as Seth watches, open-mouthed and mute with outrage. But when the combination of cake and frosting register on her tongue, her eyes roll upward and she sags dramatically against the counter. "Oh, Cyril, I forgot about your cakes." She accepts a mug of milk and drains half of it in one gulp. "I mean, normally I don't even *like* cake."

"You're picky about cake," he corrects, pouring a child-sized glass of milk for each of the kids and, finally, granting Seth his slice. "That's called being a connoisseur."

"What's conna-sir?" Nora asks, coming up for air.

"It means snob. Your mom is a cake snob."

Seth casts a skeptical eye upon his own untouched slice. "Mine's crooked."

"Hey, I'm all about content, not presentation."

Robin snorts and then chokes, coughing as she sets her plate on the table and reaches for a napkin. "Boy, aren't you."

He looks at her. "Oh, are we doing innuendo?"

"What's in-your-end-o?" Nora again.

Robin raises her eyebrows at Cyril. "Not in front of the kids we aren't."

He shrugs. "You started it."

"I know, I know." She picks up her plate and takes another bite. "I'll be good."

Seth looks between them, frowning. "What's going on?"

"Eat your cake, kid." He wipes his hands on a dish towel and pulls up a seat at the piano.

"Buddyholly!" Nora demands.

"Aren't you going to have some?" Robin asks, using her fork to point at her half-eaten slice of cake.

"I had... plenty while I was baking it."

"You? Exercising restraint? Doing manual labor voluntarily?" She shakes her head. "Who are you, and what have you done with Cyril?"

————

WHEN SHE'S IN THE BATHROOM THAT NIGHT, HE places a glass of cold water on the table next to her bed. He sorts her nighttime pills, leaving them in the little plastic cup she uses for this purpose. He tosses the dirty laundry into the hamper and straightens the comforter, turning down the top edge at an inviting diagonal.

Robin appears in the doorway, toothbrush tucked into one cheek. "What's this, room service?"

"No? I—" He doesn't have an answer.

She disappears back into the bathroom and returns, sans toothbrush. "Cyril, if this is some—"

"I'm not fucking with you."

He moves out of her way, but she intercepts him, threading her arms around his middle. When she looks up at him, face glowing with quiet pleasure, he wants to die.

"I lied," he says. "About prison."

Her eyebrows go up. More puzzled than surprised.

"Nobody stabbed me. There was some water on the floor in the kitchen, and I slipped and fell against a steel drawer handle someone had half-ripped off."

"Okay," she says, slowly. Still not sure where this is going.

"And I didn't have the entire camp playing D&D. It was me and five other guys." He swallows. "And when I said—"

She stops his mouth with a finger. "Cyril." The corner of her mouth twitches, and then her lips widen into a cockeyed smile. "Are you trying to tell me you want to have sex?"

"Chica." He looks down at her and comes back to his senses

long enough to say, "I have wanted to fuck you every minute of every day since the moment we met."

Her left eyebrow arches, and he has the feeling she is stifling a laugh. "That's... a lot of lost time to make up."

He doesn't say what they both know: that there is no making up the time they have lost, and what time they have left is unbearably small.

She tosses herself back onto the mattress. "You're on top."

"Uh, no."

"Uh, yes," she says, parroting his dour grumble. She grabs both of their pillows. "Come on. I'll show you."

He doesn't move. "Did you fucking Google how to have sex with a fat guy?"

She cackles. "I totally did. And I've got some other tips for you, too."

Being loved by her is the most excruciating ecstasy. Once she's been satisfied, it takes him what feels like an hour to finish. As he rides her, huffing like a locomotive, the rhythm in his head says *don't die, don't die, don't die.*

"Whoa," she says, giving him a shove to the side as his arms buckle. "You're not having a heart attack on me, are you?"

He grunts a negative. "I just..."

"Had sex?" She rolls off the edge of the bed, stepping into her underwear before handing him her half-empty glass of water.

"Had sex," he agrees. Everything inside of him evens out into a vaguely pleasant haze. He shoves a pillow under his head and empties the glass, watching as she picks up his shirt and hunts for the neck. "Though I'm sure the quality's not quite up to your standards."

She groans as her eyes roll upward. "I knew this was coming."

"Am I wrong?"

She drops his shirt over her head, and it unfurls like a sail. "Look. I love both my kids." She yanks the sheets straight, and, uncovering his underwear, tosses them in his direction. "For entirely opposite reasons. I love Seth for being brutally honest and I love Nora for being a clever little sneak. Love isn't some homogenized commodity, Cyril. You can't measure it out in gallons or pounds. It's..." She holds her hands out, as if to pluck the right words from the air. "It's... a point of view. It's seeing someone fully, exactly as they are, and no two people are the same. I love you for completely different reasons than I ever loved Tavis."

"Meaning, not sex."

"That's not what I—" She cuts herself off, hesitates, and then sighs. "You need me to be explicit? Fine. Tavis had the body of a Calvin Klein model, and he could go all. Night. Long." She shrugs. "But it was always kind of... about him? Not like he didn't satisfy," she adds, quickly. "You're just more... attentive?"

He shoves himself up, dropping his legs over the edge of the bed, and hooks one foot into his underwear. "Are you telling me Tavis didn't appreciate—"

"He did, he did. Just not to the same degree, I guess. I mean, having someone obsessively stalk you for a decade is creepy, don't get me wrong. But I also know I've got your undivided attention. When I'm with you, I feel like it's all about me."

"I mean... have you looked in a mirror lately? You're breathtaking."

"See, now, that's exactly my point." Her laugh is half a sigh. "To anyone else I'm just an ashy old woman with no boobs. You're delusional, but also..." She frowns, and then nods as she seems to find the words she's searching for. "You're a piano player."

"Meaning?"

She gives him a pointed look, like this should be obvious, and then rolls her eyes. "Meaning you're good with your hands, Cyril. And your timing is..." She clears her throat. "Impeccable."

He raises his eyebrows. "I'm better in bed than Tavis?"

She grins. "Let's say you've got potential. And, you know, it's also just that I'm not who I was in my twenties. Everything was so... intense, then. Now I appreciate the importance of taking it slow; having someone who makes you laugh."

"Humor's easy. I just say the worst possible thing I can think of."

She laughs. "Yeah. Like that."

She goes into the bathroom to wash up. While she's gone, he collects the pillows, piles them against the headboard, and hauls himself into position so that when she returns, she climbs under the duvet and settles against his bare skin. He puts an arm around her, and she exhales a small breath of contentment.

He knows she will die. But it seems far off from this moment, important but almost, in this moment, irrelevant. He feels satisfied, and comfortable, and...

Oh. That's it.

He's happy.

CHAPTER 30

Texture. Primer. Paint. Baseboard. Toilet and sink hookups. Cabinets. Outlet covers. Light fixtures. And then the remodel is complete.

After hauling the last load of odds and ends down to the barn, he finds Robin in the big room upstairs, staring out the picture window. She glances at him over one shoulder as he comes in, and smiles. "Kids?"

He stops beside her. "Minecraft."

She nods an acknowledgement and turns her attention back to the window, exhaling a self-satisfied sigh. "We did it. And whaddaya know? I'm still alive."

She means it to be funny. It is not. She hasn't done anything as dramatic as collapsing or coughing up blood, but in the past weeks she has visibly... slowed. It takes her longer to get out of bed in the mornings; she takes lengthy showers; her movements are accompanied by winces and stifled groans. She keeps a pillbox of painkillers in her back pocket and has, finally, declared Wednesdays to be an extra day of rest. Any attempt to discuss her status directly—not that he wants to—is met with silence. But he has eyes.

She slips a hand through his elbow. "This is my favorite view."

"Just... trees?"

"It's so green. I like seeing them from up above. Look." She points, tracing a line in the air. Seen from a distance, each tree is perfectly ordered, branches arranged around the trunk in spirals or pairs depending on type. The leaves blend in perfect waves of texture and color. "Underneath, everything seems chaotic. Like, branches grow every which way, leaves seem random. Then you get up here, and suddenly everything's... math."

She doesn't have to explain, because it's exactly why he loves code. He's never told her that, not once in all the letters he wrote. Because it wasn't something Tavis would say, and because... he had never imagined they would have something so fundamental in common.

"Order out of chaos," she muses. "Like building a house from plans, except... more."

They stand like that for a while, studying the blueprints of the world.

––––––––

THE NEXT MORNING, ROBIN TEXTS HIM FROM GRETA'S house to inform him that she's invited the couple over for lunch to see the completed second floor.

Thanks for the warning, he replies.

Just be glad I didn't invite everyone else, too. With Cooke fully vaccinated and most adults now getting the first of two shots, Greta has expanded her Sunday service watch-party from Robin and the kids to a small group of adults as well.

Cyril is constructing an improvised cheese board lunch when everyone arrives. Nora bursts in first, through the back door, kicking off her patent leather shoes as she skips through the kitchen. Robin, following on her heels, makes an "ah-ah" noise.

"You want somebody to trip over those? Go put them in the closet. Seth, go wash your hands!"

"Somebody" apparently meaning Cooke, who swings himself over the threshold on elbow crutches as his wife holds the door. "The *back* door?" he gripes. "What am I, some kind of second-class citizen?"

Robin pulls a jar of tiny cocktail pickles out of the depths of her purse and hands them to Cyril. "The fact that I built that ramp eight months ago and this is the first time you've used it tends to suggest you're a second-class *friend*," she returns lightly.

"Wait," Cooke says, trailing her as she heads into the dining room, "we're friends now? I thought I was your employer."

"That's odd," she says, over one shoulder. "I haven't seen a paycheck in a while."

Cyril puts the pickles in the fridge to chill; Greta, having followed her husband inside, takes Cyril's place at the cutting board and begins to saw salami.

"Oh, was I doing that wrong?" he asks, shutting the fridge.

"I assume you have more than one thing to prep." She nods to the board. "I've got this."

This asshole rolls his eyes, but he opens a cupboard and takes a stack of plates to the table.

"Now, where is this mythical 'upstairs' you speak of?" Cooke, standing beside Robin at the stairwell, speaks in a high, nasal tone that is impossible to tune out. He peers after the children as they bound upward. "Ah, yes. Truly lovely. Impeccable craftsmanship. Almost as if it—" he releases the handle of one crutch long enough to flourish a hand. "*Goes* somewhere."

Robin snorts. "Like you care. Table or couch?"

He nods to the table. "Maybe I do. I mean, what've you got up there, frescoed ceilings? Tiles mosaics? Tapestries?"

Robin pulls out the chair with arms. "Says the man who paid me to furnish his condo with, and I quote, 'whatever.'"

Back in the kitchen, Greta is arranging the salami in a line on the plate. Cyril collects four glasses and a couple of plastic cups for the kids and is stacking them to take to the dining room when Greta reaches into a pocket of her pleated khaki pants and produces a slip of paper. "Here."

Cyril doesn't take it. A name—Jorge—and a number are written on it in ballpoint blue. "What's that supposed to be?"

There is a crash from overhead, and then a cry. Robin, chatting with Cooke in the dining room, lets out an exclamation of irritation and starts up the stairs. Not at her usual jog, but stiff and slow.

"Jorge is twelve," Greta says, pronouncing the name with flawless intonation. "His grandmother is a member of my Bible study. She wants him to learn piano." She places the paper on the kitchen counter and taps it with her index finger. "I told her you were good." The way she says it sounds more like a threat than a compliment.

Cyril picks up the note and pockets it. "How much does it kill you to do this for me?"

Children's footsteps pound downstairs. "Ms. Greta!" Nora shrieks, bounding into the kitchen and grabbing Greta's arm. "Come see! Come see upstairs!" As proudly possessive as if she's done the work herself, rather than everything in her power to inhibit it.

Greta plucks an olive off the cheese board and pops it into her mouth. "I've seen Robin's smile." She shrugs. "Better late than never."

"Ms. Greta!" Nora pleads.

Greta looks down, finally, at the little girl. "I don't take orders." Nothing in her voice suggests she is kidding.

Nora lets her head fall back, mouth open in an impatient groan. "Puh-leeze?"

"Please come see upstairs," Seth says, returning to the kitchen to offer an assist.

Greta nods and permits Nora to lead her through the dining

room—giving her husband's shoulder a brief squeeze as she passes—and up the stairs.

Cyril pulls the pickles back out of the fridge (not cold yet, but no matter) and uses a fork to scoop some into a dish. He nestles it into the center of the cheese board and then takes the entire production into the dining room, setting it on the table in front of Cooke. "What the fuck do they see in her?" Cyril growls, as they drag Greta upstairs.

"What, you've never craved the approval of a strict teacher?" Cooke grips the arms of the dining chair and lifts himself slightly, repositioning his rear. "It's like a drug. Earn it once, and you can never get enough."

"Not interested in your sex life, thanks."

"Ha! That's funny." Cooke's intonation is flat and loud, making it abundantly clear that he finds Cyril anything but. He pulls his phone out of his shirt pocket and directs his attention, pointedly, to the screen.

They successfully ignore one another for a while: Cooke scrolls through a newsfeed as Cyril loads the table with sliced sourdough and crackers and beverages. The entire situation is awkwardly domestic—Cooke is a professional contact, not a friend. Or he was, anyway, until Cyril brought the Feds down on the guy's company. Now the man is attached to someone who is attached to Robin, who in turn is, strangely, attached to Cyril. This asshole is painfully conscious that igniting one end of this social chain could burn the entire village down. He'd do it, and gladly, except that in a matter of months this irritating little prick and his wife will be Cyril's only gateway to Robin's kids.

"Look," he concedes, finally, dropping a bowl of fruit salad on the table. "If you want to go upstairs, I can..." He jerks his head toward the stairwell.

"Offer appreciated," he snaps, without looking up. "But my wife is the one in charge of carting me around."

Why is that not a surprise? "Does she, like, throw you over her shoulder, or—"

Cooke raises his eyes from his phone without lifting his head. Then he snorts, apparently deciding not to be offended, and sits back. "Piggyback," he says, conversationally. "I find it slightly more dignified."

"You might be kidding yourself."

"Aren't we all?" He flicks at his phone again, then holds up the screen to display an article from what looks like his personal newsfeed. "Did you see this Blizzard thing? I mean, it's not going to tank them by any means, but geez."

Cyril knows enough to understand Cooke is referring to the company that produces World of Warcraft, but "No," he says, heading back toward the kitchen. "I haven't been following... anything."

"Oh." Cooke clicks his phone off. "Wait. Have you actually been offline?"

Cyril stops in the doorway. He turns around. "As opposed to what?"

Cooke clicks his phone back on, hunching over it as if he's just remembered something very important that needs his attention. "I just assumed you got your own computer."

Cyril takes a moment to process the implications of this seemingly offhand comment. Then he takes a step forward, leans over Cooke, and yanks the phone out of his hand. The little man lets out a yelp of surprise. "I'm gonna need you to explain," he growls.

"Oh. I—" Cooke reaches up, plucks the phone from Cyril's grip, and uses the edge of the tablecloth to wipe it down before dropping it back into his shirt pocket. "Assumed you would have found—"

"Found what?"

He tugs the ends of his sleeves and then adjusts his shirt collar. "I literally just loaded up her laptop with the same tracking suite you used on her cell. I showed her how to install it, so you, uh, might wanna check your phone, too."

"You—" Cyril's hands contract into fists. The fact that he *must* be polite makes the temptation to eviscerate this man unbearably strong. "You squirrelly little fuck—"

Cooke holds up one hand, as if to deflect responsibility. His fingers are shaking. "Look, Robin asked me to make sure you stayed out of trouble. And it looks like you did. No harm done."

"I should rip off your little toothpick arms."

His laugh is a dry hiccough. "You could, but you won't."

Cyril nods upward as the kids' footsteps come pounding down the stairs. "Or you'll cut me off from the kids? Even from where I stand, that's fucking low."

"Uh. What?" Cooke looks befuddled. "Why would—"

"I'm starving!" Seth exclaims.

"Me too!" Nora chimes in.

"Hands off!" Robin yells, tromping down after them. "Greta's gonna pray!"

When Greta descends, placing a hand on her husband's shoulder from behind, Cooke grasps her fingers. His knuckles are white. "Hey, honey."

"'Honey?'" she echoes, lifting an eyebrow.

"Yes. *Honey.*" He twists to give her a meaningful look. She gives slight shake of her head. "Seriously?" He exhales exasperation. "You know, for, like, when one of us needs a quick exit? You don't remember this discussion?"

Robin catches Cyril's eye. She lifts an eyebrow, as if to ask what on earth he's done. He shrugs.

Greta ends the awkward silence by lifting an open hand toward Cyril. "You want to escape... from him?"

"Oh my God, Greta." Cooke closes his eyes, pinching the bridge of his nose between a thumb and forefinger. "It's supposed to be subtle. What is even the point if you don't—" He exhales. "You know what, just—never mind."

"Mr. Cooke," she says, in the most patronizing tone possible, "the man is a teddy bear."

————

"THANKS FOR PROVIDING THE MOOD MUSIC FOR lunch," Robin says, when their guests have gone. "Even if it was only because you didn't want to talk with Cooke."

Cyril runs the water in the sink. "That smug little prick—"

"Was only doing what I asked him to do. So if you're going to be mad at someone, blame me."

"You're allowed to stalk me." He can hardly say he blames her, either.

"And he's not?" She hands him a pile of dirty plates. "He likes you, you know. Even after you trashed his company. You might have to learn to get along with him."

"Greta's the one I have to butter up." He rinses and begins to slot them into the dishwasher. "And *she* liked my playing."

Robin raises her eyebrows. "You think she's the one with the power in that relationship?"

"I don't think, I know."

"If you say so." She goes into the dining room and returns with glasses and silverware.

"Are you *sure* you wanna leave the kids with those two—"

"Don't," she says, with a firm shake of her head. "Not unless you seriously think you could take them on." She looks at him, searchingly. "Do you?"

He is silent for a moment. "I don't know."

"Well. Greta knows." She leans a hip against the counter and watches him finish loading.

He pops in the dishwasher pod and starts the wash cycle. "So now what?"

Robin pushes herself away from the counter, and, as she passes behind him, gives his ass a firm slap. "Now we haul."

Small things go up first: books, couch pillows, folding chairs, a couple of houseplants. She enlists Seth to run cords and controllers upstairs, which he does enthusiastically until he realizes it means he won't be able to play Minecraft until everything's hooked back up again. When Robin tries to cart an end table up herself, Cyril takes it from her and boosts it onto one shoulder with a grunt of disapproval. After that, he grabs the TV and then the TV stand. Robin tells the kids to move whatever they can from their bedrooms, and then follows with the Nintendo Switch and its accoutrements.

"Would you stop?" he says, yanking the electronics out of her hands. "You remodeled the house. This is just grunt work. Go read a fucking magazine."

She scowls up at him like a petulant child, hands on hips, and then shrugs. "Fine."

He helps the kids haul a few items of kiddie furniture into their chosen bedrooms, and then, at Seth's fifth or sixth request, agrees to work on hooking up the television.

Robin sits in a folding chair by the open window, tilted back on two legs with her bare feet propped up on the sill. She looks up from her architectural magazine and grins as he kneels and begins to sort through cables which have, somehow, in the short journey up the stairs, already managed to become hopelessly tangled.

"So you're gonna make me haul my fat ass up the stairs every time I want to watch TV now, is that it?" he gripes. A cool breeze luffs through the front window, tousling her hair slightly. He hadn't noticed, until then, that it has gotten a little longer.

"I was figuring I'd need some room downstairs for a hospital bed." She looks up, tongue half-out as she licks her thumb to turn the page. "You're free to rearrange, after I'm gone."

That is not something he wants to talk about. He is on his knees in front of the console. "Damn it," he says, losing the cord behind the TV stand. "Give me a hand?"

"No thanks." She licks her thumb again. "I'm enjoying the view."

She is not talking about the window. She means his ass. "I will never understand you."

"Good."

He gets to his feet, abandoning the remaining cords. She moves her legs, and with a grunt and a sigh he opens another folding chair and seats himself next to her by the window.

Seth stomps up the stairs. "Is it ready yet?"

"Sure!" Robin says, "I mean, can't you see it right there? Grab a controller."

Cyril takes the remote from the top of the TV stand and pretends to click through a menu on the lifeless black screen.

Nora, coming in behind Seth, rushes to seize one of the controllers. "Let's play!"

Seth presents Robin and Cyril with the deepest scowl he can muster.

"It's not working!" Nora exclaims, mashing buttons.

Cyril makes a passable imitation of the ka-chunk-ka-chunk of a Minecraft pickaxe.

"Oh no," Robin says, "here comes a zombie!"

"What?" Nora says. "Where?"

"Nora!" Seth exclaims. "It's *not* working. It's not even plugged in. Come on." He grabs the controller out of her hand, and before she can muster a wail, he's dragging her back toward the stairs. "Let's go play out*side*." The look he gives them as they walk off is scathing.

Robin trades a glance with Cyril. And then they're both chortling. She tries to stand, but she's laughing so hard she stumbles and collapses into him. "Oh my God," she gasps, pressing her forehead to the top of his head. She straightens, sighs, and then gives his shoulder a thump. "All right. Let's do it."

"Now what?"

She tugs him to his feet. "Couch. You and me. While the kids are out of the house."

"Sorry I asked." But he puts his hands on his knees and rises, following as she heads for the stairs.

"Do you ever wish," she says, tossing the question over one shoulder, "that they were yours?"

He's halfway down the stairs before he realizes what she's talking about. "The kids?" He lets out a bark that's half laughter, half surprise. "Jesus, no." He's never felt the slightest urge to pass anything of himself off to anyone. "They're better off without my genetic material, thanks." By every possible metric, Tavis had been the superior stock.

He doesn't have the guts to ask, *do you?*

———

"CYRIL. COME ON. WAKE UP. SHIT. SHIT."

He can hear her, feel the reverberation of her foot stomp through the hardwood floor, but he is an insect in amber, observing the world through yellow-flecked eons. He blinks, with effort, and in another instant everything snaps into sudden focus: she is standing over him, phone in hand, punching in numbers.

"Nine-one-one," a tinny voice says. "What is your emergency?"

"Yeah. My, uh—my boyfriend just passed out, and I can't get him to—"

He reaches for her leg, putting a hand over the smiling heart on her ankle.

"Jesus!" She jumps back. "Oh, thank God. Cyril?"

He blinks again. "Mm." His voice is like cotton. He tries again. "I'm good."

"No, I—yeah, I think he's okay," she says. "He's—yeah. False alarm." She listens to the voice on the other end of the line. "No, there's no obstruction. Yeah. The color is coming back. Yes. I absolutely will. Thank you. Mm-hm. Thank you." She drops to her haunches, her face suddenly close to his, and puts a hand behind his head as he lifts it. "You just keeled over. What the hell?"

With her help, he shifts onto his side and props himself up on one elbow. The room tilts. He squeezes his eyes shut and pinches the bridge of his nose. "Mm. Low blood sugar, I guess."

"Low—" Her hand tightens on his arm. Her eyes bore into his like a hammer drill. "Cyril. When was the last time you ate?"

He rubs his jaw. "My face hurts."

"I slapped you. Answer the goddamn question."

"On both cheeks? Jesus."

"You didn't have anything for lunch. The last time I saw you put anything in your mouth was—" Her eyes flicker upward as she retraces the thread of memory. "Friday morning? Which was two—almost three days ago."

He shrugs.

"God *damn* it, Cyril." Abruptly she stands, takes two steps towards the stairs, then makes an about-face and goes to the big front window. She lifts her hand, still clutching the phone, and grinds her knuckles against the glass. "You stupid fuck," she whispers hoarsely. "What were you *thinking?*"

"I mean, that seems fairly self-explanatory."

"No," she says, as if the force of that single word can simply make it not so. She spins, leveling the phone at him like a gavel. "Nobody asked for this. This is not—" Her voice catches. She shakes her head, sucks in a long, rattling breath, and lets out a high-pitched noise that is both a laugh and a sob. "Do you know what I was doing?" Tears course down her cheeks. "I was trying to figure out how they were gonna get you out of here." She flings a hand back, toward the glass. "I almost broke the fucking window."

He snorts. "That might have been a slight overreaction."

"You can't do this," she sobs. "I can't—I can't take care of you.

The kids—I—" She swallows. "One of us has to have our shit together, and it's not me."

He's failed her. Again. What a shocker. His brain still isn't firing on all cylinders, so he just sits there, watching stupidly as she sinks to her haunches and cries.

Eventually, she sniffs and wipes her eyes with the backs of both hands. "I gotta check on the kids," she whispers, rising. She doesn't look at him as she slots her phone into her back pocket and heads downstairs.

"Okay," he says, to the empty room. A minute later he can hear her voice out the window, calling to the kids outside. He runs a hand over his face to try, again, to clear the mental fog, and then braces himself against the wall and shifts to one knee. Black spots cloud his vision. He waits.

Robin's footsteps jog back up the stairs. "What are you—" She is carrying a glass of orange juice. "Hold on. Here."

He takes the glass and drains it—slowly. She sets it on the ground, and ducks under his arm to help him up. His heart feels like a butterfly. He puts a hand against the wall.

"Can you—"

"Wait," he pants.

When the world has righted itself, he takes a careful step, then nods. Though he doesn't remember doing it, they'd apparently gotten the couch up the stairs, and it's only a few steps across the room before he can sink into the cushions. Robin puts a hand on his chest. "Stay," she orders.

"Trust me, I am not going anywhere."

She brings him a second glass of orange juice and a bowl of potato salad, then stands there, hands on hips, glaring.

He eats.

"I didn't even think it was worth addressing the most laughably glaring omission in your long-ass confessional," she says. "But apparently I was wrong."

He swallows. "What are you talking about?"

She stomps down the stairs again. When she returns, she carries her parents' unframed portrait, the one that usually hangs on the wire in the hall outside the bathroom. She thrusts the stiff paper forward, so it's about two inches from his nose.

He crosses his eyes slightly to bring the photo into focus. "Uh... okay?"

"Look at my father, Cyril. Look. At. Him."

He shoves the photo back a few inches. "Jesus. I'm looking."

"The man," she says, whipping the portrait away, "is easily three hundred pounds."

"And...?"

She slaps the portrait down on the coffee table. "And I like big men."

He scoffs. "Three hundred is not—"

"No, it's not fucking five hundred pounds, Cyril. Jesus. I'm not an idiot. I'm just—" She lifts her arms, clenches her hands into fists, and lets out a wordless growl. "You, Cyril. God. You exasperating, infuriating son of a bitch. You are sweet and sarcastic and an absolutely terrible human being in all the ways that make me laugh and you're an amazing cook and a generous lover and an effortless musician. Can you just—please, for the love of God —hear me for once?"

"Maybe if you yelled a little louder."

She obliges. "I don't want you, but skinnier. Or you, but nicer. Okay? I just. Want. You."

He lifts the bowl, now empty. "Okay, but can I get some more potato salad?"

She snatches the bowl from his hand, stalks halfway down the stairwell, and releases a primal scream.

———

It is two in the morning when her bedroom door opens. He glances up from the portable Nintendo Switch screen, propped up on the dining table. He's adding onto the fortress-tower he's been building with the kids in Minecraft. It's night in the game now, and the kids hadn't secured the village, so zombies are attacking.

She stops next to him, empty water glass in hand, and surveys the wreckage on the dining table: candy bar wrappers and soda cans surround a grease-stained circle of cardboard which had, not long ago, held a frozen pizza. "Boy," she sighs, planting a kiss on his cheek, "you don't do anything by halves."

"Hey," he says, tossing her a fraction of his attention. "Throw a Hot Pocket in the microwave while you're—damn it!" The zombies are dead, but he's backed up into the stupid lava "trap" Nora had dug outside the tower, and now he's got to respawn and try to get back to the scene of the battle before all his gear disappears.

He doesn't actually expect Robin to do as he's asked, but she goes into the kitchen and the microwave begins to hum. It pings, and a moment later she drops the steaming plastic bag on the table next to his elbow. "Thanks," he grunts. He locates his gear, thankfully—he'd been carrying a diamond axe that was technically Seth's—and stows everything back in the kids' community chest.

Robin plunks her newly filled glass of water down on the table and seats herself opposite him. He keeps playing, hoping she'll decide not to say whatever it is she's going to say and just go back to bed.

She doesn't go back to bed. In his peripheral vision he sees her take a sip from her glass. Then she leans forward over the table, resting her head on one bicep. She yawns. "I just want you to be okay," she says.

"I will never be okay. Not ever. Not if you die."

"And you would be, if I didn't?"

A stray zombie shows up. He beats it to death with an axe. "Doesn't matter. That's not an option."

"Hypothetically." Her arm unfolds toward him, palm up. "Let's say the Devil appeared and offered my life in exchange for your soul."

"You're assuming I have one." He hits pause so he can look at her directly. "But yeah, I'd make that trade. I'd do whatever it took to keep you alive."

"Would you go to therapy?"

He lets out a bark of laughter. "Therapy? For my obviously massive mental health issues?"

"If I was gonna live, say, another decade."

"Sure, why the hell not." He goes back to Minecraft. A minute later he glances up and sees her eyes are closed. "Your bed might be a little more—"

"Shh," she says, sharply. "I'm imagining us. Together. Ten years from now."

"Uh... okay."

"You teach piano and run a little custom pastry business on the side. Just for fun."

He snorts. "Am I still fat?"

"Yeah. But you don't hate yourself."

"Ouch."

"I just wish—" She seems to search for the right word and, not finding it, shakes her head minutely. She yawns again. "I just wish there was something I could do to help you."

It's clear she's not going to leave him to play Minecraft in peace, so he shuts it off and slots the controllers into place onto either side of the screen. "There's nothing you can do." He shoves himself back from the table and stands, taking the Switch back to the stairwell and stooping to set it on the fourth tread. "I should be the one helping you to..." He waves a hand. "Settle your affairs or whatever, but I don't have a clue what to do, either." With the house done, there's nothing left but to sit and wait for the inevitable end.

She blinks, slowly. "You want something to do?"

He shrugs. "I could help you make videos or something. For the kids." He'd done that for Tavis—not expressly because he thought he was going to die, but because he was deployed for long stretches at a time. Cyril had taped him reading picture books and singing little songs. Things like that. Not that this asshole wants to be the one watching Robin try to articulate what her kids need to hear at graduation, marriage, having kids—

"Oh, God, no," she says. "Yeah, I... no. I can't do that."

He exhales relief. "Okay. Well. You want to take them to Disneyland or something?"

She considers that. "No," she decides, finally. "Marry me."

"I—what?"

"Marry me, Cyril." She stretches her arms, fists clenched, and then sits up, rubbing her eyes. "In person. Not just by proxy, this time."

"This is stupid."

"It'll make the legal stuff a lot easier. With the house."

"Oh, well, in that case."

He turns to retreat to the couch upstairs, but she stands and comes up behind him, snugging her arms around him from behind. She plants a soft kiss between his shoulder blades. "Who are you to deny the last wish of a dying girl?"

"Fuck you." But also: "I can't."

"Really?" She sighs in exasperation. "Can we not do this again?"

"No, I—" He pulls her arms away and turns to face her. "There's something I have to do first."

"Well, hurry up. Clock's ticking."

CHAPTER 31

"Hey, kid." He taps Seth's shoulder and, when the kid looks at him, gestures to the screen. "Wrap this up. We're gonna take a walk."

Seth looks at him like he's speaking in tongues. "A *walk?*"

"Yeah, yeah, I know. Come on."

Seth screws his face up into a scowl, but does as he is asked, tossing the controller onto the couch as he gets to his feet. "Nora!" he shouts, toward their bedrooms. "We're going on a *walk!*"

"Just us," Cyril says. "I want to talk to you about something your sister isn't gonna understand."

"I understand!" Nora declares, somehow suddenly present.

Fortunately, he'd prepared for just this contingency. "Kiddo, I left you a cookie on a plate in the kitchen. Seth and I will be back in a little bit. Try not to bother your mom."

All he has to say is "cookie," and she's dashing down the stairs. Is it just Nora, or are all younger siblings this good at working the system?

"And yes," he adds, answering Seth's expectant look, "you get one too. Later. Come on."

He lets Seth go down the stairs first, catching up with the boy as he hunts for his flip flops in the bottom of the closet by the front door.

"If this is about you and Mom getting married," Seth says, as they stump down the front steps to the sidewalk, "she already told me."

"Uh, that's funny, because I don't remember saying yes."

Seth looks up in surprise. "You don't want to marry Mom?"

"That's not—" He stops, tries to reformulate the sentence in a way that will make sense to a ten-year-old, and laughs. None of this can possibly be a surprise to the kid at this point; Cyril's been sleeping in Robin's bed for weeks. Not to mention their other nighttime activities. "I need to talk to you first."

Seth shrugs. "It's fine with me." He glances back at the house —wistfully. He is thinking of his game. Or the cookie. Probably both. "Can we—"

"Gimme a break here, kid."

"Sorry," Seth says, duly chastened.

Cyril puts a hand on the kid's head. They walk together in silence, slowly, to the end of the block. When they pause at the corner, Seth looks to him for an indication of which direction they should cross. Instead, Cyril turns to face him, putting a hand on the kid's shoulder. He remembers having to stoop slightly to do that, only months ago. "Look," he tells the boy. "The conversation we're about to have is not about me and your mom. It's about me and you. And... your dad."

"Oh," Seth says. The last traces of humor fade from his face, and his gaze falls to the ground. Silently, he takes Cyril's hand, and they cross the street, heading east towards the elementary school and away from the center of town.

Asking Seth's permission to marry Robin would have been cutesy and sweet, but it wouldn't be honest. Because if this asshole objected to fucking Robin due to a lack of informed consent, how much more is it true with this kid? Seth loves him because he's stepped into the vacuum Tavis left behind. Because the kid is ten, even if this asshole could tell him everything that went down, he wouldn't understand. All he knows is that his father is gone, and Cyril stepped in.

But someday, he's going to Google the whole thing and watch the archived news footage and read the transcripts and the op-eds and think he knows what happened. And if Cyril doesn't make the effort to tell him now, he'll never be able to forgive.

"Thing is, kid, I can't tell you everything. Some of it you're still too young to understand, and some of it is just—well, it's between me and your dad and your mom. I, uh—I wrote a lot of it down. I'm trying to write out the rest. And maybe when you're an adult I'll let you read some of it, so you can understand where I'm coming from." He sucks in a deep breath. "Here's the thing, kid. I did some really bad things."

"I know. You were in jail. Duh."

"It's not just that." He doesn't even particularly regret how that part went down. Because, in the end, going to prison meant an innocent child was saved. Nothing he might have accomplished as a free man in the past five years could possibly be worth more than that. "When your dad and your mom and I were in college—well, your dad was in boot camp, we were in college—your dad was interested in your mom. Like, he wanted to date her. But he wasn't sure what to say. So he asked me for help, and I..." He makes a writing motion with one hand. "I wrote a letter to her. And your dad put his name on it."

Seth looks at him with eyes as round as moons. "Daddy *stole* your letter?"

"No, I mean, he asked me for permission, and I... Well, I let him."

"Why?"

That's a good fucking question. He looks at the kid, and he realizes he cannot lie. Not even to himself. Cyril and Robin can do whatever they want—fuck, get married—but Seth and his sister are minors. They can't consent to anything. At the very least, he owes them the truth. "Because I... also, uh. Really liked your mom. And I didn't think she'd like me."

"Why not?"

He snorts. "Uh... I was fat and kind of a jerk." Still fat. Even more of a jerk.

"So?"

He looks down at the kid. Seth looks back up at him, unblinking. His eyes just like his mother's, except that something of his father's frank sincerity lives there, too.

And in a flash of terrible clarity, this asshole sees the past as it might have been. Where, instead of penning his feelings for Robin and passing them off to Tavis with pretended indifference, he'd confided in his friend. Where Tavis had listened to his fears and insecurities and then looked him in the eye and said that same simple word: So?

"Yeah, well, I—" He swallows, and then clears his throat. "The main thing is, I screwed up. And then I screwed up even more, because I kept on writing those letters and signing your dad's name."

The puzzled expression on Seth's face deepens into confusion. "You mean... my dad kept lying to my mom?"

This asshole knows exactly what is happening here. Seth isn't seeing his role in this—is giving him the benefit of the doubt—because he wants so badly for Cyril to be the good guy. "Look, kid," he says, as they come to the next corner. "Have you ever heard the phrase, 'history is written by the victors?'"

Seth shakes his head.

"In this case, it means I'm the one who's here, alive, telling the story." Cyril rounds the block instead of crossing again, not because he thinks he's going to wrap this conversation up in the time it takes to get back home but because he's not sure he can take much more. "If I was dead and your dad were here, he'd probably tell it very differently. You know me, and you like me, so you're seeing everything from my point of view. But in your dad's story, I'd be the villain."

A crease appears between Seth's eyebrows as he tries to puzzle through this line of thought. "You wrote letters to my mom," he says, finally. As if asking for confirmation that he's understood the situation correctly.

"Yeah."

"And my dad... married my mom."

"Yeah. But that's—I mean. That's just the first part. Because after that, your dad wanted out. He wanted to tell your mom the truth."

Seth gives Cyril a look that says he might be a kid, but he wasn't born yesterday. "My dad," he says, "used *your* letters to make mom fall in love with him, and then once he married her, he wanted to get rid of you?"

"No, it's not—" Cyril sighs. This conversation is not unfolding the way he had planned. "You know a little bit about how your dad and I tried to save Shafik. Your dad was the one who wanted to do all that, because he thought—well, it's complicated. I can't really explain all of that to you right now. The main thing is that what your dad was doing was dangerous, and I knew he was in trouble, and I had a chance to warn him, and—and I didn't."

"And he died."

"Yeah."

Seth is silent. He looks down at his feet. "Oh," he says, scrunching his toes against the foam-rubber flip flop soles. And there's so much weight behind that one word. Cyril doesn't even know if the kid remembers his dad, not really, but he's felt the weight of his absence. His mom, struggling alone. Every birthday party, graduation, or award ceremony where his peers showed up with two parents. The awkward silences where his father should have been.

They walk the rest of the way home without speaking. Cyril stops on the sidewalk path leading up to the front porch, in case the kid wants to go in alone. But Seth stops too. He stares at the ground some more, chewing on his upper lip. Then he takes a breath.

"You made a really bad choice," he says.

"One I have wished I could take back every second of every minute since."

Seth looks up at him. Expectant.

This asshole hasn't the faintest clue what the boy is waiting for. He wants to turn away, to go inside and share cookies with the kids and never speak of this again. But he can't. He won't run. Won't hide. Not anymore. He forces himself to look the kid in the eye. Pressure builds in his chest until, finally, he can't contain it anymore. "I'm sorry," he says. And with the words come tears. "I'm so sorry, kid."

There is no pause at all between his first strangled sob and Seth's skinny arms thrown wide around his middle. "I forgive you," the boy says, crying too. "I forgive you."

Finally, Cyril gives the kid a pat on the back and moves him gently away. And because Seth is ten, he opens his mouth to ask about the cookie. Cyril preempts him with a nod and a wave toward the house.

"Say that again when you're eighteen," Cyril whispers, watching the boy dash up the steps. "And maybe I'll believe you."

CHAPTER 32

This is a story about an asshole who would like the woman he loves to know that there's no greater demonstration of his feelings for her than letting her dress him in leather fisherman's sandals, linen shorts, and a cream-colored silk Hawaiian shirt.

"There," she says, stepping back to survey the whole package. "You look—"

"Like a fat tourist?"

"You look cool."

"I am, in fact, sweating bullets."

"What's the opposite of cold feet?" She disappears into their closet and, when she comes out, tucks a square of pale green silk into his shirt pocket, pausing to arrange it artfully. "You know you want me."

He hooks an arm around her ribcage, pulling her close. "I'll take you right here."

She holds a hand up between their faces, then cocks her head to one side, listening. "Car's here. Go on. I'll be out in a minute."

"You think I just take orders from you now?" He releases her.

"You always have." She shoos him with a hand. "Run along."

"Yeah, I don't run." But he goes.

She has rented a vintage Lincoln Continental limousine that looks like it just drove out of a seventies political thriller, shiny as a pair of patent leather shoes. Robin's father had kicked the bucket before Cyril ever met her, but he still feels like the old man would have gotten a kick out of it. When the driver—dressed in a suit from the same era—sees him on the porch, she steps out of the driver's seat, leaving the motor running, and bows slightly as she opens the rear door.

It's slick, after he gets himself wedged inside. A plush leather bench seat the same cream color as his shirt (had Robin planned that?) faces a diminutive analog television topped with a mini bar. Two narrow seats on either side of the television look backward, perfectly situated for a tag-along journalist or whomever the political fat cat in the back was currently interrogating.

He hears the front door slam and looks up to see Robin trotting down the steps in heels that match his shirt. She is wearing a beaded flapper dress, with a fringe that ends mid-thigh.

He keys the electric window, which to his surprise still works, albeit slowly. "Wrong era," he says.

She nods as the chauffeur opens the door again. "I look fabulous."

"That goes without saying."

She hops in next to him, tossing her little clutch purse onto the opposite seat. "Say it."

His eyes follow the slim line of her dress downward. "You are... delectable."

She slides an arm around his shoulders. "Oh, that's a nice five-dollar word. Any more where that came from?" Her eyes leave him, briefly, as the driver's door opens and the chauffeur slides in. "Thanks, June!" The driver tosses a silent wave before pulling into the street.

He clears his throat. "Does that thing, uh—"

"June? Can you roll up the divider?"

Another wave. The divider slides up. Like the windows, it's tinted nearly black.

"Did you cut her tongue out?"

Robin laughs. "I told her not to talk to you."

"What? Why?"

"Because I didn't want the chauffeur crying in our wedding photos, that's why." She leans forward, reaching for her purse, giving him a view of the back of her dress, or rather lack thereof. It hangs off her shoulders in a loose U that drops all the way to the small of her back. "Lemme text Greta and let her know we're leaving." She pulls her phone out and brings up Google maps. "Traffic's clear, at least for now. We might actually get there early."

He runs a finger from the nape of her neck to the bottom of her spine.

She smacks his arm away without looking up from her phone. "You are *not* messing up my look before we get our photos taken. Oh! I gotta text the photographer, too."

He snorts. "Photographer."

She tucks her phone back into her purse and turns to face him with a grin. "We're gonna look *amazing*. Trust me."

"We look like drug dealers."

"Or mafioso!" She grins as she tugs his shirttails down. "You look so—" She searches for the word, and then shrugs. Her smile softens. "Come here, big guy." She grabs his collar and leans in for a kiss.

They take their time.

"You look thirsty," she decides, afterward. She turns to open the mini-bar TV. It's stocked with bottles of locally brewed root beer.

"Where's the good stuff?"

She arches an eyebrow. "What, A&W? That mass-produced sugar-water? You need to give up that shit." She cranks a cap off.

The bottle fizzes, and she holds it away from her dress, laughing.

"Not on the—" He grabs the bottle and chugs the excess. "There."

"See? It's good."

He drinks to taste it, this time. "Yeah, not bad."

She leans into him, propping her feet up on the little seat across from them. "You love it."

They watch the hills roll by. With a sudden patter on the windows, rain comes down.

"Oh," he says, "now that's a good omen."

"Is it?" she asks, and then almost immediately delivers a smack to his arm as she realizes he's being sarcastic. "It's good. We need rain." For perhaps obvious reasons, the windows fog. She stretches out a hand and draws a heart in the condensation. "Tavis always loved the rain." She looks at him over one shoulder, as if to check in. "Or... was that you?"

"Me."

"Right." She settles back with a sigh. Rain patters. The heart fogs over again.

"I'm sorry," he says. "About... everything." All he's done, the time he's wasted, and everything they will never have a chance to do.

"I know."

Don't leave me, he wants to say. But doesn't. Somehow, she hears it anyway.

She tugs his arm, pulling it tighter around her. "Can we just let today be today?"

———

BY THE TIME THE CHAUFFEUR PULLS UP IN FRONT OF San Francisco City Hall, it is pouring.

This asshole should have had a suit jacket, or something, to put over her. "How the fuck are we gonna—"

"Chill, big guy."

"Really? That's the pet name you're going with?"

She lifts one shoulder. "Better than 'asshole.'"

"Is it, though?"

Outside, the chauffeur has opened the trunk and pulled out a giant white umbrella. She opens it, wrestles it for a moment against the wind, and then manages to wrangle it with one hand while she opens the car door.

"Thank you," Robin says, sliding out and waiting patiently as Cyril follows.

He wonders if the chauffeur is going to follow them up the steps, but she offers him a polite nod and extends the umbrella handle. He takes it. Robin squeezes in close to him, so he puts his other arm around her.

Then they turn, and there's a news crew. "Shit," he says.

"They're not here for us," Robin says. "Looks like a protest or something. Nobody's gonna even notice us."

"If you think either one of us is unobtrusive, you're blind."

"Well, what do you want to do, try and find a back door?" She opens the clasp on her purse and hands him a white disposable mask. "Here. Now we're anonymous."

They spot the kids and Greta—looking almost handsome in a burgundy blouse and charcoal suit pants—idling inside the entryway lobby. The kids' exclamations of greeting are rendered incomprehensible as they echo off the marble walls.

"How the hell did they beat us here?" Cyril grumbles, pausing to shake the umbrella and fasten it shut. Wrangling the kids into the car takes twenty minutes, on average, and that's without Seth's suit and Nora's frilly pink dress.

"That old Lincoln does sixty, tops." Robin laughs, opening her arms to embrace her children as they plow into her. She nods a greeting as the older woman approaches. "Greta's Mustang could do twice that on gravel."

"I don't go that fast," Greta says, taking the umbrella from Cyril. And adds, almost confessionally, "Well. Not with the kids."

Robin extricates herself from the children and checks the time. Their appointment is in half an hour. The photographer's running late, but Robin assures Cyril—like he cares—that it's fine; she apparently lives in the city and will be arriving any minute. Greta volunteers to flag her down and promptly heads back outside. Robin looks around, scanning the lobby, and then points toward a bank of windows. "I need to check in with the event office. Can you—"

He nods. "I got this. Come on, guys, let's go kill some time."

"Kill time?" Nora chortles as she makes a chopping motion. "I need a sword!"

The security guard is not going to be thrilled with the kids running laps around the rotunda, so he takes them around the left side of the staircase into the foyer leading out to Van Ness, which is a more casual area with a café and people chatting on cell phones. The patterns on the slick marble floor make a pretty good game board, and so he challenges them to move from one side of the foyer to the other without moving in a straight line or touching the borders.

The kids give up after a couple of tries, insisting it's "totally impossible," so he's hop-stepping across the floor like an idiot when Robin calls his name. He spots her coming around the other side of the staircase, beckoning them back into the rotunda.

"The photographer's here and the officiant's waiting upstairs!"

"Great," he says. "I don't suppose there's an elevator."

He's just being an ass, but she's so flustered she takes him seriously. "I mean, there is, if you—"

"It's fine."

As soon as they start up the sweeping rotunda staircase, the security guards flanking either side come forward to block public foot traffic so the prospective newlyweds can have their Kodak moment. "Here," Robin says, whipping off his mask and stuffing it into her tiny purse. The photographer, anonymous behind a giant lens, starts snapping away.

Tourists watch with upturned faces as they wait for Cyril and Robin to reach the second floor. Several people lift phones to snap photos. "Oh, yes, I'm sure I look just dashing," Cyril mutters.

"You're fine." Robin jogs two steps up and turns to face him, straightening his collar and the handkerchief in his pocket. When he tries to start up again, she presses her hand flat against his chest.

He looks down, past their photographer, to the gathering crowd below. A man with what looks like a press pass clipped to his shirt aims the telescoping lens directly at them. "Shit. There's a—"

"They can wait." Robin puts a hand on his cheek and turns his face toward her. "Look at me."

For a minute they just stand there, staring into each other's eyes. "Okay," he says. "And?"

She takes his hand. "There's no photographer. No guards. No tourists. No press. There's nobody else in the world. Just you. And me." She raises her eyebrows, still holding his gaze, and waits.

It feels like forever. And to his surprise, the world does, in fact, fade away. He watches sunlight streaming in through the windows—the rain has apparently broken—flicker off of the facets in her eyes. The slight rise and fall of her chest as she breathes. Feels his own heartbeat. Her pulse in the palm of her hand.

"There you go. Now—just take your time. Okay? Up the stairs. And then we get married."

"Wait, we're getting *married*? Jesus, I'm not even sure I *believe* in marriage." He's never really had the opportunity to form an opinion on the matter.

"It's a little too late for you to be having an existential crisis, big guy. I had to pay in advance—and let me tell you, it was not cheap."

When, eventually, they reach the top of the staircase, the photographer directs them to pause for a few more shots as Greta and the kids hurry up to join them, along with the general public. "Congratulations!" someone says. The balding officiant appears and says something about moving things along, glancing meaningfully at his watch. They follow him around the second floor to a balcony looking out over the rotunda.

And then this asshole is getting married. The officiant's voice echoes through the chamber with practiced gravity, drowning out the river rush of voices from below. The kids are wiggly but silent for once, and when Cyril turns to face Robin, Seth peeks around her elbow, grinning. Cyril winks.

Robin gasps, audibly, when he pulls out the ring. "Cyril," she hisses. "I thought—"

"I wanna see!" Nora says, loudly. Greta hushes her.

"You thought I was going to recycle Tav's ring?" he says. "Jesus, no."

"No, I just didn't expect you to—" Her voice trails off, eyes fixed on the diamond. Or diamonds, rather. It's a giant rectangular stone surrounded by a constellation of smaller stones. "Is this real?" she whispers.

"Uh," the officiant says, apparently not used to being interrupted mid-ceremony.

Cyril slips it on her finger. "With this ring," he says, prompting the officiant.

The man clears his throat. "I thee wed," he intones.

"I thee wed," Cyril repeats.

"Now, the bride may present a token of her love."

"I didn't, uh—I don't have, a, uh." Robin's eyes dart up, finally, to his. "How much did you spend on this?"

"Everything." Well, almost everything. After paying for the ring, he has about five thousand dollars left.

Her eyes go wide. "Oh my God. Cyril, I—" She swallows, thickly. "Oh my God. What are you gonna do, when—"

"It doesn't matter," he says. Nothing matters except her, here, now. This is his only chance to give her something, so he will give her everything he has. While she is still here, with him.

"Boy," she whispers. "When you fall, you fall hard."

———

THEY TAKE PICTURES ALL THE WAY BACK DOWN THE stairs, too. Stop here. Pose. Robin, you stand in front of him. Okay, no, that's not going to work. To the side a little? Yes. Cyril, turn toward her and put your hands on her arms. Okay, let's get the kids in. Ma'am, are you part of the—are you sure? Okay, that's fine. Would you mind holding my bag, then? Excellent. How about just Robin and Nora? And then Cyril and—yep, right there, just like that! Beautiful. Kid, you're a natural.

As they make their way slowly down to the rotunda, this asshole is, surprisingly, not thinking about how ridiculous he looks next to this drop-dead gorgeous woman. He is thinking about whether he will be able to look through the photos when she is gone. Or will they just sit in an album on a shelf, untouched, gathering dust? Will Nora pull it down one day, and will it break his heart to show her, but also break her heart because he'll know that no matter how much it hurt, he should have done it every day?

Maybe he'll have copies made for Greta and her husband. So that when he fails, they can help the kids remember their mother.

God. He's going to lose her.

He's going to have to watch the *kids* lose her.

She squeezes his hand. "Come back to me."

Let's get a closeup of the ring. Do you—you didn't have a bouquet, did you. Okay, Cyril, hold her hand so her fingers are—no, a little—yes. Let's see, is it still raining? Do you have an umbrella? Oh, that's perfect. This is going to be amazing. We'll go right out on the steps, and—

"Oh," the photographer says. "Looks like there's a news crew outside."

Actually, there are multiple news crews.

"Shit," this asshole says, under his breath.

"They can't be here for us," Robin says. "Can they?"

"Us? No. Me—yes." He turns to Greta. "If you can keep the kids out of the way for ten or fifteen minutes—"

"We'll be fine."

"Good." He nods to Robin. "You go with them. Once I draw them off—"

She snorts and takes her purse back from Greta. "I'm coming with you."

"Don't be ridiculous. Let me—"

"Go apeshit and get yourself syndicated and have news crews camping on our lawn again? Uh, no. I'm coming with." She pulls her phone out and taps out a quick text. "Okay. The driver's bringing the car. We just have to get down the front steps to the street."

"Uh," the photographer says, suddenly out of her element, "where should I—"

"You," Cyril says, shaking the umbrella open, "are still on the clock. Come with us."

Robin grins. "It's part of the experience!" She slips her arm through his and pats his hand. "Let me do the talking. Here. Put on your mask. Pretend it's a gag."

The instant they step outside, into what is now a light sprinkle, the cameras rush them. Five microphones are shoved into his face, and he would grab several and rip them out of the reporter's hands if he didn't have an umbrella in one hand and Robin on his other arm.

"Mr. Blanchard, when did you get out of prison?"

"Why are you at the courthouse today?"

"Is your release related to the president's call for—"

"Where are you—"

Robin holds up a hand. "Hey!" she snaps, loudly. "One at a time!" She points to a woman in black. "You."

"When was Mr. Blanchard released?"

"End of August," Robin answers. "And it was public info. You guys are ridiculously slow."

"Why are you here at the courthouse?"

He cannot resist an interjection: "What does it *look* like we're doing? Jesus, at least *pretend* to be journalists."

"Where are you living?"

"Are you still part of Anonymous?"

"Mr. Blanchard, what will you be—"

"Mr. Blanchard," Robin announces loudly, looking straight into the cluster of cameras, "is now teaching piano in Sonoma County. He is currently accepting new students, both children and adults. You can contact him at Cyril Teaches Piano at Gmail-dot-com."

And then Robin grabs his hand and pulls him down the steps, through the mob, and they are at the street, and the Lincoln is pulling into the loading zone. The chauffeur jumps out, placing herself firmly between them and the camera as they get into the back, basically photobombing everyone who gets in their way.

"Ms. Matheson," calls a voice. "Will you be taking Mr. Blanchard's name?"

"Oh, please." She laughs. "He's taking mine."

The chauffeur closes the door, but Robin keys the window down.

Cyril yanks her arm away from the switch. "What the hell are you—"

She sticks her other arm out the window and waves. "Bye!"

He leans over her and rolls the window back up. "We're gonna be plastered all over the evening news."

She brushes off her arms and hair, showering him with droplets. "You seriously underestimate the turnover rate at which current events are happening these days. I basically gave them an infomercial. You're wearing a mask, and it's drizzling. If this even makes it on air, it'll be two sentences and your mugshot."

He sighs and sits back. She pops open the mini bar and takes out a root beer.

"So you're really trying to make this piano teacher thing happen?"

She shrugs. "You'll be good at it. And you're gonna need some cash flow after buying this monstrosity." She holds up her hand to model the ring. "Is there a return policy or something? Because after I die—"

"No."

She sighs. "Well, I'm getting cremated, so if you had any fantasies about me wearing any fucking twenty-thousand-dollar ring for eternity you can kiss those goodbye. Maybe you can sell it on Ebay, or—" She snaps her fingers. "Shoot! We forgot Jamie!"

"Who the hell is that?"

She reaches to roll down the divider between them and the chauffeur. "The photographer!"

———

THE DRIZZLING RAIN HAS TAPERED TO A MIST WHEN the Continental pauses to deposit them in front of a restaurant. "Thank God I made reservations," Robin says. "I'm starving."

"What is this?" The sign says *Mandalay.*

"It's Burmese. You ever had Burmese?"

"No."

"Me either. Greta says it's fantastic."

"Oh, well, if Greta says—"

"She has better taste than you."

He hauls open one of the two solid wood entry doors, letting Robin precede him into a waiting area bordered by plastic palm trees lit up with Christmas lights and a massive gilt altar laden with incense and oranges. Left of the altar hangs a signed portrait of Jacques Pepin.

The staff is friendly but not overly cutesy; fortunately, a Hawaiian shirt and a flapper dress don't necessarily code as "just married" anywhere outside the courthouse, so they get to enjoy their braised string beans and coconut rice with relatively little fuss. Robin pokes at her phone. "Jaime made it out. She'll meet us at the gate to Chinatown in an hour."

He lifts an eyebrow. "I agreed to get married, not tour the city."

"Cyril, I am going to get as much mileage out of this dress as humanly possible." She uses her chopsticks to gesture at him. "And I don't know when you'll ever wear that getup again, so I'm enjoying it."

"I'll wear a Hawaiian shirt every day if that's all it takes to make you happy."

"HOLY COW," SHE SAYS, WHEN THEY EXIT THE CAR again, this time to no rain and a matte gray sky. "I am stuffed." She looks around, brightens, and waves. "You found us!"

The photographer, now hung with several different cameras, nods. "Don't worry about me. Do your thing, and I'll do mine." She twists an attachment onto the end of one camera and lifts it to her eye.

Cyril turns away. "Where are we going?" It seems like she's got this all planned out.

Robin points across the street, through the arch of Chinatown's iconic entry gate. "There's a little park a few blocks that
way. I brought the kids once. It's really cute."

They cross the street. "Wow," he says, as they pass a row of
tents. "Scenic." He yanks her out of the way of a needle on the
ground. "Jesus."

Robin sighs. "It's been a rough year."

The photographer stalks them down Grant Avenue, snapping
photos as Robin occasionally pauses to peer into a shop
window or comb through a street-side vendor's stall. She pulls
a card out of her purse and buys a couple of insects embalmed
in resin for the kids, handing the bag to Cyril to stuff into a
pocket.

By the time they reach the park, a breeze has kicked up and
blown away the cloud cover, leaving the air crisp, clean, and cold.
Robin pulls him toward an open square bathed in sunlight, where
a bunch of elderly folks bicker over mahjong tables.

They stop to watch three women and one man in a plastic rain
poncho sitting around a card table in flimsy aluminum folding
chairs. Robin glances up at him. "You know how to play?"

"Nope."

"And here I thought you were super into games." Her phone
pings, and she pulls it out to text, probably with Greta. She
smiles.

"Okay," he says.

Robin looks up. "Okay what?"

"Now I know how to play." He gestures to the old man in
front of them. "Which is more than this idiot can say."

"Hey!" the old guy says, startled. A woman with bright blue
eyeshadow bursts into laughter, slapping a knee for emphasis as
she translates the exchange into Chinese for her companions. The
other two women titter and nod.

"You want to join?" blue eyeshadow asks. "I'm tired of taking
this old fart's money."

"Another time," Robin interjects, tugging his elbow. "He's busy today."

"When you come back, bring cash," the lady says, eyeing him. "And your own chair."

They continue across the square and into a little garden area with a sand-colored gravel path. The photographer breaks her promise of being inconspicuous long enough to direct them toward a cement bench under a circular red bower. "It's double happiness," she says, pointing to the character formed by the wooden lattice. "Perfect for weddings."

So they stand and pose, first with Robin in front and then facing one another.

"Hold hands," the photographer says. "No, like, so the ring— yeah. Hold it right there."

Robin squeezes his fingers. "So," she says, slowly.

"Fucking knew you had an ulterior motive."

"A girl can't just take a walk on her wedding day?" She grins like a cat. "I know I didn't get you a wedding band, but—"

"I could not possibly care less."

"So sentimental. Anyway, what I was about to say was, I do have a present for you." She opens the clasp of her little purse and pulls out a plain white envelope. The seal has already been torn; she flips it open and pulls out a sheaf of three papers folded in thirds.

He takes it when she offers it to him, unfolding all three sheets at once with a firm shake. His stomach sinks as he realizes it's a medical report of some kind. Her name and medical record number are printed at the top. "What's this?"

She doesn't say anything. She just watches his face. Waiting.

He examines the paper in more detail. "A... what, CT scan?" Then he notices the date of the evaluation: three years ago. "This is old."

She reaches over his arm and flips past the first page, and then the second, which is a continuation of the numbers and acronyms on the first. The third page is a letter, also dated three years ago. He is skimming, still not understanding—*findings consistent with—mass detected in—recommend follow-up in six months*—when she taps the bottom of the page. He follows her finger down to a single word, highlighted in yellow.

Remission.

His vision narrows into a thin tunnel of light. The word grows large. Suddenly, he can't breathe.

"Cyril. Hey." She tugs his arm. "Have a seat, big guy. Right there."

He looks at the cement bench behind them. It's wet. He sits.

"He okay?" the photographer's voice says, somewhere beyond the event horizon.

"He'll be fine," Robin says. "Keep shooting." Her face appears in front of his. "Cyril?"

"I—I don't understand."

She gives him a little shove; he moves over, and she sits down next to him. "I had breast cancer. Double mastectomy, chemo, and radiation. It worked. I went into remission."

"But it came back."

"No," she says, simply.

He forces himself to look from the paper to her face. "You—you fucking had surgery. I was there—"

"Yeah. About a year ago, I started bleeding really bad every month. Like, so bad I'd be out of commission for three or four days. That's sort of a red flag for uterine cancer developing, and with the type of cancer I had, my risk was higher. The doctors recommended I get a hysterectomy, but I kept putting it off because I'd already put the kids and Greta and her husband through so much, and honestly because it was just tough to give up on the idea of having more kids. Then COVID hit, and you reached your minimum sentence date, so I talked to your lawyer and wrote a letter, and—" She shrugs. "They took like fifteen biopsies while they were in there, just to make sure. Everything came back clear."

"But you—you've been so tired—"

"Cyril, I'm not a robot. Even I can only work ten hours a day for six days a week for so long. I mean, I'm recovering from surgery, *and* I'm going through early menopause. I told you—they keep changing up my medication. My hormones have been going bananas."

"But—"

She laughs. "Are you really gonna argue this? Cyril. I don't have cancer."

He just looks at her, uncomprehending.

"I'm not gonna die." She spreads her arms, looking pleased with herself. "Gotcha!"

CHAPTER 33

"This—" he says, barely able to articulate the words. "This is—this is the most fucked up—the most fucked up thing in anyone could—"

"Oh?" she says, archly. "More fucked up than lying about your identity for seven years?"

"I honestly don't even know." He shakes his head. "I—I don't know."

"Good. Then we're even."

"Are—are you telling the truth? I mean—this isn't some—"

"Some extra meta layer?" Her grin widens. "If it was, how would you know?"

Disbelief gives way suddenly, like a broken dam. He wraps both arms around her, squeezing her so hard she coughs, and has himself a good long cry. It doesn't matter that she's lied. All that matters is that she's not going to die.

Eventually, the floodgates taper off. When he releases her, she tugs the handkerchief out of his pocket and hands it to him. "Figured you'd need this."

He blows his nose, loudly. "You're gonna have to give me some time," he says. "To, uh, get used to this."

She shrugs. "I got time."

"I just—why would you—I mean, even Greta?"

Robin laughs. "For a devout Christian woman, Greta Cooke is surprisingly willing to lie. Although I'm pretty sure the only reason she agreed to play along is because she was sure you'd get fed up and leave."

"I don't give a shit about Greta, I just—" He gets to his feet, takes a step, and then turns, shaking his head. His skull is pounding. "All of this. Everything. I—"

"What do you want me to say?" She spreads her hands. "That I never meant to let it go this far? That I planned to tell you I didn't have cancer after the surgery? I could tell you I only kept going because I realized your insane fucking puzzle box mind wasn't gonna let me in unless it was the last possible option." She sucks in a breath. "But that would be a lie."

"I'm getting the feeling I'm going to spend the rest of my life wondering whether anything you say is true." Which is, ironically, exactly what he deserves. Or perhaps it's not ironic at all. Perhaps that's exactly the point. He looks at her. "You planned this." All of it. From before he'd even gotten out of prison.

She takes a step toward him, and then again, until they're close enough to touch. She places both hands on his chest and tilts her head back to look him in the eye. "You thought you could own me, Cyril. Keep me in a little box on your desk and pull me out whenever you wanted. But you were wrong." Her fingers curl, gathering his shirt into her fists. "I'm not yours. Never was, never will be." She pulls him down, until her lips are close enough to brush his ear. "I broke you," she whispers. "And now you're mine."

She releases his shirt and steps back. Her eyes bore into him, hard as black diamonds. Her face is flushed and filled with triumph.

He stares, uncomprehending. Or not wanting to comprehend.

He looks at the photographer, still standing there snapping photos of his bloated, tear-streaked face. It clicks.

"This is it," he realizes. She's played him for a fool. Beaten him at his own game. Ridden him farther than he could have possibly expected her to go. "This is the end." She's gotten her revenge.

There's no anger. In fact, there's a kind of blunt, cauterized satisfaction in knowing she's gotten even. But mostly he's just... empty. He looks, stupidly, at the concrete bench behind him, and then at her, and the photographer. And then he walks away.

Free.

"Cyril? Cyril! Jesus Christ, where are you—Cyril!" Robin's heels clop after him. He turns—just in time to catch her as she leaps into his arms, knocking the air out of his lungs.

"What the—"

She is laughing. "Oh my God, Cyril, I *married* you!" She presses her forehead to his, arms cinched tight around his neck. "Listen to me, you colossal idiot. This is not the end. This is where we begin."

EPILOGUE

I've made up my mind to delete this absolute fucking masterpiece of masochistic masturbation probably about fifty times over the past five years. Nobody likes looking at themselves in the mirror, especially when the asshole looking back is me—in the figurative sense even more than the literal. Thing is, it's not just me anymore, is it? It's your mom and your sister and you, too. Plus my therapist said it would be "counter-productive."

Your mom's gonna think you're too young to read some of this shit, and maybe she's right. She usually is. But hell, you know what sex is, and don't think I haven't overheard the language you use with your friends. (Seriously, kid, be a little more discreet, okay? Your mom doesn't need to hear those words coming out of her baby's mouth.) If reading about your mom gets weird, well... you know how to skim. I guess what I'm saying is, read as much as you want, but maybe don't mention it to your mom for another year or two. She's already pissed I let you read *Game of Thrones*.

Just—damn it. Look. What I'm trying to say is, I'm sorry about how I reacted when you sprang those papers on me. I know it was a big deal for you, and believe me when I say it's a huge-ass fucking deal for me. I just—I dunno, maybe reading my vulgar autobiographical fanfic will help you understand that my acting like an asshole was not about you. It's just me. Being an asshole. Which I try my best to keep on the down-low with you. Your mom already knows. Anyway.

Here's the thing.

Fuck.

I'm not supposed to say shit like this because I'm technically not even related to you, but you're the best fucking thing that ever happened to me. I love you, kid. I always have. You and your sister are the very best of the two people I loved most in the world and you're better than either one of them.

I don't deserve you any more than I deserve your mom, probably even less, but if signing the papers and making it legal will make you happy, I'll do it. And I swear to God I'll try not to be an asshole. It's just... it's gonna take me a while to get used to having you call me Dad.

ACKNOWLEDGMENTS

When *Surviving Cyril* came out in March of 2017, I had no intention of writing a sequel. Robin was headed off into the sunset, alone and free. Like the characters in Rostand's *Cyrano de Bergerac*, the play from which I had drawn inspiration, Robin and Cyril were destined for bittersweet tragedy. No self-respecting woman could possibly go back to Cyril after what he'd done.

Then, in what I am sure was meant only as a complimentary off-hand comment, librarian Robin Bradford tweeted that she regretted not being able to include *Surviving Cyril* in a romance roundup because the ending didn't include a "happily ever after," or HEA, in the parlance of the genre.

Exactly, I thought—crafting an HEA for my characters was impossible!

Impossible...? Well. If there's one thing I like more than thumbing my nose at genre convention, it's a challenge.

Which is all to say: Robin, I blame you.

I'm kidding, of course. But when I started this project in the fall of 2017, I quickly realized I'd bitten off more than I could chew. That's four years from first draft to final product. While my progress was delayed by health issues and a worldwide pandemic, getting into Cyril's head was also the most difficult narrative challenge I have ever tackled. It was often frustrating, demoralizing, and emotionally exhausting—but I am intensely proud of the result. I hope readers will agree.

First thanks go to my husband, Kelson Hootman, who to my astonishment continues to take this whole "writing thing" seriously. Your unflagging support means the world to me. Next in line are my parents, John and Linda Biggers, who basically bear responsibility for the person I am today—for better or worse! Thanks for letting me be me.

It will not surprise anyone to learn that this book has been through a dizzying number of revisions. I had the privilege of trading manuscript critiques with six incredibly talented writers: Laura Santi, Karien van Ditzhuijzen, Hilary Wright, Lily MacKenzie, Julie Campbell, and Hilda Hoy.

I would be nowhere at all without the women who welcomed me as the fourth and final member in their writing group. Week after week, Janet Schneider, Valerie Stroller, and Susan Segal pored over every last sentence of this book, offering insight that allowed me to cross the finish line with my last big revision. Thank you for keeping me grounded whenever I try to get too clever for my own good!

I also want to thank the writers I have connected with online, through both Binders and the Women's Fiction Writers Association, who have provided both moral support and feedback on questions of craft. Your time and generosity have been greatly appreciated.

Last but certainly not least, my thanks go to you, dear reader. Publishing is a long and lonely road, and as a very small fish in a very big pond, I can genuinely say that every reader counts. Thank you for choosing to spend your time with these absurd characters, whom I have grown so much to love. I hope you love them too.